THE FALLEN ONE

A Medieval Romance

By Kathryn Le Veque

Printed by Dragonblade Publishing in the United States of America

This book is about the loyalty of friends,
and I have some great ones.
Mrs. Cynthia Marie Paz, thank you for always being there!

PROLOGUE

Tower of London
January, 1331 A.D.

"Bear arms as a knight again and I will be forced to kill you. These are the terms in exchange for your lives."

The words rang in his head, hollowed by the grief the meaning provoked. Perhaps they should kill him after all; surely the pain would not be as great as that which he felt at this moment. Swords, arrows, clubs; he could handle the agony of their handy work. In his eighteen years as a knight, he had been fed more than his share of injury and prided himself on his resilience. But dishonor was another matter altogether. This, he could not stomach. By his side, his brother and fellow knight spoke.

"Kill us now and be done with it," he hissed.

The man accepting their fate shushed him. "Enough."

"'Tis not *nearly* enough. Do you not understand, brother? They seek to...."

"*Quiet.*" His words were low and deliberate. "The power goes to those who are victorious in war, Sebastian. As those who have suffered defeat at their hands, we must trust in their mercy. We do not dictate provisions."

Sebastian the Red fell silent. Standing beside his older, wiser brother and their father, he swallowed the remainder of his argument because the audience chamber of kings since William the Bastard was not the place to enter into any manner of family squabble. Most especially when their visit to this place was not under the best of circumstances. They were, for the moment, among the ranks of the conquered.

Yet biting his tongue did not come easy to him. Sebastian was called 'The Red' for good reason; the mass of red hair upon his head gave clue to the fire within. His temper was quick to ignite and burned white hot. His demeanor was as red as his brother's was cool. But it was time to bank the fire within. He had no support to his argument. It was an old and not unfamiliar story among the ranks of warriors throughout history.

Sebastian, his father, and his brother had been at the head of Roger Mortimer's forces when young King Edward had rebelled against Mortimer's rule. As knights, the three of them had followed orders. Those orders had led them from the Marches to London where Mortimer had ruled with Queen Isabella for three glorious years.

During that time, his elder brother had been commander not only of the Earl of Marches' troops, but of Isabella's as well. He had commanded nearly twenty thousand men with a fair and powerful hand, and it wasn't long before he had built himself a solid reputation. He had taught the men that strength could only be truly achieved with respect, and that honor was the most important weapon a knight would wield. Those words had spread. There wasn't a fighting man in the country who did not respect the name of Mathias de Reyne, enemy or ally. Mathias had taught them all that some things transcend loyalties.

Yet the mighty had fallen. Such were the winds of war. Sebastian glanced at his brother as Edward the Third, King of England, relayed the conditions upon which he was sparing Mathias' life. The king was so very young, still trying to grasp what his role had now become. He had a horde of advisors behind him, some of them great men, feeding him carefully scripted advice. But young Edward was no fool; he was already a fine warrior and had seen much strife in his young years. He was far more of a fighting man than his father had ever been. Sebastian felt a hint of respect for the young king, but it did not ease the ache of disgrace.

As Sebastian struggled with his misery, Mathias' strong face was unreadable. Even in defeat he remained composed. He accepted Edward's sentence as easily as one might accept a favor. In truth, it *was* a favor - the de Reyne knights were related to the House of Mortimer. There was never any question of their loyalties and they should have, by all rights, followed Mortimer to the block. But they hadn't.

"You are a great knight, Mathias," Edward was rising from his throne now, coming down off the dais. It was almost as if he was begging forgiveness as he spoke. "I have known of you since I was old enough to understand this great war machine that pulses through England as blood would pulse through a living body. It seems that this country cannot survive without some measure of violence; it keeps it alive for some feverishly odd reason. I was advised to execute you along with the earl because to leave you alive is to leave a threat to my rule. But... but I cannot execute you for fulfilling your oath. You were only doing as you were ordered and you are a man of supreme honor. And I should not like my rule to be known for its heartlessness. I should like it to be known for its mercy."

Mathias gazed down at the young monarch. For such a young man, his words were old and wise. But Mathias had nothing to say by way of reply; to thank the lad seemed foolish at this point. It seemed trite. Edward sensed this; fighting against the disapproving stares that clawed against his back, he knew that most of his military advisors thought that he was making the wrong decision. Only a select few supported exile to execution; Tate de Lara, Earl of Carlisle and his greatest mentor, was one of them. Most felt that Mathias de Reyne must be eliminated for the safety of the kingdom. But Edward could not so easily erase so great a warrior.

"You, your father and your brother are henceforth stripped of your nobility and knighthoods," the young man said. "Should you ever resume arms again, you will be captured and summarily executed. Such is my decision, de Reyne; my mercy is given only once. Violate my wishes and you shall feel my wrath. Is this understood?"

Mathias nodded, once. "Aye, my lord."

"Good." Edward's gaze traveled from Mathias to Justus, the broad old man with the long gray hair, then on to Sebastian. All three men were nearly legendary in the warring community. He wished they were sworn to him. But he could not trust those who had been so close to the man who had stolen his throne. It was a regret he had.

He turned back for his chair. "You will be escorted to the city gates where you shall be released. You will never set foot in London again. You will be killed on sight."

Mathias turned away from the King. Composed for all outward appearances, the truth was that he couldn't stand to be in that place any longer, watching his knighthood vaporize into the wind. He hardly remembered exiting the hall out into the cool January sunshine and being escorted to the city limits by men who would have rather seen him dead. They even took his beloved charger and the sword of his ancestors, and all of the implements that made him who he was. Now he was no longer that which had defined him as a man.

He was no longer a knight.

CHAPTER ONE

May, 1332 A.D.
Carlisle, England

'Gazing at people, some hand in hand,
Just what I'm going through, they cannot understand.
Some try to tell me in thoughts they cannot defend,
Just what you want to be... you will be in the end.'
~ 13th Century Minstrel Lyrics

***

"Nay!" The young woman screamed. "Let her go!"

It was the middle of a busy marketplace in the middle of the day, with hundreds of people bustling to and fro. The sun was shining, birds were singing, and clouds darted across the sky in the brisk breeze. But in the middle of the busy avenue, no one seemed to be paying attention to the young woman in a panic.

She was pulling on the tunic of a rather burly man with one eye who had a young girl in his arms. The young girl was screaming and kicking as the young woman fought him for all she was worth.

"Let her go!" she demanded again, hitting him on the arm and trying to grab at the girl in his arms. "Put her down, do you hear me? *Put her down*!"

The man tried to ignore her. He was drooling, his clothing torn and stained. He had grabbed the young girl from the back of the wagon she had been sitting in and now he was trying to make off with her but her sister had other ideas. He was moving away from the wagon with his quarry squirming in his arms as the sister beat on him.

"Nay!" The sister screamed again, realizing the man wasn't about to release his prey so she grabbed hold of her sister's arms and dig her heels into the mud, trying to pull her sister free. "Release her, you animal! Father, *help me!"*

The young woman knew she needed assistance. The brute that was trying to make off with her sister was big and strong. The young woman was in a panic, struggling to keep her head. Her father and sister were down the street with the spice merchant, running errands for their mother, and she had been left with the wagon and her younger sister. The young woman had been admiring a dress merchant across the busy avenue when she heard her younger sister scream. A man had grabbed her. And the fight began.

Her young sister was crying hysterically, grabbing on to the young woman's arms by digging her nails into the flesh as she fought against her abductor. But the young woman saw that she wasn't making any headway against the man, determined as he was, so she kicked him in the knees. It was a hard kick. When he faltered, she grabbed his dirty, vermin-filled hair and yanked as hard as she could.

The man roared and tried to hit her. As he released one arm around the young girl, she slipped and ended up hanging almost up-side down. The older sister, down on one knee to avoid the strike from the brute, grabbed her hanging sister with both hands and pulled as hard as she could. Her sister slipped free and landed in the mud.

But the brute wasn't letting go so easily; he grabbed the young girl by the legs and pulled, drawing more screams from both women. People were noticing now, seeing the brutal struggle and wondering what it was all about.

Down the avenue in the midst of the bustle stood a smithy shop; they had heard the screaming, too, and a dark head poked out from the enormous shop that was blazing with fires and hammering anvils. Steam and heat rose through the thatched roof.

Mathias had heard the screaming but all he could see was people; being that it was a very busy day in spring when farmers brought their spring harvest into town, there were more people than usual. Horses, wagons, women, children, and a few knights who had arrived for next week's local tournament… they were all here. Moreover, it was a bright day with good weather, but that would change as the sun grew warmer and the smell from the sewers began to fill the air. The flies would be bad, too. Not seeing the source of the screams, he was about to turn back to his business when the cries of panic caught his attention again. Then, he saw it.

A big bear of a man had the legs of a girl in his grip, but an older girl had her arms and they were tugging her apart. Both girls were screaming and the older one was calling for help. No one seemed to be coming to her aid and Mathias thought it was a family squabble until the man let go of one of the legs he held firm and punched the young woman who had hold of the girl's arms. The blow to the shoulder sent the young woman reeling.

But she was tough. The woman was stunned but she didn't lose her grip; she continued to hold, shaking the bells out of her head before resuming her death-grip on the young girl and screaming once again for help. Meanwhile, Justus, pausing in shoeing a horse, noticed where Mathias' attention was. He could hear the girl screaming, too, but it was none of his business. Besides, he'd been banned from that kind of thing. There was no more chivalry left in his veins. That had died along with his permission to bear a sword.

"Mathias," he called quietly. "Lad, do not...."

It was too late. Mathias was already tossing off his leather apron and moving towards the struggle. Sebastian, pounding out a chorus of sparks on a piece of steel destined to be a sword for a local baron, saw his brother heading towards the struggle and thought he wanted a piece of it, too. Unlike his father, he missed the thrill of a fight or the exhilaration of a kill. Mathias, on the other hand, never spoke about it one way or the other, but Sebastian knew that his brother's sense of chivalry certainly wasn't dead. He just kept it buried.

As Mathias approached the fight, he could see that the young girl in contention between the young woman and the beefy man had been twisted around so violently that she had vomited. She had it in her hair. The young woman who had hold of the girl's arms was losing her fight; it was written all over her face. The man was winning simply because he was much stronger and the young woman was trying not to collapse because of it. She was holding on until the bloody end. It was a puzzling and violent scuffle and as it raged, Mathias walked to within a few feet of the fracas.

"What goes on here?" he asked evenly. "Why do you hurt these women?"

The brawling came to a startled halt and the woman with the weakening grip on the girl turned to Mathias with wide and terrified eyes.

"He is trying to abduct my sister," she gushed, her voice trembling. "Please help me."

Mathias cocked an eyebrow, looking at the hairy and filthy man. "Is this true?"

The man barred his teeth at him and roared. That was as much of an answer as he could give. Then he gave one hard yank and pulled the girl free of the young woman's grasp. Then he turned to run away with his prize but Mathias moved quickly.

Reaching out, he threw his arm across the man's neck and jerked him back so hard that the young girl tumbled out of his arms. As the brute fell to the ground, it was enough of a break for the young woman to grab the child and pull her to safety. Meanwhile, the fight had now moved from the scruffy man against two small women to the scruffy man against an extremely formidable opponent.

Mathias was more than ready to go to battle against the filthy man who seemed to be covered in lice and sores. Upon closer inspection, it was a fairly disgusting sight. But he made no move against the man, instead, waiting for him to throw the first punch. Poised, fists balled, Mathias stared down his opponent, waiting. As he stood there, primed and ready, a flash of red hair moved past him and Sebastian charged the dirty man, getting his kicks by grabbing him by the face and throwing him to the ground.

"Bastard!" Sebastian spat, kicking the man in the ribs. "Do you go around taking your fists to women, then? You should be taught a lesson."

Mathias reached out and grabbed his ruffian brother by the arm. "Wait," he told him, pulling him back. His focus was on the brute, now wallowing in the mud. "Were you trying to abduct that girl? Answer me or I shall turn my brother loose on you. It is better now to speak than suffer his wrath, I assure you. Answer me."

The brute, now covered in mud, only grunted as he rolled to his knees and attempted to crawl away. Mathias and Sebastian looked at each other, shrugged, and Sebastian went after the man as Mathias turned to the two terrified women. As Mathias approached the pair, Sebastian leapt on the man's back as he dragged himself through the mud and began to ride him as one would a wild horse. He grabbed the man by the hair and rode him right into the muck, laughing all the way.

Mathias heard his brother but he didn't pay any attention. He was looking at the two panic-stricken women in front of him.

"Did he hurt you?" he asked the older woman. "I saw him strike you."

The older of the pair, a young woman of exquisite beauty, gazed up at him with an amalgam of fear and gratitude. It was difficult to decipher her expression; Mathias, in fact, didn't try. All he could see was beautiful brown hair, rich with a hint of red to it, and enormous brown eyes. Her skin was pale, like fresh cream, and her features were petite and pixie-ish. He was momentarily taken aback by all of that beauty, none of which he had noticed until that moment. Now, he felt as if he'd been slapped in the face with it.

"He did not hurt me," she replied, her voice quaking.

"The younger girl, then. Is she well?"

The young woman looked at the sobbing child in her arms. "I... I believe she is well," she said. "I do not think he hurt her overly."

Satisfied with the answer, Mathias looked around. "Is there someone here for you?" he asked. "Surely you are not alone."

The young woman shook her head. "My father and older sister are in town," she replied. "They are on errands for my mother. My youngest sister and I were sitting in our wagon – that is our wagon over there – when that man suddenly grabbed my baby sister and tried to run away. My lord, I can never thank you enough for coming to our aid. No one else seemed to be willing to help but you and... dear God, I cannot possibly thank you enough."

Mathias was fairly swept up in her sweet voice and doe-like eyes. He found himself clearing his throat nervously.

"I am glad I could be of assistance, my lady," he said.

The young woman peered around him to get a look at the big red-haired man as he jumped up and down on the brute. "What will you do to him?"

Mathias turned in time to see his brother roll his burly quarry over onto his back and leap on his stomach. "I am not sure," he said casually. "I will leave the punishment to my brother because he seems to enjoy it so much."

There was a touch of humor in what could have been a deadly serious statement. It helped alleviate some of the abject terror the women were still feeling. In fact, the tension seemed to have lifted a great deal now that the young girl was safe and the culprit being taken away. There was no longer any reason for him to remain.

With a polite nod, Mathias turned away because he was unsure what more to say to her and furthermore found himself just the slightest bit giddy. In fact, he was fairly unbalanced but a word from her stopped him.

"My lord," she called. "I do not even know your name."

Mathias came to a halt, turning to face her. He thought perhaps she was more beautiful at second glance.

"Mathias," he said after a moment.

The young woman smiled and Mathias heard himself sigh with satisfaction; even her teeth were beautiful. In fact, everything about her was beautiful and he was very quickly succumbing to her very presence. With a mere glance or soft words, she was a siren luring him to his doom.

"Mathias," she repeated softly. "I am the Lady Cathlina de Lara and this is my sister, the Lady Abechail."

Mathias felt as if he had been struck, lifting the delirium of giddy fog he had had been feeling. *De Lara*, he thought. He knew that name all too well. He tried not to linger on the name, that powerful and consequential name, as his attention shifted to the slender girl in Cathlina's arms, plastered up against her sister.

The child was dark-haired, pale, and very frail looking. When she saw that Mathias' was looking at her, she buried her face in her sister's torso.

"Greetings, my lady," Mathias said to Abechail, somewhat gently. She looked as if a louder tone would cause her to shatter. "I sincerely pray you were not injured in the struggle."

Abechail was pressed as close to her sister as close as she could go. When Mathias spoke to her, she closed her eyes tightly and tried to block him out but her sister shook her gently.

"Abbie?" she said softly. "Will you thank this man for helping you?"

Abechail turned slightly, peeping an eye open from the safe haven of her sister's embrace. Instead of her sister's doe-eyed gaze, she had blue eyes that were red-rimmed and frightened. She had tears all over her face and remnants of dried vomit on her neck.

"My… my thanks," she stammered.

Mathias cracked a smile. "It was my pleasure, my lady."

Abechail's gaze lingered on him a moment before smiling timidly. She still looked horribly pale and terrified, however, and it occurred to Mathias that until the brute was properly restrained or imprisoned, the poor young girl might never feel safe. In fact, neither lady would feel completely safe. He turned to his brother.

"Sebastian," he said. "Take that animal over to our stall. There are some old stocks back behind it. Put him there."

Sebastian's ruddy face lit up. "The old binders?" he repeated gleefully. "One of them is broken, I think. I believe that is why they no longer use it."

"Then chain him to it," Mathias said. "That fool will not be free to roam as long as these ladies are in town. See to it."

With a smile on his face, Sebastian picked the muddy, lice-ridden brute up by the neck and dragged the man across the avenue towards the smithy shop down the way. People were dodging to get out of his way as he hauled the man behind him, singing a song very loudly about bearded women and knights with no libido. It was a song better suited for a tavern but Sebastian didn't care; he was happier than he had been in a long while, beating up on someone.

Mathias watched him go, fighting off a grin when he saw his father stick his head out of their smithy stall at the sound of Sebastian's voice. The shock registering on the man's face was priceless. Justus was, physically, the toughest man in England but he had a habit of showing his thoughts plainly on his face. That could make him rather vulnerable, but it also made him very humorous. Mathias had to turn away before his father saw him grinning. His expression was straight by the time he turned back to the women.

"He will no longer be a threat, I promise," he said, his gaze moving over Cathlina's features but trying not to be obvious about it. "Mayhap I should wait with you until your father returns to ensure your safety."

Cathlina shook her head. "I am sure that will not be necessary, my lord. You have already done so much for us. I do not wish to keep you from your duties."

Mathias essentially ignored her. He gestured in the direction of the wagon, a few dozen feet away. "Allow me to escort you to your wagon."

Cathlina eyed the man who was not only their savior but now determined to play their escort; he was enormously built and several inches over six feet with shaggy dark hair that had a bit of curl to it. His features were even, very handsome, and his square jaw was set with determination. But it was his eyes, rather large orbs of dark green that conveyed… something. She wasn't quite sure what she saw within the guarded green sea, but there was something there lingering just below the surface. She sensed great mystery in the searingly masculine depths.

"You are too kind, my lord," she said, pulling her clinging sister with her. "We owe you a great deal of thanks for the regard you have shown us."

Mathias herded the pair across the busy avenue, stopping short of touching her in any way, as a polite escort would have. A proper attendant would have taken the lady's elbow to show both protectiveness and guidance, but given the circumstances of their meeting, Mathias didn't think they would have taken any manner of physical contact too kindly. Therefore, he basically shepherded them to the wagon and watched Cathlina, who was hardly larger than a child herself, lift her sister up into the wagon bed.

Abechail crawled up underneath the bench seat and rolled up in a dusty oil cloth that was there. It was evident that she wanted to hide away from what had just happened. Cathlina watched her sister as the girl pulled the blanket over her head. She shook her head sadly.

"She was so excited to come to town," she said with quiet sorrow. "More excited than the rest of us. After this happening, she will never want to leave home again."

Mathias folded his big arms across his chest, his gaze moving from the swaddle-bound child on the wagon to the exquisite creature standing next to him. He wasn't one for idle chatter; in fact, he kept to himself most of the time. He was rather quiet and introspective. But something about that lovely face made him want to engage in conversation. He hadn't done that with a woman in years.

"Did you come far?" he asked politely.

Cathlina shook her head. "Not really," she replied as she looked up at him. "We live at Kirklinton Castle. Have you heard of it?"

Mathias nodded. "It is a well-regarded fortress," he replied. "It is to the north if I recall correctly."

Cathlina nodded. "It is," she confirmed. "It belongs to the Earl of Carlisle. My father, who is the earl's cousin on his father's side, was appointed the garrison commander last year. Before that, we lived in a small tower near the Roman wall further north. In fact, our home was a Roman castle hundreds of years ago and before I was born, my mother was told about a local legend that bespoke of a Roman commander and his Saxon love, the Lady Cathlina Lavinia. My mother named me for the Saxon lady of legend. She thought it would bring me good fortune."

So... she is de Lara's cousin, he thought. He was wondering how, precisely, she was related to the great Tate de Lara and now he knew. It was a sad thought, indeed, but something he wouldn't waste the energy to dwell on. He'd never had a real romantic interest in his life and realized he wasn't in danger of having one now, not with the knowledge that she was a de Lara. It was too bad, too, but he pushed the disappointment aside to focus on her sweet voice, husky and honeyed. That was a much more pleasant thought.

"Has your name brought you good fortune, then?" he asked.

"Up until today it has."

It was a cute turn of humor and they shared a small chuckle. Mathias thought he might actually be blushing but he wasn't about to touch his face to see if it was warm. He could only pray it wasn't; he'd never in his life met a lady that so easily extracted emotion from him in so short amount of time. He labored to keep his control and not look like a giddy fool in front of her.

"I am sure the events of today will not sour your good fortune," he said. "I suspect you still have many years of blessings before you."

Cathlina was still smiling at him but as she lingered on her sister's near-abduction again, her smile began to fade. She was still quite shaken by the whole thing.

"What do you suppose he wanted with my sister?" she asked hesitantly. "I have never heard of a man simply walking up to a woman and trying to steal her."

Mathias shrugged, trying to make light of the situation because it had ended well when it could have ended so tragically. He thought it was perhaps best not to dwell on what could have been before he had intervened.

"Mayhap he wanted someone to come home with him and cook him a meal," he said, mildly teasing as he skirted the subject. "Or mayhap he simply wanted a wife."

Cathlina turned to him, rather surprised. "Steal a wife?" she repeated. "I have never heard of such a thing."

"'Tis true. Those things happen."

She could sense his humored manner and it was difficult not to give in to the mood in spite of the serious subject matter. "Do you speak from experience, then?"

Mathias looked at her, full-on. His lips twitched with a smile. "I do not need to steal a wife."

"Is that so?"

"It is."

She cocked an eyebrow. "I see," she said with feigned seriousness. "I suppose women simply fall at your feet wherever you go and you can have your pick of them."

He was trying very hard not to grin; her humor was charming, and rather mocking of him, but he wasn't offended in the least.

"Something like that," he teased. "Women are always eager to marry a smithy."

Cathlina laughed softly, glancing towards the smithy stalls down the avenue. "Is that your trade over there?"

She was pointing and he followed the direction of her finger. "Aye," he replied. "My father, my brother, and me; we are the largest smithy operation in Brampton."

Cathlina dropped her finger and looked at him. "You were very brave to come as you did," she said. "I would not believe a smithy to be so brave."

He was amused. "Why not?"

She cocked her head as if cornered by the question. "Because that is not your vocation," she said, trying to explain. "You shoe horses and make weapons. You do not answer the call to arms as brave men do."

His amusement faded. *As brave men do.* He had been a brave man, once. Her comment hammered home the fact that he was no longer among the privileged, no longer in command of thousands of men who looked to him for guidance and strength. It seemed like an eternity ago when he last held a sword. Truth was, he hadn't thought much about it since the day he had been stripped of his weapons and lands and titles. There was no use dwelling on what he could not change. But at the moment, he was thinking on that very fact. He felt very useless.

"It was not a matter of answering the call to arms," he said quietly. "It was simply a matter of doing what was right."

Before Cathlina could respond, she caught sight of her father and sister coming down the avenue towards them, weaving through the crowds of people. Cathlina waved frantically at them.

"Father!" she called. "Roxane! Thank the Lord you have returned!"

Cathlina's father was a big man, muscular in his younger days but had now gone mostly to fat. He was balding and with a growth of beard, focusing curiously on his middle daughter as she called out to him.

"What is it?" he asked, depositing a burlap-wrapped bundle into the back of the wagon. "What is amiss?"

Cathlina didn't hold back. She told her father the entire sordid tale, watching the man's face turn red with anger and fright. Upon hearing the horrible story, the older sister, a dark-haired young woman who had a mere shadow of her middle sister's beauty, leapt into the back of the wagon to comfort Abechail. When Cathlina came to the part in the story where Abechail was so wonderfully saved, she pointed right at Mathias.

"This brave man came to our aid when no one else would," she told her father. "He was wonderful. He and his brother saved us. You *must* reward him."

Mathias was uncomfortable now that they were all focused on him. The father, his features still flushed with shock, made his way to him.

"Is this true?" he asked Mathias, as if he didn't quite believe his daughter's fantastic tale. "Was there truly a man to take my youngest daughter?"

Mathias could see the look of panic on the man's face. "It is true," he said. "But she is safe now. Lady Cathlina was quite brave; she fought him valiantly."

The father was stunned. He turned swiftly to Cathlina, inspecting her hands and arms for bruises before kissing her palms and turning his attention to Abechail.

The youngest daughter, who had managed to calm down somewhat since her brush with violence, was now weeping and quivering again as her eldest sister and father fussed over her. Mathias could see how shaken they all were. It was, in fact, quite touching to see how much they all cared about one another. That kind of devotion was rare.

Feeling rather as if he was viewing something intensely private, he turned to leave but was halted by Cathlina. She called his name, stopping him, and by the time he turned around, she was running at him. Her soft hands grasped his arm and those big brown eyes were shining up at him.

"Please," she begged softly. "You cannot leave before my father has had an opportunity to reward you."

Mathias had been touched by many women. He had also touched women from time to time, purely innocent gestures that meant nothing more than polite attentiveness. But he had never felt such fire from a touch as he felt now. Cathlina's soft hands were searing his flesh like brands. He could feel the heat all the way down to his toes.

"A reward is not necessary," he assured her. "It was my pleasure to assist."

"Will you at least come to Kirklinton and dine with us?" she pleaded softly. "Please allow us to show our thanks for your bravery. Do not deny us an opportunity to show you how grateful we are."

Gazing down into that sweet face, he knew he shouldn't agree. It wasn't a good idea, on so many levels. As much as he wanted to accept her invitation if only to bask in Cathlina's beauty for the evening, it simply wasn't wise. She was a de Lara and he wanted to stay far away from anything de Lara. But as he stood there with her, having her on his arm, he felt more like a man than he had in over a year. Odd how such a gesture fortified him. *She* fortified him. But he was forced to refuse.

"Your offer is very kind but I must decline, my lady," he said, trying not to sound cruel. "I can live the rest of my life on the gratitude you have already shown me. Anything more would seem greedy and excessive. I wish you and your family well."

He would never forget the look on Cathlina's face as he turned to walk away from her. It was a very difficult thing not to relent because he certainly didn't want to cause her such disappointment, but it couldn't be helped. He had done his good deed and would leave it at that.

He had work to do.

CHAPTER TWO

"Is the basket packed?" Cathlina asked.

"It is, my lady," the red-faced cook replied. "I just put the bread in. That should be all of it."

In the small, cluttered kitchen of Kirklinton, she was peering into a basket laden with goodies; pear and cinnamon compote in an earthenware jar sealed with beeswax, cherries soaked in honey and wine, pickled onions, two loaves of bread baked with cheese and garlic, and small cakes that Cathlina had made herself – a little flour, lard, eggs, butter, honey, walnuts, nutmeg and cloves made delicious little bread-like cakes. Satisfied her basket was packed to her specifications, Cathlina carefully covered it with an embroidered piece of cloth. It was her own kerchief with the elaborate letters *"CLM"*, for Cathlina Lavinia Mary, stitched in the shape of vines.

"Excellent," she said, lifting the basket off of the massive, scarred butcher table. "Thank you for your assistance"

The cook waved her off and returned to the suckling pig she had just killed. Hands wrapped around the moderately heavy basket, Cathlina headed out of the kitchen and into the yard beyond.

It was early morning in Kirklinton. In late May, the weather was warmer and they hadn't had rain for several days, which meant the ground had dried up somewhat and the mud wasn't what it usually was. In fact, it was rather dry and pleasant. Pleasant enough for a trip back to Brampton.

That was her plan, in any case. Dressed in a yellow linen surcoat with a matching linen cloak, the surcoat had lacings in the front of the bodice that, when tightened, emphasized her curvy figure to a fault. It was her favorite dress, given to her by her mother because the color had been so striking against her pale skin and dark hair. Cathlina's mother, the Lady Rosalund, was rather partial to her middle daughter. She reminded her of a sister she'd had in her youth, now long dead. Therefore, Cathlina usually had the pick of the wardrobe.

Even with the favoritism of her sometimes-flighty mother, she was still remarkably unselfish or spoilt. She was, however, quite headstrong, knowing that she would not be punished for whatever she decided to do because her parents could never bring themselves to discipline her. Cathlina knew, therefore, that she would not be punished for her latest scheme. It was simply something she had to do and her parents would have to understand that.

Kirklinton's bailey was relatively small, as the castle itself wasn't particularly large. A big, square keep constructed of bumpy gray stone sat in the middle of the complex on a slightly raised motte; there was an enclosed entry and then four rooms of various sizes on the ground floor while the second floor had three sleeping chambers and a smaller chamber used for bathing and other personal needs. On the ground floor, a trap door in the largest room, which served as a smaller great hall, led down into a dungeon-like basement for storage

The great hall was a separate structure as was the kitchen, both of them built into the curtain wall on the north side of the complex. Cathlina headed away from the kitchen and towards the stables built against the east wall. She could smell the hay and the smells of animals, and hear the braying and bleating as the beasts were fed by the stable workers.

Clutching her basket tightly, she kept looking around to make sure no one noticed that she was dressed for travel. She did not want to be stopped before she could accomplish her mission. Fortunately, everyone seemed too busy to notice.

Cathlina's horse, a lovely dapple gray mare that was part Belgian warm blood and part Spanish Jennet, was tearing at her hay when Cathlina entered the dark confines of the stables. A litter of kittens nestled near the stash of hay up against the rear of the stall and she had to take the time to pet each tiny furry creature. She set the basket down so she could cuddle the babies. As she put the last kitten down and turned for the horse, she caught sight of a figure standing next to her.

Startled, she gasped with fright until she realized it was her older sister. The Lady Roxane Marietta Anna de Lara was eighteen months older than her middle sister, a plain-looking girl with long features and frizzy dark hair. She was rather silly and not particularly bright, and she had a dreamy manner about her. With Roxane, other people's concerns or quarrels didn't interest her in the least. She was mostly focused on what made her happy. She was also quite jealous of Cathlina and often followed her, which is how she ended up in the stable.

Cathlina knew the way her sister's mind worked; Roxane was very nosy. She was the one person who couldn't know what she was doing. Cathlina's heart began to race with apprehension, wondering how she was going to prevent her sister from running for their parents when she discovered her plan to leave Kirklinton. The best way to deal with Roxane was to go on the offensive and hope to bully her into submission.

"What are you doing here?" Cathlina demanded.

Roxane cocked a thin eyebrow. "I saw you come from the kitchen," she said. "What are you doing?"

"That is none of your affair," Cathlina hissed. "Go back to the keep."

Roxane's eyes narrowed. "Tell me where you are going."

"Nay."

"Tell me or I shall tell Mother."

Cathlina's expression twisted angrily. "If you tell her anything at all, I shall tell her that you were the one who stole her store of fine wine and used it to ply Beauson so that he would kiss you!"

"You would not dare!"

"If you do not leave me alone, I most certainly will!"

"Oooh!"

"Oooooh!"

They shrieked and pointed at each other, furious and outraged. The next step was usually pulling hair but fortunately that didn't occur. Still, there was agitated posturing going on that eventually settled with Roxane backing down first. She was still making faces, however.

"I will not tell her," she finally grumbled. "But tell me where you are going. What is in your basket?"

Cathlina settled down as well, though she was still eyeing her sister with some anger. Roxane had a way of getting under her skin.

"Breads and treats," she finally said, returning her attention to her mare as she began to saddle the animal. "I am going to Brampton to bring them to the man who saved me and Abechail from the attacker yesterday. It is the least I can do."

Roxane followed her sister to the horse and actually began helping her tack the animal. "The man?" she repeated, thinking back to the day before and the events surrounding Abechail's near abduction. "The big man with the dark hair?"

Cathlina nodded as she strapped on the saddle. "Aye," she said. "He said he would not take a reward but I feel strongly that I must do something for him. Had he not intervened, surely Abechail would now be lost. He would not even come to dine with us so I thought to bring him some manner of treats to show our gratitude."

Roxane pulled the bridle off the nail on the wall above the mare's head, her manner thoughtful. "What was his name again?"

"Mathias."

"Mathias? What was his surname?"

"He did not say."

Roxane fussed with the straps on the bridle, her mind drifting to the very big, very handsome man who had saved her sisters from tragedy. He had delightful dark hair and a sculpted face.

"Mathias," she repeated, somewhat dreamily. "He was quite handsome, don't you think?"

Cathlina could hear the hopeful tone and she was irritated by it. Her sister had an eye for men, *any* man, and she could already tell that Roxane's easily-won affections were about to shift to yesterday's hero.

Cathlina had spent most of the evening thinking about the dark-haired stranger, pondering his beauteous face and deep, gentle voice. The massive arms, the unruly hair, the twinkle in the green eyes… she was smitten by the picture. The mysterious Mathias was her private joy and no one else's, and certainly not her fickle sister. She would not share a secret fantasy that would surely never be fulfilled. It was but a dream, but it was *her* dream. She turned swiftly to Roxane, a finger in her face

"You will not think of him," she hissed. "If anyone is to show affection towards him, it will be me, do you hear? I was the one he saved, you little fool. You have Beauson and Dunstan to occupy your affections. Leave Mathias alone."

Roxane looked rather surprised; her sister never spoke of a man, so this was a rare occurrence. It also made Roxane very jealous because as the eldest, she felt it her birthright to have first right of refusal on any man that crossed the sisters' path.

"Beauson and Dunstan are merely father's knights," she said. "They are not men I intend to marry."

"Why not?"

Roxane shrugged her slender shoulders. "Because they are mere knights," she repeated. "I will marry a lord."

"Then you will put Mathias from your mind because he is not a lord. He is a smithy."

Roxane's brow furrowed, just as quickly lifting in realization when she became aware that her sister was right. "You are correct," she declared. "He is not a lord. We are de Laras and therefore must marry well. Mayhap Father will convince Cousin Tate to find us wealthy husbands; do you recall when we visited last Christmas and the fine men that were gathered at Carlisle?"

"You mean when you first beheld Kenneth St. Hèver?"

"I do."

"He is a mere knight, Roxy," Cathlina said, somewhat gently, although she was thankful that Roxane was off Mathias' scent. "He is not a lord. But I am sure there are many other men of standing that Cousin Tate can align us with."

"I hope so," Roxane said wistfully. "I am growing rather weary of kissing knights."

Cathlina lifted an eyebrow at her. "You should not be kissing them at all."

Roxane shrugged with a half-hearted attempt at defiance. "I do not kiss Dunstan anymore," she said, "merely Beauson. I do believe Dunstan has a fondness for you so he is unresponsive to my charms as of late."

Cathlina finished with the bridle. "Dunstan is a nice enough man, big and strong, but he is not what I would call a smart man," she said. "Besides, he is too old. I am not interested in him as a romantic prospect. He will have to seek affection elsewhere."

With that, Cathlina finished the last strap on the bridle and moved to secure the basket on the back of the saddle. Roxane assisted her and between the two of them, they managed to tie it down securely.

"Mayhap you should ask Dunstan or Beauson to escort you to town," Roxane said. "It is a long ride to Brampton and there are dangers about. You know you should not go alone."

Cathlina shook her head as she gathered her mare's reins and turned to lead the horse from the stable. "I do not need an escort," she said. "The ride to town will take an hour or two at the most. It is a fine day for travel and I shall return in good time."

Roxane didn't argue with her, mostly because she knew it wouldn't do any good. Cathlina was stubborn and determined and Roxane was never strong enough to take a stand against her. She didn't think the ride into town was a good idea but she had already voiced her objections. Now there was nothing to do but wait until her sister returned.

The wind was picking up as they moved into the stable yard. Bits of chaff blew about as Cathlina mounted her mare and adjusted her cloak, gathering the reins. Once she was settled, she turned to her sister.

"I should be back before the evening meal," she said. "If Mother or Father are looking for me, tell them that you have not seen me. Swear it?"

"I swear it."

"Good."

"Can I have your clothing if you do not return?"

Cathlina made a face at her sister to let her know exactly what she thought of that question. Kicking her mare in the ribs, she trotted out of the bailey quite simply, losing herself in the peasants and farmers milling in and out of the open gates. Being the only castle within a several mile radius, many of the locals came here to do business with each other. It was easy to get lost in the masses of the small and crowded bailey.

Soon enough, Cathlina was on the road south towards Brampton.

CHAPTER THREE

"I am going to marry her," Sebastian said firmly. "Did you see the way she looked at me? She *wants* me."

Mathias was in the midst of shoeing a massive charger with a nasty temper. He was trying to concentrate as his brother, propped on the edge of a table, chewed loudly of his nooning meal, a large bird leg. Food flew about as Sebastian chomped and spoke.

"Could you see how attracted she was to me?" he asked enthusiastically. "Mark my words; I have found my future wife."

Mathias avoided a thrown horse-head. "You never came even remotely close to her," he said. "How can you know anything about her?"

Sebastian tore at the bird. "It was the *way* she looked at me."

"Is that so?"

"It 'tis. It was the look of love."

"How would you know? You have never seen such a look."

Sebastian snorted, pieces of food falling from his lips. "I have indeed, my fine lad," he informed him. "Every time I step foot in The Buck's Head down the street, those women give me the look. They want me."

He was deeply self-assured and Mathias couldn't resist taking a swipe at his arrogance. "They will give anyone the look that they think will pay for the privilege," he said.

Sebastian shrugged, unwilling to admit that only whores were throwing him expressions of passion. "Sometimes I do not have to pay them."

Mathias fought off a grin at his brother's damaged ego. Letting go of the horse's hoof, he went back over to the fire and pumped it hard as the flames sparked and roared.

"I would guess that Lady Cathlina does not even know you are alive," he said as he removed the red-hot shoe. "Besides, she is a de Lara. I told you that."

Sebastian was back to snorting as his brother transferred the shoe to an anvil and began to hammer. "What would the great Earl of

Carlisle say if one of his lovely relatives ended up married to me?" he wondered. "It would make us family."

Mathias put the shoe into a barrel of rainwater, watching the steam hiss up into the air. "I am sure that would not excite him half as much as it would excite you," he said, eyeing his brother. "De Lara would not want us in the family."

"Why not?" Sebastian demanded. "You served with him and St. Hèver and Pembury. You were all as thick as thieves."

"I was Tate's squire when he was a young knight," Mathias muttered. "I am not sure that makes us blood brothers."

"He loved you and you know it," Sebastian pointed out. "Besides, there is only a few years difference between you two."

"Seven years."

"He still knighted you at nineteen," Sebastian pointed out. "Two full years before most knights receive their spurs."

"That is because there was a war going on. He needed my sword."

"And I would wager he has missed it long enough this year past," Sebastian said. Then, he looked thoughtful. "In fact, I do believe you even saved his life once. He owes you everything."

"Sparing his life and saving it are two different things," Mathias said quietly. He didn't want to talk about that particular incident; in fact, he didn't want to discuss that part of his life at all. Politics had separated him from his friends. A king had stripped him of all that he was. Nay, he didn't want to talk about it in the least and Sebastian knew it, but Sebastian had jelly for brains sometimes.

But Sebastian didn't have so much jelly for brains that he didn't know he had broached a sore subject with his brother. Mathias kept himself so bottled up, however, that sometimes Sebastian wondered if the man cared about anything at all. But he knew, deep down, that he cared a great deal.

"He would be honored to have a de Reyne in the family," he said confidently. "De Lara views you as an equal, Mat. You know he does. Ken and Stephen view you as a brother. Mayhap it is time to speak of such things again. Mayhap… mayhap it is even time to contact them again."

Mathias kept his mouth shut as he removed the shoe from the water and moved to the horse. Bending over, he pulled the horse's hoof between his legs and fitted the shoe. The horse tried to move around a bit and tried to kick at him but Sebastian set his food down and went to help his brother. He held the horse firm as Mathias hammered on the shoe.

Dropping the hoof to the ground, he wiped the sweat off his brow and moved back to the fire where the remaining shoe was being heated.

"Mat?" Sebastian said quietly. "Did you hear me?"

"I heard you."

"What say you?

Mathias pulled the shoe out of the fire, his face red from the heat and exertion of wrestling with the horse. "What would you have me say?"

"Tell me your thoughts," Sebastian pushed. He could see that he wasn't getting anywhere with his brother so he ventured onward in an attempt to prompt him. "I heard something the other day that might be of interest."

Mathias was only half-listening to him. "What is that?"

Sebastian reclaimed his food and chewed on the last of the meat. "Henry de Beaumont is trying to put Edward Balliol on the throne of Scotland instead of the infant David," he said. "I heard some men speaking of it the other day. De Beaumont will need knights, Mat. Mayhap this will be an opportunity for us."

Mathias looked at his brother. "De Beaumont is allied with our king," he said frankly. "If we take up arms for de Beaumont, do you not think that Edward will catch wind of that? Nay, brother, I will not lose my head for a Scots rebellion."

Sebastian knew that would be his brother's response but he wasn't pleased with it. He tossed aside the stripped bird bone and stood up, his manner growing agitated as it so often did.

"I do not want to be a smithy the rest of my life," he hissed. "Mayhap you find comfort in swinging a hammer instead of a sword, but I do not. I will be a knight again someday, I swear it, and if it is without your support, then so be it."

Mathias wiped the sweat off his brow. "Patience was never one of your virtues."

"What is that supposed to mean?"

"It means that times change. Tides and the flow of power change. You must be patient, little brother. We will not be like this forever, but for now, it is what we must do to survive."

Sebastian wasn't satisfied with that. He was about to fire off a volley of insults at his brother's lack of courage when a soft voice interrupted him.

"Excuse me?"

It was a gentle female voice. Startled, Mathias and Sebastian turned to see Cathlina standing at the entrance to their stall; lit from behind by the nooning sun, her silhouette gave off an ethereal glow as she stood at the threshold. Wrapped in a yellow linen cloak, her dark hair was braided and draped over her right shoulder and her dark eyes glimmered as she fixed on Mathias.

"I am so sorry to interrupt," she said politely. "Do you remember me? You saved my sister and me yesterday from a brute, right out there on the avenue. I do hope you...."

Mathias cut her off, gently done. "Of course I remember you," he said, realizing in a rush that he was both surprised and glad to see her again. "Are you and your sister well?"

Cathlina smiled warmly at him, thrilled that he remembered her. "We are very well, thanks to you," she said. Then her gaze passed between Mathias and his brother. "I did not mean to intrude. I will only beg a moment of your time and then I promise I shall be gone."

Sebastian was the first one to move towards her, his enormous red-headed presence overwhelming. "Lady Cathlina," he said, a smile on his lips. "'Tis a welcome interruption, you are."

Cathlina looked at the big, ruddy-faced brother and couldn't help but be a bit put-off by him. He was smelling and sweaty and large. She instinctively took a step back as he came close.

"Thank you," she said, eyeing him. "How do you know my name?"

Sebastian pointed to Mathias. "My brother told me," he said. "I am glad to hear that you and your sister are faring well after yesterday's fracas."

Cathlina nodded. "Well indeed," she replied. "Thank you again for coming to our aid. In fact, that is why I have come. I have brought you something in the hopes of emphasizing our gratitude."

She lifted the basket in her hands and both men looked at it as if only just noticing it. Both of them had been looking at her face, mesmerized by the unexpected appearance of such beauty. Sebastian looked at the basket with interest but Mathias was on the move; he didn't want his brother frightening her, or worse. The man could offend easily.

"Your thanks yesterday was quite enough," he said, his deep voice soft. "You did not need to bring us anything."

"I realize that, but I wanted to," she said, once again completely focused on Mathias as if Sebastian did not exist at all. She couldn't seem to do much more than stare at him. "You would not take a reward and you would not sup with us, so I took it upon myself to bring you a few tokens of my appreciation. I hope you will accept them."

Mathias was genuinely touched. More than that, he was coming to realize that every time he saw the woman, she seemed to grow increasingly beautiful. He was still turned off against her being a de Lara but truth be told, every second that he gazed at her saw that resistance taking a beating. Looking at her hopeful face, he knew he could not refuse her.

"Of course we will accept whatever you have brought," he said, his eyes glimmering at her. "You did not have to go to the trouble."

She smiled brightly and he was enchanted. "It was no trouble at all," she said, moving to the nearest table surface, which happened to be littered with a mixture of tools and scraps of food. Setting the basket down, she peeled back the embroidered cloth. "I brought you pear and cinnamon compote, and different types of bread, cherries soaked in honey, and – oh! – pickled onions. Have you ever had them? They are quite delicious. The cook pickles them with vinegar and herbs."

Sebastian was extremely interested in the contents of the basket, pulling things out to smell them, while Mathias tried to control his boorish brother by putting things back where they belonged.

"I have had them, aye," he replied, smacking Sebastian's hand when the man tried to stick his fingers in the cherries. "This is most kind and generous of you, my lady. This is truly an unexpected treat."

Cathlina beamed happily, thrilled by Mathias' response but rather peeved at his brother's uncouth manners. She had the little cakes she had made all tucked down in the corner of the basket and she pulled them out before Sebastian could stick his fingers in them, handing them over to Mathias.

"Here," she said. "I made these just for you. I do hope you like them."

Sebastian was busy with the bread and wasn't paying much attention to the cakes Cathlina had presented to Mathias. But Mathias was acutely aware that she seemed to be speaking only to him; his eyes were on her as he unwrapped the cakes, hit in the nose by the clove and nutmeg smell. The gesture of bringing him gifts coupled with the delight of her lovely face had his careful control slipping.

"They smell wonderful," he said quietly. "It was very kind of you to do this."

She picked one out of the bundle and held it up to him. "Would you try one?"

He did. It was a marvelous bit of culinary achievement. "Did you make these yourself?" he asked.

"I did."

"Then they are the most wonderful gift I have ever received," he said. "No one has ever made treats for me before."

Cathlina was smiling so broadly that her face threatened to split in half. "Then I am happy to be the first," she said, noticing that Sebastian was tearing into the onions. She sighed at the sight. "Mayhap I should have made two baskets – one for you and one for your brother. It would seem he is going to eat everything before you have the opportunity to taste it."

Mathias cocked an eyebrow as he snatched the basket away from his brother, shoving the man back by the chest when he tried to pursue. Sebastian balled a fist but Mathias held up a finger.

"You have already shown Lady Cathlina what an animal you are," he said. "Would you show her that you are a brute as well? Show some manners in front of the lady, Sebastian. You are shaming me."

Sebastian tried to throw the punch but couldn't bring himself to do it. His brother was right; moreover, if he had any chance of wooing the woman, he would have to behave himself.

Lowering his balled fist, he forced a smile at Cathlina and sought to apologize for whatever brutish manners he had thus far shown when Justus entered the stall with a customer, bellowing for Sebastian. Disgruntled, Sebastian was forced away from his brother and the lovely lady.

"Good," Mathias snorted as he watched his unhappy brother stomp away. "That should keep him occupied for a while."

Cathlina watched Sebastian move away. "Your brother is quite... lively? Friendly? I am searching for the correct word that will not offend you."

Mathias laughed softly. "He is aggressive and he is a boor," he said. "But he is also fiercely loyal and strangely compassionate. It is an odd combination."

Cathlina grinned at him. "Mayhap you should hide this food from him. I have a feeling he will eat it all given the opportunity."

"He will," Mathias agreed, his gaze drifting over her delicate features. "Truly, it was quite kind of you to bring this. Where is your father so that I may thank him also?"

Cathlina's grin faded. "He is at home," she replied. "He did not come with me."

Mathias looked over her shoulder, back in the direction she had come from. "Where is your escort?"

"I do not have one."

His brow furrowed. "Did you come here alone?"

"It was not a long ride and the day was fine."

Now both eyebrows lifted in a mixture of concern and disapproval. "It is not safe for a lady to travel alone," he said as mildly as he could. "Does your father know you have come?"

"He does not."

Mathias wasn't sure what to say to that, but one thing was for certain; he was very flattered that she should risk her personal safety to deliver what she considered a reward for assisting her. In fact, he was rather stunned.

"Would you allow me to escort you home, then?" he asked softly. "I cannot allow you to return home unattended now that I know you have no escort. I hope you understand."

"It is truly not necessary. I can find my own way home."

"I am sorry, but I must insist. If you will not give me permission to escort you, then know that I will follow you all of the way home to ensure you do not run into any trouble. I can either ride with you or as your shadow; it is your choice."

Cathlina very nearly refused him again but she quickly realized that if he escorted her home, they would have more of a chance to talk. Perhaps she could come to know him better. Clearly, she was attracted to the man; now that she had seen him again, it served to reinforce her initial opinion of him. He was handsome, gentle mannered, and undoubtedly brave. There was much to be attracted to.

Unlike her sister, Cathlina didn't particularly care if he was a lord or not. Roxanne was the one with lofty goals; Cathlina had, since she could recall, merely wanted a man she liked a great deal no matter what status he held in life. She'd heard of many lords who were selfish, vain, and immoral. Being a lord didn't mean one was automatically of good character. Cathlina would rather have good character and love over wealth and status. The man in front of her was of good character; she could sense it.

"Very well," she said after a moment's deliberation. "I would be honored with your company. Are you certain you can spare the time?"

Mathias looked around the stall, at the big charger he needed to finish. Taking the basket in one hand and the lady by the other, he gently escorted her over to a stool near the wall and helped her to sit.

He set the basket down next to her.

"I must finish with this Son of Lucifer," he said, throwing a thumb in the direction of the big black charger. "When I am finished, I will be happy to escort you home. Is that acceptable?"

"It is."

Their eyes met, brown against green, and for a moment, the pull between them was stronger than they could grasp. It was difficult to describe, this attraction between two people who had no expectations or obligations to their brief association. Up until a few minutes ago, all Mathias knew of the Lady Cathlina de Lara was that she was incredibly beautiful but, unfortunately, she was also a de Lara. He had warned his brother against her. Now, he was not so apt to heed his own warning. There was something about the woman that was very, very special. He couldn't seem to take his eyes off of her because she muddled his mind so; she was bewitching. He finally had to force himself away.

"I will not be long," he said as he made his way back over to the horse, who tried to bite him. He frowned at the animal. "These animals are sometimes quite difficult to handle for those they are not familiar with."

Cathlina watched him with interest as he pulled another red-hot shoe out of the fire and began hammering at it.

"It is a very big horse," she said. "A war horse?"

Mathias nodded as he pounded. "This nasty boy has seen several battles."

Cathlina eyed the scarred horse. "We saw several knights in town yesterday when we arrived," she said. "My father says there is to be a tournament in a few days."

Mathias nodded as he put the shoe back into the fire. "So it would seem."

Cathlina studied the man as he stirred the fire; he was wearing leather breeches and a leather apron, and a rather worn linen tunic that in greater days had probably been a bright shade of red. It was very worn, and the neckline was torn just enough so she could see portions of his muscular chest. The man had the biggest arms she had ever seen, muscular to a fault, and his chest seemed to match that particular pattern. She'd never thought much about men's chests before but in peeking at Mathias', she thought his rather attractive. The man was purely big and beautiful, and her cheeks began to flush. She averted her gaze and sought to divert her innately passionate thoughts.

"Where... where were you born, Mathias?" she asked, struggling to think on something else to speak of.

He continued to stoke the fire, his face and body riddled with lusty, oozy sweat, causing his inky hair to kink up in small curls around his neck.

"Throston Castle in Northumbria," he said. "It is near the eastern coast."

"I see," Cathlina said, cocking her head as she tried to imagine where he was from. "You must have learned your trade from a very young age. Did you ever think to become anything other than a smithy?"

He pulled the red-hot shoe out of the fire again and set it on the anvil. He didn't want to tell her his deepest, darkest secret for many reasons, not the least of which was the fact that she was a de Lara. Therefore, for all she knew, he was what she saw: a smithy. There was no reason to tell her any differently because it would have been far too complicated to explain, anyway, and it might possibly frighten her away. He didn't want to frighten her away.

"Like what?" he asked, glancing up at her with a twinkle in his eye. "A farmer? A sailor?"

Cathlina took the question seriously. "You are big and brave and intelligent," she said. "Perhaps you could have found someone to sponsor you as a page or squire at a young age. You could have been a fighting man. You said you were born at Throston Castle? Who is the lord at Throston?"

My grandfather, he thought. They were heading deeper into a subject he wanted to avoid. He pounded on the shoe.

"An old man by the name of Lenox," he replied, then shifted the course of questions back onto her and away from secrets he did not wish to divulge. "Your father is a knight, is he not? Allied with the Earl of Carlisle, you said?"

Successfully diverted, she nodded. "My father is a cousin to the earl," she replied. "During the wars between the king and Roger Mortimer, my father served the earl and the king. But he sustained a very bad injury in the battle at Stanhope a few years ago and resigned from fighting. He simply administers the garrison at Kirklinton now and has knights and other men who do the fighting for him."

"What is your father's name?"

"Sir Saer de Lara. Have you ever heard of him?"

"I am sorry, I have not. I am sure he was a great knight."

"They used to call him The Axe. Father did not fight with a sword;

he liked his axe much better."

The Axe. Now, Mathias had heard *that* name. De Lara's Axe had been a feared fighter, indeed. More and more, Mathias was sure he would never divulge his past to Cathlina. Or at least, never divulge it to her father. He was coming to wonder if his attraction to her would lead him down paths he was trying very hard to avoid. If their attraction grew and he eventually pledged for her, somehow, someway, he would have to be truthful. To lie about who, and what, he was then have the truth come from someone else's lips to Cathlina's ears would have devastating consequences. Truth be told, lying was not in his blood. Truth and honor meant everything to him.

"I could make him an excellent axe," he teased softly, watching her giggle. She had the most beautiful smile. "Mayhap you will want to give your father a gift someday and employ me to make it."

She laughed softly. "I am sure you would do a very good job."

He grinned, swept up in her charm, when a pair of knights entered the stall. They didn't see Cathlina, sitting against the wall, as they sauntered into the shop, knocking over a hammer and hardly caring. They were young, arrogant, and full of entitlement. The taller of the pair, a young knight with bristly red hair, approached Mathias.

"Have you finished with my horse yet?" he demanded.

Mathias picked up an enormous steel file and bent over, pulling a hoof between his legs. "Almost," he said. "A moment longer."

"A moment longer?" the knight repeated, incredulous and outraged. "He has been here all morning."

Mathias was filing the front left hoof. "He has been here not yet two hours," he said steadily. "These shoes were specially prepared, as you requested. That takes time. I am almost finished."

The young knight pursed his lips angrily, eyeing the big smithy. "You are incompetent," he announced. "This job should have been completed an hour ago."

"I will be finished in a moment."

"I will not pay you, then. You did not finish on time."

Surprisingly, Mathias kept his composure. "I told you when you brought him in that he would be finished by early afternoon," he said. "I have finished him sooner than I estimated and you will indeed pay me the full price or I will pull every one of these shoes off of him and you can find someone else to shoe this bad-tempered beast. Do I make myself clear?"

The young knight was looking for a confrontation. He was too arrogant to back down from what he considered a challenge. "You will do no such thing," he said. "I will not let you. I will take my horse now and I will not pay you for being lazy and slow."

Mathias kept filing. "You will pay me or the horse stays here and I will sell him to the highest bidder to recoup my losses."

The young knight was outraged. "He is my horse and I am taking him."

"Not until you pay me what you owe me."

The young knight marched over to Mathias and lifted a hand to strike him, but Mathias grabbed the knight's wrist before he could follow through with the action. The knight yelped as Mathias shoved him away and tumbled over a bucket near the anvil.

This brought the knight's companion charging forward, unsheathing his sword. Mathias dropped the charger's hoof, preparing to defend himself against the armed knight, when a stool suddenly sailed into the knight's feet and the man went down. With both knights on the ground, Mathias was rather dumbfounded when Cathlina rushed up and kicked the armed knight in the shoulder. It was a hard enough kick that the man's entire body rattled.

"Shame on you!" she scolded angrily. "You foolish whelps! By what right do you try to cheat a man out of his earnings? You are a dishonor to the knighthood, both of you!"

Mathias' eyebrows lifted at her furious manner and brave tactic of throwing the stool she had been sitting on in order to disable the armed knight, but in truth, he wasn't surprised. She had shown remarkable bravery the day before whilst fighting with a man three times her size. If he thought about it, his respect for her had sprouted at that moment; she was a strong and courageous woman. Now, with this latest show of courage, his respect for her had gone from a sprout to a healthy bloom.

"'Tis all right," he soothed her, trying to steer her away from the men who were trying to gain their feet. "Please go and sit down. Do not trouble yourself over this."

Lured by the commotion, Sebastian appeared from outside the stall. His brow furrowed at the men on the ground.

"What goes on here?" he demanded.

Mathias merely shook his head but Cathlina spoke. "These men were trying to cheat your brother out of his earnings for shoeing this horse," she pointed angrily. "They tried to attack him."

Sebastian's red eyebrows flew up in outrage. "Is that so?" he said, going to stand over the young knight who had started it all. He was just starting to sit up as Sebastian loomed over him and glared. "You were trying to cheat us?"

The young knight rolled to his knees, attempting to stand up and keep a distance from the enormous red-haired knight. "He... he was slow and lazy," he stammered, his arrogance gone now that he was being challenged by two very big men. "It is within my right not to pay him for a job he did not complete when he said he would."

Sebastian reached out and grabbed the man by the neck as Justus, lured from the opposite side of the stall by all of the scuffling going on, came around to see both of his sons standing and two armed knights in various positions on the ground. The big old man with the long gray hair went straight to Sebastian.

"What are you doing?" he hissed, pointing fingers at the man in Sebastian's grip. "I have warned you against harassing our customers."

Sebastian didn't let the young knight go. "He is trying to cheat us out of paying what he owes," he told his father. "He tried to attack Mathias."

Justus looked at his eldest son. "Is this true, Mat?"

Mathias had positioned himself between Cathlina and the men tussling, including his brother.

"He tried," he confirmed. "But it is of no matter. His horse is finished and he owes a crown. If he refuses to pay, as he has declared to be his intention, then we keep the horse. Hopefully he has reconsidered, as a knight without a horse is a sorry sight indeed."

The young knight had managed to yank himself away from Sebastian and was fumbling angrily for his purse. Mathias untethered the charger and held out a hand, refusing to hand the reins over until the young knight paid him in full. By the time the young knight got the reins in his hand, he was so angry that he yanked at them and the horse took offense. A big head swung at the young knight, nearly knocking him over, as the young knight and his companion stumbled from the stall.

When they were gone, Mathias went about his business cleaning up as if nothing was amiss. Sebastian, however, followed them out and stood in the entry to the stall, watching them walk down the street with an expression that dared them to turn around and look at him. He would have liked nothing better than to go charging after them.

With the situation settling down, Justus eyed his two boys before realizing that Cathlina was standing back in the shadows. Surprise filled his expression as he gaze beheld her lingering on the fringe.

"A lady?" he said, pointing to her. "God's blood, there is a lady here. Does she have business with us?"

Mathias put his hammer on the anvil and began to remove his leather apron. "This is the Lady Cathlina de Lara," he said. "It 'twas her and her sister that we did a good turn for yesterday. Lady Cathlina has come bearing gifts to thank us."

"Good turn?" Justus was still confused. "What do you mean?"

Mathias had a half-grin on his face, his eyes on Cathlina as he spoke. "The lady's sister was nearly abducted yesterday," he said, trying not to be thankful for such an event but it was the reason that had introduced him to the lovely young woman. "Sebastian put their accoster in the stocks back behind the stall."

Justus was aware of that particular circumstance. "The animal with one eye who will not speak?"

"The same."

"He was still there last I saw."

"He will be there for a few days or until Sebastian has had his fun with him and decides to let him go." He set his leather apron down and pulled a leather vest off a nail. "I will be gone for a few hours, Father. I must escort Lady Cathlina home."

Justus' gaze was still lingering on Cathlina, thinking on the events of yesterday as Sebastian had told them. He and Mathias had all but swooped out of the sky like avenging angels. Mathias was a bit more modest, but in looking at the beauty of the lady before him, he began to suspect that one or more smitten sons was on the horizon. It would be hard to look at all of that beauty and not be bewitched by it. That spelled trouble.

"I am sure she has her own escort," Justus said. "Your presence is needed here. With the tournament beginning tomorrow, we have more business than we can handle. I cannot lose you, even for a few hours."

Mathias put the leather vest on over his rough tunic, securing the fastens that held it snug to his body. It was, in truth, a measure of protection against sharp objects, like swords or daggers, because the leather was heavily woven and fit his enormous torso like a glove; tight against his broad chest and snug against his slender waist. Since he was disallowed armor, the vest was the next best thing.

"I will not be gone long," he assured his father. "And Lady Cathlina has no escort. She bravely rode here alone but I certainly cannot let her return alone."

Justus could see the glimmer in Mathias' eyes when speaking of

Lady Cathlina and he knew the man was already infatuated. It hadn't taken long at all, but he hardly blamed him. Still, he had to discourage it quickly.

"Then I will send Sebastian to escort her," he said. "You are needed here."

The glimmer vanished from Mathias' eyes when he looked at his father. "*Not* Sebastian," he growled, leaving no room for discussion. In fact, the last time his father heard that tone, they were in battle. "I will return in a few hours and do not let Sebastian touch anything in that basket. If he does, I will put *him* in the stocks. You will tell him that."

Justus sighed heavily, realizing there was no way to discourage his eldest. Strangely enough, he was rather glad for the lady's appearance when it came to Mathias; the man hadn't shown so much interest or concern about anything in well over a year. The Mathias that had lumbered around the smithy stall since that dark January day had been morose and sullen, quiet. A mere shell of his former self. But this Mathias was much more like the Mathias of old; humorous, concerned, and interested in what was going on around him. Aye, the lady had done that much, at least. Justus had no choice but to relent.

"Return as quickly as you can," he said, with reluctance. "We shall be working long into the night as it is."

The glimmer was back in Mathias' eyes. "I will, I swear it."

When Sebastian found out where Mathias was going, he tried to follow until Mathias slugged the man in the chest so hard that he fell into a big puddle of horse urine and got covered in the stuff.

As Mathias and Cathlina walked off, Sebastian vowed to get even.

CHAPTER FOUR

For a day that had started so beautiful, the weather turned bad quickly. It was just a few miles from Brampton to Kirklinton Castle but as the weather threatened, Mathias picked up the pace.

He was disappointed, too, because the first hour of their ride had been very pleasant and leisurely. He and Cathlina had spoken of trivial things, like little stories from when they were younger or, in Cathlina's case, a grandfather who had no teeth and spent all of his time gnawing on animal bones like a dog. She had giggled through the story and Mathias had been charmed by the way she told it. The more time he spent with her, the more he felt his wall of self-protection crumbling. De Lara or no, he was deeply attracted to her.

But then the clouds rolled in and the breeze began to pick up. He watched the sky turn dark but Kirklinton was at least another hour away so he gently prodded Cathlina to move a bit faster. But she wasn't interested in returning home any time soon; she was more interested in their conversation and truth be told, so was he. Their quickened pace didn't last long before they were back to a leisure stroll.

Mathias rode a big, heavy gray charger that was well past its prime; when he'd had his knighthood stripped, they'd taken his charger as well and he missed the horse very much. It had been Justus who had purchased the old charger for his son a few months after that fateful day and Mathias was rather fond of the beast, but he soon discovered it was rather skittish. It particularly didn't like thunder. Every time the clouds rolled, the horse would jump. As Cathlina chattered on, it was taking increasing effort to control the old stud.

"Now you know all about my silly grandfather," she said as fat drops of rain began to splatter. "Tell me about your family, Mathias; I have met your father and brother. Where is your mother?"

He clucked to the big horse to soothe it. "My mother died a few years ago," he told her. "In fact, I was away at the time. My mother and I were rather close and it was always a regret that I was not with her in her final hours."

Cathlina turned serious as he spoke of his mother. "I am sorry," she said softly. "Was your mother ill for a long time?"

Mathias nodded. "She was," he said. "I tried to spend as much time as I could with her but at that time in my life, I was traveling quite a bit and could not stay by her side for an over amount of time."

"Traveling?" Cathlina asked, cocking her head. "Where were you traveling to?"

Mathias had been very careful throughout the conversation to avoid any mention of his knightly past. He'd done a good job of it so far but questions like the one Cathlina proposed could get him into trouble, so he was very careful in how he answered it.

"I was learning my trade," he replied; it wasn't a lie. He had been a young knight learning his trade - he simply didn't specify *which* trade, smithy or knighthood. "My travels took me to France and to Italy."

"You have been to Italy?" Cathlina was enthralled. "How was it? Was it beautiful? Did you go to Rome? My father went to Rome. He said the streets were paved with gold."

Mathias laughed softly at her enthusiasm. "It is a beautiful city, to be sure," he agreed. "There are many ancient and mysterious buildings. The people there told me that gods used to live in them."

Cathlina's mouth popped open in awe. "Is this true?"

He fought off a grin at her gullible astonishment. "That is what I was told."

Cathlina thought long and hard about buildings where gods used to live. "I would certainly like to see them someday," she said fervently. "Mayhap I shall travel there as well."

Mathias studied her lovely face, so pure and sweet. He wanted to offer to escort her there; he truly did. He was so upswept in the moment, feeling giddy as he hadn't felt since he had been a young boy. He would travel the world with her if only to speak on things like silly grandfathers and godly abodes. It made him feel more wonderful than he could ever recall, this beautiful young woman with the silly giggle. But the offer would not have been appropriate, and he was sorry.

"I am sure you will," he said quietly.

She caught something in his tone, something that was both wistful and genuine, but by the time she turned to him, he was looking away from her. It seemed that he had spotted something up the road and she strained to see what has his attention. He seemed concerned and that, in turn, had her concern.

"What is it?" she asked. "What do you see?"

Mathias wasn't sure, but it was men on horseback. He could see them just over the rise, heading in their direction. Soon enough, they would be upon them. The wind whipped and the thunder grumbled as he watched their distant approach.

"Men on horseback," he replied steadily. "More than likely, more knights for the tournament. More horses I must shoe."

He said it with some humor, trying to deflect any concern over the potential approach of danger. He was successful in diverting her attention and when he turned to look at her, she was smiling at him.

"It is a pity that the tournament is only open to knights," she said. "You are quite brave. I would wager that you could do very well in a tournament given the chance."

Mathias stared at her; her innocent statement brought an avalanche of memories crashing down on him. He'd competed in dozens of tournaments in his lifetime and for six years in a row had been the man to beat in every tournament from Edinburgh to Southampton. But that had been in between Mortimer's wars, and he hadn't competed in a tournament in at least four years. It seemed like a lifetime ago.

"It takes more than bravery to compete," he told her. "It takes a good deal of skill and strength."

"Do you know much about tournaments?"

"I know enough."

"I saw one tournament a few years ago," Cathlina said. "When I fostered at Lincoln Castle, there was a very large tournament one year. Our lord and several of his knights competed. It was very exciting."

A warning bell went off in Mathias' head. He turned to her. "Who was your lord?"

"Ranulf de Pennington," she replied. "He held the castle for the crown. He nearly won the joust but a big black knight under Roger Mortimer's banner beat him. Nearly drove Lord Ranulf right into the ground. We all hated him very much after that."

Mathias looked away. *That big black knight was me,* he thought ironically. Odd how the world, so big most of the time, had suddenly grown quite small. "Did you even know the knight's name or was he simply the Hated One?"

Cathlina giggled. "I do not recall," she said. "It was something like Rain or Rainton. I do not remember. If I ever meet this man, I will punch him right in the nose and call it justice for Lord Ranulf."

It was de Reyne. Mathias knew she didn't know his surname because he never told her. He thought to never tell her now lest she punch him in the nose. Moreover, it seemed as if she already had a bad opinion of him. He cleared his throat, almost nervously, and hastened to change the subject.

"So you have been to Lincolnshire," he said. "You have traveled a great deal. Many people do not ever leave the towns they were born in. You have been fortunate."

She was successfully diverted. "I was at Lincoln Castle for six years," she replied. "There was so much war going on and my father was away so often that my mother did not want her daughters away as well. I went to foster when I was eight years of age and returned home six years ago."

"That would make you twenty years of age."

"You are correct," she said. "I had my birthday last month. How old are you?"

"*Too* old."

She grinned. "It is not fair you know my age and I do not know yours."

He cast her a sidelong glance. "I am much older than you."

"How much older?"

"Thirteen years." When she began to count her fingers, slowly, he laughed. "I have seen thirty-three years."

"God's Bones," she said, shaking her head. "Are you truly so old? Why have you not married before now, Mathias?"

"Who says that I have not?"

"Have you?"

He snorted. "Nay," he said. "I was betrothed once but she found a better prospect."

The truth was that he had been betrothed to the Lady Lucy de Geneville, a niece of the Lady Joan, Roger Mortimer's wife. But that betrothal had been quickly dissolved when Roger had been captured and anyone associated with him dishonored. He didn't particularly care about it, although Lucy had been devastated. For some reason, she had fallen in love with him. He still remembered her tears when everything fell apart. Looking at Cathlina, for the first time in his life he was coming to understand, however small, the disappointment Lucy must have felt. To be separated from the person you so desperately want....

"Impossible," Cathlina cut into his thoughts. "There is no better prospect than you. Why, you are a successful craftsman with a thriving business. I would think any young lady would be honored to be your betrothed."

He gave her a half-smile, humble, but his eyes were on the knights that had now drawn much closer. In fact, they began to race towards them down the road, kicking up rocks and dirt, and the line of eight or ten men at arms behind them were also beginning to gallop. Mathias went on his guard.

"My lady," he said, holding a hand out to her and trying to remain calm. "Come to me. I would have you get on my horse and ride with me."

By this time, Cathlina saw the horses racing towards them and she was frightened. Dutifully, she directed her palfrey over to him and he took the reins to hold the horse steady.

"Those men?" she said, reaching over to pull herself onto his horse. "Who are they?"

He let go of her horse long enough to pull her up in front of him. She was warm and soft and smelled of lavender, but he ignored the very sweet sensations as he settled her on his lap. As the thunder rolled and the wind whipped her hair into his face, he let go of her palfrey so he could have full control of his steed. The old horse had a lot of strength but not a lot of speed, and he was without a weapon. He was mentally calculating the odds and several potential escape plans when Cathlina suddenly let out a hiss.

"It is Beauson," she said. Then, she started waiving frantically. "Beauson!"

Mathias had no idea what she was doing, or who she was speaking of, but he quickly realized she knew the incoming knights. He held his charger steady as the party closed in on them.

It was a well-armed group. The de Lara knights were dressed for battle, including massive broadswords and a variety of smaller weapons. The men at arms were also well equipped. Both knights threw up their visors, angry and accusing eyes moving between Cathlina and Mathias. In fact, the knight in the lead unsheathed his broadsword and pointed it dangerously at Mathias.

"If you value your life, you will let her go," he snarled. "Release her!"

"Wait!" Cathlina cried, throwing out her hands. "Put down your weapons, both of you! He has done nothing wrong!"

The knight retracted his sword somewhat but not all of the way; he was eyeing Mathias critically. The lady didn't seem harassed or injured, but the man sitting behind her was very big and very menacing looking. The sword was remained at the ready.

"What do you mean?" he demanded. "Your father is frantic, Lady Cathlina. What goes on here?"

"Beauson de Velt, put your sword away," Cathlina commanded. "I rode into town on an errand and this man politely offered to escort me home. I am perfectly fine and everything is well. Put the sword *away.*"

Beauson eyed the young lady; he was more confused now than he was when he rode up. "What errand?" he asked, genuinely perplexed. The sword lowered. "What do you mean?"

Cathlina sighed impatiently. "I mean that this man saved Abechail and me yesterday from certain harm," she said, gesturing at Mathias. "I went on an errand this morning to thank him. He is quite trustworthy, I assure you."

Beauson wasn't convinced. "Why did you not tell me or Dunstan so that we could escort you into town?"

She didn't want to tell them the truth; it was that she hadn't wanted anyone to stop her from going. She backed off somewhat, frowning.

"If I had wanted anyone to escort me, I would have asked," she said. "Now, go over there somewhere. I will gather my horse and join you in a moment."

Beauson eyed her a moment before eyeing Mathias. "I cannot leave you, my lady," he replied. "I have orders from your father to bring you home."

"You are not leaving me alone," Cathlina said testily, slithering off of Mathias' horse as he held her arm to gently ease her to the ground. "I have asked you to move away so that I may thank my escort and gather my horse. I do not wish to do this with you hovering over me like a hung dog. *Go,* Beauson. That is a command."

Beauson sighed heavily, looking to Dunstan, who was the bigger yet less bright of the pair. Dunstan shrugged and was already moving away, snapping to the men at arms as he went. They were all shuffling back down the road in a group except for Beauson; he remained. He seemed to be very interested in Mathias.

"Who are you?" he asked.

Mathias opened his mouth but Cathlina cut him off. "I told you to move away," she said, pointing an imperious finger to the group already down the road. "You will not ask his name. It is none of your business and if you do not move away, I will tell my father you were most disobedient and... and *very* naughty. Do you understand me?"

Beauson cleared his throat loudly, an unhappy gesture, and reined his horse sharply back, going to gather with the group that was now lingering about thirty or forty feet down the road. As the wind whipped and the rain began to pick up, Cathlina gathered the reins of her palfrey and made sure Beauson was out of earshot before facing Mathias.

He was still mounted on his horse, looking down at her with an expression between utter pleasure and utter longing. Cathlina could read emotions on his features and her heart began to beat strongly in her chest. She was feeling so many things that it was difficult to voice them but she was coming to realize that she was more than likely not the only one sad at their parting. Though Mathias had always been very polite and very kind, he'd never given her any indication that he might be romantically interested in her. Until now; she could see it on his face.

"Thank you for everything you have done," she said softly, sincerely. "You saved my sister and I yesterday and I will always be grateful."

He smiled faintly, feeling a tremendous pull. Those big brown eyes were sucking him in, swirling him in the maelstrom of her beauty until he was dizzy with it. He truly couldn't stomach the thought of never seeing her again but he knew to carry on any relationship with her would have been extraordinarily unwise. She was a de Lara. Still, it was hard to resist a pull he'd never felt before and a lady he very much wanted to know. Torn, confused, his disappointment was palpable.

"You are more than welcome," he said quietly. "If you should ever need saving again, please do not hesitate to send word to me."

Her grin broadened. "Are you my savior, then? Do you plan to make a career out of it?"

He laughed, leaning forward on his saddle so he could be closer to her, however small the gesture. "I would do it quite happily, but I hope you will never again need saving. To save you means that you will be in some manner of danger, and that I could not abide. I would not ever wish that for you."

She gazed at him seriously, her smile fading. "What will you do now, Mathias?"

"What do you mean?"

"Will you return to shoeing chargers for the tournament? Or will you mayhap travel to Italy again someday and relive the days of your youth?"

He shrugged. "If I go, it will not be alone," he said, a twinkle in his eye. "Mayhap I will take you along so I have someone to talk to. Sebastian can be such a bore and all he wants to do is chase women."

She laughed. "I will not chase women, I promise," she said, sobering. Her brown eyes glimmered at him. "If you go again, I do hope you will consider taking me. It would be a lovely thing to travel with you, I am sure."

The conversation was coming to a close; Mathias could feel it. They were floating along on sweet, dreamy words, bordering on flirting, and he was scrambling for things to say, feeling a desperation he'd never felt before. He didn't want the moment to end.

"Do you have plans for any more trips into town?" he asked. "If you do, mayhap you will do the honor of another visit some time."

Cathlina could feel the desperation, too. She didn't want to leave him but she knew he had to return. She could feel the stares of her father's knights on her back, heated and questioning.

"Father has made mention of coming to see the tournament that will take place in a couple of days," she said. "We will be in town then and mayhap I will see you at that time."

Mathias' thoughts were running wild. *We will be coming to see the tournament.* He began to think all manner of foolish things at that moment. In fact, he could hardly contain himself. Reaching down, he took her hand and kissed it softly.

"You will see me at that time," he said quietly. "Have no doubt that I will find you."

Cathlina felt his kiss down to her toes. Other than her father and grandfather, a man had never kissed her, and certainly not in the sweet and warm way Mathias had. Wide-eyed, she watched him turn and ride off, wind gusts and rain pelting him as he went. In fact, the rain was falling fairly steadily and she had to wipe it from her eyes as she mounted her palfrey, but she hardly cared. Mathias the smithy had charmed her, had listened to her, and had finally kissed her. That was all she cared about.

Even when her father spent an hour yelling at her for being foolish, she considered the crime well worth the cost.

CHAPTER FIVE

"We were stripped of our knighthood," Mathias said steadily. "We were told never to pick up arms again. We were never told that we could not compete in tournaments."

Justus was beside himself; as the storm raged outside and sunset turned to night, he stood in the middle of the warm, smoky stall he shared with his two sons and listened to the eldest spout nonsense. He was truly at a loss for words.

"Have you gone mad?" he hissed. "You cannot compete in the tournament!"

"Why not?"

Justus threw up his arms. "Because you are no longer a knight and only knights can compete!"

Mathias shook his head. "I am a warrior," he said in a tone that suggested no debate. "That can never be taken from me. I have had my titles and lands removed, but not my heart. I can compete and I can win."

Justus stood there with his mouth hanging open. He finally shook his head, twitching-like, as if his entire body was in an uproar. "Where has this come from?" he demanded, his gray hair swishing back and forth. "Since January one year ago, you have been quiet and obedient. You have never as much as lamented your fortune, Mathias, although if anyone had a right to, you did. Sometimes I wondered if you even cared. Now you want to do something foolish and reckless that could land us all in the Tower? I do not understand you!"

"It is not foolish and reckless."

"It is!"

As Justus told Mathias just what he thought of the man's inclination to compete in the coming tournament, Sebastian was listening, too. He had been since he had heard his brother's wild idea. He was all for doing something disobedient, but he was frankly surprised that his brother was. Mathias was usually so dutiful. He began to suspect why his brother wanted to compete and further suspected that the lovely

Lady Cathlina de Lara had something to do with it. He had begun to suspect his brother's attraction to the woman earlier in the day but now it was all but confirmed. It was amusing, really. He'd never known Mathias to care about a woman; *any* woman.

"Mat," he interjected as Justus worked himself into a fit. "Do you recall that knight who passed through here about six months ago, the one that died while we were repairing his armor?"

Mathias turned his full attention to his brother. "The one stabbed in the tavern brawl?"

"The same."

"What about him?"

Sebastian came out of the shadows, unfolding his big arms as he looked at his brother. "We still have all of his possessions," he said quietly. "Do you recall that we kept them because no one came forward to collect them?"

A light of understanding came to Mathias' eyes. "I do indeed."

Sebastian faced his brother seriously. "Father is correct; if you really do want to compete, you cannot do it as Mathias de Reyne," he said. "But mayhap you can do it as Sir Chanson de Lovern. We have everything he left – his shield, most of his armor, his joust equipment. We even have his saddlebags that contained letters regarding the death of his father, the Earl of Banbury."

Mathias' features registered the brilliance of his brother's suggestion. "I remember," he said. "Where are his items?"

"Up in the loft, I think," Sebastian said, looking at Justus. "Isn't that where you put his possessions, Da?"

Justus growled and began shaking his head. "I tried to sell them."

Sebastian nodded impatiently. "I know you did, but you never managed to because no one could afford it," he said. "The equipment is expensive and well-made, and there is plenty for Mathias to use and pose as Banbury's heir."

Justus threw up his arms again as if beseeching the heavens. "Now they are both mad," he exclaimed. He looked pointedly at Sebastian. "You cannot do this!"

Mathias and Sebastian were quite calm about it. "Aye, I can," Mathias said. "No one will know it is me. I will make sure of that. Sebastian, bring down all of that gear from the loft and let me take a look at it. As I recall, de Lovern was taller than I am but not as wide. We will have some adjusting to do."

Sebastian went off in search of the stored items. Justus, meanwhile, was doing less ranting as the reality of what his sons were planning began to sink in. Now, he was becoming frightened. He knew what Mathias and Sebastian were capable of; he'd seen it too many times. Mortimer had depended upon that cunning and determination too many times to count. Aye, he knew what Mathias had in him; the man was a beast in disguise.

"Mathias," he said quietly; raging wouldn't do any good so perhaps calm reasoning would. "Lad, if you are found out, you know what trouble this will be for you. Why risk it?"

Mathias was over by the enormous bellows, looking at a half-finished broadsword they had been working on for a local baron. It was a beautiful piece that the baron had paid handsomely for, but it wasn't finished. Justus had the skill to make beautiful swords and this one was one of his finest works. Mathias pulled it from its cage and inspected it closely.

"I have been thinking," he said, somewhat quietly. "Mayhap Sebastian has been right all along. Mayhap it is time to redeem ourselves. A tournament is a safe place to start; I will not be picking up a sword or bearing arms in the course of war. It is essentially a game of skill. With the money I win, mayhap…."

Justus was extremely interested. "Mayhap *what?*"

Mathias looked at him. "Hugh Beaumont is looking for men," he said. "We can relocate to Scotland and fight those wars the Scots constantly fight. The money will help us redeem ourselves as knights and as men, and we can mayhap marry and have families and homes."

Justus was astonished. "Marry?" he repeated. "Mat, you have never expressed an interest in marriage, ever."

"I am interested now."

Justus stared at him, mulling over his statement and remembering the very beautiful young woman Mathias had spent the afternoon with. Suddenly, it was all starting to make some sense.

"That girl?" he said. "Has she asked you to compete?"

Mathias frowned. "Of course not," he said. "For all she knows, I am a smithy and nothing more. She has not asked anything of me."

"But she has put ideas in your mind," Justus pressed. "Has she spoken of marriage?"

Mathias put the sword down. "Da, she has not said or done anything," he insisted. "But I would be lying if I said she has not made me realize what has been taken away from me. If my lands and titles had not been stripped, I could command a bride as fine as her, but in my current state… nay, she deserves more than a smithy. She deserves a man who can provide for her in a manner in which she deserves. With a wife like that, I could take on the entire world and win. She would make me proud again."

Justus' heart hurt as he listened to his son speak of things he hadn't spoken of since that dark January day. He'd always suspected Mathias' thoughts but to hear the man speak of them was heartbreaking. He'd lost so very much in a circumstance that had been both unjust and unfair, that had seen some men retain everything and some men lose everything. But it had been the way of thing.

"You will regain what is yours again someday," Justus said softly. "Alberbury Castle and Caus Castle will be returned to you as will the Westbury Barony, and you will once again be known as Baron Westbury, High Warden of the Northern Marches. When enough time passes, Edward will soften and you shall regain what is rightfully yours."

Mathias was looking at the sword, half-finished, in its iron cage. "I do not share your confidence," he muttered with sadness in his tone. "My mother was the sister of Roger Mortimer's wife, Joan. When Mortimer and the king became at odds, I had no choice but to side with my family."

Justus could feel the anxiety beginning. "You did what was expected."

Mathias snorted. "I left my friends, my king… I sided with a usurper because he was my family."

Justus' jaw ticked as he watched his son, seeing the tension in the man's body as he spoke. "Edward understands," he insisted softly. "That is the reason he did not kill you when Mortimer was captured."

Mathias' jaw ticked as he looked at his father. "He did not kill me because he was my friend," he said, his teeth clenched. "That fact and that fact alone was the only reason he did not put us all to the blade."

Justus suspected that a year of remaining silent on the subject of losing his knighthood was about to come to a head. Mathias was working himself up and Justus hastened to ease the man.

"Tate and Kenneth and Stephen pleaded for your life," he said quietly as Mathias began to pace. "They all love you, lad. You were spared because they understood your reasons for siding with Mortimer. It was not because you wished to see Edward dead. It was because Mortimer is your uncle by marriage."

Mathias' eyes flashed. "Wished the king dead or not, siding with

Mortimer killed my knighthood. Edward might as well have put me to the blade. I was dead the day I swore fealty to Mortimer."

"You are too hard on yourself."

Mathias' jaw ticked furiously. "Nay, I am not," he said, leaning on a post near the great and scarred anvil. "I am not hard on myself at all. The truth is that I should have been smarter; I should not have let family ties influence me to side with a man I knew had no right to rule England. I should have stayed with my king… and now see what my judgment has cost me."

Sebastian picked that moment to enter the room, his arms full of equipment, but Justus held a hand up to still him. Mathias was letting loose his emotion and Justus didn't want Sebastian interrupted something that was long overdue.

"This too shall pass," Justus insisted softly, urgently. "The tides of politics change as frequently as the seasons. Soon, you shall have your life restored to you. Edward is wise, lad. You have friends in very high places. The name Mathias de Reyne means something. Your castles will be returned to you, as will your titles and lands. But it will not happen if you defy the king by bearing arms in a tournament or fleeing to Scotland to fight in their foolish wars. You must be patient."

"I *am* patient," Mathias roared in an uncharacteristic display of rage. "Da, I have worked my entire life to achieve greatness few men do. It was taken away from me, mayhap justly or mayhap not. In any case, I have been patient for these long months, watching other knights ride through this dirty little village and knowing my greatness far exceeded theirs once… God's Blood, once… once I was the man all men fear. I want that back. Now, I see something I want very badly and all of those things I lost those months ago… I want it back, because I must have it in order to have *her*."

So it *was* the girl. Now they had the crux of Mathias' change of heart. Justus' gaze lingered on his eldest a moment before turning to look at Sebastian.

The redheaded knight was still standing in the doorway, watching his older brother have a moment of weakness. He had heard most of the conversation. But, unlike his father, he was unwilling to talk Mathias out of competing in the tournament. He wanted to see his brother's greatness restored, too, because if Mathias was great again, then he and Justus would be as well. Moreover, he wasn't very good in dealing with emotion so it was better to move past it quickly.

"Here," Sebastian pushed into the room and laid the equipment out on the hacked-up, sturdy work table that was nearly in the center of the stall. "This is all of it, Mat. There is almost a complete set of armor plus various smaller weapons, tunics, banners, and based on the missive regarding de Lovern's father, we could have one of the priests at Lanercost Priory draw up a bill of Patins. You will need it to enter the tournament."

Mathias, finished feeling sorry for himself for the moment, began rummaging through the armor and pieces of mail, all of which had been left by the unfortunate de Lovern. He could feel the familiar excitement filling his veins with thoughts of competitive combat and the thrill of the joust. It seemed like forever ago when last he competed.

"We will have to pay the priest well for his cooperation," Mathias said as he held up the section of shoulder armor for inspection. "We will also have to create an entire lineage for Banbury. Da, what do you know of the Earl of Banbury?"

Justus was still entrenched in their conversation, his heart still heavy and his mood morose. "Not much," he said, watching his boys rifle through the possessions of the dead knight. "I think he is related to Wallingford."

Mathias' head came up. "Viscount Wallingford? He fought with Edward. If I recall correctly, he was killed during the Despenser conflict. I was a fairly young knight at the time but I seem to remember hearing that."

Justus nodded slowly; for some reason, he couldn't look his sons in the eye. Perhaps it was fear for what they were planning on doing; whatever the case, he kept his eyes on the table with the armor on it. "I believe so," he said. "The patins should have Wallingford on it somehow. I also seem to remember hearing there was a de Braose in the family."

As the storm whistled outside and their three horses stirred restlessly in their nearby stalls, as the smithy stall also had a small stable attached, Mathias and Sebastian bent over the items to see what was serviceable. They began pulling things a part, organizing them, and eventually Justus joined them with a large lantern with oil from pressed fruit pits. Soon enough, he was looking through the equipment, too, to see what needed to be repaired before Mathias took his life in his hands and entered the tournament set for sunrise in two days.

They didn't have much time.

CHAPTER SIX

"How fortunate that the rain has moved on," Cathlina said, shielding her eyes as she gazed up into the brilliant morning sky. "Father, do you suppose we will make it before the events begin?"

Astride his fat Belgian charger that was hairy to the point of distraction, Saer surveyed the sunrise as well. Clad in his battle armor, he discovered it was too tight that morning as he had put it on, resulting in a foul mood. Everything either cut into his flesh or chaffed. He thought someone one had switched armor with him, not wanting to admit he had grown too fat to wear it. Regardless, he had squeezed into it and was now coming to regret that decision.

"Aye," he said, rubbing his irritated eyes. "The morning will be spent on men dressing and preparing their weapons. We should see the mêlée by the nooning meal, and that will more than likely last until sun set."

"Will you compete, Father?" Roxane asked.

Before Saer could reply, his wife Rosalund responded with a rude snort. "He will *not,*" she said firmly. "He will remain with his family where he belongs. Tournaments are for younger men, not old men who have seen better days."

Saer mumbled a curse under his breath at his mouthy wife. As most marriages were, it had been an arranged one between him and the Lady Rosalund de Ferrers almost twenty-two years ago. It had never been a love match. Sometimes he tolerated her, sometimes he actually liked her, but more often than not he couldn't stand to be around the abrasive and foolish woman.

Rosalund was, oddly enough, a good mother to their girls, although he secretly resented the fact that she had never produced a surviving son. The one she had given birth to when Abechail had been two years old had died within a few days. Since then, no more babies and no more heirs, and that fact had prompted Saer to act recklessly and have a son with one of the serving women. Rosalund had found out and sent the boy and his mother away. These days, Saer felt rather hollow and numb to everything, his family included. It was a sad way to exist.

"I do not expect to compete," he said, making sure he got the last word in against the wife. "I have not done so in years and have no desire to make an easy target for younger, faster men."

"But you have more experience, Papa," Cathlina insisted. "You do not need to be swift when you have more experience."

Saer turned to smile at his middle child; he did feel something for Cathlina, perhaps the only daughter he had that was worth something in his mind. Roxane was plain and demanding while Abechail would more than likely not live to see adulthood. That was what the physics said, in any case. He would feel sad when he thought about that prediction but then the numbness would swallow him up again.

The women were riding in a carriage behind him, a fine vehicle with cushioned seats and an open cab. They rarely used it, as Rosalund would only allow it to be used when she was traveling, so it was in excellent condition. Rosalund and Abechail rode in on the bench facing forward while Roxane and Cathlina sat on the bench facing backwards, but Cathlina had a difficult time remaining in her seat and was on her knees facing forward, looking over the back of the seat and down the road. She was thrilled with the trip, knowing she would see Mathias at some point. That was the only true reason she had wanted to come.

But it was a trip she almost didn't make. For her disobedience riding to town alone, her father had threatened not to take her to the tournament but she knew he would relent; watching the back of his bald head, she knew her father would refuse her nothing if she truly wanted it. She wondered how he was going to accept the fact that she wanted Mathias.

Saer knew she had ridden into town to deliver some treats to thank the men that saved her and Abechail from the one-eyed attacker, and the truth was that he was not in complete disagreement with her actions. He was, however, furious that she had gone alone, but he didn't imagine why. All Cathlina would tell him was that she didn't want to be a bother and that she could travel faster alone. He had thought it a bunch of nonsense. Any mention of Mathias had been in context with his brother, so Saer was never the wiser as to Cathlina's true motives.

She intended to keep it that way. Regaining her seat next to Roxane, who was holding a small bronze hand mirror to check her careful hairstyle, Cathlina fussed with her clothing, hoping she looked attractive enough to garner Mathias' attention. While her mother and elder sister were dressed in complicated surcoats and kirtles, Cathlina was dressed in a pale blue surcoat of simple design.

The snug bodice had a rather low neckline, displaying her white cleavage, while long sleeves held tight her arms and served as a showcase for her slender shoulders and graceful neck. The waistline was dropped and the skirt voluminous and belled, trailing behind her slightly as she walked. Although she had a heavy cloak should the rain and cold return, she wore a white shawl made from the finest linen that draped elegantly around her shoulders and arms, and her shiny dark hair had been pulled into an elaborate braid that cascaded over her left shoulder.

The truth was that she looked utterly divine, outshining Roxane in her complex red and yellow surcoat and a matching *barbette* hat, which was a round hat with a chinstrap made of delicate and soft material. Beneath it, Roxane's frizzy brown hair had been brushed and pinned and smoothed with grease to keep it from getting out of control. It was difficult being the older, and plainer, sister, and Roxane was very good at being a martyr at it. She liked to make Cathlina feel guilty for the simple fact that she had been born beautiful.

But Cathlina wasn't thinking about her petty sister at the moment. She was thinking about Mathias and how she could slip away from the festivities to visit him at his stall. She had an excuse, of course, and that was to collect the basket she had brought the treats in, and she was positive he would be very busy today of all days. Perhaps he would only give her a few moments of his time; perhaps he would only give her a smile and a word. Whatever he gave her, she would take it and gladly. She had thought of nothing else but Mathias for the past two days.

As she sat there and daydreamed over the tall, dark smithy, the carriage bumped down the road towards Brampton. The ground was heavily saturated from the rains that had pummeled the land for the past two days, miraculously cleared up before dawn. Even now, birds sailed against the blue expanse, searching for a meal, as the party from Kirklinton Castle kept up a clipped pace.

Saer, Beauson, and Dunstan were at the head of the group while ten men at arms followed the carriage, also driven by two soldiers. The road was relatively empty for the most part but as they drew closer to town, the traffic picked up. People were coming in from Carlisle to the west and points as far east as Hexham. The ladies in the carriage grew more excited as the traffic increased, straining to see all of the lords and ladies in their fine clothing. With the rains gone, it seemed that everyone wanted to be out and about. The closer they drew to town, the more it became a parade.

Entering the city limits, people were everywhere. Abechail ended up on Cathlina's lap, both girls watching the crowds curiously. A party of nobles arrived with men in silks and a fine lady in a tall wimple walking two skinny dogs on gold leashes. They saw another fine lady with a pet rabbit in her arms, and still another with a fat white goat who road on the horse with its master. It was all quite thrilling and Abechail began to lament the fact that she did not have a pet.

It was truly a day to see and be seen, but as the sun advanced in the sky, so did the temperature. The roads were quickly drying out and the muddy puddles all over town were starting to evaporate, but along with the evaporation came the smells of human habitation and dirty animals. When they reached the point on the avenue that seemed to be down-wind from the town's sludge pit, a big gusty breeze blew the foul stench right across their path. Abechail put her fingers to her nose.

"The smell!" she exclaimed, looking at Cathlina. "It smells so awful!"

Cathlina agreed, putting her fingers to her nose, too. "Papa, are we almost there?"

Saer could see that they had set up the tournament field to the north side of the village where temporary lists had been constructed. Bright red banners on tall poles were snapping in the wind, announcing the location of the games and drawing people towards the area like moths to the flame. He nodded to Cathlina's.

"Up ahead," he said, pointing. "We shall be there shortly."

Cathlina and her sisters ended up on their knees on the seats, straining to catch a glimpse of the tournament field and the banners. They entered the town from the road leading northeast, following the flow of people but veering off towards the northwest once they permeated the edge of the village. Saer wanted to circumvent the crowds that were herding towards the main entrance, taking his party through a less-crowded section of the berg and down a couple of the narrow, cramped streets.

It was mostly residential here, away from the merchants and heart of town. It was also away from Mathias' stall near the town square. Cathlina was no longer looking forward but gazing back, now watching the road to the town center fade from view. When it was gone completely, she sadly turned away, wondering now when she would have the opportunity to see Mathias.

As she formulated a plan, Saer took his party off of the avenue when they passed through a row of small homes and onto some open land.

The sun had worked its magic and dried up the overly-wet grass and Saer called a halt and commanded that their two tents be set up. There were a few other parties around at this end of town, setting up small encampments, and Saer noticed a very big one almost immediately. He made his way over to the carriage.

"Look," he said, pointing to a series of tents with a big crimson and gold standard flying over them. "If I am not mistaken, that is the Earl of Carlisle."

"Cousin Tate?" Rosalund strained to catch a glimpse. "If this is true, then we must go and greet him immediately."

Saer couldn't disagree. He grasped her arm to steady her as she climbed from the carriage. "I should have known he would come," he said. "This tournament is practically in his garden, it 'tis so close. I cannot recall the last time I saw the man."

Rosalund was straightening her gown, her eyes on the encampment in the distance. "At Christmas," she reminded her forgetful husband. "He extended an invitation for us to come to Carlisle Castle and we did."

Saer nodded at the memory. "Ah, yes," he said, tugging at the mail that was chaffing his arm pit. "I remember now. I also remember there were quite a few children running about. He has quite a brood now, does he not?"

"Five children," Rosalund said, distracted as she motioned her daughters out of the carriage. "Come along, my girls. We must greet Cousin Tate."

Roxane climbed out, fussing with her hair, as Cathlina took Abechail in hand and gently helped her out. Abechail stumbled on the uneven ground but Cathlina steadied her. The gentle breeze blew her pale blue skirt about, and the white shawl waving softly against her body as she straightened out Abechail's simply green surcoat with the white ruffles around the neckline.

"You look very lovely today," she told her little sister. "Are you excited for the games?"

Abechail nodded, curiously inspecting their surroundings. "I have never been to a tournament, you know."

"I know."

"Do men really try to spear each other?"

"Who told you that?"

"Rainey," she replied, referring to their cook's young son. "He said men drive big daggers into each other!"

Cathlina grinned. "He was also the one who told you that knights cannot see out of their visors."

Abechail looked contrite. "Well," she said reluctantly. "Some cannot."

"That is not true. If they could not see, they would crash into everything and kill themselves."

Abechail simply shrugged and averted her gaze, fussing with the sleeve of her surcoat. As far as she was concerned, Rainey knew much more than anyone else, even though Cathlina knew him to be a little boy with a big imagination. She stood there a moment, watching her little sister and thinking there was a good amount of color in her cheeks today. Usually, Abechail was so pale that to see some color in her face was unusual indeed.

The truth was that Abechail still wasn't recovered from the near-abduction two days before. A sickly child even on the best of days, the struggle had taken something out of her. Rosalund had been fearful that it might render her weak for days but as the morning came about, Abechail had been dressed before any of them. She wasn't going to allow a misadventure to spoil her fun. Besides, she spent most of her time in bed or resting due to her terrible health. She wasn't going to miss today's tournament no matter how poorly she felt.

Which wasn't too terribly, considering. Abechail eyed her older sister, knowing that the woman was watching her closely for any signs of collapse, so it was best to put on a strong front. Taking Cathlina by the hand, she pulled her along after their mother as the woman forged a path across the soft, green meadow towards the crimson tents in the distance.

As the group of ladies drew close to the collection of tents, they noticed a fair amount of heavily armed soldiers patrolling the encampment. When one of then saw the group of women approach, he went to greet them and to discover their business. No sooner had the women come to a halt than a scream went up in the largest tent and two small blond boys suddenly charged out.

The attention shifted from the incoming visitors to the escaping children. It was evident that the soldiers on patrol knew what to do, as if fleeing toddlers were the norm in their world. The little boys separated; one ran one way and one ran the other, but the soldiers in the vicinity were on to their game and easily corralled them. As angry screaming fits ensued, a finely dressed and beautiful woman with honey-colored hair emerged from the largest tent.

"Dylan!" she scolded. "Alex! Oh, good heavens... you naughty boys!"

The children were fussing as the soldiers who had captured them took them back towards the woman. She took one toddler from a grinning soldier and went to collect the second child when she caught sight of the four women at their camp's perimeter. After some serious squinting to try and gain a look at who they were, the woman's face suddenly relaxed with recognition.

"Rosalund!" she called, waving a free hand. "Greetings!"

The soldier, realizing that his mistress knew the women he had detained, allowed them to proceed into camp. In spite of the fact that the mistress had two young boys screaming unhappily in her arms, she went quickly to meet them.

"Rosalund!" she greeted happily. "What in the world are you doing here? Is Saer competing today?"

Rosalund and the girls curtsied to the Lady Elizabetha Cartingdon de Lara, wife of the Earl of Carlisle. Known by the childhood nickname of Toby, Lady de Lara was a gorgeous woman with a lush figure and almond-shaped hazel eyes. She was also quite brilliant, administering the earl's lands and making him quite wealthy. Everyone in the north knew of Lady de Lara's business savvy and how the earl depended on her. It was also well known that he was madly, deeply in love with his wife. They had a very happy marriage, indeed.

"He is not competing , my lady," Rosalund said. "We have come to view the spectacle. In fact, my youngest has never seen the games."

"Is that so?" Toby turned her attention to Abechail, so tiny and frail. "Are you excited for your first tournament event, my lady?"

Abechail was a shy girl, struggling not to be in the face of Lady de Lara, whom she had met before. "Aye, my lady," she said in a voice barely louder than a whisper.

Toby smiled, a gentle gesture even though she was still struggling with two three-year-old boys. They were putting up a fierce fight.

"Good," she said, lowering the boys to the ground but still hanging on to their arms. "Your cousin, the earl, has chosen to compete, so it should be very exciting."

"Where is our lord?" Rosalund wanted to know.

Toby tossed her head in the direction of the tournament arena "At the field," she replied. "You will, of course, join us for the evening meal, will you not? I am sure my husband would like to visit with Saer."

"We would be honored, my lady," Rosalund replied. "My husband will be thrilled to see his cousin again."

Toby opened her mouth to reply but one of the twins threw himself down on the dirt and began screaming. Toby hauled him up by his arm, smiling wanly at the collection of women.

"It is time for their naps," she said. "They do not like to rest, but they need it desperately. As do I."

"They are bright and lively boys, my lady."

"They are devils."

With that, she excused herself and half-dragged, half-carried the frustrated twins back towards the large crimson tent. Her departure was rather abrupt but Rosalund understood the need to deal with unruly children; she watched the countess carry the boys away before turning to her daughters.

"Now, ladies," she said as she took Abechail's hand. "The tournament will be much more exciting now that the earl is competing. I would say it shall be a very eventful day and now we shall have a feast to look forward to tonight."

"Mama?" Roxane asked, smoothing her frizzy hair as it began to burst free of the confines of the hat. "Do you suppose there will be any knights or lords at Cousin Tate's table?"

Rosalund glanced at her eldest. "There might be," she said. "You are not, perchance, thinking on Sir Kenneth again?"

Roxane stuck her nose up in the air and looked away. "I did not say him."

Rosalund shook her head, clucking reproachfully as she did. "Your father has told you that he is not interested."

Roxane went into pouting mode. "Why not?" she demanded. "He is a seasoned knight and a favored of the king. He is Cousin Tate's closest friend. Why can't Father approach him on my behalf? I am a cousin to the Earl of Carlisle, after all. I am an excellent marriage prospect and even though Sir Kenneth is a mere knight, I would consider him."

Rosalund sighed heavily. "Sir Kenneth is not interested in a marriage," she said. "Your father already approached Cousin Tate with the suggestion but Tate says Kenneth has many things to accomplish for young Edward and marriage is not agreeable to him at this time."

Roxane's lip stuck out. "Do you think he will be here today?"

"I do not know," Rosalund said. "If he is, then you will not follow him around like a love-sick maid. You will behave yourself."

Frustrated that the object of her affections since meeting him last Christmas, Sir Kenneth St. Hèver , was seemingly uninterested in a romantic match, Roxane turned away from her mother and tried to pretend it didn't bother her.

Cathlina watched her sister, feeling rather sorry for her, especially since Sir Kenneth had seemed to pay much more attention to Cathlina at the time. It had been a bitter situation and one of contention between the sisters for the months that followed. Cathlina had no desire to repeat that particular circumstance with her sister. For their sake, she hoped Sir Kenneth was far, far away.

Rosalund encouraged her daughters to get moving, taking the lead as she traipsed off the way she had come and headed towards the two smaller tents in the distance that were just starting to lift. The tents were of a non-descript color but someone planted a pole and mounted the small crimson and blue axe banner of Saer de Lara's house.

As Rosalund moved past the subject of Kenneth St. Hèver and began to comment on the feast, what they should wear, and perhaps what gifts they should bring, Cathlina's thoughts moved to other things as well. Mostly, she was thinking on Mathias and hoping she could escape her family for a few minutes to go and see him. It would have to be a short visit and she would have to outsmart Roxane in order to get away, but she was sure it could be done. She simply had to be clever about it.

Back over their shoulders near the tournament field, a herald trumpet sounded the first of the alerts that would draw the competitors and spectators to the arena. As Rosalund hurried her girls back to their encampment, Cathlina was verging on a plan.

CHAPTER SEVEN

"You cannot compete," Justus said, his voice low. "I have just come from the tournament field; the Earl of Carlisle is here and he is competing. He will know you on sight, Mat."

Mathias stood in one of the smaller rooms of their large smithy stall, dressed in heavy battle armor from head to toe. It was mostly mail with pieces of plate over his shoulders and a fitted breastplate that was emblazoned with the crest of Banbury. It wasn't his own beloved armor, custom-crafted protection that had been taken from him along with his precious broadsword on that cold January day, but it was acceptable. At least, it would have to do for his purposes.

Sebastian was with him, fitting the pieces left behind by de Lovern over his brother's muscled body, but neither brother so much as paused when Justus delivered his ominous news. They kept going.

"I *can* compete and I most certainly will," Mathias said as he fussed with the hauberk around his face. "With Tate competing, that will make the games far more interesting."

Justus was quickly growing distraught. "Have you lost your mind?" he hissed. "If the earl sees you, he will arrest us all!"

Mathias shook his head steadily. "He will not arrest us," he assured his father as he finished with the hauberk. "You worry overly."

Justus could see that his words were falling on deaf ears and his anxiety grew; he was already in a panic since hearing about de Lara's entry. Now, there was no stopping his fear.

"Why?" he pleaded as Mathias began to walk away to collect his tournament weaponry. "Why must you do this? I do not understand!"

Mathias picked up the first of three joust poles that he and Sebastian had worked through the night to forge; this pole was very well made with a rounded tip. The two other poles had a tip that looked like a fist and one that had a crow's foot tip because it literally looked like a bird's foot.

As Mathias pondered his answer, Sebastian came over to the table with a collection of fabric in different shades of yellow. As he began securing a large piece of fabric to one of the poles, Justus began pointing furiously.

"And there is another thing," he said. "Where did you get the banners?"

Mathias glanced at Sebastian, who was focused on his work. "We borrowed them."

Justus' eyes narrowed. "You *stole* them!"

Mathias shook his head patiently. "We borrowed them from a few merchants," he repeated. "We shall either pay them for the goods or return them, depending on the condition of the fabric when we are finished."

Justus threw up his hands. "You stole the fabric during the night because the shops were not open for business," he said. "You are thieves!"

Mathias took one of the strips of fabric from his brother and began fastening it to the top of the pole. "No one ever saw us," he said casually. "We were ghosts."

"Phantoms!" Sebastian piped up.

Mathias grinned at his brother. "They will never realize it is missing."

As the brothers jested, Justus turned away in frustration. They weren't taking any of this seriously and it was a deadly serious situation; with the unanticipated addition of the Earl of Carlisle in the tournament, the stakes were much higher than they could possibly imagine. He knew Mathias was aware; he couldn't understand why the man wasn't treating the situation with more concern. Baffled, and reaching the apex of what he could emotionally handle, he collapsed onto the nearest stool.

"We will all be arrested," he muttered, raking his fingers through his long, gray hair. "It is not fair that I should live to see my sons perish. I have done all that I can to protect them but they will not listen."

Mathias heard the man's soft utterings, casting a long glance at Sebastian before turning to his father. They knew their father was worried; the truth was that they were worried, too, but it did not deter them.

"Da," he said softly, firmly. "Look at me; I know you are concerned but there is truly nothing to be concerned over. If I thought the risk was too great, I would not do it."

Instead of looking at Mathias as he had been asked, Justus looked away. "You are taking a terrible and reckless chance."

Mathias sighed faintly. "Let me tell you why I feel this opportunity is neither terrible nor reckless," he said. "I am wearing armor that is not identifiable. It is in no way related to or indicative of Mathias de Reyne. The Patins we paid handsomely for at Lanercost Abbey is flawless; I made sure of it when the priest drew it up. For all anyone will know, I am Sir Chayson de Lovern. No one will ever see my face. I will compete, I will win, and we will have a tidy sum to do with as we please."

Justus looked at his son as if he was daft. "What if there are people at the tournament who know de Lovern? They will know you are not him."

Mathias shrugged. "I would wager to say that he was not very well known or very well liked if no one came looking for him after his death," he replied. "I am unconcerned over someone recognizing de Lovern's name or armor. He was an obscure knight, and obscure he shall remain."

"Not after you win this tournament using his name."

"Then mayhap that will allow the man some fame in death that he never achieved in life. It is the least I can do for him since I have stolen his armor and identity."

Mathias had an answer for everything. After a moment, Justus sighed heavily and looked away, shaking his head. "I hope this girl is worth the danger you are putting yourself in."

Before Mathias could reply, the young orphaned boy that they employed to clean up and run errands appeared. Stewart was a skinny child with a crown of wild red hair that looked more like bristly hay, but he was surprisingly well spoken and obedient. He focused on Justus.

"My lord," he said. "A man is here to see you."

Justus looked at the child with disinterest. "Tell him to go away," he said grumpily, then quickly reconsidered. "Who is it, lad?"

"I do not know, my lord," the child replied. "Should I ask his name?"

Justus nodded, defeat and frustration in his manner. Then, he shook his head and stood up, lumbering over to the doorway. He opened his mouth to say something to Mathias and Sebastian but thought better of it. They wouldn't listen to him, anyway. He put his hand on Stewart's stiff red hair and turned the child around as they headed out of the room.

"You would not disobey me, would you?" he asked the boy.

The child was deadly seriously. "Nay, my lord."

Justus grunted, throwing one last word out before he left the room completely. "At least someone listens to me," he said, trying to make his sons feel guilty. "Let it be the servant boy, then."

With that, he was gone. Mathias was in the process of affixing a standard to the second of the three poles as Sebastian continued to work with the third pole, the crow's foot. Sebastian glanced at his brother as he worked, their father's mood and words hanging heavy in the air between them.

"Tate's entry is a surprise," he said. "It is going to make this event a bit trickier."

Mathias was focused on his work. "I have not seen him since January last year."

"He knows we are here, in Brampton."

"Of course he does. He has been charged by Edward to keep watch over us to make sure we do not do anything foolish. We stay in Brampton so he can keep a watchful eye on three dishonored knights."

Sebastian looked at him. "If that is true, do you think you should reconsider competing today?" he asked. "If de Lara is not fooled by your disguise, Father's predictions might come true – he may have us all arrested."

Mathias shook his head. "I cannot imagine the man would arrest us all," he said. "In fact, I do believe he will appreciate the level of competition if I am his opponent."

Sebastian sighed, setting down the pole. "We did not discuss the mêlée," he said quietly. "If you compete in that, then you will indeed be taking up arms again."

Mathias looked at his brother. "I will be taking up arms in the spirit of sport, not for battle," he said patiently. "There is a difference."

Sebastian wasn't so sure but he didn't argue with him. Mathias was always the level-headed one, the brother with the most common sense and good judgment. Sebastian would have to assume he was right even if he disagreed with him. As he went back to work on Mathias' host of tournament instruments, Justus reappeared in the room.

"Mathias," the old man gasped, his face taut with panic. "De Lara is here. He has asked for you."

Mathias didn't react for a moment; he simply stared at his father as if not quite comprehending the words. But quickly enough, he realized what the man said and immediately began unstrapping the plate armor around his shoulders.

"Sebastian," he hissed. "Help me get this off. Quickly, now."

Fortunately, Justus had enough sense to close the door of the chamber, the one that opened into a store room, and then beyond the store room was the larger common room with a straw-strewn and uneven floor where the Earl of Carlisle awaited. Justus rushed to help Sebastian remove Mathias' armor and in little time, the armor was off and the mail was in a big pile on the ground.

Mathias was clad in leather breeches and a stained, worn linen tunic, which was common enough for him on a daily basis. Without another word, he pushed past his brother and father and out into the store room where they kept various implements related to their business. As Mathias passed through, he grabbed a leather apron, almost too well worn to be of any true use, and secured it around his waist. By the time he hit the big common room that smelled of horses and hay, he was fully dressed as a smithy. He spied de Lara immediately.

"My lord," he greeted calmly.

Tate de Lara, Earl of Carlisle and Lord Protector of Northern England, had been inspecting a half-finished sword tucked into a protective cage near the bellows. Upon hearing Mathias' voice, he swung around to face him.

Tate was a very big man, muscular and tall, and had a face of classic male beauty with a granite jaw and full lips. His hair was dark like a raven's wing, shorn up the back yet long enough in the front so that it swept across eyes the color of storm clouds. When he spied Mathias, those stormy eyes lightened considerably.

"Mat," he said, moving towards him with a hand outstretched. "You have not changed since the last I saw you. You are as big and ugly as ever."

Mathias cracked a grin; he was slightly taller than Tate, with broader shoulders, but the two of them could have easily been brothers with their dark hair and masculine features. Seeing Tate for the first time since he had been stripped of his knighthood was something of a shock, Mathias soon realized. He hadn't thought about how much he had missed the man until this moment. He missed him greatly.

"If I insult you in return, it might mean trouble for me," he said, his eyes glimmering. "But I will say that I am very happy to see you, my lord. It has been a long time."

Tate just stood there, holding his hand and smiling at him as he reacquainted himself with the man's face, when a knight of enormous proportions entered the stall. Mathias looked over to see Kenneth St. Hèver enter the chamber.

Very blond, with ice-blue eyes and a square, determined jaw, he may have been slightly shorter than Tate or Mathias but he was purely hard, bulky muscle with enormous hands. No man survived long in a fight against St. Hèver simply because he was so bloody strong. He was a knight' knight, a warrior all men aspire to be but seldom are. He also happened to be one of Mathias' closest friends. Kenneth took one look at Mathias and headed straight for him.

Even Tate was surprised by the amount of emotion from the usually-emotionless St. Hèver as the man threw his arms around Mathias and nearly squeezed him to death. Mathias actually grunted as he squeezed Kenneth in return, but as quickly as the two came together, they also separated. St. Hèver was embarrassed by his emotional display.

"Mat," he greeted, looking somewhat chagrined. "You are looking well."

Mathias grinned. "De Lara just told me I looked old and ugly."

"He is a truthful man."

Mathias laughed softly. "I can be grateful for my health, I suppose, even if I am a troll to behold."

Kenneth smiled, an extremely rare gesture. He had big, white teeth that he kept mostly hidden. "I do believe I was the one considered a troll," he said. "Compared to you and de Lara and Pembury, I am the shortest of the group."

"The shortest and most fearsome," Mathias reminded him. "I am glad to see you are still breathing. Having been living in obscurity for the past year or so, I have not been abreast of current events or of my friends' conditions. I am very happy to see you both alive and well."

Tate nodded. "Alive and well indeed," he said, looking around the smithy stall. "And you? It looks as if you and your brother and father have done well for yourselves. I am told this is the biggest smithy operation in Brampton."

Mathias nodded. "It keeps us busy."

There was something in his tone that suggested that was the only thing the smithy profession was good for and the truth of the situation began to weigh heavily. They hadn't seen each other since that horrible day in January when Mathias lost everything and already the crux of the situation was rearing its ugly head. It was the giant in the room that no one wanted to acknowledge yet everyone felt the presence. Tate finally honed up to it since everyone's mind was on the same thing.

"How has it been for you?" he asked quietly. "I am not entirely sure I want to know the answer, for I know how I would feel if I were in your situation."

Mathias lifted a dark eyebrow. "You do?" he asked, torn between curiosity and outrage. "How *would* you feel?"

Tate found he was having difficulty looking the man in the eye. "Hollow," he said after a moment. "I suppose I would feel hollow. What happened to you could just as easily happen to me. Such are the fortunes of war."

Mathias shrugged as if to agree. "That is true," he admitted. "But it did not happen to you. I happened to me. Feeling hollow is only the beginning. Unless you have experienced it, you cannot understand."

Tate sighed heavily and averted his gaze; he didn't dare look at St. Hèver because the man had been filled with anguish since the happening. He loved and respected Mathias deeply, and his dishonor had been a bitter thing to watch.

"There is nothing I can say to lessen your shame or anguish," he said softly. "Mat, if I could ease this at all, I surely would. You did not deserve what happened but I swear it was the only way to save your life. There were many who wanted to do to you what was done to Mortimer. The only way to prevent that was to strip you of everything and make you inert. I pray to God that you understand that."

Mathias nodded slowly. "You told me all of this before," he replied steadily. "I understand everything."

Tate gazed into the dark green eyes; Mathias was a very difficult man to read. "Do you?" he whispered, almost painfully. "Do you also know how Ken and Stephen and I spent three days and nights begging the nobles to spare your life? Do you know that Ken went to fourteen different households in one day alone, gaining acceptance to have your life spared providing we strip you of your knighthood? The day that Edward took everything from you was the day we looked upon as a victory. It could have so easily gone the other way. I would rather be speaking to you now, a mighty knight transformed into a simple smithy, than visiting your grave and wishing I could have prevented your death."

Mathias truly hadn't known all of the wrangling and bargaining that had occurred before he had been stripped but he assumed it had been something of measure. He had been in far too powerful a position within Mortimer's power structure for him to get away so easily when Mortimer was deposed. His eyes glittered at Tate.

"Yet you still feel as if you did not do enough," he ventured softly.

Tate shrugged. "It is possible," he murmured. "I did what I could. I can only pray you forgive me for what has become of you. I have wanted to say that to you since everything occurred."

"And so you have," Mathias said quietly, reaching out to grasp Tate's shoulder in a reassuring gesture. "Truly, there is nothing to forgive. I simply do not think on it any longer. My life is here and now, and I must be satisfied with that. But know that I am grateful for everything you did for me and my family during that time."

"Edward will soften," Kenneth said, watching Mathias comfort a genuinely distressed Tate. "Already, he speaks of the future and of the mighty knights he will summon. He has mentioned your name. He misses you, Mat. We all do."

A dull twinkle came to Mathias' eyes. "I am here, in the wilds of the north," he said. "I swore never to bear arms again in battle, but I can support you with my mighty hammer and flaming-hot horse shoes. I am quite good with both, you know."

Tate cracked a grin. "I would imagine you would be formidable with a willow switch should you so choose," he said. "You are formidable in any case."

"Get me a willow switch and let us find out."

Tate snorted, as did Kenneth. It was good to alleviate the tension somewhat and both men were eased to see that Mathias had patiently and honorably accepted his sentence. In truth, they had expected nothing less. Mathias had always been exceptionally honorable, but still, that didn't lessen the tragedy of the circumstances.

"Speaking of formidable," Mathias took the opportunity to shift the subject. "I hear you are competing in the tournament today. Good news travels fast."

Tate nodded, struggling to move past the heartbreak of Mathias' situation. "I am," he replied. "So is Ken. It is unfortunate that you are not. It would be like old times."

Mathias wasn't sure which direction to take with his reply. He could agree with the statement or he could confess his intentions. He wasn't so sure he should do the latter, at least not at this point, so he settled for a neutral reply.

"If it was like old times I would be defeating you both," he said with some humor. "Mayhap it is best that I stay clear of the competition."

Kenneth fought off a grin. "I seem to recall that I defeated you in the mêlée the last tournament we competed in," he said. "Coventry, wasn't it? I knocked you off your feet."

Mathias cocked an eyebrow. "I tripped."

"Tripped or fell, the result was the same."

"You are too confident. If you do not cease this foolish boasting, I shall ask de Lara permission to compete against you in tournament to knock some of that arrogance out of you."

It was a calculated statement. Mathias wanted to see how Tate would react to the idea of him competing in a games based on the very war implements he had sworn never to wield again. Even though he had skirted the subject with his father and declared that he wasn't, in fact, taking up arms, the truth was that at some point, he would be wielding a weapon if he advanced in the games. That being said, his statement to de Lara constituted a pivotal moment, one that Mathias found himself greatly anticipating. Before Tate could respond, however, a small figure entered the stall.

"Cousin Tate! What a wonderful surprise to find you here!"

CHAPTER EIGHT

The men turned in the direction of the delighted utterance to see Cathlina standing in the doorway. Clad in a pale blue surcoat with a sheer white scarf around her head and shoulders, she looked like an angel. At her abrupt appearance, however, silent shock filled the air.

Mathias, in fact, was frozen. He had never seen anything so beautiful, but in the same breath, he had no idea what to do. Her appearance was unexpected and, at the moment, unwelcome. He was terrified for what was to come now, terrified that Tate would tell her everything about him and then all would be lost. Already, he felt a huge sense of loss.

"Cathlina?" Tate was the first to speak, his voice a mixture of surprise, pleasure, and disapproval. "What in the world are you doing here?"

Cathlina extended her hand to Tate, which he caught in his massive glove. She beamed up at him as he held her hand tightly. "Father brought us to see the tournament," she said. "We have only just left your lady wife; she says you are to compete today."

Tate nodded. "Indeed," he replied. "I am competing, as is Sir Kenneth. Surely you remember him?"

Cathlina turned to the big blond knight standing behind her; she hadn't really noticed him when she entered the stall because he was back in the shadow of the wall. He was smiling at her, his ice-blue eyes rather soft. So the great St. Hèver *was* here; she wondered how her sister was going to react to his presence and she further wondered if St. Hèver had gotten over his infatuation with her. As he bowed his head towards her in greeting, she was rather hoping so.

"Sir Kenneth," she said, forcing a smile. "It is agreeable to see you again."

Kenneth bobbed his head at her again. "It is agreeable to see you as well, my lady," he said. "You are looking very well."

It was as close to a compliment as the serious knight could come and somehow, Cathlina sensed that his infatuation for her had not burned itself out. There was something in the depths of the ice-blue eyes that told her so. Quickly, she turned her attention back to her cousin.

"We are very excited to see you both compete," she said. "Abechail is so excited that she cannot eat. This is her first tournament, you know."

Tate was still holding on to her, now shaking his head. "I did not know," he replied. "How is she feeling?"

Cathlina's smile faded. "She is the same," she replied. "The physics say her disease is worsening. Sometimes she spends weeks in bed, coughing that awful stuff out of her lungs. The physics tell my parents that it is only a matter of time before... well, before she is no longer with us. Mother cannot abide their word; she believes God will heal Abbie. I pray that he does."

"As do I," Tate said softly.

Cathlina nodded sadly, trying not to think of her sister's sorrowful state. But thoughts of Abechail reminded her of what had happened the day before, the very reason why she was in the smithy stall, and her attention shifted from Tate to Mathias, standing a few feet away.

"Yesterday, in fact, Abechail would have suffered a terrible fate had it not been for this smithy," she said, pointing to the man. "He saved our lives and I am sure he is a very good smithy, so if you have come to solicit work from him, I would ask that you do so. We owe him our gratitude at the very least."

Tate and Kenneth looked at Mathias and he could read the surprise on their faces. But with Tate, there was more than surprise; there was amusement and perhaps approval. It was difficult to say. Tate let go of Cathlina's hand as he focused on Mathias.

"Is this so?" he asked, more to Cathlina than to Mathias. "What did he do?"

Cathlina was back to smiling broadly, her gaze nothing short of adoring on Mathias. "When we were in town with Father a few days ago, a man tried to abduct Abechail," she told Tate. "He just lifted her right out of the wagon and tried to make off with her. I tried to stop him but he was too big for me to fight. I cried for help but no one would come. Just as I thought all was lost, Mathias stepped in and saved us. He was wonderful."

By this time, Tate was listening seriously. "What did you do?" he asked Mathias.

Mathias tried to downplay his heroism. "A fool half out of his mind tried to take the little one," he said, rather quietly. "It was not as great a feat to stop him as she implies. Sebastian took the fool out back and put him in the stocks."

"Is he still there?"

"He is."

Tate cocked an eyebrow. "Then see his is properly punished."

"He has been in the stocks for two days, naked to the elements. I have left his punishment to Sebastian who seems to take fiendish glee in torturing the man."

Tate cracked a smile. "I would believe that," he said. "Still, you shall be properly rewarded for assisting my cousins. What would you have?"

Mathias could see Cathlina standing a few feet away, her lovely face upturned to him, her eyes alight with admiration. The first thing that came to mind was a serious request; Cathlina was here and his mind was on the tournament and his very reason for wanting to compete. She was looking at him with such respect; he wanted to see that in her face when she looked at him, always. What was taken away from him, perhaps he could gain back just a little. Tate could do that for him. He could also deny him. There was only one way to find out.

"What would you be willing to give?" he asked deliberately.

But Tate wasn't catching on, at least not to the seriousness of the question. He shrugged his shoulders. "Money?" he asked, then looked around the stall. "You do not seem to be in any need of money. What else is there?"

"The tournament."

Tate looked at him as if confused by the statement. "What about it?"

"Let me compete."

Tate continued to look at him as if the words had no impact on him, as if it was the most common question in the world. But when the statement finally did sink in, he lifted his eyebrows. Then, he turned to St. Hèver , who gazed back at him with his usual stony countenance. Tate gazed at Kenneth, pondering Mathias' request, before cocking his head curiously.

"What do you think, Ken?" he asked. "Shall we permit it?"

Kenneth seemed to be fighting off a grin. "I am not sure," he said. "I am not entirely sure I want to be pummeled today."

"Nor am I," Tate said. "But it would make it a good deal more fun."

"It would, indeed. It would make the pummeling worth every moment."

Tate's gaze lingered on Kenneth a moment longer before returning his attention to Mathias. It was evident he was weighing the request and the serious implications of it. Finally, he simply shook his head.

"As much as I would like to permit it, I do not believe it would be a good idea," he said quietly. "You are Mathias de Reyne. Everyone knows who you are and what you represented, once. Hearing your name would drive those loyal to the king mad with want to kill you, or worse – it would drive those who had been loyal to Mortimer into thinking perhaps his cause was rising from the ashes. It is too soon for your name to be known again, Mat. I am truly sorry."

Mathias wasn't surprised at the response but he was disappointed. Still, he struggled not to react.

"As you say, my lord," he said, holding up a good front that it didn't matter. "Mayhap you are correct in your reasoning. One can never know."

Kenneth came out of the shadows, approaching Tate. "I do not agree with your assessment," he said, sounding very much as if he was pleading on Mathias' behalf. "Everyone knows that Edward is soundly in control of England. Mathias is just one of the many knights who fought against the king. The country is united now and so is the kingdom. It is time to forgive and Mathias' presence in the tournament today will reinforce that we are all united now for Edward."

Tate looked at Kenneth, fully aware that the man was siding with one of his dearest friends. The words were coming from the heart, not the head.

"Mayhap that is true," he said, "but there is a greater possibility that knights who fought for Edward are competing today and they will make every effort to kill Mathias. Like it or not, he still represents Mortimer."

Kenneth wasn't usually so verbal. He was normally the strong, silent type, but the subject matter had him running off at the mouth.

"I fought for Edward and I do not want to kill him," he reminded Tate quietly. "I think you are giving too much credence to the hatred bred by men. Above all, Mathias is one of the greatest knights this country has ever seen regardless of who he sided with."

"Ken," Mathias put a hand on Kenneth's shoulder, pulling the man away from Tate before the friendly discussion grew heated. "He is correct; mayhap it is still too soon for me. He is trying to keep me out of danger as he always has."

"You can take care of yourself," Kenneth said frankly. "If I, Tate or Stephen had been in your position, I can say without a doubt that we would not have submitted with the grace and honor you have displayed throughout this ordeal. Mat, your greatness cannot be contained forever. At some point, you are going to have to emerge into the light again. Why not start now?"

"Because of what Tate said," Mathias said, pointing to de Lara. "What if it is too soon for men to forgive? Mortimer and Isabella not only usurped the rightful king but they also murdered the king's father. People have not yet forgotten about that."

Kenneth, who as more consummately cool than any man alive, threw up his hands in a fit of emotion. "If you truly believe that, then why did you side with the bastard?"

Mathias kept his composure, although it was beginning to fracture. "You *know* why. He was my uncle. I had no choice. In order to please my dying mother, I promised her that I would support her sister's husband."

Kenneth knew that but suddenly, emotions were raw again and it was as if the past year of healing had been stripped away. He felt pain and sorrow again, but instead of arguing about it, he went with his nature and shut his mouth. The past could not be undone, anyway.

With a heavy sigh, Kenneth turned away, catching sight of Cathlina as he did so. He had forgotten she was there, as they all had. The subject they had discussed in front of her was a volatile one and the expression on her face suggested she was perhaps as deeply entrenched in the subject matter as they were. It was, in truth, a passionate and fascinating story, not one easily ignored. When Kenneth locked gazes with Cathlina, she pointed at Mathias.

"Who...?" she began, then reconsidered the question. She started again. "Mathias is not a smithy?"

Kenneth turned to look directly at Mathias. He was looking at Cathlina, too, having completely forgotten she was there. He felt like an idiot. She had heard all that he hoped she would not hear and now he would have to explain it to her and pray she understood. But somehow, he was more apt to believe that she would flee the stall and never look back. Already, he felt the sorrow of her departure but before he could answer, Tate replied for him.

"He is not a smithy," Tate said quietly. "Mathias de Reyne is one of the greatest knights I have ever known. We served together for many years before the madness between Edward and Roger Mortimer and, as you heard, Mathias sided with Mortimer. Because of this, he was stripped of his titles and lands, and has found a living now as a smithy. He is one of my greatest friends and one of the truest, most honorable men I know. You were very fortunate that he came to your aid, Cathlina. He is a very great man."

Cathlina's eyes were wide as she gazed at Mathias, digesting what Tate had told her. The truth was that she was overwhelmed with it all; it was too much information, too important and severe. Her head was starting to swim with it.

"I see," she said, although she didn't mean it. She didn't truly grasp half of what she had heard. "I... I brought him some treats yesterday to thank him for helping my sister and me. I have only come for the empty basket. I did not mean to... I fear this is something I should not have heard. I did not mean to interrupt your business."

"You did not interrupt anything," Tate said, seeing how stunned she was. "Where is your father? He can escort you back to your encampment and I shall see you later at the tournament."

Cathlina was feeling many different things at that moment; disappointment, fear, surprise, sorrow... it was difficult to isolate just one. All she knew was that too many emotions were welling in her chest. Mostly, she felt foolish. Her eyes were on Mathias as she spoke.

"My father is not here," she said, her voice tight and the least bit trembly. "I came alone. Mathias... I mean, my lord, if you will give me my basket, I shall be along my way."

Mathias could see how upset she was and he felt so incredibly guilty. "I will retrieve it," he said softly. "Then I will escort you back to your family."

"Nay," she said abruptly, already moving out of the stall. "I do not... you should stay here. I do not need an escort."

Mathias, Kenneth and Tate were all moving after her she tried to flee. "Cathlina," Tate called after her. "Sweetheart, please let Ken escort you back. You do not have to...."

It was too much; Cathlina took off at a dead run, disappearing in between a couple of stalls in a silky flash of pale blue linen. Mathias didn't even wait for Tate or Kenneth – he took off as well, following her path. He had to find her and soothe her if he could but he was sure he couldn't. She ran because of him. Still, he felt desperate to explain himself even if she didn't want anything to do with him. He wanted everything to do with her.

Cathlina was small and fast, but he was big and faster. Moreover, he knew this town and she didn't. Mathias was able to follow her path quite easily. She had ended up out behind some small cottages to the north side of the village and as he emerged from between a pair of structures, he could see her in the distance, walking through knee-deep green grass with her head bowed. As he slowed his pace, Kenneth came running up behind him.

"There she is," Kenneth said. "I shall retrieve her."

Mathias put out a hand to stop him. "Let me do it," he said. "I am the reason she ran. Let me take her back."

Kenneth looked at him. "What do you mean?"

Mathias sighed faintly, his gaze on the distant figure. "I suppose you could say that we have become friends," he said quietly. "It is not a pleasant thing to discover your friend is not who you thought he was."

Kenneth understood somewhat. He also realized that tendrils of jealousy were snatching at him but it wasn't in his nature to act upon them. He wasn't the type. Moreover, he'd had his chance with Cathlina back in December when her family had visited Carlisle. His attraction to her had been mild but she clearly hadn't been interested in him. He hoped Mathias had better luck with her.

"A friend?" he repeated. "Or something more?"

Mathias shook his head. "Nothing more," he assured him. "Moreover, a woman like that is out of my class."

Kenneth's eyebrows furrowed. "She is not out of your class," he said. "Why would you say such things?"

"If you had a daughter, would you allow her to marry a dishonored knight?"

Kenneth shrugged; he had a point. "Your dishonor will not last forever," he said. "In fact… if I were you, I might not listen to de Lara's assessment of your status. If I was in the same situation, I might compete in the tournament anyway. I might borrow my friend's bay charger, a rather new and inexperienced beast, but one of very fine stock and eager to learn. Mayhap my friend would have him tethered in de Lara's encampment so that I could slip in and take him. It is not as if de Lara told you not to compete. He simply said it would not be a good idea."

Mathias looked at him. "What is this? Insubordination from Kenneth St. Hèver , the perfect knight?"

Kenneth merely looked away, watching Cathlina struggle through the tall, wet grass. He didn't comment on his suggestion, instead, letting it settle in Mathias' mind. He shifted the subject.

"She is a beautiful girl," he commented, his gaze lingering on Cathlina before turning to Mathias. "Her father is very protective of her, however. Take heed he does not come after you with his axe if he thinks you have eyes for his daughter."

"I never said I had eyes for her."

Kenneth's white eyebrows lifted. "Liar."

"I am not."

"Then why did you run after her when she fled?"

"To make sure she did not come to harm."

Kenneth gave him a disbelieving look before turning away and returning the way he had come. Meanwhile, Mathias went after Cathlina.

The morning dew was still heavy in the grass as he tramped through it. Cathlina still had her head down and her pace had slowed, and as Mathias drew closer he could see that her hands were at her face. She was moving them around. Eventually, she lowered her hands and he could see a white kerchief clutched in the fingers of her left hand. He came up behind her and put a gentle hand on her shoulder.

"Cathlina?" he said softly.

She jumped and whirled to face him. Her eyes were red and watery and her pert little nose was red from crying. Seeing Mathias behind her, Cathlina tried to move away from him quickly but the heavy grass made it difficult.

"I do not need your assistance," she assured him. "I do not need the basket, either. You can keep it."

"Cathlina, stop," he begged softly, reaching out to gently grasp her. "Please let me explain what you heard."

She shook her head, her kerchief at her nose. "There is no need to explain," she said. "I heard what Cousin Tate said; you are a knight pretending to be a smithy."

"I am not pretending to be anything. I am what you see."

She disputed him with a sharp wave of the hand. "But... but you know my cousin, the Earl of Carlisle," she said, sniffling into her wadded kerchief. "He said you were a great knight. What in the world are you doing posing as a smithy and fooling people into thinking you are a simple man?"

"Is that what you think? That I was trying to fool you?"

She shrugged, blowing her nose. "It does not matter to me who you are.

"Then why are you weeping?"

She came to a halt and scowled at him. "I am not weeping for you if that is what you think."

He fought off a grin. "I had hoped that you were."

Her scowl turned to curiosity. "You do? Why?"

He removed his hand from her elbow now that he was sure she wasn't going to run off; he could see that he had her attention. Feigning shyness, he looked away.

"Because I have rather enjoyed coming to know you," he said, trying to get a look at her from the corner of his eye to gauge how she was reacting. "I was very much looking forward to seeing you today. "

Cathlina's tears were almost completely forgotten. "You *were*?"

"I was."

Cathlina was seemingly at a loss. It was evident that she wanted to say something to him but perhaps propriety was preventing her from speaking her mind. The tears had been replaced by a rather warm glimmer. The fact that he seemed to be attracted to her outweighed her confusion at the moment. Suddenly, she didn't feel like running from him anymore.

"I am not sure what to say to all of that," she said softly, "but I suppose I could tell you that I was looking forward to seeing you, too. I have been looking forward to seeing you again since I met you. Coming to your stall in search of my basket was merely an excuse."

He looked at her, a smile on his full lips. "I had hoped that it was," he said, his voice deep and gentle. "In fact, I was trying to think of another excuse after the basket had been used up. Surely there was something else I could retrieve from you, or mayhap you would leave your kerchief behind so that I could return it to you."

Cathlina's chest was swelling with hope. In fact, it was becoming difficult to breathe as she gazed into his dark green eyes. But as she bathed in the joy of the knowledge that he was evidently feeling the same allure she was, the weight of Mathias' conversation with Tate was pressing upon her. Her expression grew serious.

"Why were you pretending to be a smithy, Mathias?" she asked softly. "I do not understand half of what Cousin Tate was saying, but am I to understand you are an outlaw?"

Mathias shook his head, thankful that she was at least receptive to hearing his story. He chose his words carefully.

"I am not an outlaw," he said quietly. "In order to explain myself, it is easier to start from the beginning. Do you remember when we spoke of my mother and I mentioned that she had died a few years ago?"

"I do."

"She was an older sister to Roger Mortimer's wife, Joan," he went on. "My mother was close to her sister and as she lay very ill, she made me promise that I would always support Joan's husband no matter what. Unwilling to disappoint her, I agreed. Therefore, when Mortimer and Isabella took the throne from young Edward, I fought with Mortimer and when he was ultimately captured and killed for his treachery, I was stripped of my titles and lands for my participation."

The second time around, and with Mathias' clear and gentle explanation, she was able to grasp the scenario better. It was still overwhelming information but somehow, she quickly coming to accept it. In fact, it made a good deal of sense; Mathias was a very big and very muscular man, and didn't look like any smithy she had ever seen. There was something clean and powerful about him, like a god in the midst of a sea of pagans. Now, it was all starting to make sense.

"So you served Mortimer?" she asked.

He nodded slowly. "I was the captain of his armies."

It was difficult to comprehend that as much as her cousin Tate had been the right arm of Edward, so Mathias had been the right hand of the hated Mortimer. So much death and destruction in a power struggle that had nearly torn the country apart, and Mathias and Tate had been in the middle of it. Tate had emerged greater than before but Mathias, by virtue of his loyalties, had emerged a fallen man. He was the fallen one. The information threatened to overwhelm her again but she fought it.

"What were your lands and titles?" she asked.

"Does it matter?"

"Not really," she said. "I was simply curious."

His gaze lingered on her a moment before he spoke "I was known as Baron Westbury, High Warden of the Northern Marches," he said. "Alberbury Castle and Caus Castle on the Marches were mine as well as seven thousand retainers under my direct command. But that is over and done with now. I am, in fact, a smithy these days because when my titles were taken from me, I was forced to swear that I would never again bear arms in battle in exchange for my life."

She gazed up at him with her big brown eyes as she digested his statement. "Your brother and father, too?"

"Them, too. We had to find some way of making a living and by virtue of our profession had some proficiency at metal working, so it seemed like a logical choice."

"So you live as peasants."

"We do what we must in order to survive."

She could imagine him at the head of a great army. It was very easy to picture. As she thought on him clad in armor and bearing weapons as a powerful warrior, now reduced to wearing a leather apron and wielding a hammer, she began to feel sorry for him. She couldn't help it.

"What will you do now with your life?" she asked seriously. "It seems that Sir Kenneth did not think your exile would last forever. When your greatness is restored, what will you do?"

He lifted his eyebrows thoughtfully. As he did so, horns from the tournament field began to sound, calling the combatants to the arena for the practice bouts. Mathias fully intended to participate but before he could, he had to get Cathlina moving. He extended his elbow to her.

"Let me take you back to your family," he said. "The tournament will be starting soon."

Cathlina took his elbow without hesitation and he began to lead her back the way they had come. Things were calm now between them, and the feel of her hand against his arm was comforting and natural. It had been so long since Mathias had felt a woman against him, in any form, that the simple touch of her hand was enough to set his heart fluttering.

"Please answer my question" Cathlina said as he helped her navigate a muddy puddle of mashed grass. "What will you do once your honor is restored and you are a mighty knight again?"

He shrugged. "I will have my titles and property returned to me at some point," he said as they walked. "I never believed otherwise. When the time comes, I will assume my place in the king's stable of knights. I will swear fealty to him."

"When do you think this will happen?"

"It is difficult to know. Time has a way of healing bitter memories. Mayhap it will be next year, or mayhap in ten years. I do not know."

"And you remain so patient?"

He thought he had been very patient, but remembering his conversation with his father whereupon he discussed winning the tournament and using the proceeds to start a new life in Scotland, perhaps he hadn't been patient at all.

"Nay," he shook his head ruefully. "I am not as patient as I would like to think. Something has happened recently that has made me reconsider my patient stance."

"What has happened?"

He gave her a side-long glance. "I met a young lady who has made me think that mayhap there is more to life than scratching out a living as a smithy," he said. "She has opened my eyes to a great many things."

Cathlina had no idea he was speaking of her and she began to feel a good deal of disappointment and jealousy.

"Oh," she said, somewhat subdued. "Then... then I wish you good fortune in your future endeavors."

He could tell that she didn't mean it and he suspected why. In fact, her reaction gave him great hope and happiness. As they passed through the small cottages and onto the avenue that led towards the smithy shack, he put a big hand over the small fingers clutching his elbow.

"I have a question to ask you, Lady Cathlina," he said. "May I be so bold?"

She picked up the damp hem of her skirt to prevent it from dragging in the dust and creating mud. "Of course."

"Are you spoken for?"

Cathlina was watching the dusty road pass under her feet, her damp slipper with a brown ring around the bottom. The softly uttered words were not the combination of words she had expected and when the meaning struck her, she looked at him in shock.

"Am I...?" she repeated, eyes wide. "Why... why would you ask?"

"Cathlina!"

The shout came from down the avenue. Cathlina and Mathias turned to see Tate approaching. His expression was filled with concern, with relief, as he quickly came upon them. His focus was completely on Cathlina.

"Cathlina, are you well?" he asked. "I am happy to see that Mathias was able to find you."

Cathlina looked rather embarrassed, her gaze moving between Tate and Mathias. "I... I am well," she assured Tate. "I am sorry if I caused you concern. I was... well, I am sure my father is looking for me. I was simply trying to make my way back and lost my way."

Tate took her from Mathias. "I will take you to him."

Cathlina looked at Mathias in panic as Tate pulled her away. "Mathias," she called, but realized she couldn't say what she was thinking. She scrambled as she thought of a way to phrase it. "In… in answer to your question, it depends on who is asking. Were you inquiring for yourself, perchance?"

Mathias' eyes glimmered at her as Tate tried to lead her away. "I was."

She grinned. "In that case, I am not."

He laughed softly, watching Tate urge her down the avenue with him. Cathlina giggled, waving at him as he waved back. It was a sweet moment in spite of Tate's presence, the looks between Cathlina and Mathias full of potential and promise.

Mathias lowered his hand, watching her disappear from view with her enormous cousin, the vision of her smiling face the last memory he held to him. He held it close as he headed back for the smithy stall, keeping the vision of her as his inspiration. All his life, he'd been told what cause to fight for whether or not he truly believed in it. That sense of duty had cost him everything. He wasn't going to make the same mistake again. Now, he had his own cause to fight for.

He had a tournament to participate in.

CHAPTER NINE

By the time the tournament festivities began around mid-day, the breeze had picked up and the standards surrounding the field were snapping briskly. Fat, puffy clouds danced across the blue expanse of sky, carrying with them the threat of rain as they passed. In the tournament arena below, the perimeter of the competition area was packed with spectators.

The lists containing the crowd were small and hastily constructed, and they were already full of people. There was a section for the Earl of Carlisle's family, now full of Toby and her five children – Roman, daughter Catherine, the rambunctious twins Dylan and Alex, and baby Sophie. There was also a seat for Tate but since he was competing, Saer sat upon it and laughed at the antics of his cousin's children. The rough boys were busy playing knights, pushing each other down, and adding to the fun. Watching the rough twins roll their older brother was great entertainment.

Cathlina, Roxane, Abechail, and Rosalund had a rough bench to sit on but it was enough. They had a great view of the field. At their feet on the rough-boarded floor was a linen cloth spread out containing a small table with food upon it. There was an abundance of fruit, bread, cheese, plus little puddings in wooden cups that were made from mint and lemon and honey.

There was also something that they had never seen before, something that the young de Lara children scooped up out of a earthenware bowl and shoved gleefully into their mouths; upon tasting the dish, Cathlina and Abechail were told it was called *pastos,* a dish consisting of long, cooked sheets of wheat and eggs, all mixed up in a sauce that consisted of cheese, milk, nutmeg, and a few other ingredients. It was creamy and delicious. It was a dish that Tate and Toby had collected on their travels to Italy years go and the de Lara children ate it quite regularly.

As the earl's young children and Abechail sat on the floor of the lists and ate, Cathlina and Roxane were more interested in the knights that were now starting to take the field for practice. The first series of games would be the joust and a big wooden guide had been built in the center of the arena to keep opponents from crashing into each other as they made their charge. Even now, workmen were finishing with the reinforcement of the guides as the field marshals kept close watch on both the workmen and the knights that were thundering around the field.

It was beginning to get exciting. Saer came off of his seat and stood at the railing with Cathlina and Roxane, watching the knights take the field astride their massive war horses. Saer had allowed Dunstan and Beauson to enter the competition to represent Kirklinton Castle, and they entered the field fairly early clad in the colors of the house of Saer de Lara. Their tunics bore a big yellow axe right on the chest.

"Papa, are you disappointed that you are not competing?" Cathlina asked as a big knight in a green and black tunic blew past.

Saer watched the knight, too, scrutinizing him. "I am not," he said flatly. "Although tournaments were great sport when I was young, I am afraid it is indeed a younger man's sport. If I were to compete today, I would be easily defeated."

"Did you win many tournaments?" Roxane wanted to know.

Saer's attention was on the Earl of Carlisle now making an appearance on the field, a big man on a black and white charger bearing a tunic of crimson and gold. Toby and her oldest son, a handsome and well behaved lad named Roman, began to yell and wave at the earl. Tate thundered onto the field and the crowd, seeing that the earl had arrived, began to cry for him as well. Behind Tate came another knight bearing the earl's colors astride a muscular dappled gray charger. When the two of them thundered out into the arena, the energy level of the crowd surged.

"Who is the other knight bearing the earl's colors?" Roxane asked, squinting at the distant figure.

Saer was squinting, too. "I believe it is St. Hèver ," he said, then cast his daughter a long glance. "You will not make a nuisance of yourself with him, do you hear? The man is not interested in marriage."

Roxane's lip stuck out in a pout as she turned away from her father, trying very hard not to watch every move St. Hèver made as he deftly controlled his horse on the other side of the arena.

"I was not going to," she sniffed, offended. "I simply wanted to know who it was, 'tis all."

Saer cocked an eyebrow as if he didn't believe her, returning his attention to the knights that were now starting to circle the arena, warming up their chargers. Cathlina glanced at her sister, trying not to make eye contact because she was sure her sister was already upset about the fact St. Hèver was here and Cathlina didn't want to confess that she had seen the man earlier. It would only inflame Roxane. As the chargers rushed past, kicking up clods of earth, she sought to change the subject.

"There are quite a lot of knights here," she said to her father. "How many do you think there are?"

Saer watched de Lara blow by him, followed by St. Hèver. "At least thirty or forty men," he said. "They have already drawn lots to see who will compete against each other. See that wall on the opposite side of the arena? They will hang banners there so we will know who is competing against whom."

"Papa?" Abechail wedged herself in between Roxane and Saer, tugging on her father's sleeve. "Papa, there is a vendor selling candied fruits. I saw a girl with some. Can I please have some?"

Saer didn't want to leave now that the knights were warming up, but he couldn't very well let Abechail go by herself and he certainly couldn't deny her. Hurriedly, he grabbed her hand and very nearly pulled her off the lists. Young Roman was invited to go along as Saer and the two children went in search of sweets. Cathlina and Roxane didn't much care, fixed on the knights as they were.

As they were watching Tate and Kenneth make practice runs along the guide, a knight on an enormous bay stallion entered the field. Bearing a tunic of straight yellow without any of the elaborate embroidery the other knights had, he was a massive man in heavy protection as he thundered across the arena, struggling with his disobedient horse. The charger was very young and very excitable, and it was difficult not to notice the pair as the charger kicked up his white feet and generally behaved madly. He was so beautiful, however, that the struggle between man and beast became mesmerizing to watch.

Cathlina's attention was divided between Tate, Kenneth, and the new knight with the wild horse. Soon enough, she was only watching the knight with the excitable horse, as was nearly everyone else around her, because the pair was making practice runs along the guide. When they made a run past another horse, the excitable bay tried to savage the other charger and the field marshals were called in. It was one thing for the big chargers to savage each other in battle but quite another to have it happen in a tournament.

"Mayhap they will not let him compete," Roxane said to her sister, pointing at the knight with the agitated horse in the middle of the arena as he spoke with two of the field marshals. "That horse is very mean."

Cathlina shrugged. "They are all very mean," she said, indicating a knight off to their left whose horse was muzzled with a great steel cage. "Look at that horse; they have to put a barrier around his mouth."

They were both watching the knight with the muzzled horse when two big chargers suddenly roared up beside them. Dirt flew up, hitting Roxane in her greased-up hair, and she shrieked. Cathlina found herself carefully picking the dirt out of her sister's hair as Tate and Kenneth lifted their visors.

"My lady," Tate said to his wife, who was rising from her seat to greet him. "Do you have a favor for me to carry before this great and terrible production begins?"

Toby grinned her lovely white smile, fumbling around in her long sleeve before pulling free a small white kerchief. As she went to hand it to him, the twins decided they wanted to ride with their father and started climbing up on the railing to get at him. Cathlina and Toby pulled the boys down as they demanded to go with their father. As Toby admonished the twins on their behavior, her beautiful five year old daughter, Catherine, calmly went to her father and extended a little posy she had picked that morning on the way to the arena. Tate took it from the little girl as if it was the finest treasure.

"Thank you, Cate," he said, smiling at her. "This is the best favor I have ever received."

As the little girl beamed, Kenneth put in. "And there is no favor for me?" he asked her. "I am deeply hurt, Catie. I thought you loved me best."

Cate giggled as Roxane spoke up. "You may have my favor, Sir Kenneth," she said, pulling forth an elaborate and heady-smelling piece of silk from her bosom. She held it out to him, feigning shyness and batting her eyelashes. "I would be honored if you would carry it."

Fortunately, Kenneth was adept at keeping an emotionless façade. His first instinct was to recoil and run away, but he fought it. He faced Roxane's offensive bravely.

"I am honored, Lady Roxane," he said, although he didn't mean a word of it. "But you must not feel pity for me. There are dozens of young knights here that would be very proud to wear your favor. Surely you do not want to give it to an old knight like me."

Roxane was flattered and offended at the same time. She looked around at the other competitors, rather uncertainly, until Cathlina came to her rescue.

"She does not know any of the other competitors, Sir Kenneth," she said. "Since you do not have a favored young lady today, my sister honors you with her offer. She will cheer you louder than anyone."

Roxane was back to her false modesty pose as Kenneth began to sweat. But he knew he couldn't get out of it so he simply nodded.

"I am humbled, my lady," he said without a hint of defeat in his voice.

Roxane smiled brightly as she extended the kerchief. Kenneth took it and, with a smell that nearly knocked him off his horse, quickly tucked it into his armor and tried to get it as far away from his nose as he could. With a stiff bob of the head, he slammed his faceplate down and thundered off. Roxane watched him wistfully.

"Mayhap Father should ask him again if he is agreeable to a betrothal," she whispered to Cathlina. "He seemed very pleased by my favor, don't you think?"

Cathlina wasn't so sure but she nodded anyway. "I do," she said. "He is very handsome. You would make a fine match with him."

Her heart full of admiration for Sir Kenneth, Roxane moved away from the rail to regain her seat as Cathlina remained, watching the knights as they finished warming their horses and, one by one, began leaving the field. She noticed that Tate was still lingering at the rail, holding his wife's hand sweetly and kissing her fingers as they murmured soft words between them. She noticed how much in love they were, a love that most women wanted but seldom achieved. Love, like the kind her cousin shared with his wife, was very rare. Her heart tugged a bit for want of that kind of love. She wondered if she'd ever be fortunate enough to have it.

Tate kissed his wife one last time and lowered his face plate, charging off in the same direction Kenneth had taken. Cathlina continued to linger by the rail, watching the knights, her mind wandering to Mathias and wondering if she should try and slip away to see him now that her father was occupied. Her mother kept close watch of her, however, and she casually turned around to see that her mother and Roxane were in intense conversation. No doubt plotting on how to wrest a betrothal out of Sir Kenneth, Cathlina thought wryly. She thought the man had looked rather stricken when he had been forced to take Roxane's favor because he was no-doubt fearful of what that would lead to. Fighting off a smile at the memory, she was caught off-guard when the knight on the wild bay charger suddenly pulled up to the railing.

"My lady," he said in his glorious deep voice. "Are you spoken for?"

Cathlina was prepared to ignore the bold knight and turn her back to him when something in his voice made her stop. There was something strangely familiar about it and she looked at him, cocking her head in an increasingly inquisitive manner. She had heard those words before, earlier in the day, in the same soft and deep timbre. Could it be...?

"I asked you a question, my lady," he said, his voice considerably quieter. "Are you spoken for?"

A light of recognition went on in Cathlina's head. She could hardly believe it. "That depends," she said quietly, leaning forward on the rail to gain a better look at him. "Are you asking for yourself, perchance?"

"I am."

"Let me see your face."

The knight reined his foaming charger as close as he could, turning sideways so he was closer to the railing and closer to Cathlina. His visor was still lowered on his fearsome helm but she knew he was looking at her. The corners of her mouth twitched.

"Open the visor," she said softly, eyes glimmering with the mirth and surprise of the situation. "Let me see if I recognize your eyes."

"Will you give me your favor if you do?"

Her smile broke through. "I will do it quite happily."

The visor flipped up and Mathias' dark green eyes were twinkling back at her. "Do you know me?" he whispered.

Cathlina nodded. "I do indeed."

The corners of his eyes crinkled. "I am glad."

Cathlina eyed him, glancing around to make sure they weren't being watched. "What are you doing here?" she asked, trying not to be overheard. "I heard my cousin tell you not to compete. He said men would try to kill you because of your association with... well, you *know*."

"He did not give me a direct order not to compete," Mathias replied carefully. "Moreover, no one will know who I am. My name is Chayson de Lovern. For the duration of the tournament, that is who you will address me as."

Her brow furrowed in confusion. "De Lovern?" she repeated. "Who is that?"

"It is me."

"Does Cousin Tate know what you are doing?"

"He does not, so I would appreciate it if you would keep this between us. No one knows."

She still appeared bewildered but didn't question him further. But she did want to know one thing.

"Why are you doing this?" she asked softly. "Why would you risk yourself so?"

He wrestled with the horse when it threw its head, waiting until it settled down before returning his attention to her.

"Because there is a young lady who has made me think that mayhap there is more to life than scratching out a living as a smithy," he said quietly, his gaze riveted to her. "I am doing this because she is not yet spoken for and I am hoping that if I win this event, it will restore some of my honor and she will agree to let me court her."

This time, Cathlina knew he was speaking of her. She couldn't help the grin on her lips or the flush of her cheeks. She wore the simple but delicious surcoat of pale blue and the white linen shawl around her neck and shoulders; the shawl was the only thing she had that she could give the man so she pulled it off of her shoulders and wadded it up, extending the ball to him. As Mathias took it, she spoke.

"I would have agreed to let you court me if you had only and truly been a simple smithy," she said softly. "You do not need to prove your might in order for me to take notice. I took notice of you the day we met."

He had the balled-up shawl in one big hand, gazing at her with more emotion than he could ever recall when it came to a woman. His chest was warm and tight, his heart fluttery. It was the oddest sensation but wholly wonderful. He had to fight the urge to dismount the horse and take her in his arms, for never in his life had he wanted to hold a woman so badly. His entire body fairly ached with desire. Bringing the shawl to his nose, he inhaled deeply the scent of roses. A common enough scent but one that was as sweet and beautiful as she was.

"When men ask you if you are spoken for, what will you tell them?" he asked, his word muffled by the shawl.

She lifted an eyebrow. "I am not sure," she said. "Until you ask if you can court me, I suppose I am still unspoken for. You have not asked at all."

"May I court you, my lady?"

He said it without hesitation and she laughed softly. "I was hoping you would."

Mathias suddenly slapped his faceplate down. At the same time, Cathlina felt a body next to her and she turned to see Roxane standing at her left hand, curiously looking at Mathias who, by now, was thundering back across the arena.

"Who was that?" Roxane wanted to know.

Cathlina sighed. "A very nice knight by the name of de Lovern," she said. "He asked for my favor. Since you have already given yours away, I saw no harm in giving mine to him. What do you care, anyway? You have the mighty St. Hèver at your feet."

Predictably thrown off the subject to de Lovern and on to St. Hèver, Roxane smiled happily and took her sister's arm as they regained their seats. The field marshals were clearing the arena in preparation for the first bout and spectators were settling in for a thrilling day. The excitement in the air was palpable as the horns began to sound, announcing the count-down to the first round.

This day, of all days, would be memorable.

CHAPTER TEN

"Did the earl see you?" Justus wanted to know. "God's Bones, the man is not a fool. He will know you on sight, Mathias. You cannot deceive him."

Back behind the smithy stall in a small corral used for horses waiting to be shod, Mathias held fast to the big bay stallion he had just confiscated from de Lara's encampment. The horse was excitable and beautiful, and as he held the beast still while Sebastian adjusted the saddle, he wondered what had become of his own lovely charger he had surrendered along with his weapons and armor. The horse had been with him for seven years, a beautiful animal the color of silver, and he knew the horse had been coveted by many. He was sure the animal was part of some nobleman's collection, possibly even the king's collection, and was very well treated. Still, he missed the horse.

"I spoke with de Lara at length this morning," Mathias replied. "You know this; you saw him when he was here."

"I saw him," Justus said impatiently. "Sebastian and I purposely hid away when he came. We knew he had much to say to you."

"He had much to say to us all," Mathias said, somewhat quietly. "I told you that he apologized again for what occurred. It was all things we have heard before, words of anguish and hope. He still feels very guilty for what happened."

"He should not," Sebastian said as he swung the saddle onto the charger's back. "We made our choice and accepted the consequences."

Mathias struggled with the charger that didn't want to stand still. "Even so, the man has a conscience."

"Conscience or no, he will arrest us if he discovers what you've done," Justus said, agitated. "I did not raise you to be foolish, Mathias."

Mathias was helping his brother with the leather straps that secured the saddle to the horse's body.

"Nay, you did not," he said, grunting when the twitching horse bumped into him. "But you did raise me to be bold, brave, and determined, and that is exactly what I shall be."

Justus knew there was no discouraging him. Mathias was stubborn in every sense of the word. It was a character flaw or a character strength depending on the situation, so the old man sighed heavily and stood back as his sons prepared the enormous charger with pieces of tack they'd accumulated over the past year. The equipment wasn't nearly as elaborate as some of the knights in the competition, but it was adequate. It would have to do.

Mathias was going to go through with this charade regardless of what Justus said. Therefore, rather than fight his son, he stepped in to assist. The three of them had soared to the top of the power echelon together and had fallen back down again together, and if Mathias was to be arrested for doing something he very much wanted to do, then Justus would be by his side for that also. As always, the de Reynes would serve together, following a tradition set forth by Justus' great-great-grandfather, Creed de Reyne. He, too, served with his brothers. The de Reynes were a loyal bunch.

As Justus moved to the back of the horse to fuss with the plain yellow banner on his haunches, Sebastian moved up to the bridle where his brother was.

"Where did you get that favor," he asked, pointing to the balled-up shawl on the pommel of the saddle.

Mathias glanced at it. "From a certain young lady."

"Lady Cathlina?"

"Aye."

"The same lady you warned me against because she is, in fact, a de Lara?"

"The same."

Sebastian was the last one to judge his brother, but even he shook his head after a moment. "From a man who sees reason in all things, I am impressed with your willingness to be reckless. I sincerely hope she is worth it."

Mathias looked at his brother, depth of sincerity in his expression. "I would not be doing this if she was not. She is worth all this and more."

Sebastian believed him.

***

There were twenty seven knights competing in the Brampton tournament, and most of those were from the north. There were a few that made a profession out of tournaments rather than battles, and those men were gaily bedecked with banners and followed by countless women begging for a lock of hair or a glimpse of their smile.

One knight in particular had big plumage feathers sticking up out of helm, quite full of himself until St. Hèver cut the plumes in half with his sword. Kenneth said it was an accident but most knew it wasn't. He had been annoyed by the prideful knight's boasting just as the other competitors had been. When Kenneth had hacked off the plumes, the knights within eyeshot had roared with laughter.

Including Tate. It had been a bit of comic relief in the midst of serious tournament preparation. He and Kenneth had been preparing their chargers for the coming bouts; Kenneth had drawn the second bout against a big bald knight named Quinton de Gare while Tate wasn't going until the seventh round against a knight named Chayson de Lovern. After the mutilated plumage incident, they returned to their equipment as Kenneth prepared to shortly compete.

"What do we know of de Gare?" Tate asked him as he fixed a leather strap that had broken. "The name sounds familiar but I cannot place him."

Kenneth grunted. "You are not going to like the answer."

Tate's head came up. "Why not?"

Kenneth glanced at him as he finished adjusting his stirrup. "He was sworn to Hugh Despenser the Younger," he said. "I remember seeing him years ago when the Despensers wrought their havoc. Do you not recall him as a younger man? He had hair then."

Tate thought hard. "I recall a Jasper de Gare."

"His brother."

Tate sighed sharply and returned to what he had been doing. "I remember them now," he said. "Quinton is a big man but, if I recall correctly, not a very good warrior. Jasper was the warrior."

"You would be right."

The continued to prepare their equipment in silence for a few moments until Tate spoke again.

"My opponent," he said, "what is his name? De Lovern? I believe that is Banbury's heir."

Kenneth was extremely careful in how he reacted or what he said; he was well aware that de Lovern was Mathias. He hadn't seen the man since the incident with Cathlina de Lara that morning but an hour later, his big bay charger had been missing and was now the mount of an unknown knight named de Lovern, who happened to be Tate's first round opponent. The way the man moved, his skill with a horse, and the way he handled his weaponry made it very, very clear to Kenneth that Mathias had taken his advice. He had entered himself in the tournament and, by a stroke of luck, drew Tate as his first opponent. *Oh, the irony*, Kenneth thought.

"I have not heard of him before," Kenneth said casually.

"He is riding a charger that looks very much like the one you purchased in York last month."

"Is he? I had not noticed."

Tate finished with the strap he had been repairing. "Did you check to see if your horse is missing?" he asked. "Mayhap de Lovern stole it."

"If he has, I will run him through."

"I will run him through for you. Since he will be competing against me, I will have more of an opportunity than you will."

"I would not worry about it. Simply have a clean round and do not get hurt. It would forever scar your wife and children if you did."

"Do not worry about me," Tate said, looking over his horse to make sure he was prepared. "By the way; where is Mathias?"

Kenneth was still fussing with the stirrup, or at least pretending to. "I have not seen him since this morning."

It wasn't a lie. Tate continued to check his saddle. "I thought he might at least come to watch."

Kenneth looked at him, then. "Would you?" he asked. "If all of this had once been yours and now you were denied what came naturally to you, knowing you were the best of the best, would *you* come to watch?"

Tate finished checking his saddle and looked at Kenneth. "Nay," he said flatly. "I would come to compete."

Kenneth didn't know how to respond; he held Tate's gaze steady before shrugging his shoulders and turning back to his stirrup. Tate eyed his very blond, very big friend a moment before moving to walk past him.

"If you happen to see de Lovern," he said quietly, "tell him I plan to knock him on his arse and take your horse."

Kenneth watched the man walk away. A faint smile creased his normally emotionless-lips; it was certainly going to be an interesting bout, and one he was looking forward to.

He knew Tate was, too.

***

Kenneth's round against de Gare had been three very violent passes, resulting in two shattered joust poles for each of the competitors, but in the end Kenneth emerged the victor. As he made his victory pass in front of the roaring crowd, he was obliged to stop in front of Roxane and accept her blessing. He did so, but he didn't take her hand and kiss it as most knights would have. He simply gave her a salute and rushed off.

Roxane was fairly upset that he hadn't kissed her hand but she was soon distracted from her sorrow by a very young knight in the fifth round. He was tall and slender, with red hair, and he was very solicitous with Roxane before his bout. Either he hadn't noticed St. Hèver or he was too arrogant to care, because soon enough Roxane was enamored with the brash young knight who took to blowing her kisses after he won his bout against a fat knight who lost his balance and fell off after the first pass.

The sixth bout came and went without fanfare, as the knight from Gloucester unseated a knight from Ashbourne in the first pass. It was uneventful and the crowd grew restless until they realized that the Earl of Carlisle was up next against an unknown knight named de Lovern. Pages ran out to rake the field, filling in any holes, and the guides were checked to ensure they were steady. After the field marshals checked everything, the flags of Carlisle and de Lovern were placed on the board and the crowd began to roar.

Mathias was the first to enter the field. The wild charger had settled down and was a truly beautiful and somewhat tame beast as he cantered across the field and took his position at the far end of the guide. Tate entered after him aboard his black and white steed and the crowd went mad, cheering excitedly for their earl. Mathias settled in, adjusting his borrowed gloves as Sebastian, his red hair tucked up under a skull cap, aided his brother with his lance.

"De Lara likes to aim for the neck," Sebastian said quietly as he handed his brother the crow's foot pole. "He will start out aiming for your chest but bring the pole up at the last minute."

Mathias nodded patiently. "I know," he said. "I have competed against the man many times."

"Watch out for his tactics."

"I intend to."

"And do not lose St. Hèver's horse. He will murder you."

Beneath his lowered visor, Mathias wriggled his eyebrows in agreement. That was an understatement.

The field marshals made the call for ready and Sebastian scattered as Mathias moved his horse into position. The pole went down, into the cradle position as it was called, and the marshals dropped their flags. The game was on.

Mathias kept his eye on Tate as their steeds thundered toward each other. He had blocked out the crowd and everything else, focused on his opponent. More thunder and the distance closed swiftly. Tate brought the tip of his pole up, right at Mathias' neck, but Mathias was fast. He shifted in the seat so the pole brushed past him while at the same time, he aimed for de Lara's big head. Rather than spear the man head-on, he turned it so the broadside of it hit de Lara right in the forehead.

The earl teetered but he didn't go down. He did, however, drop his pole, which was considered a victory for Mathias. The crowd, seeing that perhaps this unknown de Lovern was indeed as worthy contender, cheered the man for his small victory. Mathias, without a scratch, headed back to the starting point. Sebastian was there to meet him.

"He will be out for blood now," Sebastian said, a grin on his face. "You made a brilliant move."

Mathias handed the joust pole to his brother while he flipped up his visor and re-adjusted his gloves. "He is going to aim for my head the next time. I will need to be vigilant or he will push me right off the horse."

Sebastian was still grinning. "How does it feel?"

Mathias looked at him. "What do you mean?"

"The tournament," he said, his voice softening. "How does it feel to be back?"

The corner of Mathias' mouth twitched. "Like I never left," he said. "Where is Father?"

Sebastian looked over his shoulder towards the crowd. "He is here, watching. He is terrified for you."

Mathias snorted. "Mayhap; but at this moment he is as excited as we are, I promise you."

Sebastian chuckled, handing the joust pole back to his brother. As the field marshals called for the opponents to take position, Mathias slapped his visor down and spurred the charger to the start position. The flags were dropped and the destriers lurched forward.

Sebastian had been correct; Tate aimed for Mathias' head but it didn't come until the last second. Mathias had to move out of the way quickly to avoid being unseated and in doing so, ended up hitting Tate squarely in the chest. The wooden support of the joust pole splintered, sending shards flying into Tate. It wasn't until the earl reined his charger to a halt at the end of the guide that he realized two big shards had punctured him; one in the hip and one in the shoulder. They were embedded fairly deep, deeply enough so that he had to be helped from his charger.

As Mathias and the crowd await the verdict on whether or not Tate could continue, it took both the physic and Lady de Lara to convince Tate to forfeit the match. The projectile embedded in his hip was causing a great deal of bleeding and Lady de Lara was very distressed about it. Reluctantly, the Earl of Carlisle conceded his match to Chayson de Lovern.

The crowd, sensing that perhaps they had a people's champion in de Lovern, began to cheer him madly as he made his way off the field. But before Mathias left completely, he turned towards the lists where Cathlina was leaning on the rail.

Cathlina saw him coming; she'd been at the rail since the bout had started, her heart in her throat at the two violent passes that Tate and Mathias had made against each other. She was only now starting to breathe easy, easier still when she saw Mathias heading in her direction. In fact, her heart began to beat madly and her palms began to sweat, so very thrilled that he was about to acknowledge her. But that was before her father came to stand next to her, scrutinizing the man who had forced his cousin to withdraw. Her excitement took a pause.

"Who is that knight?" he demanded.

Cathlina looked at her father. "His name is Chayson de Lovern."

Saer scowled. "I know his name," he said. "What I want to know is who he is. Where does he come from? And why did he ask you for your favor?"

Cathlina patted her father patiently on the shoulder. "Father, do not work yourself into a fit," she said. "He was very polite to me. He seems to be rather skilled, don't you think?"

Saer pursed his lips irritably. "Either he is very skilled or suffers the blessing of blind luck to oust Tate de Lara from the first round," he grumbled, turning away from the rail. "I will go and see how my cousin fares."

Cathlina continued to pat him on the shoulder even as he walked away. Frankly, she was thrilled he was leaving. "Make sure he is well tended, Papa," she called after him. "Stay with him if you must."

Saer acknowledged her with a wave, muttering something more to his wife as he left the stands. Meanwhile, Cathlina had returned her attention to Mathias, who had resumed his quick pace towards her. He had paused when he saw Saer, waiting to see which direction the man would take. As his charger, sweaty and foaming, bumped up against the railing, he flipped up his visor.

"How was that?" he asked. "Did you enjoy it?"

Cathlina beamed. "You are very skilled. Most impressive."

His dark brows lifted. "It was unfortunate the lance splintered," he said. "I was looking forward to confiscating de Lara's horse."

Cathlina giggled. "Mayhap next time."

He shrugged. "Mayhap," he said, looking around. "Have you eaten yet?"

Cathlina shook her head. "Not yet. I have been busy watching men joust."

He looked at her, then. "Would you be willing to sneak away from your father yet again and join me for a meal?"

Cathlina knew her mother and sisters were behind her, but they were mostly occupied watching Tate and Toby's children because Lady de Lara was with her injured husband.

"My father has gone to see how Cousin Tate fares," she said quietly. "I believe I could steal a few moments away from my mother. Where shall I meet you?"

"At the entrance to the lists."

"I shall be there."

Winking at her, Mathias shut his visor and cantered back across the field, exiting it to the north. Cathlina returned to her seat, watching her sisters play with the twins and the two year old baby girl, Sophie. Abechail seemed particularly enthralled by the baby, which was good to see. Abechail was in bed so much of the time that it was good to see her excited about something.

Cathlina sat next to her mother a nominal amount of time before making her move to leave. She didn't want to seem suspicious, as if she was running off with a clandestine purpose, so she sat tight, making small talk, until very casually, she yawned.

"Mam, I must find the privy," she said, rising to her feet. "I want to be back before Dunstan's round."

Rosalund had the baby in her arms. "Take Abbie with you."

Cathlina struggled not to throw a tantrum. "Abbie does not need to go," she said, looking to her little sister on the floor. "Do you, Abbie?"

Abechail couldn't figure out why her sister was giving her such a strange, nearly intimidating, expression. She looked between her mother sister. "Aye, I will go," she said, struggling to her feet. "I need to use the privy also."

Cathlina rolled her eyes and looked and looked at her mother. "I do not want to take her," she said flatly. "The last time I was left in charge of Abbie, something terrible happened and I could not bear to go through that again. Please do not make me take her. I am afraid."

Rosalund understood somewhat but she thought that Cathlina was being ridiculous. "Do not be so silly," she scolded. "Take your sister with you and return shortly."

Cathlina shook her head; she was already scooted down the stairs. "I will not," she declared. "I will go alone and be back shortly. If Abbie needs to go, then Roxane can take her. I do not want to!"

With that, she was gone before her mother could argue with her. She knew that she would be in for a scolding when she returned but she didn't care; she wanted to see Mathias and couldn't do it with her baby sister hanging about. There was romance in the air, her very first beaux, and she was giddy and reckless.

Fortunately, she didn't have far to go. As soon as she bolted out of the entrance, an enormous hand reached out to grab her. She gasped with fright until she saw who it was; deep green eyes twinkled back at her.

"What took you so long?" he asked. "I nearly died of anticipation."

Cathlina giggled. "You look healthy enough," she said. "Besides, I had to escape my mother. I cannot be too long or she will start to worry."

"Ah," he said, taking her hand and tucking it into the crook of his elbow. "Since we have so little time, what would you like to eat? Something sweet and fattening?"

Cathlina relished the feel of him; his enormous body was warm against her, his fingers clutching hers as they headed down the avenue. She was walking on clouds, thrilled and happy to be with him. "You choose."

"Do you trust me to?"

"I do."

He grinned as he led her down the avenue, feeling as prideful as a peacock with her on his arm. She was radiant and beautiful, and he felt extremely fortunate. The streets were crowded with people who had come to town to see the tournament and they dodged groups of women and children as they headed to the food vendors. Already, the smells of roasted meat and baking breads assaulted their nostrils as they entered the area with vendors shouting the culinary virtues of their dishes.

There was a man selling mutton in a honey and cinnamon sauce, all served up on great slabs of toasted brown bread. Mathias purchased a slab for Cathlina and a slab for himself, taking her to the steps of a nearby cottage where they sat down on the stone steps and delved into their meal. Cathlina picked at the meal while Mathias shoveled, but all the while, their focus was on each other.

"Are you staying in town tonight?" he asked her as he slurped up the sauce.

She nodded, nibbling on the big hunk of bread. "We brought our travel bedding and our shelters," she said. "We set them up on the edge of town next to Cousin Tate's encampment."

He nodded as he shoved a big bite in his mouth. "Then this is quite an adventure for you."

She grinned as she licked her fingers. "It is," she agreed. "We rarely travel from Kirklinton, mostly because Mother does not like to travel. Oh, she pretends that it is father's issue and that he does not like his children exposed to the wicked world, but we know it is Mother. She tells my father that there are wicked people about. Why, when Abechail was nearly abducted, it only reinforced her stance. She was none too excited about us coming to town for the tournament, but Father had promised Abbie so he could not very well refuse her."

Mathias listened to her, the sweet lilt of her voice, and knew he could listen to her speak forever. "Your little sister," he ventured. "If it is not too bold to ask, what is her affliction? You said she was unwell."

Cathlina sobered as she picked at her bread. "It started a little over a year ago," she said. "Abbie was perfectly healthy and then she developed a cough she could not get rid of. She began coughing up blood and had pain in her chest. She lost a good deal of weight and her skin turned such an odd gray color. The physics have all told us that there is something wrong with her lungs. They think it is a cancer of some kind and there is nothing they can do for her. She spends days and weeks in bed taking potions that the physics make for her, but every day she seems to weaken more and more."

Mathias had stopped chewing, listening to her tragic story. "I am truly sorry for you," he said quietly. "I wish there was some way to help her."

Cathlina smiled sadly. "As do I," she said. "We try to pretend that nothing is wrong. We go on with our days and treat her as we have always treated her because she does not want to feel different."

"Does she know she is very ill?"

Cathlina nodded. "She knows," she said softly. "She uses it to her advantage; she has coerced my father into buying her a white pony, a goat, and three puppies. She has an entire menagerie of pets."

She was giggling as she said it, perhaps trying to deflect her own horrific sadness, and he grinned because she was. It was evident that she was greatly distressed by it but didn't want to give into the anguish, not just yet. That would come soon enough. Mathias shoved the remainder of the meal into his mouth and chewed.

"She is a very fortunate lass to have you as her sister," he said, gazing at her with some admiration. "I saw you try to fight off her abductor. You are exceptionally brave."

Cathlina shrugged modestly. "I was terrified out of my mind," she admitted. "I did not realize what I was doing. All I knew was that I could not let the man take her."

"It was your bravery that saved her."

She grinned, embarrassed, not knowing what to say to him. She wasn't used to having praise heaped upon her, but he did it quite freely and she wasn't hard pressed to admit she liked it. It made her feel very special. She put a bite of mutton in her mouth and chewed daintily.

"Do you know who you compete against in the next round?" she asked.

He shook his head, brushing off his hands on his boots. "Nay," he replied. "They will not draw lots until this round is complete."

"Have you competed in many tournaments?"

"Many, indeed."

"Here you are!" Came an unfamiliar voice into the conversation. "I have been looking everywhere for you."

Mathias and Cathlina turned to see Sebastian walking up on them. The man's skull cap was removed and his long, curly red hair flowed freely to his shoulders, dusting the top of the frayed and stained peasant's tunic he was wearing. Mathias stood up as he brother approached.

"Sebastian," he greeted, indicating Cathlina. "You remember Lady Cathlina."

Sebastian looked down at the perfectly beautiful woman seated on the stone steps with the trencher on her lap. He nodded his head in her direction. "Of course I do," he said. "She makes wonderful cakes."

Cathlina grinned as she set the trencher aside, her sweet face upturned. "I am glad you enjoyed them," she said. "It was the least I could do for your assistance."

Sebastian could see, in that instant, what had his brother so smitten. He hadn't had much opportunity to speak with her since their introduction and he could see that she was indeed a lovely and well-spoken young woman. If she had Mathias' attention, then she must be something special, indeed.

"It was our pleasure," he said as a twinkle came to his green eyes. "In fact, I still have the brute in stocks back behind the stall. I can give you a stick and you can beat him if you wish."

Cathlina giggled. "As righteous as that sounds, I am afraid I must decline. I will leave the beatings to you."

"Are you sure?"

"I am sure."

Sebastian was grinning because she was. She had a charming little manner about her. His gaze lingered on her a moment longer before turning his attention to his brother.

"The pole you smashed on de Lara is not repairable," he told him. "Unless I can find another length of wood, we will have to use the remaining two and hope those do not shatter."

Mathias scratched his forehead in resignation. "I suppose that was to be expected," he said. "How is de Lara?"

Sebastian shrugged. "St. Hèver said he is well enough," he replied. "The only reason he forfeited was because his wife was so upset. He plans to watch the rest of the tournament from the lists."

"Then I am pleased he is not overly injured," Mathias replied. "I suppose I should visit him. I will tell him I heard of his injury and wanted to see how he fared."

Sebastian shook his head. "He knows, Mat," he said, lowering his voice. "Ken said that Tate knew you were posing as de Lovern. If you go and see the man, do not insult his intelligence."

Mathias merely lifted an eyebrow in response, not particularly surprised that de Lara spotted him in disguise. As he was debating how to handle the situation, he heard a growl behind him.

"You dark bastard… de Reyne, I knew it was you."

Mathias and Sebastian turned to see the big bald knight that St. Hèver had defeated in his first round of the joust standing several feet away. Quinton de Gare had two other men with him, swarthy warriors that were as dark as they were dirty, and they were all quite focused on Mathias and his brother.

Mathias recognized Quinton; the man had served Mortimer in the ranks of lesser knights, a fairly dumb and unskilled but extremely strong warrior. There had been times when Mathias had been forced to render discipline on the man for various infractions, which wasn't unusual with the lesser fighters in a large army, but Mathias never thought there had been any bad blood between them. Honorable men took their punishment or chastising honorably. At least, that was the expectation.

But Quinton's tone and words didn't suggest honor or respect. Instinctively, Mathias moved away from Cathlina, who was still sitting on the steps with her half-eaten meal in her hands. He didn't want any hostilities aimed at her.

"De Gare," he said evenly. "I saw that you were competing in the tournament."

Quinton snorted rudely. "Competed and lost," he said, agitated. "What are you doing here? I heard the king locked you up in the Tower."

"He did not," Mathias said. He didn't want to engage the man in any level of conversation so he moved to the point. "Is there something I can do for you?"

De Gare grunted, looking between him and Sebastian. His focus lingered on Mathias' brother. "Sebastian the Red," he muttered. "I had heard you were dead."

Sebastian was tensed, ready for a fight. That was simply the way his mind worked. "Not yet," he replied.

De Gare's attention lingered on the brothers; there was something raw and condescending in his expression, like a man who doesn't know when to keep his mouth shut. Everything he was thinking was written on his face or preparing to lash out on his tongue.

"You were so high and mighty," he rumbled. "The both of you thought you ruled England along with Mortimer. Now you're in the gutters like the rest of us."

Mathias didn't respond; he simply turned away, heading for Cathlina so he could escort her away. Sebastian stood there and postured angrily, his fists working, but he too was smart enough to turn away from whatever de Gare was attempting to stir up. Unfortunately, de Gare chose to follow them as they walked away.

"You are scum, de Reyne," he said, listening to his friends titter. "You thought you were so much better than I was. But you are scum, do you hear?"

Mathias had Cathlina by the elbow, quietly leading her away while she looked up at him with frightened eyes. She didn't like the big, scary beast of a knight following them but it occurred to her who he was. She had seen St. Hèver soundly beat him in the joust. She also saw that he had a pitcher in one hand, presumably alcohol of some kind. He was well on his way to being quite drunk.

"Have you nothing to say to me, de Reyne?" de Gare continued to follow. "You know that everything I have said is true. You are scum and you live in the gutters like the lowliest rubbish. Does your woman know what trash you are?"

Sebastian grunted, fairly aching to throw a punch, but Mathias called him off with a shake of the head. He didn't want any fighting near Cathlina.

"Dirty, filthy, rotten whoreskin," de Gare snarled. "You are a pig, de Reyne. Where is your mighty army now? Where are your weapons? You live like an animal!"

Cathlina, in between Mathias and Sebastian, turned to the red-headed brother. "I will take that stick, now," she said softly.

Sebastian cocked an eyebrow at her; he wasn't sure if she was serious or not. As he shook his head faintly, Cathlina's dark eyes bore into him.

"A stick, Sebastian," she said again. "You will give me a stick."

Sebastian looked rather fearful, glancing at his brother as he spoke. "I will not."

"De Reyne!" de Gare boomed. "Turn around and face me, you filth. For the punishment and humiliation you dealt me when we served Mortimer, I intend to extract justice from your hide. Turn around, I say!"

Cathlina had enough. She was furious and hurt on Mathias' behalf to the point of irrational behavior. She was very protective over those she loved… those she loved. *Of course*! She thought. *I must love Mathias 'else I would not want to kill for him.* He had saved her life, once. Now it was time to return the favor.

As they moved down the avenue, they passed a metalworker's shop. The man had all manner of iron crosses, small shovels, fire implements, and the like on display. Yanking her arm from Mathias' steady grasp, she rushed to the display of iron instruments and grabbed the first thing she came to, which happened to be a very sharp fire poker. Before Mathias or Sebastian could stop her, for they didn't realize what her intentions were until it was too late, Cathlina rushed at de Gare and his contemptible companions. She swung the poker at de Gare's head, catching him in the face. As he fell back, she swung it again and caught him in the chest. Blood seeped out from two wounds.

"You are a vile and horrible man," she hissed. "How dare you speak to him in such a manner. You are a worthless excuse for a knight and only feeling sorry for yourself because St. Hèver soundly beat you in the joust. Go back to whatever hole you crawled out of and I shall not see your face again for if I do, I shall tell the Earl of Carlisle and have him deal with you. Is that what you want? A fight with a man who can destroy you with a flick of his hand? Go away from me, you beast. Go away before I kill you!"

It was a shocking and extraordinarily brave action. Mathias and Sebastian rushed up, standing on either side of her and fully prepared to deal de Gare and his companions a heavy beating if they so much as moved in Cathlina's direction. But de Gare, with a bloody gash on his cheek and the pitcher of spilled ale across his legs, looked up at Cathlina with shock first and then rage.

When he tried to get up, Sebastian planted a ham-sized fist in his face and knocked him back to the mud, unconscious. After that, his companions fled. Mathias snatched the poker from Cathlina's grasp and tossed it, turning her around in the direction they had come. But the moment he spun her around, they both came to an abrupt halt.

Saer de Lara was standing behind them with Abechail on one side of him and Roman de Lara on the other. By the look on his face, Mathias knew the man had seen the entire incident.

CHAPTER ELEVEN

"De Reyne," Saer hissed. "Of course I know the name. I know the man's reputation. He was Mortimer's devil. Everyone knows who he is."

Tate stood across from his cousin, trying to stay neutral about the situation. He had heard Mathias' side of it, and a sobbing Cathlina's, and the stories were much the same. But Saer's story was something concocted by an overprotective and zealous father, how he happened across his daughter in the company of two ruffians in the midst of a street fight. Tate was trying to balance the entire situation out and keep Mathias from Saer's wrath.

"Did you also know he is one of my closest friends?" Tate asked softly. When he saw the look of surprise on Saer's face, he nodded. "We fostered together. There is no finer knight in all of England that Mathias de Reyne."

Saer threw up his hands. "How can you say that?" he demanded. "The man sided with Mortimer and tried to kill us all! He is everything we fought against, everything we hated, and I cannot believe that you would defend him so."

"He sided with Mortimer because he is related to the man," Tate fired back, struggling with his temper. "He had no choice. We all side with our family, do we not? His only true crime was that he was related to a man who tried to usurp the king. That has no bearing on how good and true a knight he is."

Saer didn't want to listen. He turned away, wandering aimlessly through Tate's crimson tent. Cathlina sat near the door on a small stool, her eyes huge at her father. She knew she was in for a row but she was also quite defiant about it.

"Father, he is the man who saved us from the man who tried to abduct Abbie," she said with surprising strength. "He is kind and decent and considerate, and I will not hear you say anything terrible about him. He does not deserve it."

Saer looked at her as if she was mad. "Not deserve...?" he sputtered. "You have no idea what you are saying. The man is wicked!"

Cathlina shot to her feet. "He is *not* wicked," she said, her voice growing louder. "What you saw earlier in the street was my fault. That terrible knight was saying such awful things about Mathias and I'd had enough of his slander. Mathias defended Abbie so I returned the favor. I would not let someone speak so terribly about you, or Mother, or anyone else that I cared for. Mathias was trying to walk away from the confrontation but I did not; I struck that horrible knight and I do not regret it."

By this time, Saer had ceased his agitated movements and was peering at her strangely. "*Care* for him?" he repeated. "What does this mean?"

Cathlina wouldn't back down. "Just that," she said. "I care for him, Father. He is sweet and wonderful and virtuous. He has asked to court me and I have agreed."

Something happened to Saer at that moment; his color changed from a sweaty red to a yellow ashen.

"*Court* you?" he repeated, shocked. "I… I cannot believe my ears. If he wanted to court you, then he should have come to me first. Moreover, I will not let the man who headed Mortimer's war machine court my daughter. It is unthinkable."

Cathlina regarded her father carefully; she was quite capable of manipulating him but she could see that he was starting to take a very firm stand against Mathias that would not tumble like the walls of Jericho. Once Saer was set on something, it was very difficult to change his mind. She had to strike hard and fast if she was going to win this battle. Aye, it was indeed a battle.

"Father," she said after a moment. "You will listen to me and listen well; I love Mathias. There, now I've said it – I love him. It is my intention to be his wife. You only have one choice in this matter; you can give us your blessing. If you do not, I will take the first opportunity to run away and commit myself to the cloister. Is this perfectly clear?"

Saer stared at her. In the next moment, he was charging across the tent and grabbing her by the arm, yanking her from de Lara's tent. Cathlina struggled against her father, pounding on his hand to force him to release her, but it was of little consequence. Saer had her firm. Tate went after them, mostly to make sure Saer didn't inadvertently hurt his daughter, but by the time he quit the tent, he had to prevent Mathias from charging Saer.

Mathias had been lingering several feet away from the tent with Sebastian and Kenneth, waiting to be dealt his scolding by Saer and, more than likely, Tate as well when he saw Saer dragging Cathlina from the tent. She was struggling and fighting, and he snapped. Only Tate and Kenneth's strength prevented him from charging Saer and breaking the man's neck. Cathlina saw Mathias and began to scream.

"Mathias!" she cried.

Mathias lurched in her direction but Tate and Kenneth held him firm. "Nay, Mat," Tate hissed. "Let them go. I will go and speak to them later on your behalf but for now, let them go. You have no choice."

Mathias was as coiled as a spring. He watched Saer drag Cathlina across the meadowed expanse that separated Tate's encampment from his. She was fighting and kicking all the way. He dragged her into a tent made of canvas and rope, and shortly they heard sharp smacking sounds and Cathlina screaming.

After that, there was no way to corral Mathias because Tate started running in the direction of Saer's encampment and Mathias was on his heels. Kenneth and Sebastian barreled after the pair, everyone crowding into Saer's larger tent where Saer was giving his daughter a very sound beating on the bottom. Tate grabbed the switch in Saer's hand and Mathias grabbed Cathlina.

"Enough," Tate snarled at his cousin, tossing the switch aside. "Are you truly so weak and foolish that you would beat your daughter? What on earth is wrong with you?"

Saer was shocked to see a host of knights in his tent, interfering in his fatherly duty, but more than that, he was furious. He looked at Mathias with Cathlina cradle against him, sobbing.

"You may not have her," he hissed. "You, who controlled Mortimer's forces and orchestrated the deaths of thousands of men. I lost friends to you!"

Mathias had Cathlina held against his chest, his embrace soothing and protective. "As I lost friends to you," he said quietly. "Such is the nature of war, de Lara. You can point fingers at me as much as you wish but you are equally guilty."

Saer stood there, looking at the man he had fought so zealously against. He felt sick watching the man with his arms around Cathlina. In truth, he was overwhelmed with all of it. He hadn't suspected anything between the smithy and his daughter although perhaps he should have considering she had left Kirklinton without an escort to go and see the man. She had told him that her visit was purely to thank the man for helping fend off Abechail's attacker but in hindsight, he should have been wiser. Saer just didn't want to imagine that his

Cathlina, his pride and joy, had designs on a man. Now to find out that the man had once been a hated enemy was nearly too much to take.

"Mayhap," he said softly, calming somewhat as his fury cooled and the reality of the situation began to settle. "But look at you now; a smithy? A once great-knight reduced to shoeing horses and shoveling dung? And you expect to make a life for my daughter living as peasants?"

Cathlina looked up at Mathias, total trust and admiration in her expression. Mathias glanced at her, feeling her confidence fortify him. But before he could respond, Tate spoke.

"Mathias' exile will not last forever," he said quietly. "I will speak with the king to that regard. Mayhap is indeed time to forgive and forget those events which tore this country asunder."

Saer looked at him. "But what if young Edward will not forgive?" he said, shaking his head. "Tate, if we were speaking of your daughter, would you allow her to marry a dishonored knight, knowing what kind of life that would mean for them? As a father, I want the best for my daughters and even if de Reyne was not a dishonored knight, I would have extreme reservations about allowing my daughter to wed him."

"Why?" Tate asked softly.

Saer began to grow agitated again. "Because the man fought with the enemy and very nearly cost us our lives," he said. "Would you let *your* daughter marry him?"

Tate nodded before the question fully left Saer's mouth. "Knowing the character of the man as I do, I would be proud for my daughter to marry him."

Saer grunted and turned away, eyeing Mathias, his daughter, and even Kenneth and Sebastian. He had a tent full of knights, seasoned men who had shaped the course of the country, but he was torn and despondent. He couldn't decide if it was truly because of Mathias and all he had once stood for or if it was because he didn't want to lose Cathlina. His little girl had become a woman and he'd hardly noticed.

"Then you must allow me to think on this," he muttered, looking at Mathias. "All I have heard is from my daughter stating that she wishes to marry you. You have not come to me, as a man would, and spoken to me of her."

Mathias conceded the point. "You are correct," he said. "However, in my defense, there has not been the opportunity and your daughter and I have only recently spoken of such things. It was not the proper way to go about the situation and I offer my apology. However, now that we are face to face, I will tell you now that it is my intention to marry your daughter. At present, I will be able to provide quite well for her as a smithy's wife and in time, she will have all of the titles and wealth that I can provide for her when my titles and lands are restored. Of this I have no doubt. I assure you that my intentions are quite honorable."

Saer watched the man as he spoke, his body language and the fact that he never once broke eye contact. That spoke of respect. It eased him somewhat but not completely; he was still having a difficult time swallowing everything. It was too much for him to absorb at the moment and he finally waved a dismissive hand at the group.

"I must think on it," he said. "I will give you no answer today."

"But soon, Father?" Cathlina said, wiping the last of her tears from her eyes.

Saer whirled on her, pointing a stern finger. "That is enough from you."

Cathlina frowned as Mathias stepped in. "I understand and respect your need to think on my request," he said, giving Cathlina a squeeze so she would remain silent. "I also trust that you will make the right choice. I will eagerly await your word."

Saer only shrugged. Tate caught Sebastian and Kenneth's attention, silently ordering them from the tent with a nudge of his head. When they left, he turned his attention to Saer one last time.

"I trust I will not need to come running back here to prevent you from beating your daughter," he said. "If it happens again, I will take her with me back to Carlisle. I will not let you harm her because you are angry. Is that clear?"

Saer looked at Tate as if the man had hurt his feelings. "I was not beating her," he said. "I was spanking her for her insolence. She needed it."

Tate cocked an eyebrow. "A technicality," he said, his voice low. "I do not approve of hitting children, no matter how insolent they are."

Saer, feeling emotionally exhausted and defeated, simply turned away. Tate's attention lingered on the man before turning to Mathias and Cathlina.

The pair was huddled together, the hulking presence of Mathias wrapped around Cathlina. She looked so small and fragile in his arms. Tate touched her affectionately on the cheek before turning to Mathias.

"You have a tournament to finish," he said softly. "I would suggest you go and prepare for the second round."

It occurred to Mathias that he'd not spoken to the man since

Sebastian had mentioned Tate's knowledge of his deception. He tried not to look too contrite. "Was I that obvious? I thought I did rather well at concealing my identity."

"You did a fine job," Tate agreed. "But you forget how well I know you. Your move of hitting me on the helmet in the first pass confirmed what I already suspected. Go, now. I will make sure Cathlina is taken care of."

Mathias looked down at Cathlina, swathed in his enormous embrace. He quite honestly didn't want to let her go but knew he had little choice. Leaning down, he kissed her very sweetly on the cheek before releasing her. Then he looked at Tate.

"If he touches her again, I will kill him," he said simply.

Tate knew he meant it. He'd seen what Mathias could do in battle and had no desire to push the man. So he nodded.

"He understands that," he said quietly. "Give me my cousin and be on your way."

"You will take her to the lists where I can see her?"

"I will."

Mathias' gaze lingered on Cathlina a moment before kissing her hand gently and quitting the tent. Cathlina watched him leave, her entire being focused around him and the memory of him. She couldn't focus on anything else. When she finally shook herself from her trance, she caught sight of the grin on Tate's face. She smiled, embarrassed, silently acknowledging all of the sweet and giddy things she'd been thinking. He laughed softly.

"If you are ready, my lady, I will take you over to the field," he said.

"Nay," Saer said from across the tent. "I want to speak with her first."

Tate's smile faded as he looked to his cousin. "Go ahead," he said. "I shall wait right outside the tent."

Saer turned to look at him with as much defeat in his expression as Tate had ever seen. The Axe he'd known all those years looked old and tired. Children growing up and resisting parental directives had a way of doing that to people.

"No need," he said wearily. "I just want to speak with her a few moments. I will bring her over to the field myself"

Tate cocked an eyebrow. "You will not beat her."

Saer shook his head, resigned. "I will not beat her."

"Swear it?"

"I swear"

"Then I will see you over at the field."

Mathias won the joust later that day without his favored lady in the lists. Once he realized what had happened, he went to Tate with a plan and begged the man to help him. The whole story about Henry Beaumont and fighting for the Scots came in to play, and Tate was more than willing to listen. Had he not loved his wife so much, it would have been difficult for him to understand Mathias' willingness to sacrifice everything for the chance at a new life with the woman he loved. As it was, he understood completely.

Tate was not hard to convince, and an appropriate scheme was hatched.

CHAPTER TWELVE

Kirklinton Castle was bottled up tightly and had been for three days. Patrols were doubled and the wall walk was crowded with sentries. Ever since their flight from Brampton's tournament back to Kirklinton, the castle had been sealed up. Now, everyone was waiting, watching the road, preparing for what was to come.

It was like a deathwatch. No one knew what to expect or why the defenses were doubled as if preparing for a siege. Dunstan and Beauson had been told not to let anyone into or out of Kirklinton and they held tight to their directive. They didn't truly know the full extent of their orders or the reason behind it other than Saer had ordered them to forfeit their rounds at the tournament for the harried return home. The crying girls had been loaded up into the carriage and back they had all come. Now, the soldiers were moving through their duties in stressful silence as the family remained locked up in the keep.

Cathlina was inconsolable. She had fought so much on the way home that Rosalund was forced to hold her down the entire way, alternately scolding her for her behavior and comforting her. All Saer would say was that she had behaved terribly and as a result, the entire family had to leave the tournament to return home. It wasn't until they reached Kirklinton that Saer told his wife the entire story. His side of it, of course, and Rosalund was appalled.

Therefore, Cathlina was confined to the keep. She had someone watching her constantly so she would not try to escape and run back to Mathias. Abechail had slept with Cathlina since they had returned, the sickly little sister doing her best to comfort her distraught sibling. Eventually, Abechail and Roxane learned the reason for their sister's distress and although Roxane remained distant and pouting, Abechail never left Cathlina's side.

Cathlina woke up on the third morning since their departure from Brampton with Abechail in her bed. But they were not alone; Abechail's pets, the spotted goat and the three brown puppies had joined them. As the puppies wriggled and licked, Cathlina tried not to become too annoyed.

Climbing out of bed, she called for warmed water and was provided with linen towels and two big basins of warmed lavender water. As the sun began to rise and the activity about the castle swung into its normal routine, she bathed with a bar of lumpy lavender soap and donned a clean linen shift. It was big and voluminous, with a ruffle around the bottom, and she pulled a red silk surcoat over the top. The surcoat had a corset that laced up and she sighed distractedly as she laced up the coat, her mind wandering to Mathias as it did a thousand times a day. He was all she could think of, like the strains of the siren song that never went away. She fairly ached with it all.

By the time she was brushing her hair, Abechail was up. Abechail took the brush from her sister and brushed her hair while Cathlina sat and stared from the lancet window overlooking the southeast section of the bailey. As Abechail put the brush down and began to braid, Cathlina gazed across the rolling green land, visions of Mathias and their future spread out before her. She could only see him as a restored knight, stronger and taller and prouder than anyone, a knight that belonged to her and her alone. She could imagine the castle they would live in and the strong sons they would have. She could feel his hand on hers, his lips on her flesh. She imagined what it would be like to kiss him. She prayed she had the opportunity to find out.

Lost in her daydreams, she didn't notice that Abechail had braided her hair elaborately and wound it all up and around her head. In truth, it was quite lovely, as Abechail had a talent for dressing hair even at her young age. She would often practice on her sisters, although Cathlina's silky hair was much easier to manage than Roxane's frizzy strands. As Cathlina admired her little sister's handiwork in a polished metal mirror, the door to the chamber opened and Roxane entered.

There were two chambers on the top level of the keep and both of them were occupied by the three girls. They shifted around in the beds, sometimes sleeping in one bed or the other, or two of them would sleep together while one slept alone. It had always been thus; moreover, the same went for their clothing – they all shared the same surcoats because they were all relatively the same size, although shifts and shoes remained personal. Roxane, in her shift, had come hunting for just the right surcoat for the day's dressing.

She stuck her nose in the air when she saw Cathlina in her beautifully braided hair and headed straight for a massive wardrobe that sat low and squat against the wall. The moment she opened it, clothing burst forth and fell on the floor. Frustrated, Roxane started digging through it.

"You must be more organized," she said to both sisters. "These are all wrinkled!"

Abechail wandered over to her eldest sister. "You were in there the last," she pointed out. "This is your mess."

Roxane turned to Abechail, her lips puckered furiously. "Never mind," she snapped. Then she noticed the dogs and goat over near the bed. "And why are the barn animals in here? I am telling Mother!"

"For Heaven's sake, Roxane," Cathlina stood up from her stool. "Shut your yap, do you hear? You never have a kind word for anyone, you selfish wench. All you ever do is complain!"

It was the opening volley to the hair pulling event which would start shortly. Abechail scooted in between her sisters as they came close to one another to stop the inevitable progression.

"Oh!" Roxane gasped. "Look who's calling me selfish? We had to leave the tournament because of you!"

"We left because Father was angry!"

Roxane put her hands on her hips, sassy. "We left because *you* behaved outrageously with the smithy that saved Abbie from that awful brute," she said. "Father said you were horrible and wanton!"

"Father is imagining things."

"I am going to tell him you said that!"

"Go ahead," Cathlina scowled. "I do not care what you do. I could not possibly be in any more trouble than I am now."

"I hope he spanks you!"

Cathlina rolled her eyes and turned away. "You are simply upset because I have a handsome man who pays attention to me," she said. "You throw yourself at men and they never notice you. Do not blame me because you are as ugly as a toad."

Roxane shrieked and threw herself across the room, fully prepared to yank out all of Abechail's careful braiding, but Abechail put up her hands and prevented her sister from making contact with her artistic hairdo.

"Stop it, Roxane," Abechail pushed her away. "She is right and you know it. You are jealous!"

Roxane's mouth popped open in outrage. "You nasty little goat!"

She gave a yank on Abechail's long hair and Abechail came right back and slapped her cheek. Soon, Cathlina was breaking up a fight between Abechail and Roxane, and Abechail was winning. The sickly little sister had smacked Roxane on both cheeks and was going in for a punch.

"Cease, the both of you," she said, exasperated. She looked at Roxane, struggling for calm. "Roxane, I am sorry if you are upset because we left early but in case you have not yet understood, I am upset that we left, too. I certainly did not want to leave, but I had no say in the matter. You know how Father is when he is determined to do something."

Roxane backed down somewhat, eyeing her sisters who were siding against her. Still hurt, and huffing, she turned back around for the wardrobe that had vomited its contents out all over the floor.

"'Tis simply that…," Roxane began, pausing as she picked a dark green brocade off the floor. "There was a knight and he viewed me most favorably. I am not sure how Sir Kenneth will react when he realizes there is competition for my affections."

Cathlina looked at Abechail, who rolled her eyes. Cathlina fought off a grin. "Is that so?" she said. "I am sure Sir Kenneth will survive. What is the name of his competition?"

Roxane quickly forgot her irritation. "Sir Anthony de Ferrer," she said dreamily. "He serves the Earl of Billingham."

"I see," Cathlina said, moving to help her sister with the green dress because it was tangled up in some other things. "Did you get the opportunity to speak with him?"

Roxane nodded. "A few times," she said. "It was very brief, of course, for propriety's sake. I did not want to appear unseemly."

"What did he say? Does he want to court you?"

Roxane came off her cloud a bit. "Not exactly," she said. "But he was very kind and courteous. I told him where I lived and he said he would make a point of coming to visit me."

She seemed quite convinced on the knight's sincerity, so Cathlina merely looked at Abechail and wriggled her eyebrows. Time would tell. As the sisters began pulling garments off the floor and placing them back in the wardrobe, shouts could be heard from the sentries in the ward.

The girls, with clothing in their hands, ran to the window and jockeyed around to try to gain a better look. Their view cut off nearly half the bailey, including the gatehouse, but they could see the road beyond. On this clear and fine day, they could see a collection of men in the distance. It was clear very quickly that it was an army, heading their way.

The girls fell back from the window and began scrambling. "It is Sir

Anthony!" Roxane gasped. "He has come to court me!"

"With an entire army?" Cathlina scowled as she shoved pieces back into the wardrobe. "That is a lot of men, even for you."

When it occurred to Roxane what her sister meant, she scowled fiercely. "Coming from a reckless and wanton woman, you have no room to accuse me of loose behavior."

Cathlina threw a balled scarf at her sister, hitting her in the side of the head. "At least I have the opportunity to be reckless and wanton without having to bribe my partner. Only a man in need of alcohol or money would be foolish enough to look at you."

After that, they forgot all about the incoming army. The fight was on.

***

"You left very suddenly," Tate said, eyeing his cousin across the table. "I thought mayhap something terrible had happened."

Seated in the great hall of Kirklinton, which was a long room built against the wall of the bailey, Saer looked at his cousin over the top of the wine pitchers. He thought on his answer carefully before opening his mouth.

"Cathlina was not herself," he said. "Moreover, Abechail is a very frail girl. She started feeling very poorly so we thought it best to come home immediately."

Tate nodded his head but it was clear from his expression that he didn't believe him. The hall was full of de Lara's senior soldiers and knights, all having their fill of Saer's hospitality. Kenneth was there, seated next to Tate, and the big blond knight held a fairly grim expression at this point. They had come out of their way on their travels back to Carlisle and the man wasn't happy. Mostly, he wasn't happy at Saer's behavior but he kept his mouth shut. There was a good deal he wanted to say to the man but couldn't, for obvious reasons. This wasn't his fight.

"I am sorry to hear that they are unwell," Tate finally replied. "It was unfortunate that you missed an exciting tournament."

Saer wasn't particularly interested in speaking of the tournament because it would bring up the subject of Mathias, which he was unwilling to discuss. Still, he would not let his cousin bully or badger him about the subject. As far as he was concerned, the situation was over with.

"There will be other tournaments," he said shortly, changing the subject. "Where is your lady wife? I have not seen her since your arrival."

"She is in the bailey with our children," Tate replied. "Did you see the rather large covered wagon we have? It is nearly like a home on wheels. It contains beds and a table to eat on. We often travel with it because of the children. It is much sturdier than a tent."

Saer was intrigued with the thought of a home on wheels. "I did not see it in Brampton," he admitted. "A home that travels, you say? It sounds interesting."

Tate nodded. "It is," he said. "The children are napping right now, so she has them all tucked in at the moment. You will see her later. Speaking of later, where is Cathlina? I would like to see her now."

Saer stiffened. "Why?"

Tate cocked an eyebrow. "Let us be frank," he said. "You fled Brampton after I told you not to beat your daughter. If I was the suspicious type, I would say you did not listen to me. Show me Cathlina so that I may see she is safe and uninjured."

Saer was outraged. "Is that why you came?" he demanded. "To see if I have hurt my own child?"

"Where is she?"

"In the keep with her sisters."

"Produce her for me so that I may see for myself."

"And if I do not?"

"Do you truly wish to know?"

Saer backed down; he knew he couldn't resist his powerful cousin and he tried to remind himself that the man only had Cathlina's best interests at heart. Still, he felt violated as a father. Cathlina was his child, after all, and his cousin was making demands. Demands made him unhappy.

"You may see her," he said after moment. "You will see that she is uninjured. And this nonsense with de Reyne… her mother and I have been discussing the matter."

Tate took a big drink of his wine. "And?"

Saer sighed heavily as if displeased with whatever it was he was about to reveal. "And we have realized that Cathlina is a young woman now," he said. "As a girl, she was content to remain under our roof and do as she was told. But she is a young woman now. She desires a home and family of her own."

Tate agreed. "That is very true."

Saer looked at him. "Therefore, her mother and I have decided to seek eligible men for her hand in marriage. It is time she is married."

Tate could feel Kenneth tense up beside him. "But Mathias has already offered for her hand," he reminded him. "You told the man you would think about it. Well?"

Saer stood his ground. "I will not see her married to de Reyne," he said frankly. "Tate, surely you can understand my position. Cathlina is a beautiful girl and will command a fine and wealthy husband, and not one who has been disgraced. De Reyne is unworthy of her. If she truly wants to marry, then I will ask you to help me find her a suitable match. Surely, as an earl, you can find all of my daughters suitable matches."

Tate sighed heavily, glancing at Kenneth to see what his reaction was. Kenneth, however, remained stone-faced. Saer saw the looks pass between the men and turned to St. Hèver.

"You were interested in Cathlina once," he said. "Would you consider her again? With your strong and guiding hand, she would make you a very fine wife in time."

Kenneth tried not to look shocked now that the focus was on him. Had the offer been made back at Christmastime, he would have accepted it without hesitation and in truth, for a split second, he really did consider it. He couldn't help it. But he shot that idea down immediately; he could not do such a thing to a friend. Mathias loved the girl and he would never betray the man so. He struggled to come up with a reply that would not offend Saer.

"As... attractive as your offer is, I must decline," he said. "I am afraid that I am... that is to say, I am already spoken for."

It was a flat-out lie but it was the only way he could think of that would not offend anyone. He looked at Tate, the ice-blue eyes silently pleading for assistance, and Tate caught on to his panic. He, too, began thinking very quickly.

"Aye," Tate put in, hoping he didn't sound nervous or uncertain. "Ken is betrothed... well, of course he is betrothed to my wife's... sister."

Saer lifted his eyebrows. "I was not aware your wife had a sister."

"She is younger," Kenneth put in, desperate to be off of the subject. "The family lives near Harbottle. In any case, Cathlina already has a perfect suitor who would be very good to her. I have been friends with Mathias de Reyne for many years and you would not find a man of better moral character or virtue in all of England. You really should reconsider your stance against him."

They were back on Mathias, brilliantly executed by Kenneth, where Saer did not want to be. Tate took charge before Saer could say anything. He didn't want the conversation deteriorating because he had a purpose for being here. It was more than just a visitation; it was a covert operation, and he was a key part of it. He didn't want to get kicked out in a huff before his scheme had a chance to come to fruition.

"Let us speak of your daughter and her marital prospects later," he said. "For now, let us speak on other things. It appears as if you have done some construction to the north side of the castle. Will you show me what you have done?"

Saer still wasn't over the discussion about Cathlina and her marital status as it related to Mathias de Reyne, but he graciously allowed Tate to take charge of the conversation. In fact, he was resigned to it. He'd had very little control over life in general since that moment he saw Cathlina in the street brawl flanked by two enormous men.

The men that were seated rose from the great feasting table as Saer began to explain to Tate how he needed to build a troop house to contain the soldiers because with three young women in the family, Rosalund was uncomfortable with the men sleeping all about the great hall and lower level of the keep. She wanted them away from her girls. Tate followed Saer out into the bailey where the sky was brilliant blue and a soft breeze snapped across the land. Kenneth, a few senior soldiers, and three lesser knights followed.

Outside, there were more soldiers and people milling about. As Saer took Tate and a few men over to the new troop house, Kenneth broke off from the group and made his way over to the big, wooden wagon where Toby and the children were. There were a few soldiers standing guard, milling about, and one enormous knight in full battle armor, including a helm. If one looked closely enough, one could see the faded Banbury emblem on the big breastplate. Kenneth walked right up to the knight, lingering in the shadows of the wagon.

"Tate will keep him busy," Kenneth said to Mathias. "Cathlina is in the keep. I will go in and bring her out to you. Take your charger and go wait for us outside of the walls."

Mathias flipped up the visor and looked around. "I saw a grove of dense trees off to the east when we were riding in," he said. "I will wait for you there."

Kenneth looked around to make sure they weren't being watched. "You have the letter from Tate introducing you and your brother and your father to Henry Beaumont, correct?"

"I do."

"Where will you pick up your brother and father?"

"They are riding to Longtown as we speak," he said. "I am to meet them at the Ladyseat Inn and then from there, we ride to Scotland."

Kenneth looked at his friend, seeing hope and excitement in his eyes. "Are you sure you want to do this?"

Mathias nodded without hesitation. "More than anything in the world," he said, his voice softening. "A week ago, I was bitter and defeated... a hammer in my hand when it should have been a sword. Then I heard cries for help and went to the aid of the most beautiful woman I have ever seen. Fate brought us together, Ken, and I'll not let God nor Kings nor fathers keep us apart. With the money I won in the joust, it is as I told Tate – I intend to start a new life in Scotland with my new wife, once again an honored knight where I should be. This is *my* life, Ken; I intend to live it."

Kenneth smiled faintly. "Will you ever come back to us?"

"I suppose that is up to Edward."

"I will convince him."

Mathias felt the sincerity in Kenneth's words. "When you do, send for me. I would like to resume my rightful place with you and de Lara and Pembury. You will tell Pembury what has become of me, will you not?"

Kenneth's smile broadened. "You can tell him yourself," he replied. "The night that Tate wrote the missive you carry for Beaumont, he sent a messenger for Pembury. The man has been in Berwick for Edward because the Scots have been besieging the city. Tate has asked him to meet you in Edinburgh at a place called the Barrel and Bucket. From there, you will travel north to Beaumont's home near Loch Drumilie. It's called the Devil's Den, as it sits in the Devil's woods. If Beaumont is not there, he may be further north near Aberdeen. You may need to hire a guide to find him. This will not be an easy journey, Mat; are you sure you want to subject your lady to it?"

Mathias thought about Cathlina on a driven ride straight through Scotland in search of a rebel. Well, the Scots viewed him as an English rebel. It would not be easy but it was the chance of a lifetime. He had to take it.

"We will persevere," he assured him softly. "So Pembury is to meet me in Scotland? Will he accompany me to Beaumont?"

"He will indeed," Kenneth replied. "Tate has told him to stay by your side until you are both recalled by Edward."

Mathias was deeply moved; Stephen of Pembury had been closer to him than even Tate and Kenneth, a mountain of a man he loved like a brother. He loved them all like brothers, now going against the king's directive to get him out of England and on to a new life. He was no longer the Fallen One now; he would prove himself the Redeemed One with the assistance of the most prestigious knights in England. He had God, the angels, good fortune, and the earl they used to call Dragonblade on his side. He was a lucky man.

"I will look for him once we reach Edinburgh," he said quietly. "Go and get Cathlina now. I will be waiting."

Kenneth slapped him on the shoulder and left, moving off across the bailey towards the keep. Mathias didn't waste any time; he collected his charger, the big bay stallion that Kenneth had now given him, and left the castle grounds, heading off of the road and into a dense collection of trees about a quarter of a mile from the castle. It was there he waited for Kenneth to bring Cathlina to him.

It was well past sunset when they finally appeared.

CHAPTER THIRTEEN

"Mathias!"

He heard his name in the darkness, watching Cathlina race through the darkened bramble towards him. It was so dark that she ended up tripping, but jumped to her feet with the agility of a cat and continuing on her way. Mathias' arms opened up to her and she hurled herself into them.

She was all hair and flowing fabric. Mathias held her tightly, relishing their first real embrace with more emotion than he believed himself capable of. Behind her, silhouetted by the moonlight that was straining to penetrate the canopy of trees, he could see Kenneth coming up behind her. He had something clutched to his chest and when he lowered his arm, Mathias could see the outline of a satchel.

"What happened?" he hissed and Kenneth. "What took so long?"

Kenneth seemed irritated, unusually for the usually unflappable knight. "God's Bones, don't ask," he said, handing Mathias the satchel even though he was still embracing Cathlina. "When I went to locate the lady, she was with her sisters and the eldest one would not let us out of her sight for a couple of hours at least. She made me sit and converse and then when I tried to get Cathlina alone to tell her of your intentions, she followed us. And you will not believe this part – your intended had a red welt on her cheek and when de Lara saw it, he accused her father of beating her again."

Mathias looked at Cathlina in the darkness, trying to get a look at her face. "The bastard," he hissed. "What did he do? Did he hit you again?"

Cathlina shook her head as he ran his enormous hands all over her face. "It was Roxane," she said. "We had an argument this morning and… well, sometimes we are known to slap each other. It was not my father at all."

Mathias' eyebrows shot up. "Your *sister* slapped you?"

"She did."

"I hope you slapped her back."

Cathlina broke out in giggles. "Of course I did. I pulled her hair for good measure, too."

Mathias chuckled, hugging her tightly, so thrilled to have her in his arms. As he embraced her, kissing her cheek, Kenneth entered the conversation again.

"You can imagine with all of that madness going on, the hours dragged out," he said. "Suffice it to say that it has taken this long to bring your lady to you. Now, you need to get out of here before they start looking for her. I must go back and keep the sister occupied until you are well on your way."

Mathias looked at Cathlina. "Did Ken tell you everything?"

She nodded eagerly. "He said you are running off to Scotland and wish to take me with you," she said. "Oh, Mathias, I can hardly believe it. I thought I was never going to see you again!"

He grinned at her, his white teeth reflecting the muted moonlight. "Hardly," he said. "But Ken is correct; we must flee and we must do it now. Are you certain you want to go with me?"

"Of course I am!"

"It means marriage. I will marry you as soon as possible and you will be wed to a knight on the run."

She shushed him. "I do not care," she said. "All that matters is that we are together, whether you are a smithy or a dishonored knight or the king of bloody England. I do not care about any of that. Let us leave before my father finds out!"

He laughed softly, turning to Kenneth and reaching out to take the man's hand. The handshake was firm, full of the reassurance of a good parting.

"I will do what I can to stall them," Kenneth said. "Get as far as you can tonight. By morning, surely they will discover her missing and the search will commence."

Mathias nodded quickly, taking Cathlina in hand and rushing her towards the charger. The beast was munching on undergrowth as he lifted her up.

"I will send you word when and where we settle," he told Kenneth. "And you have my deepest gratitude for what you have done, Ken. I will always be in your debt."

Kenneth simply waved him off, watching Mathias vault onto the back of the charger and direct the steed further into the darkness of the forest growth. He had to avoid the road because the castle sentries could see the land for at least a mile in all directions, including the road. Mathias had to get them out of the range of the sentries. When they finally faded from view, Kenneth turned back to the castle.

By the time he returned to the great hall, he was fending off more marriage innuendoes from Saer and Roxane, and cursing Mathias under his breath for having to endure such a thing. Tate, too, was playing the stalling game, plying Saer with enough wine to get the man ragingly drunk so that they feasted long into the night.

No one realized Cathlina was missing until well into the next day and to add an additional stalling tactic, Tate took charge of the search parties and told Saer to remain with his family and await word. Tate then moved his army away from Kirklinton and sent at least three advance parties out in full view of Saer.

The search parties, however, all had secret instructions to sweep through Brampton, stop at nothing, and proceed to Carlisle Castle post-haste. Instead of searching for Cathlina as he promised he would, Tate simply took his army and his family home, but he made a good show of a search for Saer's sake. One week later, Saer received a missive from Tate, written carefully by Toby.

Have no worries for your daughter is in excellent hands. Will send word later.

He never did.

CHAPTER FOURTEEN

It was the middle of the night by the time Mathias and Cathlina reached Longtown, a berg near the Scots border that had seen more battles than most. It was a strict blend of Scots and English, a mixed bag of nationalities. It was also a wild and lawless town.

There was a small church just south of the town, built of stone and surrounded by a graveyard that was overflowing its perimeter. Decades of battles had seen to that. It was cold and misty as Mathias reined the weary charger up to the door and dismounted, pulling an exhausted Cathlina off behind him.

She was unsteady on her feet, yawning and sleepy, but she had never complained during their long ride north. The road hadn't been particularly good and the horse excitable, making for slow going. As he tied the charger up near a heavy growth of grass and vines that the horse could feast on, he took Cathlina's hand and led her do the ancient iron and wood door. The big iron knocker made the entire structure shake.

It took four separate tries on the knocker before someone attempted to answer the door. By that time, Mathias was irritated and when the timid, sleepy man opened the door, he shoved his way in and pulled Cathlina along with him. The man, very dirty with wild hair and missing teeth, hovered fearfully.

"Are you the priest here?" Mathias asked him. "My lady and I wish to be married immediately. Rouse who you must in order to accomplish this."

The man shook his head and tried to run off, but Mathias would have no part of it. He grabbed the man by the neck and held him fast.

"Did you hear me?" he said, less friendly this time. "My lady and I wish to be married immediately. You will perform the ceremony."

The priest shook his head again, yelping when Mathias squeezed. "I am not the priest," the man said. "I must get him."

Mathias was weary and brittle, translating into a harsh manner. With Cathlina tightly in-hand, he followed the man as he scurried back into the darkness and into the rather large church built of big blocks of brown stone. Cathlina clung tightly to Mathias, peering at her surroundings and thinking them to be dank and spooky. Everything smelled of the candles they used that were rendered from fat, a heavy and greasy smell that had the ambience of a burnt body. It was a rather sickening smell.

In fact, Cathlina put her fingers to her nose as she followed Mathias to the rear of the church. The frazzled man threw open a small oak door which ushered them into a sort of common room. There was a table and the remains of a meal on it, and old straw scattered about that had the smell of urine. As Cathlina and Mathias paused, the frightened man opened another small room and hissed at the occupants. They could hear voices on the other side, both irritated and curious. Eventually, a man in a stained nightshirt emerged, pulling on his brown woolen robes.

"I am Father Malachy," he said, rubbing his red and crusty eyes. "What is it that you wish?"

Mathias pulled Cathlina against him. "I am Sir Mathias de Reyne," he said. "My lady and I wish to be married immediately."

The priest rubbed his eyes again to get a better look at them both. He seemed particularly interested in Cathlina; wrapped in a dark blue cloak with a rabbit skin lining, she appeared rather small against Mathias' bulk.

"This is most irregular," the priest said. "One does not simply walk into a church and demand marriage. It is a process by which the couple is made ready to accept God as supreme creator of their lives. You must live for Him. Where is the lady's family? Have they given consent?"

"I can pay you ten gold crowns," Mathias said impatiently. "Can we dispense with this lecture and get on with it?"

The priest looked at him, shocked by the amount of money the man was willing to pay. His curious, apprehensive gaze passed between Mathias and Cathlina.

"Are you running from someone, child?" he asked Cathlina.

She shook her head. "Nay, Father."

"Is he forcing you to marry him? Is he brutish?"

She giggled; she couldn't help it. "Nay, Father, he is not forcing me and he is not brutish. We simply wish to be married."

"If he is forcing you, you must tell me. You will be safe here, as I will protect you."

Cathlina found the statement hysterical; the priest was about her size and Mathias was a giant by comparison, well over six feet in height and all manner of power about him. Mathias caught her mirth and merely rolled his eyes.

"Am I forcing you?" he asked.

She put her hand over her mouth to stifle the uncontrollable giggles. "Well," she said. "Mayhap. But I am going along with you happily."

He shook his head at her. "Silly wench," he grumbled affectionately. "Let us have him marry us before you condemn me further."

Mathias was already digging out the coins; the priest could hear them jingling. With a shrug, because he couldn't sincerely see any reason to deny them and it was clear that the lady wasn't in distress, he herded them into the main part of the church and, with the frazzled man and another acolyte as a witness, joined Mathias de Reyne and Cathlina de Lara in marriage.

After paying the priest the promised coinage, Mathias mounted his wife on the skittish charger and in the dead of night, headed into Longtown and the Ladyseat Inn.

***

Cathlina awoke the next morning in a strange room, to strange sounds, and for a moment had no idea where she was. It was daylight outside but she could hear the gentle patter of rain on the windowsill. She lay there a moment, looking around the room without moving her head, struggling to orient herself. She could see her cloak and satchel over near the wall on a chair that had been made from twigs. It leaned heavily. As she stared at the chair and her possessions, gradually, it all came back to her.

Lady de Reyne. She was Mathias' wife now. It didn't seem real, not in the least, and the surge of joy and excitement she felt at the thought was palpable. After their hasty marriage at St. Michael's Church, they had spent another hour in misty weather hunting down the Ladyseat Inn.

Once they finally found it, it was dead quiet and still except for a few drunken patrons, but they had managed to find Justus and Sebastian sleeping soundly in a small room. Since the inn was full, they vacated the room to give Cathlina a bed to sleep on. She'd tumbled in to bed with hardly a word to either of them. She was asleep before her head hit the pillow.

Propping herself up on an elbow, she looked around to see that she was quite alone in the very little room. She didn't even know of Mathias had slept with her. It was cold, too, because the fire was out and the hearth was a big, sooty mess. Climbing out of bed, the first order of business was to get dressed and find her husband.

She was still in the dark green linen surcoat she had worn from the day before but her shoes and hose were off, indicating that Mathias must have removed them after she fell into an exhausted sleep. The floor was cold as she hopped over to the chair that contained her cloak and satchel, and the first thing she saw was her hose neatly rolled up on top of the bag. Her shoes were underneath the chair. Setting her hose and shoes on the bed, she opened up her satchel and began to dig around inside.

Given that Kenneth had afforded her ample time to pack a satchel before whisking her off to Mathias the day before, she had managed to pack everything that mattered to her although it had been tricky with her nosey sister around. Inside her satchel was an oil cloth bag, resistant to water, and she dumped the contents out on the bed. It contained a frayed reed tooth-brush, a bag of soda mashed with lemon for her teeth, a big bar of lumpy soap that smelled of lavender and a phial of flax seed and lavender oil that kept her skin from drying out. She also had a comb and a variety of things for her hair. Her sanitary supplies were also tucked into the bag, linen and absorbent moss that were used during her woman's time.

Her satchel contained four surcoats, hose, undergarments, shifts, and her boots. She pulled out a clean shift and a lovely pale gold surcoat of simplistic fashion with long belled sleeves, snug bodice, and a rounded neckline that showed off her slender neck and shoulders. She found herself wanting to dress for her new husband, wanting to please him so badly in appearance and manner. All of this was still so new and unreal to her, the adventure of a lifetime that she was more than ready to partake.

Taking her bar of soap and a small linen rag from her satchel, she found a small bucket of cold, stale water near the door. It was only half full and she had no idea how long it had been there, but it was clean water and that was all she cared about. Quickly, she stripped off the shift and surcoat she slept in, washing her face and body in the cold water. Drying off with her used shift, she donned the new shift and the gold surcoat. Her hair went into a thick braid that draped over one shoulder, and hose and boots went on her feet. She was just packing everything back up when the door to the chamber creaked open.

Mathias stood there, hand on the door latch and a surprised look on his face when he saw that Cathlina was up and dressed. His expression of surprise quickly turned to one of appreciation.

"You are awake," he said, his voice soft. "I thought you might still be sleeping."

She shook her head, feeling nervous at the sight of him. Was he glad they had married? Did he regret making such a life-changing decision? Her stomach was in knots with apprehension and excitement. She smiled timidly.

"I woke up a few minutes ago," she said. "What time is it?"

"Mid-morning," he said, coming in to the room and shutting the door behind him. "Are you hungry?"

She nodded as she quickly finished packing. "Quite," she said. "But I am ready to leave when you are. I am sorry I slept so long; you really should have awoken me earlier."

He smiled, drinking in the sight of her, still in disbelief that he had actually married her. "You were exhausted," he said softly. "Besides, it gave me time to purchase some things when the merchant stalls in town opened."

She cocked her head curiously. "What did you purchase?"

He nodded, digging into a pocket in his tunic and pulling forth something small. Cathlina didn't see what it was until he held it up into the light. Then, she could see that it was a golden band encircled with pale green stones. It was exquisite.

"I wanted to get you this," he murmured, reaching out to take her left hand and making a point of sliding the ring onto the third finger. "I was ill-prepared with a wedding band last night when we were married so I wanted to make amends. My father picked this out, actually. He said you would like it."

Cathlina looked at the ring, astonished. "It is the most beautiful ring I have ever seen," she whispered. Then she looked up at him, her big brown eyes glittering. "For me? You would really give this to me?"

Mathias cupped her beautiful face in his big hands, swallowing up her head. He simply stared at her, drinking in every contour, every line of her face.

"I hardly slept last night," he whispered, "because I found myself awake, watching everything about you. You slept like the dead, with hardly a move or sound, and the entire time all I could think was that it was difficult to believe that you finally belonged to me. Cathlina, I have not even known you for a full week. Do you realize that? But it does not matter because I cannot remember when I have not known or longed for you. You took a knight who was dishonored and resigned and ignited something in him again. I cannot explain it any more than that; you have made me want to live again."

His words were so deep and so touching. Cathlina instinctively reached out to touch his face, feeling his flesh against her fingertips. When she came close to his mouth, he kissed her fingers gently but that was not enough; he wanted to taste her lips and he did, slanting over them tenderly at first but then hungrily. The more he kissed, the more he wanted. It was their first real, true kiss, better than all of the first real, true kisses in the history of the world because it was with her and she was the sweetest thing that had ever walked the earth. He knew that and he loved her for it.

Cathlina had never been kissed by a man in such a fashion. Their marriage last night had consisted of a chaste kiss to the cheek and any other kisses from Mathias had always been to her hand, so this roaring suckle of passion was something that sent her head spinning.

Caving against his heat, his maleness, she was completely under his control as he dominated her. His lips were warm and firm, and she mimicked him as he suckled her lips. When his tongue gently pried its way into her mouth, she experienced it curiously, then passionately, and tasted him as he was tasting her. When his mouth finally left hers, she nearly collapsed, breathless.

"If we keep going, we shall never leave this place," he said hoarsely. "Unfortunately, we must leave immediately but rest assured that we shall take up where we left off tonight. I have a new wife and I intend to know her."

Cathlina knew what he meant and, as she tried to catch her breath, managed to blush. Her mother had been frank with her and Roxane when they had crossed over into womanhood about what was expected from a husband and being extremely naïve and curious at that time, she had gone so far as to seek out an experience to find out what, exactly, her mother had meant.

He had been a young knight, no longer serving her father, and their tryst had been over before it began when he had spilled his seed over her shift in his excitement. After that, her curiosity had been sated and she never thought about such things again until this moment. Now, with a husband she was quickly coming to adore, she was rather apprehensive about the event and the fact that there more than likely wouldn't be blood on the sheets. She wasn't sure what to tell him.

"Then let us leave right away," she said, going to gather her satchel. Mathias took it from her as she collected her cloak. "Do you suppose it would be all right for me to take a piece of bread with me while we travel?"

Mathias smiled as he ushered her out of the door and into a very narrow corridor that led directly to an uneven flight of stairs leading into the main room of the inn.

"Better than that," he said, "I have had the innkeeper pack a basket with food for us."

Cathlina turned to look at him, gratefully, as they descended the stairs. "You have thought of everything,"

"I have a wife to tend to. I must see to her comfort."

She smiled sweet at him once they reached the bottom of the steps. Mathias set her satchel down and helped her on with the heavy cloak, politely securing the stays around her neck. The activity brought out the innkeeper and his wife, who had a big basket packed with bread and cheese and other things. As Cathlina took the basket and peered into it, hungrily, Justus and Sebastian entered the structure from the street. They approached Mathias but their focus was mostly on his new wife, whom they only saw fleetingly the night before.

"The horses are ready," Justus said. He dipped his head at Cathlina when their eyes met, smiling hesitantly. "My lady."

Cathlina grinned at that man. "That seems rather formal considering I am now your daughter."

"I have never had a daughter. I am not sure how to behave."

She laughed softly. "Pretend I am one of your sons, only prettier and nicer."

He chuckled because she was. "I will try to remember that," he said. "Welcome to our family. I pray you find us agreeable."

Cathlina cocked an eyebrow. "Agreeable or not, we are all going to get to know each other very, very well over the next few days, I would suspect. I will tell you now that I like flowers and hate the taste of fish, that I can cook somewhat, and that I demand a clean and orderly existence. My mother taught me to be a frugal chatelaine so I do not like to spend money unless it is absolutely necessary. Is there anything else you wish to know?"

By this time, all three of them were looking at her with varied degrees of amusement. Sebastian was even snorting.

"I did not even know those things about you and I am your husband," Mathias finally said.

She shrugged flippantly, although it was in good humor. "That is the risk you take when you marry someone after having only known them a week. Now, you will tell me something about you that I do not know so I can see what I have gotten myself in to."

Sebastian burst out laughing as Mathias fought off a grin. "I like to spend money, I love the taste of fish, I hate flowers, and I demand everything around me be as disorderly and smelly as possible." His grin broke through when he saw her laughing. "Sebastian has a temper and fists of steel, my father likes to complain, and I believe we are all a big, bloody mess. Will you help right us, my lady?"

Cathlina shook her head at him. "It sounds as if you are all quite hopeless."

"That is true."

Mathias winked at her, took her elbow and, with his brother and father, escorted her to the door of the tavern. It was raining outside, turning the road into a great boggy mess. The humor faded from Cathlina's face when she saw the state of the weather but she didn't say a word; she simply pulled her hood over her head and allowed Mathias to lead her out into the rain.

Two steps into the soupy avenue and Mathias handed her satchel over to Sebastian so he could pick her up. He swung her into his arms and carried her across the road to where the horses stood, tethered beneath the shelter of a big oak. He placed her on his saddle as Sebastian and Justus went to their horses to prepare them for departure. As Cathlina pulled her cloak more closely around her, Mathias dug around in his saddle bags and came up with a length of oiled cloth, a rain cloak, which he wrapped tightly around his wife. Then he mounted behind her and collected his reins, motioning for his father and brother to follow.

And so they were off, riding north into Scotland as the gentle rain fell and the soft wind blew. The roads were in fair to poor condition because of the rain so it was slow going as they went. The road had a few travelers on it, mostly farmers moving their stock or wagons, but they stayed well away from the party of three big men and one small lady. With the cold gray mist over the landscape, it was a quiet and lonely journey.

Early on in the ride when the rain had turned to mist that was far wetter than the rain, Cathlina had covered her head up with the oil cloth in a vain attempt to stay dry while she dug around in the basket that the innkeeper had given her.

Surprisingly, there was a nice variety of food and she nibbled at the brown bread with currants, oatmeal pies that had some kind of meat mixed in with them, cheese, small apples and several pears. She ate until she could eat no more, offering Mathias something to eat and having the pleasure of feeding him because he had both hands on the reins because the charger was still rather skittish. He would eat whatever she fed him and try to steal kisses in between.

Unused to games played by men, or anything having to do with romance, Cathlina was rather embarrassed at his affectionate attempts in front of his father and brother, so she ended up burying her head under the oil cloth so he couldn't get at her. Mathias laughed long about that antic.

It was near sunset when the rain finally let up and the waning afternoon produced deep blue skies. The sun came out and, although cool, shed light upon brilliant green fields that glistened with moisture. The River Esk ran off to the east, a wide expanse of watery ribbon that snaked its way through the landscape and just as the sun went down, they passed through a small berg that sat on the river's edge.

The temperature had dropped with the clear sky and it had turned very cold as they came to a halt in front of one of the many taverns that lined the river. Cathlina could see at least three others down the avenue with laughter and drunken people spilling out of their glowing innards. Mathias handed her down to Sebastian, who carried her to the threshold so she wouldn't get her boots muddy in the puddles that smelled like urine. She thanked the redheaded brother, her basket of half-eaten food from the morning still in her hand as he put her on the ground.

Justus and Sebastian escorted her inside as Mathias went to see about securing two rooms for the night. The inn wasn't very busy, at least not like the other ones in town, and Mathias soon realized it was because the man's prices were fairly high. Moreover, the inn was one-storied and fairly small, and they didn't have rooms to let for the night. They did, however, have small cottages down by the river's edge that cost a decent amount of money for just one night's lodging. Mathias didn't care at that point; he paid for two cottages and four meals.

The inn was on a slight rise and the cottages tucked down below next to the water. They were constructed of sod and rock, which made them little more than a cave, but Mathias quickly discovered that they were dry and surprisingly comfortable. The innkeeper and a serving wench brought down buckets of wood and peat for the fires and soon enough, Sebastian had two blazing fires smoking in the hearths.

It was warm in the little caves quickly. Both of the cottages had one rather small bed and a small table with stools instead of chairs. Dried grass and straw was thick on the mud floor to provide some insulation. Not strangely, Cathlina was very comfortable inside the little cottage because anything was better than being on the back of the skittish charger, so she very happily settled in, checking the bedding and making sure there was water in the basin and a chamber pot under the bed. When the meal was finally delivered by two serving wenches, she had them set it upon the table in her cottage.

The smells of beef drew the men into the small cottage as Mathias, Justus and Sebastian crowded in to eat. Just as if they were back home in their smithy shack, Justus and Sebastian grabbed the stools and settled in around the table where huge knuckles of beef awaited them. There were also an abundance of carrots boiled in brine, turnips, and big hunks of warm brown bread. It was a feast and they dug into it with gusto as Mathias pulled off big pieces of steaming beef for his wife so she wouldn't be left out. She had been crowded out by the hungry men.

Cathlina giggled as he handed her a slab of bread with the beef piled on top because he was rolling his eyes at the manners of his brother and father and even went so far as to smack his brother on the side of the head because he was eating like a barbarian. Food was flying everywhere. Mathias took his own meat and bread, sitting down beside Cathlina on the bed.

"How far do you plan to take us tomorrow, Mat?" Sebastian asked as he stuffed meat in his mouth. "If I recall this road, there isn't a tremendous amount of civilization until we reach Edinburgh."

Mathias nodded as he chewed on his meal. "A positive aspect," he said. "Hopefully it means less Scots to question us and wonder what we are doing in their lands."

"What will we tell them if we run across any?" Justus wanted to know. "With a woman along, I do not suppose you would be inclined to fight your way out of a confrontation."

Mathias looked at Cathlina, shoving bits of bread in her mouth. "That would not be my first choice," he said, his gaze lingering on her sweet beauty. "The armor and mail we have is limited from what we could scavenge. Sebastian and I split the armor I used for the tournament and you have an old mail coat that hardly fits. It will make a fight even more dangerous."

Sebastian shrugged. "At least the weapons we have are superior."

Justus sighed faintly. "There is an old baron somewhere who will wonder what became of the sword I was making for him."

Sebastian snorted. "We have more weapons on us than a small army," he said. "We stripped the stall of anything valuable before we left it – hammers, blades, or tools. Woe betides the idiot foolish enough to attack us."

"Cathlina, can you use a weapon, lass?" Justus asked, half in jest. "We are speaking of battles and not including you in the conversation. Mayhap you can fight as well."

Hearing her name, Cathlina's head came up from her bread and she appeared thoughtful. "I have never tried," she said with a glimmer in her eye, "but I am great aim with an open palm."

Mathias grinned. "That means someone would have to get close enough to you for you to slap their face. I hope that is never the case."

"I can pull hair, too. And punch."

"Let us hope it does not come to that."

They shared a small laugh as they finished up the remainder of their meal. Sebastian, having inhaled his fill of the beef, belched loudly and began collecting the rubbish to throw outside. Now with the meal dwindling, fatigue was overtaking him.

"You did not answer my question, Mat," he said as he got up and opened the cottage door. "Where do you plan on taking us tomorrow?"

Mathias finished the last of the ale in his wood cup, cheap liquor but satisfactory considering it was all they had. Already, he could feel the warmth in his veins, soothing his weary body.

"It will be a long day," he said. "It is at least a day's ride on a swift horse to reach Hawick. I would like to try and make it there tomorrow night. But I think our first priority must be commissioning armor that fits us but I do not suspect we will find such a smithy until we reach a larger town like Edinburgh. Until then, we will have to be careful and make due."

Sebastian tossed the stripped bone outside. "Then we will leave early," he said, wiping his hands off on his dirty breeches. "Come along, old man. Let us leave the lovers alone."

Justus was still chewing on a piece of bread, looking rather surprised when Sebastian pulled him to his feet. But he just as quickly realized what the man was saying; Mathias had a new wife, something he was still unused to. It had been just the three of them for years since his wife passed away. Now, there was a new female added to the mix and in all honesty, he still wasn't sure how he felt about any of it. Times were changing and he was forced to accept it. He looked at Cathlina with a grin.

"I apologize," he said. "I am a dense old fool. Good sleep to you, my lady."

Cathlina fought off a smile as she pointed a stern finger at him. "You must call me Cathlina. You did it once before."

He nodded, still grinning. "Cathlina, then."

As Justus quit the cottage, Sebastian came up, his dark green eyes working her over for the moment. He, too, was fighting off a smile.

"Good night to you, sister," he said. Then he pointed at Mathias. "Come bang on my door if he is too brutish with you and I will put him in his place."

Cathlina laughed softly, blushing furiously. "You are a beast," she said, pointing at the door. "Out with you."

Sebastian chuckled and did as he was told, leaving the cottage and following his father out into the night. When they were gone, Cathlina went to shut the door behind them but noted that the water bucket near the door was nearly empty. They would need water for the morning. She picked it up by the rope handle.

"I would collect some water before we retire," she told Mathias. "I shall be right back."

He shook his head as he moved for her, extending a hand. "I will get it for you."

Cathlina was already moving out of the door. "I will get it," she insisted. "You have done all of the work all day and I have done nothing. Let me do something."

He simply lifted his shoulders as she made her way outside to the riverbank barely twenty feet away. The moon was just starting to rise, making the gently flowing waters of the river look like streams of diamonds. Everything was glittering, cold and bright.

He could hear his father and brother in the cottage next door, arguing over something, and the faint noise from the tavern behind them wafted upon the cold air. He watched Cathlina go to the edge of the river and crouch down, splashing the water with her hand before dipping the bucket into it.

Mathias' gaze lingered on her a moment, thinking of the night to come, before turning around and moving to the fire to stoke it. He wanted it warm when his wife took off her clothes. He was in the process of working it into a rolling blaze when he heard Cathlina scream.

Mathias was up and out of the cottage faster than he had ever moved in his life. Even as he was running at her, he could see that she was quite alone. There were no threats that he could see. Sebastian and Justus were running towards her as well, all three men descending on her, preparing to do what was necessary in order to protect her. But by the time they reached her, she was giggling uncontrollably and splashing her hands in the water. She seemed to be having a marvelous time.

"What is the matter?" Mathias demanded. "Why did you scream?"

Cathlina looked up at the three edgy men behind her and stood up, apologetic. "I did not scream," she said, bewildered, but then her features relaxed with understanding. She put a wet hand on Mathias's arm. "I am sorry; I suppose I did scream but it was not one of fright. I was startled when the otter came out of the water and nibbled on me."

"Otter?" Mathias repeated. "What otter?"

Cathlina was crouching down again, splashing her hands in the water. She was calling to something, something they couldn't see in the darkness, but suddenly a flash of black wet fur shot out of the water and into the bucket next to Cathlina. She squealed with laughter as an otter about the size of a large fish, perhaps ten or twelve pounds, played around in the bucket, dumping it over and then slithering back into the river. Cathlina was delighted.

"See?" she pointed to the river. "An otter. He seems to be quite tame."

Sebastian crouched down next to her, watching the otter frolic in the moonlight. "I have seen them around in the burns and lakes," he said. "They are little thieves; they will steal your meal if you don't watch out."

"I think he is wonderful," Cathlina said as the otter came back on shore and scooted right up to her. She was able to pet it but when Sebastian tried, it barked at him. She looked at her brother in law apologetically. "Mayhap he only likes girls."

Sebastian made a face and stood up, watching the otter play and wriggle at Cathlina's feet. "It's to bed for me," he said, yanking his father by the arm. "Come along, old man. Back to bed."

Justus was fairly intrigued by the otter but allowed Sebastian to pull him along. As they moved back to their cottage, Cathlina remained crouched on the river's bank, giggling at the otter that was very playful. He would slither out of the water and rise on his hind legs, making grunting sounds at her as she pet it. But he thought she had something to eat for him and would grab and nibble at her fingers, much to her delight. Soon enough, the otter was back in the bucket, rolling around in it.

Mathias stood over the pair, hands on his hips as he watched the fun. In truth, it was very sweet to watch. Cathlina had such a glow about her, such beauty and innocence, that he wasn't surprised that creatures sensed it. The otter was being very playful and affectionate with her. He finally reached down and put a hand on her dark head.

"As much as I would like to stand here all night and watch you play with the otter, I really think we need to get some sleep," he said. "Get your water and let us return inside."

Cathlina knew he was right. She tried to coax the otter from the bucket and when he finally slithered out and back into the river, she rinsed the bucket out a couple of times before finally collecting the cool, sweet water. Mathias took the bucket from her and they made their way back up to the cottage. They were about to enter it when a flash of wet fur bolted past them as the otter ran into the cottage. Both Cathlina and Mathias watched with surprise as the otter leapt onto the small bed and began burrowing in the covers.

"Oh!" Cathlina cried. "He will get everything wet!"

Mathias was much calmer than his wife. Shaking his head at the antics, he set the bucket down as Cathlina went to the bed, trying to remove the happy otter. The animal didn't want to come out, however, and she spent a good deal of time trying to coax the furry creature forth. Finally, she simply trapped him in the coverlet and wrapped him up, carrying him like a swaddled baby to the door. Setting the blanket on the ground, she gently unraveled it until the otter rolled out.

"Now, you stay out here," she scolded as she backed into the cottage. "You cannot sleep with us. Good night to you, my little friend. I will see you on the morrow."

Even after she closed the door, she could hear the otter grunting outside and scratching at the wood. Mathias threw the old iron bolt and pulled her away from the door.

"Come along to bed, now," he said. "We will be up before dawn and you must get some sleep."

Cathlina nodded as she moved to her satchel and began removing her clothing. It occurred to her that their marriage would be consummated very shortly and she struggled not to feel nervous about it. Now, the travel of the day had passed and the evening meal was finished, and all that was left to do was settle down for sleep. She could hear the otter scratching at the door as she began to unfasten her surcoat.

"I do hope he will go away and settle down," she said, eyeing the door.

Mathias pulled his mail hood off. "He will," he said, turning to face her and holding out his arms. "Help me with this, please."

Cathlina went to him, dutiful and eager, but really didn't know what he meant. She'd never undressed a man before. Mathias indicated his arms.

"Pull on the mail," he said.

Cathlina took hold and pulled, nearly falling over with the weight of the mail when it came off. Mathias had to grab hold of her so she wouldn't end up on the floor. She grinned at him.

"I suppose I am not very good at that," she said.

He winked at her. "You will get better. As the wife of a knight, you'll have to."

She watched him drape the mail over the table to dry it out. He then began to pull off his other clothing; tunic and then undershirt, revealing his naked and magnificent chest. He was very broad in the shoulders, neck and chest, with heavily muscled arms. His torso was trim, with a fine matting of dark hair from his neck to his belly. Cathlina stared at him, absorbing the sight, digesting it, and realizing that it made her very hot simply to gaze on the man. Her cheeks were flushing madly and she lowered her gaze to focus on her own clothing.

Nervous fingers fumbled with the ties on her surcoat. She could hear Mathias moving around, no doubt removing the rest of his clothing. The mere thought made her fearful and excited at the same time. She was just moving to unfasten the back of the dress when Mathias came up behind her.

His body was big and warm against her back. "Here," he said huskily. "Allow me to assist you."

Cathlina merely nodded, removing her hands and feeling him deftly undo the stays. She lifted her arms and he pulled the dress up over her head, leaving her clad only in her shift, hose and boots. Mathias pulled up a stool and sat her on it. Carefully, he lifted her shift to her knees and began untying her boots.

"I realize we have only known each other a very short amount of time," he said softly, "and in essence, you married a stranger. Nothing is more nerve wracking, I am sure, than being a bride on her wedding night. But did you stop to consider it is fairly nerve wracking for the groom as well?"

She smiled timidly, watching him as he pulled her right boot off. "I had not thought on it."

"You should," he said, setting her boot aside and moving to remove the other. "I have never had a wife before."

"But you have had... a woman before?"

He paused slightly in removing the boot, thinking carefully on her question, before continuing. "Well," he murmured, "I suppose if we are to establish honesty in our marriage, I cannot lie to you about such things."

Cathlina grew serious. "You do not have to tell me if you do not want to," she said. "I should not have asked."

He looked up at her. "As my wife, it is your right to know about me, even the personal things. Aye, I have been with a woman before."

Cathlina expected that answer. She tried to imagine the women he might have been with, wondering if she could compare with their beauty. Surely they must have been the most beautiful women in England. But she didn't want him to suspect her thoughts so she lowered her gaze, trying to think of something to say, when he interrupted.

"This concerns you," he ventured softly. "I assure you I have not spread myself around like some men have. I have no bastards that I am aware of. I do not carry diseases of any kind."

She looked up at him as if horrified by the thought but wasn't fast enough to mask her shock. Mathias, seeing the expression on her face, looked rather stricken himself.

"I do not believe I am doing myself any favors by running off at the mouth," he said. "I am sorry. I did not mean to disgust you. I simply meant to ease your mind."

Cathlina nodded faintly, thinking on his words and trying to figure out how to explain her thoughts. "I must agree that there should be complete honesty in our marriage," she said. "Therefore, I must confess my own."

"What is that?"

"I am not virgin."

CHAPTER FIFTEEN

Mathias stared at her. After a moment, his manner cooled dramatically. "You will explain."

Cathlina could see, in that instance, that her honesty had not been well-met and she struggled to explain to him in a way that wouldn't send him in to a rage. In fact, she started to tremble, now very sorry that she had opened up to him. It had been a mistake.

"I was very young," she said, struggling not to cry from the expression on his face. "I was around fourteen years of age and... at Lincoln where I fostered... the servants and soldiers constantly coupled. As young girls, we used to spy on them. When the lady of the castle explained the ways of men and women to the young women in her charge... the way she told us of coupling made it seem so... she spoke of it as if it was nothing precious or unusual. She spoke of it in little detail and told us that we must discover for ourselves one day what a curious and detestable act it was. We decided that one of us would find out what she meant and tell the others and... oh, Mathias, I was stupid and irresponsible. I was so young... I did not know at the time that my virginity belonged to my husband. My foolish companions at Lincoln never told me that part of it and when I found out, I swore never to tell my parents. I could have very easily not told you but... well, you said we must have honesty in this marriage so I told you. I am sorry if I disappointed you."

Mathias continued to stand there, staring at her. He truthfully had no idea how to feel. Cheated crossed his mind, as did deception, but she had made it clear deception was not the case. She had told him something she very well didn't have to; she could have explained away the lack of blood on the marital sheets a number of different ways and that, of course, would have been deception. More than anything, he realized he felt vastly hurt and disappointed. Someone had touched his sweet Cathlina first. It was his own fault really; he married her so swiftly he never discovered such things. Now it was too late. But truth be told, even if he had known, he would have married her anyway. He felt too strongly about her not to.

With a heavy sigh, he planted himself on the bed, pondering her revelation. His expression was like stone until he looked up and saw the tears in her eyes. He could feel himself ease up somewhat, understanding the fear and regret she was feeling. He could see it in her face.

"You will tell me in exact detail what happened," he said quietly.

She sniffled, nodded, and quickly wiped the tears that were starting to spill. "I was in the great hall and he was...."

"Nay," he cut her off. "The act itself. Tell me what he did to you."

She blinked at the request but dutifully recalled the event in as much detail as she could. "He...," she said, swallowed hard, then began again. "It happened so fast. He put his hand up my shift and his fingers... he put them inside me. I could not see very much because my skirts were up around my neck but he lay atop me and... are you sure you want to hear this?"

"Go on."

She reluctantly obliged. "Very well," she said quietly. "He lay atop me and I felt something... you know, like his fingers, only it seemed bigger, but then he groaned and climbed off of me. He told me how beautiful I was, kissed my cheek, and that was the end of it. When I tried to put my skirts down, there was a big wet spot on them. My friends said it was where he spilled his seed."

"Then he did not penetrate you?"

She shrugged. "His fingers did," she said softly. "I do not really know if anything else did."

"Did you feel pain? Was there blood?"

She shook her head. "There was no real pain at all," she said honestly. "To be truthful, I do not recall seeing any blood."

Mathias thought on that, realizing he felt marginally better about the situation. He was coming to see a very clumsy attempt that evidently went nowhere. From what she described, it was barely anything at all but she had bared her soul as if she had wildly fornicated. That seemed not to be the case at all and as much as he found it rather shocking that a well-bred lady should have behaved so, he realized he was fighting off a smile. His little Cathlina was a bit of a foolish rebel, which oddly pleased him. He was starting to feel rather inadequate against her perfection.

"Then I would wager to say that you are still virgin," he said. "From what you have told me, it does not seem as if he completed the deed."

Cathlina stared at him, shocked to hear words of understanding coming out his mouth. It was not what she had expected at all. She nearly collapsed with emotion, with relief.

"Mathias, I am so sorry," she hissed, squeezing her eyes shut as she put her face in her hands. "I was so young and stupid. I had no idea how serious it was until later. You must understand that I am truly and deeply sorry. I pray you will forgive me."

He looked at her lowered head a moment before reaching out a hand to touch her silky hair. "I suppose we have all been foolish in our life," he said. "You have been truthful with me and I appreciate it. But I will say this; coupling between a husband and wife is sacred. If no one has told you that before, I will tell you now. We are married now and I am the only man you can have relations with. Is this clear?"

She nodded before he even finished his sentence. "You do not need to even say such things," she said. "I understand it all too well and I would be true and faithful to you in any case."

"Just so we understand one another."

"We do indeed," she assured him. "Even if I did not adore you, you are still my husband and I would never so much as look at another man. You are the only man in my world, now and ever more. What I did those years ago… as I said, I was very young and very foolish. I did not understand the gravity of it. I have grown up since then."

"Say it again."

"Say what?"

"That you adore me."

Cathlina smiled, her eyes glimmering. "I do adore you," she said softly. "Did you not realize that?"

He smiled in return, a genuine smile, somehow feeling closer to her after her heartfelt and astonishing confession. He'd never felt so close to a woman and as the moments passed, he could feel himself being sucked deeper and deeper into her world. Leaning forward, he captured her face in his big hands and his lips slanted hungrily over hers.

By the light of the fire, Mathias kissed Cathlina as passionately as he had ever kissed a woman in his life. She was so very soft and sweet, pliable to his whims, and soon enough he picked her up and set her on his lap. It was a rough movement but one of extreme excitement; she ended up straddling him, still in her shift and hose. But other than those items, she wore nothing underneath.

Mathias knew that and it excited him almost beyond coherency. Cathlina's arms were around his neck as his big arms encircled her, his mouth suckling the breath from her. His hands began to roam, feeling her slender torso through her shift before moving to the flesh of her ankles. As his mouth moved to her jaw, her neck, his hands moved up her silky legs until they came to rest on her knees. He couldn't even remember feeling anything so wonderfully soft and it fed his desire.

She didn't flinch as his hands snaked down her thighs and came to rest on her hips, but he did feel her tense. When his fingers danced up her torso, he felt her shudder, and he couldn't resist gently groping her breasts. When he did that, she tried to pull away purely out of embarrassment and apprehension, but he stopped her.

"Stay, stay," he whispered, holding her fast with one big arm while his free hand very gently fondled her. "This is something you will like, I promise."

Cathlina was torn between overwhelming sensations and natural anxiety. "But... is this what men do?"

He laughed softly as he kissed her mouth. "This is what husbands do."

Her eyes were open, watching him as he kissed her. When his mouth trailed down her jaw to her shoulder, she looked down to see his big hand fondling her soft, full breasts beneath her shift. Her nipples were hard and he toyed with them, causing her entire body to tremble. It was curiosity and it was fascination, watching her husband as he touched her body. She should have been very frightened by it all but she truly wasn't. Something about Mathias' touch made her feel warm and wriggly inside. When he finally pulled the shift over her head and latched onto a nipple, sucking tenderly, Cathlina's reaction was to gasp and clutch his head. The sensual sensations were too much for her to contain.

Mathias could hardly believe how responsive she was to him. The harder he suckled her, the more she bucked and groaned, until a hand moved down her belly to the thatch of dark curls between her legs. Since she a straddling him, her legs were already wide apart and he stroked her, feeling her leap. In fact, she put her hands on his shoulders and tried to climb off of him but he wouldn't let her; he suckled her breasts steadily, holding her against him with one hand while the other went to work between her legs.

She was already very wet and hot, and he carefully inserted a finger into her. Cathlina gasped at the tender intrusion but stopped trying to push away from him because he was holding her too tightly. There was nowhere to go so she sat atop his lap, her head back and eyes wide open to the ceiling, struggling to process everything he was doing to her. She knew she mostly liked it but there was natural fear there as well. It was nothing like her silly tryst with the young knight back at Lincoln Castle; this was an encounter between a man and his wife. This was an encounter between her and Mathias... *her* Mathias.

Therefore, she simply wrapped her arms around his neck and held on fast when he stood up and carried her over to the small rope bed. He laid her down in the soft light of the fire, pulling off his tunic and lowering his breeches between heated kisses. She was wet and ready for him, and he wouldn't wait any longer.

Very carefully, he edged his phallus into her quivering body, feeling her tense as he gained headway. He nursed at her breasts to distract her as he recoiled and thrust again, listening to her grunt as he seated himself deep. She didn't cry out or try to push him away, but rather seemed willing to accept all he was doing to her. He found that kind of bravery admirable, adding to his already- strong feelings for the woman.

When he was finally deeply embedded in her, he began to thrust, gently at first but with increasing power. Cathlina lay beneath him, her legs spread wide apart as she welcomed her husband into her body for the first time. He was skilled and he was gentle, and he succeeded in building an odd heat within her loins that made her want to wriggle her hips against him. She learned early on that bolts of lightning surged through her body every time they came together and she was intent to seek the lightning that seemed to grow brighter with each successive thrust.

Something was building inside of her the more he moved until finally, the thunder rolled and the lightning exploded deep within her loins. She began gasping so loudly as wave after wave of ecstasy rolled over her that Mathias had to put his hand over her mouth to keep her quiet. But her pleasure threw him over the edge and in one great and powerful thrust, he spilled himself deep.

Even when it was over, he didn't want it to be over. He wanted to remain as they were for the rest of his life. He continued to stroke in and out of her, feeling the warm wetness of what he had put in her, and utterly and incredibly happy for the first time in many years. Beneath him, Cathlina lay still and quiet. He finally lifted his head and looked at her.

"Are you well?" he asked huskily. "Did I hurt you?"

She met his gaze. "Nay," she whispered. "You did not hurt me in the least. You were quite gentle."

"I tried."

"You succeeded." She grinned at him because he was smiling at her. "But... I was thinking...."

"What?"

"The lady of Lincoln was quite wrong," she murmured. "This was not a dispassionate act at all. She must have had a terrible husband."

Mathias laughed softly. "I hope to never fall into that category."

Cathlina touched his face, inspecting the masculine lines. "I do not expect that you will," she murmured. "Already, you have proven yourself quite wonderful."

Mathias kissed her, without all of the blazing passion now that his lust was sated but more with emotion and sentiment. It was stronger than all of the lust in the world. What he felt for her was coming from the heart, not the loins. It was both frightening and wonderful. From this moment on, they were irrevocably joined.

When Mathias finally rolled off of her and settled in for sleep, Cathlina stopped him. He had no idea why until she got up from the bed and peered closely at the linen beneath them. When she spied what she had been looking for, she pointed it out to him with a somewhat joyful expression. Mathias grinned when he saw it.

There was blood on the fabric.

CHAPTER SIXTEEN

One week later
Edinburgh

Edinburgh was bigger than Cathlina could have ever imagined. The largest city she had ever been to was Carlisle, and that seemed big enough, but Edinburgh was overwhelming in its size. Coming in to the city from the south, they could see it spread out on the horizon like a great cloak of men, buildings, and animals. A faint haze of smoke hung in the sky above the city, indicative of its large population.

Astride a small brown palfrey that Mathias had purchase for his wife in Hawk, Cathlina had watched the approaching city with great awe. Riding with the friendly otter in a basket, now named Midge and officially a part of their group, she had been very excited to realize they had come to one of their primary destinations. But Midge kept jumping out of the basket and gleefully running up and down the road until Mathias would climb off his steed and dutifully chase the animal down.

Since nearly the moment she had met him, Cathlina had become very attached to little Midgy and when it came time to leave Langholm, Midgy had followed them down the road and Mathias knew he could not deny his wife her furry little friend. There was no use even trying. He had proven to be a cute little companion and had been hours of endless entertainment. For days they had simply let him run beside them as they traveled but coming close to the city as they were, Cathlina was afraid he would be stepped on or otherwise hurt, so she kept him in the basket as much as she could.

As Edinburgh loomed, Mathias and Sebastian and Justus seemed to view the city with less awe and more suspicion, since it was a city full of Scots and they were clearly not Scots. To most here, they were the enemy. But they had to pass through Edinburgh to not only locate Sir Stephen of Pembury but also to make their way to Henry Beaumont's fortress north of the city. Still, they had a lot of business to conduct in Edinburgh and Mathias wasted no time in his search for the Bucket and Barrel.

At the first inn they stopped at once they entered the city limits, the barkeep couldn't tell them exactly where the Bucket and Barrel was but he thought it was perhaps near Edinburgh Castle. Unwilling to drag Cathlina all over the dirty streets of Edinburgh in search of the fabled Bucket and Barrel tavern, Mathias sought lodgings at the present inn but was directed to a man who had a bigger inn and more room.

This foray took them down the dirty and stone avenue that was literally awash with human excrement until they came to a very large inn called the Green Pony. Inside the rather vast structure, the owner was able to provide them with three very satisfactory rooms on the third level; two big sleeping chambers and a smaller sitting chamber that were all connected together. It was high above the common room and had a great view of the city. Mathias paid for a week's lodging up front and slipped the otter into the rooms buried under heavy cloaks.

Cathlina was thrilled with the rooms; they were cozy and moderately clean, and she and Midgy could watch all of the comings and goings from her perch in the sitting room. At one point during their first day there, Sebastian stole a big copper tub from the nearby livery and brought it up to the rooms so they could have a place for Midgy to swim. The otter was happy as a lark in his big copper tub, swimming and frolicking, but he still barked when Sebastian came near him. Sebastian took up making faces at the animal every time he saw him. Sometimes he would even bark back.

On their second day in Edinburgh, Mathias and Sebastian had located the Bucket and Barrel Inn. It was a fairly large tavern and fairly well kept, but Stephen of Pembury was not in residence. Day after day they returned to the tavern to sit and wait, with no luck, while Justus remained with Cathlina. To keep occupied, Cathlina had gone to the street of Merchants early in their stay and had purchased several items including a knitting needle and yarn as well as a deck of lovely painted cards all the way from Rome. When Cathlina and Justus would grow tired of card games, he would sit and snore in his chair while she would work on a knitted tunic for Mathias. She was clever with the yarn and the garment was turning out beautifully.

The time with Justus had been well spent, however. Cathlina had come to know her father-in-law as a man with a vast amount of knowledge in many things. He was intelligent and wise, and it was very clear how much he loved his sons. They were everything to him. Cathlina would sit and knit, listening to him tell stories about Mathias and Sebastian when they were children and of the mischief they would get in to.

He told stories of them playing with sticks as very young lads and pretending they were swords, a game that seemed innocent enough until Mathias nearly blinded Sebastian. After that, their mother, the Lady Penelope, forbid them their swords but Justus would let the boys play when their mother wasn't looking. It made for charming story-telling and Cathlina was coming to like Justus a great deal. In fact, she missed her own father less with Justus and his endless library of stories.

As the days passed, she tried not to think of her family, now left behind and undoubtedly frantic over her disappearance. She thought perhaps to send them a missive once she and Mathias got settled in Henry Beaumont's ranks, but she hadn't the nerve to ask her husband yet. Everything was so new and uncertain still. She even missed Roxane and she especially missed Abechail. Her baby sister was very heavy on her mind for she knew Abbie would have loved Midgy. She hoped she was able to introduce them one day.

Eight days after their arrival in Edinburgh, the day dawned misty and windy, and Mathias and Sebastian enjoyed a meal of bread with melted cheese and warmed cider before the fire before setting out for the Bucket and Barrel.

Midgy, having slept in under Mathias and Cathlina's bed, came slithering out of the shadows and sat on his hind legs, grunting for food. He ate fish, which wasn't too difficult to come by in Edinburgh, and Mathias found a man who would deliver a bucket of fish to them daily but he usually came later in the morning. The innkeeper wasn't suspicious, fortunately, because Mathias told him that his wife had a fish fetish and that was all she would eat. For someone who hated the smell and taste of fish, Cathlina put up with it for Midgy's sake.

This morning, Midgy was impatient but didn't want the bread and cheese the men were eating. Mathias finally gave him a smooth, round rock to occupy him, one of his favorite toys they had collected on the journey north, and Midgy ran back into the bed chamber with it. Mathias and Sebastian heard Cathlina shriek as the otter jumped on the bed and began burrowing.

"Midgy, *no*!" Cathlina said, her voice hoarse and sleepy. "Your nose is cold! Stop nibbling on my toes!"

Mathias and Sebastian grinned, listening to Cathlina as she scolded the otter and then evidently settled down with it. The bedchamber grew rather quiet. But then they began to hear signs of life coming forth as Cathlina got out of bed and went about dressing for the day. Midgy came rushing back out into the sitting chamber to jump in his half-filled copper tub and play with his rock.

Mathias finished the last of his cider and set his cup down. "I will bid my wife farewell before I go," he said, grunting wearily. "Pembury had better make a show of it soon or we shall have to move on without him."

Sebastian stood up and stretched his muscular body. "How long will you give him?"

Mathias paused by the bed chamber door. "Another week and then we leave," he said. "I do not know what has become of the man but we cannot wait here forever. However, the armor we commissioned will not be ready for another week. We have to wait at least that long."

Sebastian shrugged in agreement and went to finish his own cider as Mathias entered the bedchamber. There was a small fire burning in the hearth, peat that smoked a great deal. Since it was rather dark in the room, Cathlina had lit a couple of tapers as she moved about getting dressed for the day. Mathias found her bent over the basin, washing her face and neck with lavender soap.

"Sebastian and I will be leaving shortly," he said, putting a gentle hand on her back. "I will see you this eve."

Cathlina rinsed off her face and looked at him. "How much longer do you intend to wait for this Pembury?"

Mathias lifted his eyebrows. "Sebastian and I were just discussing that," he said. "The new armor we commissioned will not be finished for another week, so I will give him at least that long. Then, we must move on."

"Where?"

"To Henry Beaumont's lair," he told her. "Remember I explained to you why we are here?"

She wiped off her neck. "Aye," she replied. "You are going to pledge fealty to Henry de Beaumont and fight in his wars for the Scots crown."

"Correct," he said. "De Lara has sent Pembury to accompany me north but if the man does not show, then I will have no choice but to push north and find Henry without him."

She looked at him seriously. "Do you think something has happened to him?"

Mathias shook his head firmly. "Pembury? Bloody unlikely. The man is invincible. I am sure he is on his way but if he does not come soon, he will have to catch up to us. I cannot wait much longer."

Cathlina opened her mouth to say something but Sebastian was suddenly at the door, knocking swiftly. "Mat?" he hissed. "Someone is at the door."

Mathias was on the move, unsheathing the big, sharp but unadorned broadsword that had accompanied him north. Telling Cathlina to bolt the bed chamber door, he shut it softly and moved for the door that opened up into the corridor outside. Sebastian had collected his broadsword and together, the two of them went to answer their caller.

"Who comes?" Mathias demanded.

"Open the door or I will break it down."

Sebastian immediately tensed for a fight while Mathias cocked his head curiously; the voice was deep and booming, but there was something about it that he thought he recognized. The words didn't frighten him at all because somehow, someway, he could sense mirth. Aye, he recognized the voice now. Yanking the door open, he lashed out a massive balled fist and made contact with some portion of a body; he wasn't sure which. He struck out as hard as he could.

The man at the door fell back as Mathias made contact with his throat. Slamming back into the wall of the corridor, he didn't try to fight back. He was too busy gasping for air because Mathias had hit him squarely on the Adam's apple. As the man slumped against the wall, Mathias and Sebastian stood over him.

"How many times have I told you not to stand so close to a door when issuing threats?" Mathias scolded. "Next time, it could be more than a fist that comes out at you. It could be a broadsword."

The man had his left hand wrapped around his neck, gazing up at Mathias and Sebastian with a mixture of irritation and humor. Clad in heavy and expensive battle armor, he was well prepared for any manner of armed offensive but a fist to the neck, where he only had a mail hauberk, had him reeling.

"You bastard," the man rasped. "I shall get you for this, I swear it."

Mathias just shook his head; it was readily evident that he knew the man, as did Sebastian. After several long seconds of pregnant and tense silence, the man against the wall suddenly burst out in chuckles, which caused Mathias and Sebastian to follow suit. Soon, the three of them were laughing uproariously.

"Pembury," Mathias reached out a hand to pull the man off the wall. "Where in the hell have you been? I have been looking for you for a week."

Stephen of Pembury took Mathias' hand and pulled himself up. He was an enormously muscled man standing eight inches over six feet and was easily taller than even the tallest man. In fact, Pembury was a giant wherever he went. With his dark hair, chiseled features and cornflower blue eyes, he cut a striking figure of male virility and power, and had more than his share of female admirers. He was enormously strong, intelligent and obedient to a fault. He also happened to be Mathias' closest friend and the two of them came together in a hug that reaffirmed the bonds of that friendship. Then Mathias pulled him inside the sitting room and shut the door.

"I have been at the Bucket and Barrel for two days," Stephen said, still rubbing his throat. "The innkeeper told me that two men had been coming daily looking for me but I could not be sure it was you. I had to be careful, you know. Yesterday, I hid while I paid a man to follow you back here. When he described the men he had followed, I was certain it was you. And here I am."

Mathias shook his head as Sebastian grinned. "Here you are," Sebastian said, very happy to see him. "Where have you been keeping yourself for the past year? We heard you were with Edward in Scotland."

Stephen nodded as he pulled off his helm and moved to make himself more comfortable. "Mostly in Newcastle and Berwick," he said. "The Scots have been a handful, fighting each other for the throne and then battling the English for independence. I have hardly seen de Lara or St. Hèver. How are they?"

"Well," Mathias said. "We just left them, in fact."

"That is good," Stephen said as he set his helm on the nearest table. His cornflower blue gaze sought out Mathias. "And you? How have you been this year past?"

The last time Mathias and Stephen had seen each other was shortly after Mathias had been stripped of his title. It had been a painful parting and, frankly, Mathias didn't remember too much of it. All he had remembered clearly was the anguish.

"I have been well," he said quietly. "My brother and father and I were living in Brampton, operating a rather successful smithy business. It has been a quiet year and one of reflection.

Stephen nodded in understanding. "You were entitled to some much-needed rest."

"I received it."

"And now you are ready to return to us?"

Mathias shrugged. "It is time to move on with my life and resume my chosen profession," he said. "Edward will simply have to understand that. I cannot remain a smithy for the rest of my life."

Pembury shook his head firmly. "You are too great for that," he said, eyeing Mathias. "I have been waiting for this day, in fact. I knew it would come sooner rather than later. I have some things for you."

Mathias looked at him. "What do you have?"

Stephen smiled faintly. "Your sword," he said softly. "I have your sword, your equipment, and your charger. I brought them with me."

Mathias' features when slack with shock. "You did?" he asked, awed. "I… I had turned them over to the court's magistrate. I had no idea where they had gone."

"I took them," Stephen said, his manner quiet. "I could not stand the thought of them falling into hands that were unworthy to hold them, so Tate acquired them from the magistrate and turned them over to me for safekeeping. He did not tell you that?"

Mathias shook his head, still stunned. "He did not."

"Then mayhap he wanted to surprise you."

Mathias chuckled as he realized with great joy that the possessions he valued above all else would be returned to him.

"I am surprised," he agreed, grinning. He sobered. "You realize that all of you – Tate, Ken, and you – are going against the king's directive. He stripped me of my title and told me if I held a sword again that it would mean my life. Now all of you are helping me defy him?"

Stephen's good humor faded. "What happened to you could have happened to any of us," he said softly. "You had your reasons for siding with Mortimer, Mat. We all knew that. What happened at the end… Edward stripped you in order to save your life. We had to do it even though it was a travesty. But now this… they can take away your titles but it does not diminish who you are as a man and a warrior. We knew your time would come again and we are here to ensure that it happens."

Surely no better friends in the world had ever existed. The bonds they all shared ran deeper than blood or kings. It ran deep into the heart. Mathias was deeply touched and humbled by the show of support.

"Thank you, my friend," he said quietly. "I cannot thank you enough for your thoughtfulness."

Pembury smiled in return, his big teeth straight and white. "You would have done the same for me," he said. "Now, what is this I hear? We are to swear fealty to Henry de Beaumont and fight for his foolish cause?"

Mathias nodded. "We are," he said as he eyed the man, "but I am not entirely sure how you are going to swear fealty to him if you are already quite sworn to Edward?"

Stephen shrugged. "Tate has sent Edward a missive asking for my leave," he said. "You know that Edward cannot deny Tate anything. He worships the man."

"Tate is his uncle; indeed he does."

"Therefore," Pembury continued as he grabbed around for a cup to fill with the remainder of the warmed cider, "you and I are bound for our Scots adventure. Oh, and Sebastian, too."

Sebastian, standing near the hearth, sneered at him. "You should be so fortunate to have me on your side, Pembury."

Stephen lifted a cup in agreement. "I certainly would not wish to fight against Sebastian the Red. Those Scots had better run if they know what is good for them."

He drank deeply of his cup as Midgy decided to purge forth from his copper tub and make an appearance. As Stephen began to pick at the bread still left on the table, the otter raised up on his hind legs next to him and began grunting, begging for food. Stephen nearly bolted out of his chair at the sight and only by sheer courage managed to keep it. His eyes were wide on the furry creature.

"God' Bones," he exclaimed. "What in the hell is that?"

Mathias caught sight of Midgy and grinned. "My wife's pet."

Now Stephen was truly astonished. "Your *wife*?"

Mathias nodded as he headed to the bed chamber door and rapped softly. "Cathlina?" he called. "Open the door, love."

They could hear the iron bolt being thrown and the door quietly opened. A woman of astonishing beauty stood in the doorway, her sweet face both curious and apprehensive as she looked at the men in the chamber. Mathias put his arm around her shoulders and pulled her out into the light.

"This is the man we have been waiting for," he told her. "This is Sir Stephen of Pembury."

Cathlina's face relaxed into a smile as she gazed upon the massive man with the bright blue eyes. "My lord," she said, dipping in a polite curtsy. "It is good to finally meet you."

Stephen was still wrestling with his astonishment that Mathias had not only taken a wife, but that he had brought her along. He bowed his head in her direction.

"Lady de Reyne," he said. "It is indeed a pleasure to make your acquaintance. I had no idea Mathias had married."

She grinned as she looked at her husband. "Ask him to tell you how it came about," she said. "It is a rather sordid tale."

Stephen smiled because she was. He looked at Mathias. "I can already tell she is far too good for you."

Mathias bowed his head in agreement. "You would be correct," he said. "Now that you have met her, you know that she will be traveling with us. I could not leave her behind for reasons I will explain to you at another time."

Stephen accepted his statement without another word. He went to reclaim his cup but saw that the otter had it, now rolling it around on the floor. As he hunted around for another cup, Justus emerged from the second bed chamber and greeted him like a long-lost son. Pembury was thrilled to see the old man, tougher than most men half his age. He had fought with three kings, starting with Edward I. Stephen greatly admired Justus de Reyne.

As he and Justus sat down to conversation, the otter was running amuck because it was hungry and Lady de Reyne was trying to pacify the animal. Sebastian wasn't paying much attention to her but Mathias was, and Stephen could see in those brief few moments how enamored the man was with his wife. Not that he blamed him, for she was a lovely little thing, but he had to admit he was concerned.

They would be traveling into enemy territory for the purpose of swearing fealty to a man who was fighting for the Scottish throne. This was a serious endeavor, as much as any of the wars between Edward and Mortimer, but now Mathias was bringing his wife along with him who would only be a distraction. Stephen wondered just how effective Mathias would be with his attention divided.

He prayed the distraction would not be deadly.

CHAPTER SEVENTEEN

Three weeks later

In the expanse of dense forest north of the town of Perth known as the Devil's Wood, a mighty fortress tucked back in the hills known as the Devil's Den served as the highland base for de Beaumont and his operations in Scotland. It was a different design from most English castles in that it was mostly massive walls built from brittle gray stone and the interior contained a single stone tower and several wood and thatch outbuildings. Dogs, horses and men mingled freely, and English troops held strict vigilance over the countryside. They were in enemy territory.

Which is why Mathias and his party were nearly mowed down by archers when they approached the day before, but Mathias has the good sense to keep everyone out of archer's range while he sent Stephen to announce their arrival. He thought about sending Sebastian but with his flaming red hair and big build, he looked like a Scot and Mathias didn't want to lose his brother to a slurry of panicked sentries. Therefore, he sent Stephen in all of his godly English glory to announce their intentions and deliver the missive he carried from de Lara.

The decision had worked in their favor and soon they found themselves in the bosom of the Devil's Den. While Henry was too busy to see them the day they arrived, he provided adequate accommodations and saw them at sunrise the next day. Leaving Justus with Cathlina, Mathias, Stephen, and Sebastian attended Henry's audience.

The great hall of the Den, as it was locally known, was a vast place with a pitched roof, stone walls, and two enormous hearths. It was full of Englishmen, mixed with Scots, all of them loyal to Henry who had immersed himself in Scotland's politics for well over twenty years. He was part of the contingent that fought at Bannockburn, and lost, and became what was known throughout England as a group of disgraced nobles called "The Disinherited". For some reason, however, Henry managed to maintain power in a world that had seen many of his compatriots stripped. Henry fought for the side that suited his politics best at that time, English or Scots, but mostly, Henry fought for himself. He was an opportunist of the greatest degree.

It was this short, gray-haired, and rather powerfully built man that now gave audience to Mathias, Stephen, and Sebastian. His manner was both welcoming and disdainful, an odd combination.

"Mathias de Reyne and Stephen of Pembury." Henry Beaumont had a crisp and almost condescending way of delivering his speech. "Two of the greatest knights in young Edward's arsenal stand before me. And let us not forget Sebastian the Red; a mighty man indeed. One cannot help but wonder why you are all here?"

"Was it not satisfactorily explained to you in the missive I delivered to you from the Earl of Carlisle, my lord?" Mathias asked. "The earl has sent us to support your cause."

Henry was no fool; he had been doing this for a very long time. "My cause?" he asked. "Or Edward Balliol's cause?"

Stephen, who had been entrenched in the Scots politics well over a year, spoke. "Edward does not believe the rightful heir to the throne of Scotland is the infant, David, son of The Bruce," he replied steadily. "It is his opinion that the House of Balliol is the legitimate heir. Edward is the son of the former king, John Balliol, descendent of Isabella of Angouleme, and of John de Warenne, Earl of Surrey. That makes him more royal than most, my lord."

Henry watched Pembury carefully as he spoke; the man was a well-known puppet of King Edward but had a sterling reputation of his own. There was no one in Scotland or England who could speak poorly of the man. De Reyne, however, was another matter; he had been Roger Mortimer's genius, the brilliance behind Mortimer's might. Henry had fought with de Reyne before during the years he supported Mortimer and Isabella but, unlike de Reyne, he fell from favor, switched alliances, and helped plot Mortimer's downfall. De Reyne had stayed the course with Mortimer, like a good soldier. Aye, Henry was particularly interested in de Reyne.

"Spare me the lineage lesson, Pembury, for I know it better than you," he said, turning his attention to Mathias. "You, however, intrigue me greatly. Mortimer would not make a move without you and I know for a fact that it was your military mastermind that put the man upon the throne for three years. Well? What say you? What happened to you when they cut off Mortimer's head?"

Entrenched in Scotland and his own political issues, de Beaumont evidently had not heard of Mathias' dishonor. Before Mathias could respond, Pembury intervened.

"He was spared, my lord," he said, looking at Mathias and silently begging the man to keep his mouth shut. "We are in the service of the Earl of Carlisle now who has sent us here to support your cause. Will you accept our fealty, my lord?"

Henry accepted Pembury's explanation of Mathias' service record since Mortimer unfortunately parted ways with his head; there was no reason to doubt the man considering Mathias' reputation.

"It is as simple as that?" he asked, as if waiting for a caveat. "I have your swords and your loyalty?"

"The earl has deemed it so, my lord," Pembury replied steadily. "He wishes Balliol on the throne and not a child who will be ruled by the nobles, and especially not Moray. We are here to ensure that."

He had a point. Henry's gaze lingered on Mathias a moment before finally rising from his chair. Flicking a wrist at the three knights, he began to walk from the hall.

"Come with me," he said.

Dutifully, Mathias, Stephen, and Sebastian followed. They headed out into the vast bailey of the Den, swarming with men and animals. There was an encampment of troops, both English and Scots, against the southern wall with make-shift shelters and cooking fires. They had to pass through the edge of the encampment in order to reach the keep, which rose three stories above the bailey. Henry took them inside the very cramped and stuffy cylindrical tower and they mounted the narrow stone steps to the second floor. When they came to the landing, Henry rapped on the only door on that level. After a muffled response, he opened the door.

The room beyond was the entire circumference of the tower. A fire smoked in the hearth and two big dogs, shaggy hounds, slept near the fireplace, lifting their heads when they saw visitors. There was a bed, and clutter, and a table near a lancet window were a solitary man sat hunched over a scatter of vellums. When he saw the men entering his chamber, he rose to greet them.

"My lord," Henry said as they entered the room. "I should like to introduce you to some of the major players in young King Edward's battle against Roger Mortimer. Be introduced to Sir Sebastian de Reyne, Sir Stephen of Pembury, and Sir Mathias de Reyne. Good knights, this is Edward Balliol."

The three knights bowed respectfully to Edward, who scrutinized the group closely. Middle aged, with a paunch in the middle and piercing brown eyes, he was an intelligent man and very ambitious. He knew the names that Henry had spoken of. Aye, he knew them well.

"De Reyne," he said, approaching Mathias. "I know of you. You were Mortimer's commander."

Mathias nodded shortly. "Aye, my lord."

"Your reputation precedes you."

"Thank you, my lord."

"Why are you here?"

"Because the Earl of Carlisle has offered their services to our cause," Henry said, glancing at the three big knights. "It is evident that he does not wish to see the infant David upon the throne and what Tate de Lara wants, King Edward wants. We are in the presence of greatness, my lord. These men will win you a kingdom."

Edward looked at the knights, filling up his chamber with power and glory. He hardly knew what to say. "This morning when I awoke, I had no idea that this day would bring such news," he said, moving from Mathias to Stephen. "I am rather speechless with the military might I am faced with. Did you bring men with you?"

Mathias shook his head. "Only me, my brother, Pembury, and my father."

"Is Carlisle planning on sending an army?"

Stephen answered. "I am told four hundred men will be making the journey from Carlisle in a few weeks. The earl wanted to make sure we were well received and settled before sending men."

Balliol nodded shortly, thinking of more men to reinforce his cause. "Very well," he said. "We will sit and talk now. I want to understand what your presence here truly means."

In the stuffy room that smelled of dogs and smoke, Henry pulled up a stool but the other three remained standing. They were about to hear the plans for their immediate future and the reclamation of a throne for the House of Balliol. For Mathias, it was as if he was back with Mortimer, huddling for battle, feeling the power that he wielded flow through him like the rich red blood that filled his veins. Power and blood were one in the same. He could breathe battle, smell it and taste it, once for Mortimer and now for Balliol.

This was what he was born and bred to do, his destiny as God had given it to him. The year he had lived as a smithy, he realized, had only made him hungrier for his true vocation. He was a knight, through and through, and no one could take that away from him. As he sat around that small table, he realized that this was the beginning of his redemption.

Matthias de Reyne was back.

***

Midgy was wreaking havoc.

In the accommodations assigned to Mathias and his party, the otter was a festive creature who had no idea that knocking things over, spilling water, slithering into the fireplace and then emerging with soot all over his body which, in turn, got all over people and objects, was a bad thing. He was just curious and happy, as he usually was, until he got black soot all over Justus' lap when the old man was sleeping in a chair. Justus woke up and yelled at the otter, which promptly stood on his hind legs to beg food from the irritated old man. Cathlina had quickly distracted the animal with toys.

They were lodged in one of the small huts that lined the Den's outerwall, built from river rock with a heavy thatched roof. There was one big room and one smaller adjoining room, and a fireplace that was open on both ends and servicing both rooms. Midgy was having a great time with the pass-through hearth.

"Justus?" she asked as Midgy tried to burrow his way into Mathias' saddle bags. "Do you suppose you can find a pot or a tub for him to play in? It would keep him out of the hearth."

Justus eyed the otter, who was grunting happily. "Aye," he said, rising wearily from his chair and upset that his nap had been interrupted. "I will see what I can find."

He opened the door to the bailey of the Devil's Den with the intention of hunting down the stables when he caught sight of his sons returning from the keep. Pembury was walking beside them, his hulking presence unmistakable. Cathlina came to the door to watch the approach of the knights, their enormous forms shadowed by the setting sun. When Midgy tried to squeeze by and make a break for it, she caught the otter and held him fast.

Mathias smiled wearily as he came close, his gaze locking with Cathlina's. She smiled in return and he took both her and the otter in his arms to kiss her. Midgy squirmed and tried to break free.

"Are you hungry?" he asked her. "Henry has invited us to sup with him in the great hall, so put on your best gown, my lady. Let these fools see what a true beauty looks like."

Cathlina scooted back into the chamber excitedly as the knights filed in and shut the door behind them. Her possessions, as well as Mathias' bags, were in the smaller of the rooms so she disappeared into the smaller chamber with Midgy. They could hear her rummaging around.

"Mathias!" she called. "I need your assistance!"

Mathias had just removed his broadsword, the prized possession that Pembury had returned to him. Setting it down on the table, he disappeared into the smaller chamber and they could hear his deep, steady voice and her excited one. When it became clear he was helping his wife with her dressing, Justus turned to Sebastian and Stephen.

"Well?" he asked. "Is Henry agreeable to our service?"

Stephen planted his bulk on a small chair. "He is," he said. "In fact, he is very happy to have us. It would seem he has an important outpost he wants us to man, one in Fife near Kinghorn. He has a small contingent there now but it has taken a beating. He is hoping by putting more seasoned men there, the area might know some peace. More than that, he would like us to work on an alliance with the neighboring laird. He wants the man's support."

Justus lifted his bushy eyebrows, thinking that Henry was about to throw them all into the fire at a border outpost.

"That is no place for a woman," he hissed.

Stephen shrugged as if he had no say in the matter. "What else is he going to do? Leave her here? You know he will not."

Justus fussed, knowing it was a moot point. Instead of complaining, he went to sit down and wait for Lady de Reyne and her husband to make an appearance.

Inside the smaller chamber, Mathias had helped his wife from her plain yellow surcoat and helped her don a deep, rich scarlet brocade, the nicest surcoat she had brought with her from Kirklinton. The bodice laced up the front, emphasizing her slender torso, and she tied and re-tied it until she had it correct. By that time, Mathias had wandered back out into the other room to await her and she could hear soft conversation between the men. She was very excited to be supping in another castle because other than Lincoln Castle, Carlisle Castle, and two or three others she had visited while fostering at Lincoln, she had rarely supped away from familiar venues.

With her clean surcoat secured and Midgy rolling around on the small bed behind her, Cathlina pulled forth her comb and small polished bronze mirror. She missed Abechail and her talented fingers, for she was not nearly as clever as her little sister, so she ended up braiding her hair and wrapping it around her head like a halo. Big iron pins held her hair in place and in truth she looked quite lovely. Collecting her dark blue cloak, she emerged into the room where the men were.

"I am ready," she declared to the host of expectant and appreciative eyes that turned in her direction. "But what shall we do with Midgy while we are gone?"

Mathias could hear the otter grunting and playing in the other room. He looked around the chamber and spied a big bucket near the hearth, used to clean out the ashes. He picked it up and tossed it at his brother.

"Go and get some water," he said. "Hurry; we will wait for you."

Sebastian was outraged. "I do not even like that hairy rat," he declared. "Why must I go?"

Mathias simply pointed at the door. Sebastian made faces, mostly at Cathlina, who bit her lip to keep from laughing as he stomped from the hut. Midgy came out of the chamber at that point, skittering around on the floor looking for something to find mischief with. He ended up jumping on to Stephen's lap and the knight shoved him back onto the floor. Cathlina came to the rescue with his favorite smooth rocks, distracting him, and in a short time, Sebastian returned with the bucket of water.

Cathlina had him set it down near the hearth, whereupon Midgy jumped into it and, being too big for it, splashed most of the water out onto the floor. But he was happy and it was time to leave.

"Off we go," Mathias said, ushering everyone from the hut. He eyed the otter as he closed the door. "Behave yourself, beast."

Big brown otter eyes blinked back.

***

The great hall of the Devil's Den was filled with smoke and loud men. From the moment Mathias escorted his wife inside, he was coming to think it was a very bad idea to have her here because the only other women were serving wenches and the moment they walked into the hall, they passed a pair having sex behind a pillar. Cathlina looked away quickly and pretended not to notice while Mathias didn't acknowledge it. He knew fighting men and he knew how they were; sex in a hall, in a stable, or in any other convenient place wasn't unheard of in the least. They took it where they could get it but Mathias didn't want his wife exposed to that kind of debauchery.

Mathias directed Cathlina over to the great feasting table that was crowded with men. All of them were drinking heavily. De Beaumont and Balliol sat at the far end of the table and, seeing Mathias and the other knights, waved them over. They had to walk the entire length of the hall to get there and there was increasing attention on Cathlina as they went. One drunk man even went so far as to reach out and grab a fistful of skirt, prompting Mathias to land a blow so heavily into the man's face that blood gushed from every facial orifice. Like a dog guarding his bone, the territory of Cathlina was readily established.

Cathlina was rightly terrified by the time she reached the end of the table and Henry introduced himself and Balliol. She was polite but stiff, taking a seat on the bench between Mathias and Justus as servants swarmed around them to bring them food and drink. It was so loud in the hall that it was seriously difficult to hear any conversation they might attempt.

"I was unaware that Mathias had brought his wife," Henry said with a hint of disapproval. "Where were you born, Lady de Reyne?"

"Near Brampton, my lord," she replied, startled when two men down the table started a fight. She tried not to watch it as she focused on Henry. "My father is a cousin of the Earl of Carlisle and commands the garrison of Kirklinton for him."

Henry's eyebrows lifted. "You are the earl's cousin?" he repeated. "How interesting. Now de Reyne is related to de Lara by marriage. An arranged one, I am sure. What is your father's name?"

Cathlina already didn't like the man; he spoke quite condescendingly, as if she was no more than an ant beneath his feet. He seemed quite aloof to her.

"Saer de Lara, my lord," she replied.

Henry cocked his head. "Saer de Lara," he repeated as if attempting to remember something buried deep in his memory. "Saer... Saer... why does that sound familiar to me?"

"More than likely because her father served the earl in the wars against Mortimer," Mathias replied, claiming a metal cup full of rich red wine. "They called him The Axe because that was his weapon of choice."

Henry's brow furrowed. "The Axe," he hissed. Then, his face washed with recognition. "I seem to remember a Saer de Lara on campaign for young Edward's father. The Axe, did you say? I do recall him, I believe, but this man traveled with a whore wherever he went. I remember this because when he was done with her, he would hire her out to other knights. I think her name was Abbey. Could it be the same man?"

Cathlina's mouth flew open in outrage. Mathias could see the storm coming and he clamped his hand over hers, silently begging her to be still. He could feel her trembling with rage and shock.

"Even if it is, do you think it entirely appropriate to discuss those details with his daughter?" he said in a tone that conveyed his displeasure. "I believe you owe my wife an apology. That was most tactless."

Henry looked surprised by Mathias' statement and even more surprised by Cathlina's red-faced expression. When he realized what he had said, he started to chuckle.

"Aye, I suppose it was," he said, taking another drink of his wine. "My lady, I do apologize. Sometimes I speak before I think, especially when I have had a half a bottle of wine. I pray I did not offend you overly."

Cathlina didn't say anything; she averted her gaze, staring at her lap. She was afraid that she was going to blast the foolish man with insults so it was best not to say anything at all. As a large trencher of mutton and gravy was put in front of her, and then the others, Henry continued on as if nothing slanderous had occurred. He focused on Mathias.

"You will leave on the morrow for Kinghorn Castle," he said. "As I told you earlier today, it is a small outpost near the sea, only a Pelé tower and enclosure really, but it is strategic. It stands at an important port and is a two day's ride to the east."

Mathias and Stephen were listening carefully. "Aye, my lord," Mathias replied. "We shall be prepared to depart at dawn."

Henry nodded his approval, his gaze moving between Mathias and Stephen. Today had brought unexpected reinforcements to his upper command structure and he was deeply pleased. He glanced at Balliol before he spoke.

"There is something more that we did not discuss with you earlier," he said, lowering his voice. "I wanted to be quite sure with Balliol before telling you, but know this; we are not sending you to Kinghorn simply to man an outpost. We are sending you there to be the first contact for the rebel force with is due to land at Kinghorn within the next month. With King Edward's approval, we have more than eighty ships in several Yorkshire ports awaiting word to sail to Scotland to once and for all claim the throne for the House of Balliol. The armada is under orders to make port at Kinghorn, where they will be met by you. You will lead the army into Scotland under the flag of Balliol and take them straight to Perth, where I will be waiting with the majority of my army. The infant David and his regent, the Earl of Moray, are in Perth. It is time to end this once and for all."

So it was a battle march. Mathias and Stephen understood all too well. "The king made no mention of this to me, nor did de Lara," Stephen said.

"It has been in the process for some time," Henry said confidently. "Mayhap they wanted me to tell you directly. In any case, you now fit quite nicely into those plans."

Mathias digested the information. "How many men will sail?"

"Two or three thousand. It will be a sizable force." Henry sat back in his chair, his somewhat amused gaze passing between Mathias and Stephen. "You have both done this before, on a much greater scale. Before me I have the two sides of the greatest battle for the English throne our country has ever seen – Mortimer's forces against young Edward's. With your skill and knowledge, victory for Balliol is assured."

So there it was, all of it. The discussion they'd had earlier in the day didn't allude to what the true purpose was for sending them to Kinghorn. Now they knew. Mathias couldn't even think about what he had brought Cathlina into; certainly, when he'd decided to flee to Scotland to join de Beaumont's forces, he knew he would be exposing her to some level of danger but he had been confident he could protect her in all aspects.

Now, there was a massive battle on the horizon and at some point he was going to have to leave her to fight. He already knew he would have to leave either his father or Sebastian behind to protect her, and he knew neither one of them would take it very well. Unless, of course, he sent her back to Kirklinton.

He sighed heavily, realizing that sending her home was the only safe thing to do. He was getting in over his head here in Scotland and he could not lose control of the situation where it pertained to his wife. As he mulled over the circumstances and what he must do about it, something suddenly whizzed by his head.

Startled, he grabbed Cathlina and forced her to get down as Sebastian and Stephen bolted to their feet. Across the table from them stood several men, all of them glaring daggers at Mathias. Before Mathias could say a word, Sebastian unsheathed his broadsword and leapt onto the table.

"You bastards," he snarled, kicking aside food and drink, and splashing a nearly full cup of wine on to Cathlina. "You will answer for that."

Broadswords were being unsheathed. Mathias thrust Cathlina at his father. "Get her out of here," he commanded. "Take her back to our rooms and bolt the door."

Justus pulled Cathlina away from the table as Mathias and Stephen unsheathed their weapons. Sebastian threw himself at the group of men who had thrown the pewter cup at Mathias' head, swinging sword and fist. He was an animal. Mathias and Stephen jumped into the fray as Henry and Edward quickly moved away from the table and out of the range of the fight. They ended up moving with Justus and Cathlina as they headed for the exit. Inside the hall, the battle was on.

Shouts of 'Mortimer's dogs' could be heard as the room deteriorated into a full-scale brawl. Evidently, there were three or four men who had fought for young King Edward and they knew who Mathias was purely by reputation. The fact that Stephen of Pembury was with him had no bearing; they were out for Mortimer blood and went after Mathias and Sebastian with a vengeance. Some men scattered but some stayed to fight; over near the hearth, there was a beating happening.

Mathias had been set up on by two men, trying to drag him to the ground and kill him. But he was faster, and better, than they were; using his massive elbow, he smashed one man in the face, effectively disabling him, while he pummeled the other man with an enormous fist. The broadsword, gripped tightly in his left hand, didn't come in to play until the man pulled a long, slender dirk on him, and at that point, Mathias brought his sword up and gored the man in the belly.

It was a bad fight. Pembury , with his size and strength, had wiped through four men and was looking for more as Sebastian, yelling and grunting, had disabled three. Then he began to run after other men who were attempting to flee. All the while, Cathlina and Justus were over near the door, watching the chaos when they should have very well left; Justus was watching because he very much wanted to be a part of it and Cathlina was watching because she was terrified for Mathias. She was very afraid something awful was going to happen to him.

But she had nothing to worry over. Once Mathias was finished with his two opponents, he fended off two or three more, easily disabling or dispatching him, depending on whether or not they pulled a weapon on him. His fists were like battering rams, destroying all they touched, and his sword, having not seen action in well over a year and a half, glittered wickedly as it did as God and Mathias intended. It was an instrument of death, and Mathias used it with uncanny skill. It was truly something to behold.

"Cathlina," Justus tugged on her. "We must leave. If Mathias sees that we are still here, he will become angry."

Cathlina knew that but she couldn't seem to tear her gaze away from him. It was mesmerizing. Unfortunately, Mathias caught sight of her, too, and his normally calm demeanor flared. He was furious that his father hadn't taken her to safety, furious that Justus has allowed her to see such carnage. Storming across the hall and punching one fool who tried to come at him, he caught Cathlina just as she and Justus were trying to make their escape.

Tossing his wife up over his shoulder, he planted a trencher-sized hand on her bottom to let her know of his displeasure. It made him feel much better so he did it again, listening to her howl. She had disobeyed him and now she was going to pay the price. Carrying his yelping wife off across the bailey, Mathias took Cathlina to safety himself.

Justus ran back inside and joined the last of the fight.

CHAPTER EIGHTEEN

Cathlina had only seen the sea once in her life, and that had been when she was a small girl. Her father had taken the family to the sea near Maryport in Cumbria where they had spent a week with one of Rosalund's cousins. Cathlina had loved the sea, the power and majesty of it. Now, as they drew near Kinghorn, she could smell the salt in the air.

In the summer season, the weather was beautiful and pleasant. There was no need for cloaks or heavy clothing during the day; in fact, as they drew near the coast, Cathlina was clad in a simple linen surcoat with a wide neckline and a soft linen shift beneath, and she was perfectly comfortable. The sun was warm and she would close her eyes, turning her face upwards to bask in it. It was perfectly lovely.

Seagulls screamed overhead, perhaps at Midgy who was running along beside the party from the Devil's Den. There were all manner of road ditches containing water, and they had passed several lochs and ponds on their journey, and Midgy made sure to swim and frolic in every one of them. He also caught himself several fish, gorging happily. Cathlina didn't worry about him because he always stayed close and even if he fell behind because he was swimming, he always caught up. He was a happy boy.

Cathlina was happy as well. Mathias rode ahead of her astride a big silver charger that Pembury had brought north with him and Cathlina had found out that the horse had been .Mathias' before he had been stripped of everything. Mathias wore his custom-made armor with the Westbury crest emblazoned in the breastplate, also delivered by Pembury. It seemed that Stephen had held on to Mathias' possessions all of this time, waiting for the moment when he could return them to his friend.

Now, Mathias looked like the legends of old, the mythical knights who were larger than life. Even though he wasn't Baron Westbury any longer, he still wore his emblem with pride. As Midgy raced along the road beside them and slid through great puddles of mud, Cathlina directed her palfrey up to the front where Mathias was.

"Greetings, husband," she said.

He turned to her with a smile on his face. "Greetings, love," he said sweetly. "We should be at the outpost within the hour. It should be over the next rise."

Cathlina nodded, inhaling the sea air deeply. "This is so beautiful," she sighed. "Everything is so… so violent and primitive looking, like the rocks and the sea has collided here and the carnage is scattered among the hills. I have never seen anything like it."

He looked around at the sky and rugged landscape. "You should have been a poet."

Cathlina giggled. "I do not think I would be very good at that," she said. "I cannot write."

He looked at her over his shoulder. "But you can speak of beauty in such ways," he said. "I will write it down for you."

Cathlina shrugged, embarrassed, watching Midgy as the otter found another small pond and dived in. Even though the mood between them was light, and had been for two days, she still felt the need to clarify something.

"Am I forgiven, then, for not leaving the battle in the great hall the other night?" she asked softly.

A faint smile creased his lips. "You were forgiven the moment I spanked you," he said. "But you will not disobey me again."

"Never," she swore, eyeing him in his imposing and functional protection. "You look very handsome in your armor. Does the blue and yellow lion tunic belong to Westbury?"

He shook his head, fingering the tunic he was wearing over his armor. "Nay," he said. "This is de Beaumont's colors. The Westbury standard is black and white."

"Do you think you will be able to wear it again soon?"

He nodded, slowing his charger down so she could ride beside him. When she came close, he reached out and took her hand, gently holding it in his massive glove.

"Hopefully very soon," he said quietly. "That is why I am here, love. It is my hope that in fighting a war supported by King Edward to ensure my loyalty to him, a victory attained will once again restore me in the eyes of the crown. Everything I do, I do for our future. It is important to leave a legacy for our children."

Cathlina smiled as she thought on the children they would have, sons in their father's image and perhaps even a daughter or two that looked like her. She prayed nightly that they would be so blessed but as she thought on their children, she began to think of her own siblings. Those thoughts brought about images of her father and what de Beaumont had said about him. Her good humor faded.

"What do you suppose de Beaumont was speaking of when he said he thought my father traveled on campaign with a whore?" she asked. "Why would he say something so outrageous?"

Mathias shrugged. "He is an intelligent man but not very diplomatic," he said. "You must understand that he has known literally thousands of men in his lifetime. It would be so easy to mistake one for another. I am certain he was thinking of someone else when he spoke of your father."

Cathlina thought on that. "He did mention that the whore's name was Abbie," she said, almost in passing. "I have a sister with the same name."

"A coincidence."

"Are you sure?"

"I can always write your father and ask him if it would ease your mind."

She looked at him, sharply, only to see that he was grinning at her. Fighting off a smile, she shook her head.

"I am not entirely sure he would take it too kindly," she said.

Mathias laughed softly and kissed her hand, letting it drop gently. Midgy suddenly bolted onto the road, grunting and startling the horses, especially the big bay stallion that Pembury was now riding. The beautiful young horse had made the rounds from St. Hèver to Mathias to Pembury. As Stephen struggled to calm the animal, the group heard a good deal of howling off to the left.

Men in tartans of orange and black were descending on them, spilling out of a grove of young trees that backed up to a small range of rocky hills. There was quite a gang of them, unorganized, but they had significant numbers. Waving weapons and clubs in the air, their intention was obvious.

There was no delay in the reaction of the knights; they swung around to face the onslaught, bellowing orders to the infantry that had accompanied them from the Devil's Den. They were trained for war, cool in a crisis, and none calmer or more succinct than Mathias.

"Father!" Mathias yelled at Justus. "Take my wife and ride as hard as you can for the outpost. *Go*!"

Cathlina was swept up in the panic but she was only concerned for one thing at the moment. "Midgy!" she cried. "Where is he?"

No one could tell her. The otter was nowhere to be found and furthermore, Mathias was more concerned about people and not pets. He grabbed the reins of her horse, forcing the animal to move as Justus thundered up and smacked her palfrey on the behind. Both horses took off, tearing down the road towards the outpost while Mathias, Stephen, and Sebastian charged out to meet the incoming Scots.

As soon as Justus and Cathlina crested the rise in the road, they could see the outpost about a mile ahead. The sea was on the horizon, a glistening band of water that was clear and inviting. Had the circumstances not been so harrowing, the view would have been gorgeous and peaceful.

As it was, Cathlina hardly noticed. By the time they reached the outpost, the heavy iron gates were open and men were coming out to assist. She was weeping for her husband's safety and for her otter, which seemed to have disappeared. Justus quickly ushered her inside the enclosure and towards the small keep. When they reached the door, he practically shoved her inside.

"Stay here," he ordered, throwing her satchel at her in his haste. "Bolt the door and do not open it for anyone you do not know. Is that clear?"

Fearful, sniffling, Cathlina nodded. "It is."

Justus turned and ran back to his charger as Cathlina slammed the door. It was an old door, warped from the salt air, but very heavy and braced with big iron bars. She threw the massive iron bolt and stood there a moment, hugging her satchel and leaning against the door trying to catch her breath. She could hear shouts and movement out in the bailey, feeding her sense of fear.

Struggling to calm, she backed away from the door, holding her satchel tightly against her chest as if it would bring her some comfort and protection. Then she started to look around, at the dark and dreary stone prison with tiny lancet windows cut into the walls. The Pelé tower was small, smelling of mold and damp earth, and as her eyes grew accustomed to the darkness, she could see green moss growing at the base of the walls. There were water stains everywhere.

She was standing in a small entry with a low ceiling. Immediately to her right, she could see through the darkness a very steep and narrow flight of steps built into the thickness of the wall that led up to the dark first floor. The ground floor had just one room, it appeared, with a hard packed dirt floor, a table and a few chairs, a cold hearth, and possibly a well in the corner. She couldn't really tell but it didn't matter at the moment. It looked as if it had been well lived in. There was a single tiny lancet window cut high in the wall to allow for some ventilation and light.

Timidly, Cathlina mounted the narrow steps to the first floor. It was one big, open room with two small windows, a broken down rope bed, and other bedding strewn about the floor. It smelled like a sewer. There was also a small alcove that protruded over the stairwell and she peered from it, realizing it was a small watch tower of some kind. There were windows, very narrow and long, cut into it and she could see very well to the north and to the west. She could see the bailey below and how men were scrambling to the walls and how the great iron gates were now closed. Unable to see over the walls clearly, she took the second flight of steps cut into the wall and ended up on the second level.

This level also only had one big room and a privy cut into the same small alcove that was above the watch tower on the first floor. The privy had an even better view of the landscape and she could clearly see the battle going on to the west. Shocked, she stood up on the privy seat to watch the happenings. Having never seen a battle before, it was a frightening and awesome sight.

Cathlina stood there for a very long time watching the battle. It was far enough away that she couldn't make out any individuals, but she could clearly see the chargers, including the big silver beast, and that was how she started keeping track of her husband. Mathias was a very busy man.

Every so often he would disappear into a sea of men only to reemerge and then plunge back in again. For the first hour or so, men seemed to be in a big boiling mass and she could hear the cries over the wind. Then, the battle seemed to weaken somewhat and it became clear there were dead and dying on the ground as the bulk of the fighting moved closer to the outpost. Men on the walls of the castle watched the battle but no one made a move to assist, mostly because those they could spare were already in the fight and they didn't want to open the gates again and risk a breech.

The day drew long, the skirmish active, and the sun eventually set as the battle continued in the dusk. The old Pelé tower was becoming very dark and very cold, and Cathlina knew she needed to at least light a fire and get herself organized. Eventually, Mathias and the knights would return and she wanted to make sure they had some comfort after the horrific day. Climbing down off her privy perch, she went about her tasks.

The first thing she did was take stock of any supplies in the tower and she came across more than she thought she would. There was a stash of peat on the ground floor along with kindling and she was able to start a fire in the first floor hearth. The second floor hearth proved a little more of a challenge because as night fell, the fog rolled in and the air became very moist. Trickles of water dripped down the chimney to the second floor hearth and dampened things up quite a bit but Cathlina prevailed. When a fire was burning in the second floor hearth, she made her way down to the bottom floor again and inspected what she thought was the well.

It was indeed a well and the water level was high. Since men had been living in the tower, there were cooking pots and a store of food on the ground level. Cathlina inspected the sacks and scrap that were all organized, more or less, under a small table that was wedged into a corner.

She came across a sack of little brown dry beans, some dried turnips, hoards of dirty carrots, and a half-eaten fowl of some kind that was cooked until it was charred. There were also stiff brown chunks of dried meat that was very salty. Pulling forth a fairly large cooking pot from the remains in the hearth, she took a small bejeweled dirk out of her satchel, cut everything up that could be cut, and threw it all into the pot with enough water to fill it. Then she put the pot on the arm over the fire and let the snapping fire do the rest. She wasn't sure if the stew would be any good, but at least it would be something.

After that, she went to check the battle again to see that it had moved to the north but was still going on. The sun had almost set completely but the tower was fairly well lit thanks to the two fires burning. Growing anxious, and the slightest bit bored, Cathlina ended up cleaning up the remainder of the tower and fashioned beds from the blankets and other items strewn about. She knew that Mathias and the knights would return and she wanted to make it as comfortable as possible for them. Moreover, it was easier not to think of what horrors might befall her husband if she was busy doing something. She had to stay focused. She had to prepare for Mathias' return.

By midnight, in spite of her best efforts to stay awake, she fell asleep in a chair next to the fire.

***

Mathias had no idea how long he had been pounding on the old iron door to the tower when it finally opened. It was the dead of night and he was carrying his father, who had been hit by an axe in the chest. Justus was very conscious, and very active, and trying very hard to pretend his wound wasn't bad when it was. Once the tower door opened, he shoved inside and dragged his father along with him.

Cathlina gasped when she saw Justus being carried in by his son. "My God," she said. "What has happened to him?"

As Mathias set Justus down in the nearest chair, Sebastian and Stephen entered the tower. They were dirty and somewhat roughed up, but neither was injured. Mathias made sure his father wasn't going to topple over before turning to his wife.

"An axe wound," he said, his voice hoarse from exhaustion. "He took a blade squarely to the chest although the mail stopped it somewhat. It could have been much worse."

Cathlina had never seen a battle wound before. In fact, she had never even been around a battle until today. She stood there, unsure what to do, as Mathias and Stephen began pulling Justus' protection off. They moved carefully and with skill. Cathlina struggled not to become ill at all of the gore.

"What can I do?" she asked her husband. "Please tell me what I can do."

Mathias was trying to pull the damaged mail coat off of his father's chest without causing the man too much pain. Pieces of the mail were stuck in the wound, which was starting to coagulate. Stephen seemed to be guiding him, instructing him quietly on how to accomplish the task.

"Hot water," Mathias finally told her. "Can you find something to boil water in?"

Cathlina nodded eagerly and fled. She went on the hunt for a second pot she had seen while organizing the tower and soon came across it with some of the other items she had stacked up. Drawing water from the well, she filled the pot to the rim and lugged it over to the burning peat, setting it in the coals and trying not to burn herself in the process.

Meanwhile, Stephen had brought his saddle bags and pulled forth a big leather satchel shoved deep into them. As Cathlina watched curiously, he began pulling out all manner of mysterious instruments. There were things that looked like tongs and other things that looked like knives or hooks. Everything was made from either iron or steel, wrapped carefully in linen to protect it. Cathlina watched the man as he efficiently and concisely began arranging what he would need to tend Justus.

Mathias was standing over his father, trying to keep the man calm. He was also watching Stephen work. When he glanced up and saw his wife standing a few feet away, watching everything going on with apprehension and concern, he caught her attention.

"Are you well, love?" he asked softly.

Cathlina looked at him as if he had gone mad. "Am *I* well?" she repeated. "God's Bones, Mat, you are the one who just fought a battle. Are *you* well?"

He smiled faintly. "Well enough," he said, watching her as her attention was repeatedly drawn to Stephen and what the man was doing. "Stephen is a healer, and one of the very best in all of England. He used to be a Hospitaller knight. He will heal my father."

Cathlina had heard of the Hospitaller order, men meant to tend to the sick and poor pilgrims in the Holy Land but who were also fearsome fighters. She had never met one before and was properly awed. Before she could voice her respect, however, Stephen spoke.

"Mat," he said, hovering over Justus as the man slouched back on the chair. "I must cauterize this wound. You must put this on the fire and get it nice and hot."

Mathias went to Stephen's side, accepting the small iron implement from him to put upon the fire to heat it. It was about as long as a man's forearm with a flat end. As he tried to stoke the heat in the hearth so they could get a proper burn on the end of the instrument, Sebastian came up behind his father and put both hands on his shoulder to steady him. Cathlina thought he seemed particularly subdued, unusual for the normally fiery man. He was exhausted like the rest of them. When their eyes met, she smiled timidly.

"Are you well, Sebastian?" she asked.

Sebastian nodded his head, returning his attention to what Stephen was doing. "I am," he said, pausing for a moment. "I... I tried to look for Midgy. I did not see him at all, but with all of the water around here, I am sure he has found a safe place. I will look for him again in the morning."

Cathlina was touched and saddened; touched that he should go to the trouble and saddened because her beloved pet was still missing. "You *do* like Midgy," she said to him. "You pretend not to care for him but I know you do."

Sebastian pursed his lips irritably. "Untrue."

She smiled as she made her way over to Sebastian and Justus, putting a hand on Justus' arm as she focused on Sebastian.

"You are not telling me the truth, Sebastian de Reyne," she declared, though it was gently done. "I know you are just as worried as I am."

Sebastian looked away. "You are mad."

Cathlina laughed softly, looking to Justus as Sebastian tried to avoid her. "And you?" she said, squeezing the old man's arm. "You will be none the worse for the wear when this is all over. I will feed you great and fattening things while you recover."

Justus looked up at her, a strained smile on his face. "I would hope you would tend a foolish old man," he said. "In fact, I smell something cooking now."

Cathlina gestured towards the floor above them. "I found some food scraps and put a stew in a pot," she said. "I do not know how it will taste but at least it will be something warm."

Justus merely nodded, grunting because Stephen was picking bits of mail out of the wound. Cathlina smiled encouragingly at him as she patted his arm one last time and returned to Mathias, who was kneeling by the hearth and trying to work up a substantial flame. It was the blacksmith in him, the innate ability to heat metal. She crouched down beside him.

"Who were those men?" she asked softly.

Mathias was poking at the peat. "Scots from Clan Wemyss," he said. "They have been harassing the outpost fairly steadily for months now. This was just another raid."

Cathlina pondered the statement. "There seemed to be a lot of men."

"There were enough."

"Did they go home?"

He nodded. "They did indeed," he replied. "But they will be back. The outpost commander says they have been hitting harder and harder each time, with more and more men from other clans."

Cathlina leaned against his back, watching him as he fussed with the fire. "What does this mean? What will happen?"

Mathias didn't say anything for a moment. When he did, it was softly uttered as he turned to look at her sweet face, so close to his own.

"It means I should have never brought you here," he whispered. "I knew when I came here that I would be facing battle of some kind, but in my mind, you would be safely bottled up somewhere far from the fighting. It appears that it will not be the case. I cannot have you in the midst of hostile territory where fending off raiders will be a daily event."

She looked at him with her big brown eyes. "What will we do?"

He kissed the end of her nose. "As much as I loathe the thought, I fear that I must send you back to Kirklinton," he murmured. "I have no choice. I cannot have you here in the midst of a war."

Her brow furrowed and her eyes narrowed. She moved away from him. "You cannot send me home," she hissed. "You are my husband. My place is with you."

Mathias could see the brewing storm. "Love, I have no choice," he said. "I cannot take the chance that the next raid will tear down these walls and those barbaric Scots will get at you."

She was growing angry. "I can take care of myself."

"They will kill you after they have made sport of you. Do you understand what I am telling you?"

"You want to send me away!"

"I want you safe."

Infuriated, and sickened at the thought of going back to Kirklinton and being separated from Mathias, Cathlina opened her mouth to argue with him but noticed that Sebastian was listening. She didn't want him to overhear. Bewildered, angry, she turned away from the group and hastened up the stairs to the first floor.

Mathias let her go. With a heavy heart, he removed the cauterizing iron from the fire and brought it over to Stephen, who had Mathias and Sebastian hold their father down while he seared the wound.

Cathlina heard the howling on the floor above them and smelled the burning flesh. It scared her to death.

CHAPTER NINETEEN

Midgy came back the next morning. Sebastian had been out at dawn looking for the creature and found him swimming happily in a tidal pool near the castle. He had come right to Sebastian when the man had called to him. Sebastian had promptly wrapped the animal up in his rain cloak and carried him back to the outpost.

Cathlina had been thrilled, of course. She had thanked Sebastian profusely and then fed Midgy some tidbits of the dried meat. But that wasn't enough for the otter and when Stephen, Mathias, and Sebastian broke their fast with the remainder of the previous night's stew, Midgy sat up on his hind legs next to the table and had begged for food. They threw him a few pieces to keep him quiet. Then, he promptly trotted over to the well and threw himself in.

Cathlina gasped as she rushed to the well, watching her otter swim around in it about eight or ten feet down. Mathias and Sebastian got out of their seats and came over to watch.

"Midgy, come out of there!" Cathlina said as she lowered the bucket. "Get into the bucket!"

Midgy only wanted to play with the bucket. Sebastian shook his head at the antics and returned to the table while Mathias took the bucket rope from his wife and began hauling up the playful otter. Cathlina had hardly spoken to him since he told her of his intentions to send her back to Kirklinton and he didn't like the silence. It was their first true disagreement since they had known one another and his stomach was in knots. He'd hardly slept because of it.

Mathias watched his wife as she removed the otter from the bucket, scolding him, and then running after him when the creature made a break for the stairs and raced up to the first floor. Mathias followed.

The first floor was where they had brought Justus after Stephen had finished working on him. They had fashioned a pallet for him near the hearth to keep him warm and as Mathias mounted the top of stairs, he could see that the otter was trying to burrow in Justus' bed and the old man was trying to kick the animal out. Cathlina was on her knees beside the bed, grabbing the happy otter and pulling him out by his hind feet. She apologized to her father-in-law and the old man waved her off, fighting off a grin.

"He will not get any rest if you do not keep the otter away from him," Mathias said as he walked up on them. "I have no idea why that creature likes you so much, but he does."

Justus grunted, feeling weak and uncomfortable. "For the same reason women do," he said. "It is my blinding good looks."

Mathias shook his head as Cathlina giggled. "Frightening is more like it," he said, making a weak attempt to insult him. "How are you feeling this morn?"

Justus grunted as he shifted around, trying to find a comfortable spot. "Better," he said. "I will be on my feet by tonight."

Cathlina cocked an eyebrow. "I believe it is Stephen who will tell you when you can get on your feet."

Justus scowled at her. "I'll not take orders from that mountain of a man who fancies himself a competent healer," he scolded her. "If I want to stand, I will stand."

Cathlina bit her lip to keep from smiling. "You had better behave yourself or I will put Midgy back on the ground and let him burrow in your bed."

"I shall throw him out the window if you do."

Cathlina couldn't help the laugh as she turned away, carrying the otter with her. Mathias stood over his father for a moment longer even though he was cognizant of the fact that Cathlina was mounting the steps to the chamber they had slept in on the second floor. He waited until she was out of earshot before crouching beside his father.

"How are you really feeling?" he asked quietly.

Justus inhaled thoughtfully. "Very tired," he said. "But it will pass. I will heal."

Mathias nodded, his manner somewhat subdued. "I know you will," he said. "As you have healed many times in the past. You are immortal, I think."

Even in his uncomfortable state, Justus could see by Mathias' expression that something was amiss. More than that, he was intuitive when it came to his son. "What is wrong?" he asked quietly.

Mathias glanced at him. "What do you mean?"

"You are a sullen man with much on his mind. Why?"

Mathias averted his gaze, pausing a moment before answering. "I told Cathlina that I am going to send her back to Kirklinton," he said, his voice lowered. "She is understandably unhappy but I feel it is the right thing to do. With the impending battle march on the horizon, I must send her someplace safe and she would not be safe if she remained here at Kinghorn. Most importantly, I am at a loss as to who to send with her as an escort. You cannot go, I should not go, Stephen will not go, which leaves Sebastian. He will not want to go."

Justus sighed heavily, feeling pain in his chest as he did so. "She must leave immediately," he said. "Based on the viciousness of the Scots we saw yesterday, the longer she remains here, the greater the danger. I would not send her with a big contingent of men, however."

Mathias shook his head. "Absolutely not," he said. "It would attract too much attention."

"One knight should be sufficient."

"Who, then?"

Justus shrugged as much as his stiff body would allow. In the glow of the weak fire, his swollen eyes glittered at his eldest son. "You," he said softly. "You should take her. You would worry endlessly if it was anyone else no matter how much you trust them. Moreover, you must face her father with what you have done."

Mathias pursed his lips wryly. "He may very well throw me in the vault and you would never see me again."

"Then take her to Carlisle and let de Lara escort her back to her family.

Mathias liked that idea. "A better option."

"When are you leaving?"

"Tomorrow before dawn," he said as he eyed his father. "It will take us at least six or seven days to reach Carlisle and five to return if I am fortunate and the weather holds. I can move much faster alone. I will be gone two weeks at the most but hopefully less. There is a lot that could happen while I am away."

Justus knew what he meant. "We will ably defend the outpost in your absence," he said. "And if the ships from Yorkshire arrive, we will send you word. Will you be returning the way we came?"

"Aye."

"Then we will send someone to find you along that route should it come to it. Meanwhile, remove your wife. She is not safe here."

Mathias thought on that a moment longer before nodding his head and patting his father on the arm. "Your advice is sage," he said as he stood up. "My thanks."

Justus watched his son head for the narrow stairs that led to the second floor. He was such a proud and powerful man, and Justus had always been wildly proud of him, but he couldn't have been prouder of him at any time in his life than he was at this moment. The sometimes selfish and always arrogant knight he had seen through Mortimer's days had grown a heart in the last year and a half, but it was none more apparent than at this moment. Justus knew that the lovely Lady Cathlina had a good deal to do with that. She had made his son more than just a knight; he was a man now, and a good one.

Justus closed his eye and attempted to go back to sleep, ignoring the gentle argument that was now gaining steam over his head as Mathias explained to his wife the way of things from now on. As Justus tried to ignore the increasingly loud voices, he felt something around his feet. Lifting his head, he could see something moving in the covers, heading towards his chest. He wasn't surprised when Midgy appeared, grunting happily as he gave scratchy kisses to Justus' chin.

"Settle down, you silly beast," Justus said, positioning the otter so he wasn't lying on his wound. "Settle down if you want to stay here."

Midgy did. When Mathias descended the stairs an hour later, the first thing he saw was his father and the otter, all wrapped up in blankets, sleeping peacefully next to the fire.

They were both snoring.

CHAPTER TWENTY

The trip south seemed oddly faster than the trip north. Perhaps it was because Mathias was moving much quicker than he had on the ride north, as if he was being trailed by Scots and was working as hard as he could to put distance between his wife and danger.

Whatever the case, they left her brown palfrey behind and rode double astride his muscular silver charger because Mathias didn't want to have to worry about his wife on a separate horse. He wanted her with him, and on an animal he trusted. But most importantly, they kept the otter bottled up so he could not escape and run off, costing them valuable time. Cathlina had him swaddled up like a babe in her arms, and the otter rode fairly contentedly that way.

No amount of pleading or arguing could convince her to leave Midgy behind. Mathias had tried, Sebastian had even tried, but ultimately she refused to leave her pet. She was upset enough that Mathias was taking her hone and, in truth, he didn't have the heart to forcibly remove her from her pet, so he let the beast come along purely to keep her happy.

But Cathlina wasn't happy. She was miserable at the thought of being separated from Mathias, especially since he was evidently heading towards a massive battle, Scots against Scots, with the English participating purely for their own benefit. Mathias, her sweet Mathias, was in the middle of it. When they had come north, she knew why and she knew that he would be involved in military operations, but she had no idea the reality of it. A concept was one thing but the reality was quite different. The knowledge of it all was overwhelming her.

Mathias knew this and it ate at him. Cathlina had become increasingly distant from him since they had left Kinghorn to the point where they would ride for hours and not speak to one another. He tried to break the ice, to engage her in conversation, but she would barely answer him or not at all. She was nothing like the adorable chatterbox he had come to know. She was sullen and withdrawn no matter what he tried to do to break her out of it. Her behavior was tearing him all to pieces.

On the fifth day on the road to Carlisle, they entered Langholme near sunset. The river was flowing softly by the familiar town and the smells of cooking fires hung heavy in the air. It was the magical time of twilight and Mathias headed for the same inn where he and Cathlina had stayed on their way to Edinburgh. He hoped it would break her from her mood with only good memories associated with it. At that point, he was willing to give anything a try.

The man at the tavern remembered them and rented them the same cottage for the night. Mathias ordered a meal to be sent to them as Cathlina took her satchel, and the otter, and headed for the cottage down the narrow path towards the river. Midgy, smelling his home, leapt from her arms and immediately dove into the muddy river, swimming happily. Cathlina watched him for a few moments as Mathias unlatched the cabin door and took their possessions inside.

As Mathias started a fire, Cathlina remained outside, watching the otter play. There were other otters around, now coming out to join in the fun. As Cathlina stood there and observed, Mathias came out of the cottage and walked up behind her.

"You must be exhausted," he said softly. "Come inside and rest awhile. Our meal should be down shortly."

Cathlina shook her head, watching Midgy play. "I am not tired," she said.

Mathias sighed faintly. "Cathlina," he murmured. "Love, it has been days since you have spoken civilly to me. I realize you are upset; I am upset, but I do not want to spend my last few days with you in tense silence. Please do not shut me out. I cannot bear it."

Cathlina's gaze was still on the otter but she could feel his words like stabs to her heart. Her eyes began to fill with tears and before she realized it, they were pouring down her cheeks. Pain filled her, such as she had never known.

"This has all happened so fast," she whispered, lips trembling. "We have been living a fool's dream, Mathias; we married hastily, we ran from my father to Scotland so that you could restore your honor as a knight, and now we are returning home again, only I will be returning home in shame and you will be returning to Scotland to fight for glory. You have no right to take me home and leave me there alone to bear the shame for what we have done. It is cowardly."

Mathias' jaw ticked as he struggled not to become overwhelmed with emotion. "I am taking you home for your own safety," he said. "How many times do I have to tell you that? Would you rather stay in Scotland where your life would be in danger every minute of every day?"

"Why not?" she whirled on him, shouting. "Why *not?* Your life is in danger every minute of every day, so why not mine? You married me because you wanted to share your life with me, but you are not. You are casting me aside like so much rubbish because you do not want to be bothered with me. Your glory and your restoration of honor are far more important; I was convenient to you until a few days ago, until you learned what de Beaumont wanted from you, and now I am inconvenient so you are returning me where you found me."

He looked at her, horrified. "Is *that* what you think?" he asked, incredulous. "That I find you convenient or inconvenient depending upon my whim?"

"Aye, I do," she said, now in his face and matching him outrage for outrage. "There could be no other reason for taking me back to England. While you are at it, you should pin a note to my chest that says how sorry you are for taking me without permission but now that you are on your way to being a great knight again, you no longer have need of me."

He was pale with bewilderment and anger. "That is a horrible thing to say."

Cathlina wouldn't back down; the tears were falling with a vengeance. "I was a comfort and companion to you when you were just a smithy," she sobbed. "You loved me and found me charming, and all was well. But now that you are a soldier again, you no longer have need of me. I wish you were just a smithy again, Mathias; I hate the selfish warrior who loves battle more than he loves me."

He stared at her, astonished. She couldn't have done more damage than if she had stabbed him through the heart. Perhaps that physical pain would have been preferable to the emotional pain he was feeling at the moment.

"You once told me that you did not care if I was a smithy, a dishonored knight, or the bloody King of England," he said softly. "All you cared about was that we were man and wife."

She jabbed a finger at him. "I said that all I cared about was that we were together," she said. "Mathias, when you take me back to England, we will not be together. You will achieve your knightly redemption without me by your side. Is this really what you intended all along?"

Mathias sincerely didn't know what to say to her. He didn't want to admit that some of her words made some sense. He didn't want to acknowledge it.

"I love you, Cathlina," he said hoarsely, looking lost and defeated. "I am so sorry you feel this way, but it is not the truth. I swear to God, it is not the truth."

She wept painfully, turning her back on him. "Take me home, Mathias," she wept bitterly. "Take me home and then return to Scotland. But when your battles are over and your glory is restored, do not come for me. I do not want you to. I will never be the thing you love most in this world; your vocation and your world as a knight will. I will always come second."

Mathias could hardly breathe for the pain in his heart. In fact, he put a hand over his chest as if to hold in the anguish. He simply couldn't believe what he was hearing.

"What can I do to prove to you that you are the most importantly thing to me?" he begged softly. "Tell me what to do and I will do it."

Cathlina wiped at her face, clearing room for the new tears that were falling. She shook her head. "You will not do it."

"You cannot know that unless you tell me what it is."

She sniffled. "Do not go back to Scotland," she said. "Come back with me to Brampton and resume your life as a smithy. Forget you were ever a knight and let us live simply and without violence. Let us go back to those first days of our acquaintance when the world was so new and bright, and there were no battles to interfere in our world. I want it to be like that, always."

He sighed heavily and hung his head, mulling over her statement. "Is that what it will take?"

"Aye."

"You are asking me to leave my father and brother and friend behind, men who are depending on me to do what I said I would. They are depending on me to fight with them."

"I am depending on you to be my husband."

"I cannot do both?"

"You can if you take me back to Scotland with you so we are not separated."

"I will not put you in danger."

"Then you have a choice; give up de Beaumont's wars and return with me, or go fight for the Scots and forget you ever had a wife."

Mathias found himself weak with emotion, with the overwhelming stress of what she was saying. She was giving him no choice at all. He couldn't understand why she didn't see that.

"Before I took my wedding vows with you, I took another oath," he muttered, feeling despondent even as he said it. "I took an oath of the code of chivalry. I became a knight long before I ever became a husband. You are asking me to choose between you and a timeless code of honor that has become the very fabric of my being. As much as I love you, and I love you more than any man has ever loved a woman, I have an honor within me that cannot be undone, not even by you. I will not leave my father and brother and friend in Scotland, fighting a war that I dragged them in to. You know why I had to do this; I thought you understood a knight's heart, *my* heart, but I see that I was mistaken. All you can see is what you want to see and demand that I prove my love to you as if my word and actions are not good enough. I find that uncommonly selfish and petty. Tomorrow, I will take you back to Carlisle Castle and I will return to Scotland to do what I said I would do. When it is over, make no mistake that I will return for my wife, and we will be together until the end of my life. If you want to hate me for doing as I must, then I cannot stop you. I am sorry it has come to this."

With that, he turned and went inside the cottage, leaving the door open so she could follow. Cathlina, however, didn't follow; she stood there, staring at the spot she had last seen him standing, wondering how the situation had turned so terrible.

She loved Mathias; she loved him with all of her heart and, deep down, she knew he loved her too. She understood the chivalric code, but she also understood her own wants; her husband with her, safely, and not off fighting Scots who threw their axes into men's chests. It was a reality she couldn't accept and at the pinnacle of it was her terror that Mathias would never make it back to her. She was terrified that she was going to lose him.

Breaking down into painful sobs, Cathlina collapsed right there on the river bank with Midgy frolicking several yards away.

When Mathias came out of the cottage an hour later to look for her, he found her sleeping the sleep of the dead on the cold river bank. Sweeping her into his arms, he hugged her tightly as he took her back to the cottage. When they slept, it was in each other's arms.

***

She could feel his hot breath on her neck.

It was early morning as the sun strained to break free of the horizon, sending pillars of golden light through the window, filling the tiny cottage with illumination. Cathlina and Mathias were burrowed down deep in the little bed, smothered by covers in their warm and wonderful world. Cathlina could feel Mathias' massive body wrapped around her, his naked hip next to her hand. Feeling him, smelling him, brought about warm and passionate feelings. Half-asleep, Cathlina stroked his hip with her hand, wriggling her bum back against him.

Mostly asleep, Mathis still responded to her, as he always did when she was close. There was something about the woman that sent liquid fire through his veins that he could not control. She was still clad in her surcoat and shift from the night before but his hands snaked up her skirts as his mouth latched on to her ear. She trembled giddily as he suckled a sensitive little lobe, his hands already pulling her legs apart and pushing her skirts out of the way.

Cathlina groaned as he entered her from behind, thrusting deep into her heated and moist body. He held her pelvis against his as he found his rhythm, performing the primal mating ritual that joined his body to hers. He pulled her left leg up, holding her fast so he could gain more freedom of movement as his mouth moved to her neck and gently nibbled. The more he thrust, the more inflamed he became, biting her shoulder and listening to her gasp with the pleasure-pain of it. Letting go of her leg, he flipped her onto her back and mounted her once more, long and hard.

Cathlina was swept up in their love making, her hand on his face as he repeatedly impaled her on his enormous phallus. Mathias kissed her deeply, his tongue invading her sweet mouth, tasting her as if he was feeding a massive hunger that refused to be sated. He pulled at her surcoat, freeing her breasts, and his tongue lapped up the tender nipples greedily as he continued to thrust. A hand moved to the junction where their bodies were joined and he rubbed her mound, feeling her buck and gasp beneath him.

When she finally found her pleasure, he answered with a massive climax of his own. His seed was spilled, filling her deeply and fully, and he whispered his love for her over and over, telling her how very much he adored her. Exhausted, Cathlina kissed him tenderly before snugging down against him and falling back asleep.

Mathias, however, remained awake. Even though the sun was rising and they needed to start their day, he was loathed to get out of bed, wallowing in this delicate cocoon of warmth and love. After the night they'd had, the things that had been said, he wanted to forget it all like some horrible nightmare. Worse still, he was coming to wonder if she wasn't right; was his knighthood more important than her? Was he being selfish? He didn't think so, and he hated it when he started to second-guess himself. As Cathlina snored softly, he carefully disengaged himself from her and got out of bed.

Mathias was very quiet as he donned his clothing but once he began to put on his armor, the noise awoke Cathlina. He passed a glance at her after putting on his noisy mail coat and saw that she was awake and looking at him. He smiled timidly.

"Good morn, love," he said softly. "Did you sleep well?"

Cathlina nodded, sitting up in bed as she watched him pull on his hauberk. "I did, but I had a horrible dream," she said, rubbing her eyes. "I had a terrible dream that we quarreled."

His jaw ticked faintly as he straightened out the mail hood. "That was no dream," he muttered. "I am afraid we did quarrel. I am sorry if I hurt you; you know I would never knowingly do that."

Cathlina blinked her sleepy eyes, thinking back to the previous night and the things that were said. She started to get misty but rubbed her eyes again to mask it.

"Then nothing has changed," she whispered sadly. "You are still taking me home and then returning to Scotland without me. I do not know why you should apologize for choosing your own wants over mine."

He didn't want to start arguing with her again. He put his shoulder protection on and began strapping it to the breastplate. "I have a duty, Cathlina," he said softly. "I am sorry if you cannot understand that."

"You have a duty to me as well. I am sorry if *you* cannot understand that."

"I will not have this conversation with you again. The subject is closed."

Cathlina shut her mouth. Silently, she climbed out of the bed and began stripping of her clothing, completely ignoring Mathias as he finished dressing. There was a bucket of water on the table and she proceeded to pull out a clean shift, clean surcoat, her precious lavender soap and a rag. As Mathias pulled on his boots, she stood in her shift and washed her face, neck and arms, rinsing off in the very cold water and drying herself with the hem of the shift she was wearing.

As Mathias finished dressing and just sat and watched, she pulled off the shift she was wearing, exposing her luscious nude body to the weak morning light. Mathias inspected her hungrily, her sweet curves and remembering how they tasted upon his tongue. But she quickly covered up, pulling the clean white shift on and then a red linen surcoat on over it. In little time she was completely dressed, braiding her hair into one thick braid and draping it over one shoulder. All the while, Mathias sat and watched her, feeling the pain of their disagreement like daggers. It was all he could do to breathe.

When Cathlina had finished dressing, she packed everything up in her satchel and opened the front door, calling for Midgy. She was back to ignoring him so Mathias quit the cottage and went to the livery to collect his charger as his wife tracked down the errant otter. He paid the stable boy to groom and saddle his horse, and by the time he returned to the cottage, Cathlina was standing on the riverbank sniffling. He went to her.

"Are you ready to leave?" he asked. When she turned around and he saw that she was weeping, his manner softened. He thought it was still because of him. "Love, I am truly sorry you are so upset but I will not continue to discuss it."

She shook her head and wiped at her eyes, pointing to the river. "It is not that," she said. "Midgy has not come back. I fear he is gone."

Mathias could see that she was genuinely upset and his hawk-like gaze perused the area. "This is where we first found him," he said gently. "Do you suppose he has returned to his family? It is quite possible, you know. I would not worry that something has happened to him. He more than likely simply went back to his family."

"Do you think so?"

"I do."

She was sobbing softly, looking over the river. "I hope not," she said. "I will miss him so."

Even though she was angry with him, Mathias threw caution to the wind and put his arms around her, kissing her forehead. To his surprise, she didn't stiffen or pull away. She continued to sniffle softly, watching the river and hoping her otter would make an appearance. But there was no sign of Midgy. Mathias sighed softly.

"We cannot wait for him," he said gently. "We must be on our way."

"Can I call for him a little longer?"

He wriggled his eyebrows and released her from his embrace. "Just a few more minutes and then we really must leave," he told her. "I will go to the inn and procure some food for the journey, and we will leave when I get back."

Cathlina nodded and began walking the river bank, calling for her pet. Mathias watched her a moment, feeling sad for her, for the situation in general, before heading up the path to the tavern. By the time he returned nearly an hour later, as he wanted to give her plenty of time to hunt for her pet, he found her sitting outside of the cottage with her satchel in her lap, waiting for him. When he walked up to her, she didn't look at him. Her gaze lingered on the gently flowing river.

"Midgy has not come back," she said sadly.

Mathias sighed softly, his gaze moving out over the river. "We cannot spare more time to look for him now but if it will make you happy, I will return when time allows to search for him."

"Promise?"

"I do."

She squared her shoulders. "Then we may leave now."

Mathias knew how she must be hurting but he respected the fact that she was trying to be strong about it. He grasped her elbow gently and helped her to her feet, not saying a word. At the moment, he wasn't entirely sure what to say. They were facing a difficult enough day ahead without the added sorrow of the missing pet. No, he wasn't sure what to say to her at all.

The horse was waiting by the tavern, tied to a wooden post shoved deep into the ground. The dirt was surprisingly dry and dusty in the mid-summer season and the lower legs of the silver charger were already a dusty brown. As Mathias escorted her to the charger, they passed by a towering rose vine that grew up all around the south side of the tavern and was bursting with small white roses. Cathlina reached out and plucked a piece of the vine that had four or five roses on it. She held it to her nose as Mathias lifted her up on to the charger.

Mathias mounted behind his wife, collecting the reins of the charger and directing the animal onto the main road south. All the while, Cathlina sat silently in front of him, smelling the roses. When they took the bridge over the river, she didn't look to see if Midgy was anywhere to be found. It was as if she had given up. There was too much on her mind and Midgy was the last straw. When they were about a mile south of the town, Mathias heard her break down into soft sobs. Whether it was for him or the otter, he didn't know. He didn't even ask, for nothing he could say would ease either situation. He didn't want to make things worse. She withdrew completely, and Mathias let her.

He let her cry.

CHAPTER TWENTY ONE

Tate de Lara wasn't simply astonished to see Mathias and Cathlina ride into the outerbailey of Carlisle Castle; he was bloody well shocked. He had been in the gatehouse, a squat, intimidating red-stoned building, when a solitary rider had been sighted coming in from the northeast. Tate had paid very little attention until he happened to see the rider at close range and realized there were two people astride the charger. Moreover, he recognized the charger. Mathias and Cathlina were returning.

He had sent a soldier running for St. Hèver, who was in the great hall, before making his way to the gatehouse entry about the time Mathias and Cathlina were entering. He moved quickly to the horse, looking up at the exhausted pair with great concern.

"What has happened?" he demanded. "Why are you here?"

Cathlina looked as if she had been weeping and Mathias, drawn and pale, handed her down into Tate's waiting arms. As Tate gently took Cathlina, Mathias dismounted behind her and handed his charger off to one of the any soldiers crowding around them. He followed Tate and Cathlina across the expansive bailey towards the enormous keep.

"Mathias, tell me," Tate asked again, his arm around Cathlina's shoulders. "What happened? Why have you returned?"

Mathias unlatched his helm and removed it, revealing damp dark hair beneath. "It is not safe for her in Scotland," he said simply. "I found Pembury and we subsequently located de Beaumont, but the wars he is fighting are more than we imagined. He is planning a full-scale invasion and he wants me to help lead it. He has nearly eighty ships prepared to set sail from Yorkshire ports to help him gain the throne for Edward Balliol, who is now in resident with de Beaumont."

Tate looked at him with surprise. "Balliol is with him? The last I heard, he was in France."

Mathias sighed wearily. "He is here now," he said. "He is very confident that he can wrest the throne from the infant David. He thinks the regent, the Earl of Moray, is one to be easily defeated. I am not convinced, however. I think the infant has more support than we realize."

Tate was seriously listening to him and not paying attention to Cathlina at all. "Why would you say that?"

They were drawing near to the keep now and Mathias could see Toby emerge, shielding her eyes against the morning sun to see who was approaching. As Cathlina scurried forward ahead of the men, Mathias and Tate came to a halt and faced one another.

"Because de Beaumont is convinced that he will have superior numbers to reinforce him from England," he said quietly. "The man is experienced and intelligent, but he does not seem to realize that he is in Scotland siding with Scots that are just as passionate about Balliol as Moray is about the infant. Moreover, Moray commands thousands and even now, de Beaumont cannot have more than eight hundred men. I have seen the thin numbers for myself."

Tate listened to him carefully. When Mathias was finished, he sighed heavily as he pondered the information. "Is this true? I can hardly believe it."

"It is true."

Tate simply shook his head in disbelief. "I wonder if King Edward knows this."

"If he does not, he should," Mathias said. "But it will take weeks for the news to reach him. We cannot wait for direction. What is happening in Scotland is happening now, which is why I brought Cathlina home. Although I had hoped to start a new life with her in Scotland, it is too dangerous for my liking. I will have to bring her home and pray her father forgives us for marrying without his blessing."

Tate tried to sound confident. "He will," he said. "The man is not unreasonable, and he will appreciate that you thought of his daughter's safety by bringing her back to England. Moreover, if the danger is as bad as you say it is, you would be ineffective because you would be worrying about her constantly."

Mathias lifted his eyebrows in an ironic gesture. "Cathlina does not see it that way," he said. "She thinks that I am abandoning her and that I no longer have use for her now that I am once again a knight."

Tate was pensive. "Women do not often times see what it is that makes us do what we do," he said. "It took Toby years to accept that I am a fighting man and that war is in my blood. It does not diminish my love for her."

"I wish Cathlina saw it that way."

Tate clapped him on the shoulder and turned him for the keep.

"Leave her here with us," he said. "Toby will explain what it is to be a warrior's wife. Mayhap she would take it better from another woman."

Mathias nodded. "I will admit that women are mysterious creatures," he muttered. "Sometimes it is so simple to speak with her, then other times...."

Tate grinned as they prepared to mount the steps to the massive keep. Toby and Cathlina stood at the top of the steps, Cathlina in Toby's embrace. Tate and Mathias gazed up at the pair with expressions of fear, awe, and respect.

"I understand you completely," Tate murmured. "They are indeed mysterious creatures. Come into the keep and let us discuss this over a pitcher of ale."

Mathias balked. "I cannot," he said. "I must return to Scotland immediately. I have only come to deliver my wife for safekeeping."

"And so you have," Tate replied. A flash of armor caught his attention and he turned to see St. Hèver heading in their direction from the stable block. He gestured at Kenneth. "It sounds as if you could use reinforcements. Mayhap I should send Ken with you."

"I would take him gladly."

Kenneth jogged up to them, his concerned attention on Mathias. "What are you doing here?" he asked the same question Tate had. "What has happened?"

"Rumblings in Scotland," Tate answered for him. "Mat has brought his wife back here for safekeeping, but it sounds as if the entire country is about to tear itself apart."

Kenneth wasn't surprised. "De Beaumont is a skilled military man and a deft politician," he said. "He is also a troublemaker. What seems to be the issue?"

"Eighty-eight ships preparing to sail from ports in Yorkshire to deliver English support for Edward Balliol, who has arrived from France and is now prepared to assume his role as king with de Beaumont's support," Mathias said. "The situation is more critical than we suspected."

"Did you find Pembury?"

"I did. He is in the middle of it with me, as de Beaumont has asked me to aid him in leading the charge."

Kenneth's gaze lingered on Mathias for a moment before turning to Tate. "I am bored to tears here in your happy little earldom," he said. "Short of going out and stirring up trouble just so I will have something to do, I would ask permission to return to Scotland with Mat and aid him in doing battle with the Scots."

Tate looked at the two of them, seasoned knights he had fought with innumerable times and, in Mathias' case, fought against him in heartbreaking moments. It had been a very long time since he had swung a sword with Mathias flanking him. Moreover, if what Mathias said was true and a massive battle for the Scots throne was imminent, then perhaps it would be prudent if he was a part of it, too. Edward Balliol on the throne would be allied with young King Edward and Tate, as always, fought for young Edward's interest. Aye, perhaps it was time he be a part of it.

"I am bored as well," he said after the moment. "But as you have asked permission from me, I must ask permission from my wife. Let me think about how to accomplish that without sending my wife through the ceiling in a fit of rage."

Mathias gave him an expression that suggested fear and hope. "May I attend you and study your technique? It would seem I am in need of a lesson on how to handle a wife."

Kenneth caught on to the intimation. "Are you saying that you cannot handle that tiny woman you married? Mat, I am shocked."

"Don't be. I am willing to admit I am a novice where marriage is concerned."

"Let me guess; she does not want you to go to war and leave her here."

"How did you know?

"Because I have seen it too many times. You are not alone, my friend."

Tate began to head towards the keep. "Come along," he said to the two of them. "Come and witness my superiority when handling my wife."

"I would wager on Toby's superiority first," Kenneth said.

As Tate and Kenneth chuckled, Mathias grinned only because they were. He felt no humor. All he could feel was the abject sorrow with the situation between him and Cathlina, terrified that he would leave to return to Scotland and things would never be the same between them. He had been questioning his decision to return for a few days now because so many things she said to him made sense. But there were things that didn't.

In any case, he had to leave before the day was out and he fully intended to hash things out with her before he left. There were things he had to say to her that she needed to hear, and he could only pray they would make a difference. He didn't want to see such a beautiful relationship wrecked because of bad decisions or misunderstandings.

One he left for Scotland, he could only pray that he had a marriage to return to.

***

Although it was reluctantly, Toby indeed gave permission for her husband to take one thousand men into Scotland to aid Henry de Beaumont and Edward Balliol's cause. Because Tate was so close to the Scots border, he usually kept around two thousand men at any given time at Carlisle Castle, and another thousand at Harbottle Castle, another outpost about a day's ride to the east. Saer de Lara had eight hundred men at Kirklinton, men sworn to Carlisle, but Tate refrained from calling upon them. He didn't want to spread his resources too thin.

Because he had so many men to muster, it was later afternoon by the time he organized all of his men and had the quartermasters bring forth the wagons. Given that he didn't want to start a battle march at sun set, he made the decision to stay the night and start for Scotland before dawn. Mathias had made a push for leaving that day but when he saw that wasn't going to happen, he was secretly glad; it would mean one more night with Cathlina. Perhaps he could make her see his side of it.

Cathlina had spent the entire day with Toby as Tate, Kenneth, and Mathias went about organizing the troops. Even though Mathias was deeply involved in mustering the army, his thoughts kept drifting to Cathlina. Like the waves of the sea, crashing onto him again and again, thoughts of his wife tumbled down on him until he could think of little else. Already, he missed her, and he knew it was only going to get worse.

The sun was setting as they wrapped up the last tasks with the assembled army and told the men to eat and sleep early because they were departing before sunrise. Mathias, in the midst of mustering the army, brought up the subject of the Treaty of Northampton, part of the treaties established with Robert the Bruce before his death that, among other things, prevented the English armies from crossing north of the River Tweed.

Tate was aware of this, as was King Edward and every other fighting man in England, but Tate was clever – he broke up his army into several divisions, each one commanded by a knight or another senior soldier, with orders to cross the river in smaller separate units that could not constitute the definition of an army, and then join up into a collective group once they reached the outskirts of Edinburgh. It was a technicality but really all they could do if they didn't want to lose precious time.

With the army assembled and the logistics of their campaign north ironed out, the trio of knights headed up to the keep and entered the enormous structure with the great hall on the first level. When they entered, it was already warm and fragrant with the scents of rushes and roasting meat. As Tate headed for the feasting table, his children caught sight of him and rushed him.

Tate laughed with delight as his aggressive twins tried to take him down by the legs. Roman, his eldest, challenged his father with a woodened sword and Tate raised his arms in surrender. Meanwhile, Tate's oldest daughter, five-year-old Cate, went to Kenneth because her father was being mobbed and she liked Kenneth, anyway. She didn't know the tall, dark knight with him but eyed Mathias curiously as she took Kenneth's hand.

"Hello," she said.

Mathias smiled faintly at the beautiful little girl. "Good eve to you, my lady."

"Who are you?"

"My name is Mathias."

Cate inspected him a moment longer before deciding he was worthy of her attention. She took his hand, too, and led both Mathias and Kenneth to the feasting table. "Sit," she said.

They did. Cate planted herself between them, feeling quite special to have two big knights on either side of her. Servants began appearing, placing plates of freshly baked bread on the table, and Cate was happy when Kenneth broke apart a loaf and presented her with the warm, soft, white middle. As she chewed happily, Toby entered the hall from the stairwell with her youngest daughter on her hip.

"Good men," she greeted, watching her husband as he manhandled the wild twins into their seats. "How goes the troop movements in the bailey?"

Mathias and Kenneth had their wine in hand and were already drinking deeply as Tate replied.

"We are prepared and ready to depart before dawn," he said. "I intend to march straight through to Edinburgh where we will then take the ferry crossing to Dumferline. From there, I will hold the army stationery until I find out where de Beaumont is and the status of the situation. I will send you a missive at that point to let you know what is happening."

Toby wasn't particularly thrilled by any of it but she forced a smile as she sat her youngest child to the bench. She had been through this drill too many times not to have learned how to gracefully accept that which she could not change.

"I would appreciate that," she said. "You will also let me know how Mathias is so that I may tell his wife."

Mathias looked up from his cup. He could tell just by her tone that she must have had a long talk with Cathlina; it was, in fact, written all over her face as she met his gaze steadily.

"I did what I could, Mathias," she murmured. "I hope that it is enough. She is not unreasonable; she is simply frightened."

Feeling embarrassed and off-balance that someone else had to intervene in his personal problems, Mathias cleared his throat softly. "Where is my wife?" he asked.

Toby poured some boiled fruit juice for her younger children into small wooden cups. "I put her in a chamber on the top level," she said. "She has said she does not wish to join our meal. I thought mayhap you could persuade her otherwise."

Mathias averted his gaze, staring at his cup for a moment before silently rising from the table.

"Top floor, did you say?" he asked.

"First door on the left," Toby replied.

Mathias quit the great hall without another word. The stairs of the keep were built into a corner turret, spiral madness that connected all four levels. Mathias mounted the steps all the way to the top floor of the keep where there were three oak and iron doors fitted into the stone walls. He went to the door immediately to his right and knocked softly.

"Aye?" It was Cathlina. "Toby, truly, I am very grateful for your concern, but I am exhausted and simply wish to sleep. I will see you on the morrow, I promise.

"It is your husband," Mathias said quietly.

There was a very long pause before someone threw the bolt on the opposite side of the door. Very slowly, it opened, and Cathlina's face appeared in the dim light. Their eyes met and, for a moment, no one spoke. They just looked at each other. Finally, Cathlina spoke.

"I thought you had left," she said softly.

For some reason, her quiet statement enraged him. He shoved the door open, pushing her back, as he came into the room and shut the door behind him. When he faced her, it was with his hands on his hips.

"Do you truly think I would leave without bidding you farewell?" he demanded.

Cathlina backed away from him because of the hazard in his tone. "I...," she stammered. "I... I thought, well, that you were in a hurry so mayhap you had already rushed away."

He was growing increasingly exasperated. He pointed at the bed with a big finger. "Sit down."

It was a command and she knew it. Obediently, because she had never truly seen him enraged, she scooted over to the bed and planted herself. The mattress, a combination of straw and feathers, sank dramatically and pillows toppled off. Mathias picked up the pillows and threw them back on the bed angrily.

"Allow me to clarify something, Lady de Reyne," he said, standing in front of her. "I would never leave you without bidding you farewell, no matter how foolish you have behaved or no matter how badly you have hurt me. Are we clear on that fact?"

Cathlina, looking at him with big eyes, nodded. He continued. "Secondly, you are my wife. I have told you that I love you and that has not changed. I have, since the moment we met, showed you uncompromised attention and affection. I have never once intimated to you that my knightly honor was more important than you, nor do I love war more than I love you. I do *not* love war; it is my vocation and it is in my blood. It is a part of me. I am sorry if this is shocking to you, but you knew before we were married what my true vocation was and what my plans were. At no time did I surprise you with any of this, did I?"

He was looking for an answer and Cathlina was tongue-tied. As she shook her head, weakly, he sat down on the bed and threw his arms around her. She shrieked as he fell onto his side, taking her with him. Now she was trapped in enormous arms, feeling his heat and life. His hot breath was in her face as his eyes bore into her.

"You have behaved appallingly for the past several days but I tell you now I will no longer stand for it," he growled. "You are a grown woman and my wife, and your behavior is not befitting either position. You have married a knight and the sad fact of the matter is that knights fight battles. It is not because they want to but because they must. I do not want to leave you, but I must. Because you are the most important thing in the world to me, I must do all I can to ensure your safety and in this case it meant removing you from Scotland. It is because I love you more than anything that I do this. Am I making headway into your thick skull? I do not go to war because I want to but because I have to. My heart does not go with me because it is here, with you. I will return for my heart, and for you, because both are my world. This war I fight is because I said I would and for no other reason. Is this in any way unclear?"

By this time, Cathlina was looking rather beaten. "Mathias, I…."

He cut her off. "Tell me that you love me."

Her features softened. "Of course I love you," she murmured. "That is why…."

He cut her off again. "I know why," he said. "I know the reason behind everything. Now, will you *please* stop behaving like a spoiled child who is not getting her way in all things and start behaving like the wife of a great knight who loves her with all of his heart?"

Cathlina stared at him a moment longer before offering him a weak smile. "Are you telling me that I can never again pitch a fit, for any reason?"

"Never."

"That is not fair. I may have good reason some time."

"If you do, I will evaluate it at that time."

She giggled, putting her arms around his neck. Her small fingers caressed his dark head as she gazed into his dark green eyes. She relished the feel of him in her arms, his life and love against her. She couldn't hold out against him any longer; her anger was gone. She could no longer maintain it because her love for him was stronger than her fear.

"I am sorry if I hurt you," she whispered. "I did not mean to. I have no excuse except this is all so new to me. I do not want anything to interfere in our beautiful world, especially not a Scottish war. I suppose I did not know any other way to react than with fear and anger."

He was calming now that the situation between them was easing. He could only pray that she was truly seeing reason.

"I understand," he said softly. "But tomorrow, I ride for Edinburgh and I do not want to have to worry that you are harboring resentment towards me. It would destroy me, Cathlina."

"I would never resent you," she murmured. "But I do worry about you. Am I not even allowed to do that?"

"Of course you can worry. But do not take that fear out on me."

Cathlina sighed faintly. "I will try."

"Swear it?"

"I do," she agreed. "I… I am very proud of you, Mathias. I am proud of you whatever you do, whether you are a smithy or a knight. I told you that once before. I meant it."

He smiled faintly, cupping her sweet face with a big hand. "I know you fell in love with a smithy but ended up with a knight," he said. "All I ask is that you trust that I will always come home to you, Cathlina. And even when we are separated, know that my heart is with you."

"As mine is with you," she murmured, running her fingers across his lips and watching him kiss her flesh. "I do love you so, Mat. I am just so frightened for you."

"I know," he kissed her hand and then her forehead. "But, as I said, you must trust that I will return to you."

"I do," she said, closing her eyes as he hugged her close. "Please forgive me for being so cruel."

"There is nothing to forgive," he murmured into her hair. "But I will say this; I will miss you terribly. I look forward to my return more than you do."

She smiled, looking up at him. "Will you have me remain at Carlisle while you are away or may I return to Kirklinton?"

He tucked a stray bit of hair behind her ear that was tickling him in the nose. "That is your choice," he said. "If you wish to return to Kirklinton, I am agreeable. I am sure you want to see your family."

"I do," she admitted. "I miss Abechail and even Roxane. And I would like to see my parents. "

"Then you may go to Kirklinton if it makes you happy."

Thoughts of returning home brought about more thoughts of their future and what would become of them once he returned from Scotland. "Where will we live when all of this is over?" she asked. "I would like to think on something positive while you are gone."

He lifted his eyebrows thoughtfully. "Hopefully Westbury will be returned to me when de Beaumont's armies are victorious," he said. "We will be going to the Welsh Marches."

"I have never been there," she said. "What is it like?"

He thought on Alderbury Castle, a place he hadn't seen in a very long time. "Very mountainous," he said. "There are dramatic rivers and tall mountains, green hills and big valleys. I think you will like it a great deal."

"I am sure I will," she said, stroking his cheek. "I am looking forward to raising our children there."

He smiled faintly. "As am I," he murmured, kissing her soft mouth. "Many, many children."

His words were drowned out as he slanted over her lips hungrily, feeding on the adoration and passion he felt for the woman. All was well between them and that was all he cared about. He could focus on the army, and Scotland, tomorrow because tonight, all he could think of was Cathlina. He would give her every last bit of himself tonight and tuck the memories away to comfort himself with for times when he was feeling particularly lonely. Tonight, there was only the two of them, bathing in a warmth and a love that was only once told of in legend.

Tonight, it belonged to them.

CHAPTER TWENTY TWO

Two months later

August had burst upon the north of England in a riot of wildflowers. Everything that could possibly bloom was blooming because it had been very wet a few weeks earlier in the season and now it was sunny and warm. At Kirklinton Castle, it was now a game to coerce Saer into allowing the elder daughters out of the castle long enough to collect a wagonload of flower. He didn't like the girls out and exposed so much but he couldn't resist their begging, so he usually ended up escorting them to the meadows where the blooms were calling their name.

In spite of the glorious weather, Abechail's health had been in rapid decline the past few months but more succinctly in the last few weeks. She was confined to bed mostly now because she was too weak to go about her daily routine as she usually had. Rosalund had the servants move her bed near the windows so she could at least look outside and she spent most of her time feeling the warm caress of a breeze on her face and watching the birds ride the drafts. Still, no one spoke of her illness or her impending death. Rosalund wouldn't allow it and no one else was willing to face it, so Abechail fell into steady decline as the world went on around her.

Still, there was some joy in the de Lara household now that Cathlina was returned. She had come home about a month earlier, escorted by the Earl of Carlisle's men, rosy and beautiful and happy. She also happened to be Lady de Reyne and pregnant, although she hadn't figured it out yet until her mother had informed her what the symptoms her body was displaying meant.

Then, no one could be angry at her for running off and marrying Mathias, and Saer certainly couldn't be upset with Mathias considering where the man was and what he was doing. The escort from Carlisle Castle had been sure to tell him that he was now fighting in Scotland for Henry de Beaumont. Moreover, Mathias was to be the father of his grandson. Odd how old angers and prejudices towards Mortimer's former attack dog suddenly dissolved with a child on the way and the fact that he was now evidently a restored knight.

Therefore, now in mid-August, things were nearly normal again; Roxane and Cathlina argued from time to time, Saer spent a good deal of his time on patrol of Carlisle lands with the earl in Scotland, and Abechail and Rosalund spent most of their waking hours together. Life was good for the most part, and it was typical, and no one tried to think on the horrors hanging over their head. For now, they pretended it was all happy because it was easiest to cope that way.

The third week in August dawned warm and pleasant, as most of the days of the month had been. Cathlina rose before Roxane, as was usual, and called for warmed rosewater to bathe in. Surprisingly, she was feeling very well in early pregnancy with none of the illness that she'd heard tale about. Her belly was taut and slightly rounded, but that was the only sign that she was pregnant other than her womanly cycles had ceased. Daily she dreamed about telling Mathias of his son and wondering if his excitement would match her own. Hourly, she thought of him and of his trials in Scotland, praying he was well. She had become very pious over the past few weeks, praying daily at Kirklinton's small chapel for Mathias' safety and Abechail's health.

After she bathed, she donned a soft yellow surcoat and shift, of lightweight linen in the warmer temperatures, and braided her long hair in two pretty braids to keep her heavy hair off her neck. Then she scurried next door to Abechail's chamber and crawled onto the bed with her younger sister, who was just starting to awaken. Abechail giggled sleepily when Cathlina lay down beside her and gently tickled.

"Awaken, Abbie," she said, kissing her sister's cheek. "How are you feeling this morning?"

Abechail was as pale as death but smiled at her sister. "The same," she said. "How is the baby? I cannot wait to see him."

Cathlina fought back the gut-wrenching sadness of Abechail's future, instead choosing to indulge the girl. There was no use in doing otherwise; if she was to dream, make them great and pleasant dreams.

"You will have to wait until spring to see him," she said. "What do you suppose his name shall be? It should be something grand."

"What would Mathias name him?"

Cathlina shrugged. "We have never spoken of children. I do not know."

Abechail sighed faintly, her gaze inevitably moving to the lancet window near her head where she could see the brilliant blue sky beyond.

"A grand name would be an ancient and powerful name," she said. "Do you see the birds outside? There is a family of hawks in the stones near the gatehouse and I have given them all great names."

"What are their names?"

"Magnus, Maximus, Tiberius, and Lucius," she said. "I have named them after Romans."

Cathlina grinned. "Where have you heard such names?"

Abechail looked at her, a twinkle in her eye. "The same place you have," she said. "Father has told me stories of the Romans who used to live here. He said there was a Roman fort not far from here and Magnus, Maximus, Tiberius, and Lucius were the soldiers there who held off an entire clan of Scots one day. They were very brave."

Cathlina laughed softly. "I think that Father mayhap made the story up."

"It is a true story!"

Cathlina hugged her. "As you say, little pigeon," she said affectionately. "Now, then; do you feel like going outside today? Roxane and I found an entire field of blue bells nearby. You would love to see them."

Abechail's weary eyes lit up. "I would," she agreed. "Do you think we can go this morning?"

Cathlina nodded and climbed out of the bed. "I will go speak to Father now. I will return shortly."

Abechail had a bit of pink color in her cheeks at the excitement of going outside this day. Cathlina quickly left the chamber, nearly running her mother down in the landing outside the door. Rosalund had Abechail's morning meal in her hands and only by swift action managed to keep it steady when Cathlina crashed into her.

"Heavens, Cathlina," Rosalund exclaimed. "Slow down, child. You must take care of that babe you are carrying and tripping down the stairs in your haste will see him come to great harm."

Cathlina kissed her mother on the cheek. "I will not trip down the stairs," she assured her. "Abbie says she feels well enough to ride out today. May we go?"

Rosalund looked dubious. "I am not sure," she replied. "Let us see how she feels after her meal. Sometimes she sleeps the rest of the morning after she eats."

Cathlina knew that but she struggled not to let the mood dampen. "Very well," she said. "But I will go to the stables and have the carriage prepared anyway. Surely a small trip will do her some good."

Her mother didn't reply as she continued to Abechail's chamber, mostly because she would not comment on her daughter's impending fate and they all knew it. Replies were not expected. Cathlina therefore continued to the lower level of Kirklinton's keep and out into the mild summer day.

As she crossed the bailey and stopped to pet a friendly dog that usually hung around the great hall, she noticed that the portcullis was lifted and her father was speaking with several soldiers. She also happened to notice that they were bearing Carlisle colors. Curious, she headed towards the gatehouse. Perhaps it was news from Scotland and she was eager to hear it.

Saer saw her approaching from the corner of his eye, her yellow surcoat billowing in the breeze. He turned his attention to her even though the Carlisle soldiers were still speaking. When she finally came upon them, he held up a hand to silence the soldiers.

"Cathlina," he said. "I am glad you are here. It seems that we have news from de Beaumont's wars."

"Truly?" she was very excited to know. "What is it?"

Saer motioned at the sergeant from Carlisle. "This is my daughter, Lady de Reyne," he told him. "You will tell her what you just told me."

The sergeant bowed towards Cathlina. "My lady," he said. "I bring news of a great victory in Scotland at Dupplin Moor. Henry de Beaumont and his English allies have triumphed over a great Scots army. Edward Balliol is now upon the throne. We are told that your husband was instrumental in planning and executing a battle against a greater Scots force. He was victorious, my lady. Balliol owes his crown to him."

Cathlina was stunned but in the same breath, she felt nothing but pride and joy at that moment. She thought her heart my actually burst with it all.

"Is he well?" she asked eagerly. "What of the Earl of Carlisle and his other knights? Are they all well?"

The sergeant nodded. "We are told they all survived except for Sir Justus de Reyne," he said. "The man had been wounded in a previous battle and succumbed to his injuries."

The smile vanished from Cathlina's face. "He... he is dead?"

"Aye, my lady," the man replied. "His body was sent back to Carlisle along with the announcement of victory. Lady de Lara said we should come immediately to inform you."

Cathlina stared at the man a moment longer before glancing to her father. Then she turned away.

"Poor Justus," she murmured, struggling not to burst into tears. "Mathias must be shattered. Oh, my poor love."

Saer watched his daughter as she wrestled with her grief. He did not know Justus de Reyne but she obviously did and was saddened. He turned back to the sergeant.

"You were also telling me about Carlisle's concerns for our safety," he said. "You will continue."

The sergeant nodded swiftly. "Lord de Lara states that the defeated Scots have fled south and there is rumor that the Earl of Mar intends to attack Carlisle holdings in revenge for Carlisle's participation in the battle," he said. "If they do decide to attack, the earl and his army will not make it back in time to fend them off. You are to secure Kirklinton until the earl returns from Scotland and the threat can be more readily accessed. He fears the Scots will try to attack before he can reach home."

Saer could see all aspects of that potentially devastating information; if the Scots reached Carlisle or Kirklinton before Tate returned with the majority of his army, the results would be horrific.

"Is the threat credible?" he asked the man.

The sergeant was serious. "We were told that when the battle for the throne was over, the armies of the defeated scattered," he said. "De Lara fears they have scattered south and are heading our way."

Saer pondered that information carefully. "If that is true, then I think mayhap we should vacate Kirklinton altogether and ride for Carlisle Castle," he said. "Kirklinton is a smaller outpost and cannot withstand a massive Scots offensive."

"It would not be wise to leave now, my lord."

"Why not?"

The sergeant shook his head to emphasize his point. "You must not risk transporting your family over miles of open road," he said. "We have no idea where the Scots army is; they could be upon us tomorrow for all we know. You would be safer to stay here and reinforce your lines."

By this time, Cathlina had turned around and was looking at her father with some fear. He caught her expression, immediately thinking of the grandchild she carried. Nay, he could not risk her. He could not risk any of them. His instincts told him to get to Carlisle Castle for safety but he wouldn't go with his instincts. He would remain at Kirklinton because he couldn't chance getting caught on the open road.

Resigned, he was reluctant to agree.

"Then I shall do that," he said. "Who is in charge at Carlisle?"

"Sir Kenneth St. Hèver has come home with Justus de Reyne's body. He is in charge of Carlisle's defenses until the earl returns."

St. Hèver was a superb military commander; Saer knew that from his days fighting with the young king. Nodding curtly, he waved the sergeant on.

"Tell St. Hèver we shall hold tight here," he said. "I will await word from Carlisle when the threat has passed."

The sergeant saluted smartly and turned on his heel, taking the other Carlisle soldiers with him. As he went, Cathlina went to stand next to her father, watching the party from Carlisle mount their horses and depart. She lifted a hand, shading her eyes from the sun as she watched them fade in the distance. Once they were gone, she looked up at her father.

"Are you concerned?" she asked him.

He was but he didn't want to tell her that. It would only upset her. Forcing a smile, he put his arm around her shoulders and gave her squeeze.

"Nay," he said, brushing off the suggestion. "The Scots always bypass Kirklinton in favor of attacking the larger target of Carlisle. But just to be safe, we will lock ourselves up tightly until the earl tells us the threat has passed."

Cathlina began a slow trek back across the bailey, thinking of Justus and feeling very saddened over his death. The sergeant said that he had succumbed to a wound from a previous battle; it must have been the axe wound to the chest. Perhaps it had become infected. Whatever the case, his body had given out and now he was dead. Her heart truly ached for the old man she had become so fond of. She was sure Mathias and Sebastian were deeply grieved.

As she thought on Justus, she could hear her father in the gatehouse, shouting orders to the soldiers to secure everything tightly. So much for her journey with Abechail to see the flowers; she had a feeling it would be a very long time before they were allowed out of the castle. But her husband was alive and well, and that was all she truly cared about. She was deeply grateful.

The keep loomed before her and as she headed into the big stone structure, she thought of all of the things she could do for the day to keep busy. She was looking forward to some pleasant time with her sisters and mother as she awaited Mathias' return. They had sewing and other things to occupy their time; aye, it would be time well spent.

She had no idea that in a very short while, boredom would be the least of her worries.

CHAPTER TWENTY THREE

"I am sure, given your role in de Beaumont's victory at Dupplin Moor, that the king will restore everything to you and then some," Tate said, his mouth full of well-cooked mutton. "You have earned it and I will vouch for the fact. If I have not said this before, then I will say it was a pleasure to see you in action once again, Mat. I have missed you."

Seated around a fire in the midst of the southern Scottish moors, Mathias, too, was stuffing himself with mutton. They had two of the big beasts roasting on an open pit, sending succulent-smelly greasy smoke into the night air.

It was two weeks after the victory of Dupplin Moor and finally, they were returning to England. Mathias had voiced his thoughts on whether or not Edward would be receptive to allowing him to resume his knighthood for good and Tate had responded. In fact, Pembury, de Lara, and even Sebastian seemed to think it was a certainty that the Westbury barony would once again be Mathias' before the year was out.

"As I have missed you and the smell of battle in the air," Mathias said humbly. "Let us hope that the king is receptive to my petition to regain my honor, for I truly do not know what else I can do to prove my worth and loyalty to the king if my showing at Dupplin is not enough."

"There is nothing more to do. You have done more than any one man should be expected to. You have once again proved your superiority as a knight and as a tactician. Edward will gladly welcome your fealty."

Mathias was hopeful but tried to keep it contained. "I hope he will. I will eagerly give it."

Tate nodded as he shoved more meat into his mouth; it was the first time they had stopped in two days, following the trail of Scots heading south. Word had come a week prior when they were in Scone with de Beaumont, tying up the loose ends from the battle of Dupplin Moor, that an army of Scots led by the Earl of Mar were heading south into Carlisle lands. Tate had promptly rounded up his men and, with nine hundred additional men from de Beaumont including an entire fleet of longbow archers, quickly headed south.

Scouts had brought back regular reports as they had thundered south; first, they had been four days behind the Scots army, then it was three, and then it was two. But now, they were still a day behind and the Scots army had crossed the border into England. Carlisle was a mere day's ride from the border, shorter if the ride was swift. No one wanted to mention the fact that there was no way to catch the Scots; they would reach Carlisle before the de Lara army did. No one wanted to send the earl or Mathias into a state of panic with their wives and children bottled up in a castle under siege.

Therefore, Sebastian and Stephen drove the army like slave masters, hardly stopping to rest or eat. Tonight was a rare occurrence because the men had been on the road for almost a week without stopping more than a couple of hours to rest. Even now, they knew that this rest would be short also; they would eat, they would try to catch what rest they could, and then they would continue.

Mathias could hardly eat even though he knew he should. The battle, the campaign, and his father's passing had taken away his appetite and tried to take away his spirit. Sebastian had taken Justus' death even harder and was more brusque and violent than usual. He had been positively fearsome in battle. The man had no idea how to deal with his feelings but when he and Mathias were alone, he would speak of his grief as if it was of little consequence. Mathias wouldn't speak of his at all. Together, they were trying very hard to deal with something that was greatly impacting their lives and neither one was sure how to soldier on without their father. It was an impossible concept.

Meanwhile, Mathias was also dealing with his performance at Dupplin Moor and the Scot's army heading towards Carlisle where he had sent his wife to safety. That, more than anything, was fracturing his control. The calm and consummate commander was sometimes as brusque and brittle as Sebastian, which was unusual. Several times he had asked to ride ahead to Carlisle Castle but Tate had held him back, sending Kenneth instead. He wanted someone there without an emotional investment in the place, someone who would hopefully make decisions based on reason and not emotion. Even so, Mathias and Tate were following Kenneth's trail to Carlisle at a maddening pace. The sense of urgency filled the very air they breathed.

After supper on this warm august night, Mathias found himself lying down on his bedroll, gazing up at the blanket of stars across the night sky. He could see Cathlina's face in the diamond night, the glistening of her brown eyes in every twinkle of the stars. As he lay there thinking about the texture of his wife's skin, something hit the ground beside him and he looked over to see Sebastian flat on his back, staring up at the night sky. Mathias returned his attention to the stars.

"All will be well, you know," Sebastian said after a moment. "Even if the Scots make it to Carlisle Castle before us, we are not far behind them. They will barely have time to lay in an attack before we box them in against Carlisle's walls and destroy them."

"Mayhap."

"It is true. You know it is true."

Mathias sighed faintly, folding a big arm behind his head as he watched the night sky. Thoughts other than his wife began to populate his mind now that he was thinking about Carlisle and the battle that lay ahead.

"It was so easy," he murmured, "so very easy to think logically at Dupplin. It was so simple to see how overwhelmed we were by the superior Scots forces and to know that the only way to defeat them, or at least gain the upper hand, was a surprise attack. So we swept over their camp in the night when they were sleeping and decimated their ranks. But when the battle continued in the morning and were able to use the terrain and the archers to our advantage, everything happened as it should. It was as if God was on our side and victory was assured. But now, with renegade Scots preparing to close in on Carlisle where Cathlina is, I cannot help feeling foolish, as if I scattered them to her doorstep. I feel as if I have failed her because the very reason I sent her to Carlisle in the first place was for her safety. Now see what has happened."

By this time, Sebastian was propped up on one elbow in the grass, watching his brother beat himself up over something he had no control over. He hastened to reassure the man.

"You established the criteria for battle that will be utilized for years to come," he insisted. "You were brilliant in positioning our army and using the longbows against the Scots foot infantry with their spears. As fast as our archers could reload on the slopes, that is how fast they killed the Scots infantry downslope as they tried to reach us. God knows how many English lives you saved, Mathias. The fact that the Scots army broke apart and fled is a testament to your brilliance, but you could not have known in which direction they were fleeing or what target they had in mind."

Mathias sighed faintly. "I will not receive the credit for this battle," he said softly. "Henry de Beaumont will be chronicled as the mastermind behind the victory, and I am accepting of that. Had we fallen, he would have been chronicled as the defeated. In any case, I am no longer concerned with Dupplin Moor or the long-reaching implications of the battle. I am only concerned with reaching Carlisle and my wife."

Sebastian lay back down in the grass and gazed up at the stars. "Father was proud of you, you know," he muttered. "He knew what you had done. He went to his grave proud of you."

"Proud of *us*," Mathias corrected. "He was proud of *us*. I will admit that it was difficult to face battle without him. It is the first battle I have ever fought without my father by my side."

"For me, as well," Sebastian said. Then he pointed to the sky. "But he is up there, watching over us. He is with Mother, and that is where he has wanted to be all along. I do not grieve for him because he is finally at peace with her."

Mathias rolled his head over, looking at his brother as the man stared up at the sky. "That is a very astute thing to say, little brother," he said. "But we still have each other, and I have Cathlina. We will still make a fine, strong family."

Sebastian snorted. "I suppose I must find a wife now. You married the only woman I had ever had an eye on."

Mathias sat up in a huff. "God's Bones, Sebastian," he gruffed as he rose to his feet. "You have had your eye on innumerable women in my lifetime. Cathlina has a sister, you know. Mayhap you should focus your attention on her."

Sebastian looked up at his brother with interest. "Which sister? Isn't the younger one ill?"

"She has an older sister, Roxane," he said. "She is the one Cathlina fights with."

Sebastian grinned. "So the sister has spirit? I like that. Aye, mayhap I will give her a second look when we arrive at Carlisle."

"Then let us get the men roused so we can move within the hour."

Sebastian bolted to his feet with the lure of a woman dangling before him. The sooner they get to Carlisle, the sooner he could get an eyeful of the Lady Roxane de Lara. As Mathias rolled up his bedroll and began heading to the corral where the chargers were tethered in the thick green grass, he began to hear the shouts of sentries. Immediately, the bedroll hit the ground and both he and Sebastian had their broadswords readied as they jogged across the encampment, heading in the direction of the alerts. By the time they reached the source, Tate and Stephen were already interrogating the man who had breached their boundaries. Mathias moved closer and saw that it was one of their scouts.

"I barely escaped, my lord," the man was telling Tate. "They saw the patrol and set after us. I was fortunate to have reached you."

Tate's features were grim. "Tell me what you saw."

The scout took a few deep breaths and then downed a cup of wine handed to him by another soldier. He wiped his mouth with the back of his hand before replying.

"Our patrol crossed into Longtown, north of Carlisle, when the tracks of the Scot army veered off to the southeast," he said. "We followed and saw that they had closed in on your garrison at Kirklinton Castle. But it seemed to me as if it was not the entire army so I sent two men to Carlisle Castle and they came back to tell me that the castle was under threat by a substantial army of Scots. It would seem they split their forces and were raiding both castles, my lord."

Tate was trying not to look too worried. "What else did you see? Were the castles holding?"

The scout nodded. "They were, my lord. It appeared to me that the Scots were only just starting to dig in. They were building ladders. It did not seem as if any real battle had yet begun."

"How long ago was this?"

"At least a day, my lord."

"Twelve hours?"

"Or more, my lord. I am not entirely sure how long I have been running because I had to make a few detours in order to lose my pursuers."

Tate saw Mathias' face in the darkness and their eyes met, locked on each other, and silent thoughts began to pass between them. The siege of both castles was unexpected and wholly disheartening. Tate finally motioned to Stephen and Sebastian, who moved back through the encampment shouting for men to pack their belongings and prepare to depart. As the army began to stir, moving to carry out the orders, Tate moved to Mathias.

"We will have to split the force," he said with quiet urgency. "As much as I do not relish doing so, Kirklinton will need aid. Mat, you will take four hundred men to Kirklinton and make short work of the Scots there. Then you will move on to Carlisle to reinforce me. I will send a messenger this night to Harbottle Castle and empty her of her might force. That should bring another one thousand men to Carlisle and with those numbers, we should make short work of the Scots."

Mathias was still rattled by the scout's report and struggling not to show it. He was his usual cool and collected self, but inside, he was a mess.

"Send Pembury to Kirklinton," he suggested. "Cathlina is at Carlisle and I…."

Tate cut him off. "I need Pembury with me," he said. "You are better suited to the kind of siege Kirklinton will need. You will crush them, Mat. I am depending on your emotion in this case to send a clear message to the Scots. Moreover, it will put you in good with Saer if you save his castle. He would forgive you everything."

"But…."

Tate put a big hand on his shoulder and shook him gently. "No more talk," he said, though it was not unkind. "You have your orders. Go now and prepare for our ride; it will be hard and fast through darkness, so be vigilant. If all goes well, you should see Kirklinton come the morning."

Mathias wasn't pleased but he didn't argue. "Sebastian goes with me," he said.

Tate nodded firmly. "Absolutely," he said, slapping him on the back before heading off into the darkness. "Have the perimeters of the camp broken down and I will see you at the head of the column in an hour."

Mathias watched Tate fade off into the darkness. He wasn't exactly sure what he was feeling at the moment other than terror and disappointment; he wanted to ride with Tate to Carlisle because that was where he left his wife, but on the other hand, he had his orders. He would be seeing Cathlina a little later than he had hoped.

With a heavy sigh, this time one for courage, he stalked off into the darkness, shouting orders to the men around him as he went. Soon, the entire camp was scrambling to assemble and by the light of the three-quarter moon, the Earl of Carlisle's army moved south. By morning, he did indeed see the walls of Kirklinton but it was not as he had expected or hoped.

Kirklinton was in flames.

CHAPTER TWENTY FOUR

They came in the late afternoon.

Three days after the warning from the Carlisle soldiers, men began emerging from the trees about a half mile from Kirklinton Castle in a solid line of legs and weapons. Oddly enough, it wasn't the glint of weapons that gave them away; it was the tartan that blended in to the foliage because it gave a strange rippling effect when they moved. Kirklinton's sharp sentries were the first to see it and the shout went up. The Scots were on the approach.

Cathlina had been with Roxane and Abechail in Abechail's small bower, keeping her company by telling her stories and playing card games with Cathlina's lovely painted cards that Mathias had bought her on their travels through Scotland. Every time Cathlina held up a card to her sister or lay it upon the table in a fan pattern with others, she was reminded of Mathias and of how much she missed him.

The afternoon had been waning and they were thinking on the approach of the evening meal when the sentry's cry went up. Startled, Cathlina and Roxane had jumped up and run to the lancet window that faced the gatehouse only to see the Kirklinton soldiers scrambling upon the walls. They really couldn't see beyond the walls from Abechail's chamber so they raced into their larger bower which had more a view of the north and west. That was when they saw the line of men moving across the clearing towards the castle, like a tide of ants at a distance, heading in their direction.

"Look!" Roxane gasped, pointing. "Men! Do you see them?"

Cathlina did, indeed. Her heart sank but strangely, she didn't panic. Her big brown eyes stared at all of the men approaching the castle. The closer they loomed, the more detail she could make out as she and Roxane clung to each other anxiously.

"They are carrying clubs and axes," she said with apprehension in her tone. "They do not look like Mathias or other knights we have seen. Remember how the knights in the tournament were dressed?"

Roxane nodded fearfully. "They were dressed in mail and armor, and...." She suddenly stopped and pointed out of the window. "Look at the knights on horseback. See them back behind the men on foot?"

Cathlina did and her fear began to grow just a little. "I do."

"They are here to attack us!"

"It is possible."

Together, they continued to watch the Scots come forth from the foliage, moving across the warm summer grass and trampling on the wildflowers the women had taken such delight in. Then, they simply stopped. Confused, Cathlina and Roxane watched anxiously for them to make a move that would throw them all into the midst of a battle, but they remained still. Then, it appeared as if someone gave a command because the men began moving; some of them settled in where they were while others moved back into the trees and soon they could hear the distant sounds of chopping. In short order, trees began falling.

"What do you suppose they are doing?" Roxane asked apprehensively.

Cathlina had no idea. She had never seen a battle before. "I do not know," she said. "But Father will. He will come and tell us what is happening."

As the women clutched each other in mounting fear, Rosalund entered the chamber. Her usually cold and austere face was flushed with exertion and fright.

"Come, girls," she said, clapping her hands and nearly startling Cathlina and Roxane out of their skins. "Your father has asked that we remove ourselves to the vault and lock ourselves in. We must collect all the supplies we can before we do this. Hurry; there is no time to waste."

Cathlina and Roxane rushed after her. "Lock ourselves in the vault?" Roxane repeated. "Why would we do that?"

Rosalund hustled into Abechail's room where the girl lay, weak and ill, upon her bed. She ignored Roxane's question as she stroked her youngest child's pale face.

"We shall return for you," she said calmly. "Your Father wants us to be safe and will lock us up in the vault until this is over."

Unable to see out her window at what was occurring, Abechail was understandably frightened. She clung to her mother's hand.

"What is happening?" she asked, verging on tears. "Have the Scots come?"

Rosalund nodded patiently. "They have, my lamb," she said. "Your father says that they are building ladders so that they may mount our walls. If they are able to get in to the bailey, then it will only be a matter of time before they breach the keep. Your father feels that if we lock ourselves in the vault, they cannot get to us."

Abechail's eyes were tearing up but she nodded. Rosalund stroked her daughter's hair one last time before returning her attention to Cathlina and Roxane.

"Roxane," she said. "You will collect as much water as you can from the well and take it to the vault. Use buckets and pitchers and anything else you can find. Have a house servant assist you. Go, now; there is no time to waste."

When Roxane fled, she turned her attention to Cathlina. "And you, my dear, will collect blankets and bedding and take it down to the vault. I will also have you bring chamber pots. I am having the servants stash as much food as we can collect. Hurry on with your task, now."

Cathlina had been moderately calm until Rosalund had revealed the plan to hide in the vault. If her father was already making such preparations, then the impending battle must be a terrible one indeed. That knowledge made it most difficult to remain calm.

"If Father wanted us to stay to the vault, then shouldn't we have stored supplies earlier?" she asked. "It seems foolish to do this at the last hour. We have known for days that the Scots could come."

Some of Rosalund's patience left her. "We knew nothing for certain," she snapped. "Your father prepared as he saw best. You will not question his decisions."

Cathlina shook her head, exasperated and afraid. "I am not questioning his decisions," she said. "I am simply asking why we did not do this sooner. Now we must rush about while the enemy is building ladders against us."

"Psh," Rosalund shushed her. "Go now and do as you are told."

With shaking legs, Cathlina rushed off. She could hardly believe this was happening, that the Scots were preparing to knock down her front door. She had moved beyond thoughts of her father's lack of preparation and on to Mathias. Hadn't he sent her back to England to prevent this? Confused, terrified, and praying that Mathias would somehow know of her danger and come to her aid, she raced in and out of bed chambers, collecting what she could carry before taking it to the vault.

The dungeons of Kirklinton were built under the great hall. The hall itself was built using one of the curtain walls for its northern perimeter wall and on the western portion of the hall were alcoves for the servants and a small doorway that led down a flight of stairs into the great vault.

Originally used as storage, Saer had converted it into the prison because the gatehouse had a tiny bottle prison that was barely big enough for three men. The vault had two great iron grates, one at the top of the stairs and one at the bottom. The vault itself had a dirt floor and big barrel ceiling, the stones carefully placed to support the weight of the hall above. It was big, and cold, and branched off on a ninety degree angle from the staircase so anyone coming down the steps could not see into the room. They could only see a very small portion of the entire vault. That would hopefully work to their favor.

Cathlina worked steadily gathering bed linens and fashioning four relatively comfortable pallets down in the vault. She placed them as far away from the door as she could get them in order to keep them as far away from danger as possible. Furthermore, she had the cook hunt down large sheets of oilcloth sometimes used to protect the rabbit hutches in the kitchen yard from the elements. She lay those down on the ground underneath the pallets to keep the cold away.

As she emerged from the vault and headed out into the bailey towards the keep, she could see that there was a good deal of activity upon the walls. Men were shouting and she could see a rush of soldiers heading for the wall turrets. It was nearing the nooning hour by this time and as she neared the keep, her father and mother suddenly emerged. Her father was carrying Abechail in his arms and her mother was running along beside.

"Cathlina, come!" her father said briskly as he ran past her. "There is no more time. Into the vault!"

Cathlina's terror surged as she followed after them, nearly tripping on her skirts in her haste. "Where is Roxane?" she cried.

"At the well," her father said. "I will fetch her. You must come with me *now.*"

Cathlina ran after them without another word. Truth was, she was too frightened to speak; this was her first siege, her first battle, and she fought back the tears of terror. Dear God, if only Mathias knew of her plight; he would let nothing stop him from protecting his wife. A wife who happened to be carrying the child he did not yet know about. As Cathlina ran through the great hall and down the stairs into the vault after her parents, she wiped the tears off her cheeks. She prayed she would have the opportunity to tell Mathias of his son. It was all she prayed for.

Saer handed Abechail over to Rosalund, who bedded her daughter down gently on one of the pallets Cathlina had made. Swiftly, he turned to Cathlina, who was panting with fright and exertion behind him.

"Come with me," he said, taking her arm.

He pulled her over to the stairs and pressed something cold and hard into the palm of her hand; it was an old iron key. When Cathlina saw what it was, she looked at him curiously.

"The key to both gates," he told her softly. "You must keep it safe because as long as you have it, the Scots cannot get in. Do you understand?"

Cathlina nodded seriously. "Of course, Father."

His gaze lingered on her a moment before cupping her face in his hands and kissing her forehead swiftly. "Take great care of yourself and my grandson," he muttered. "Know that you are very special to me, Cathlina. I love you very much."

Cathlina's eyes welled with fat tears. "I love you, too," she sniffed. "All will be well; you will see. You will meet your grandson in the spring."

Saer seemed to grow misty-eyed but instead of making a fool of himself with more sentiment, he simply raced up the stairs. Cathlina followed, slamming the big iron gate behind him and locking it. Then, she moved down a few steps and waited for him to return with Roxane.

They weren't long in coming; Roxane and Saer returned shortly, Saer carrying a heavy bucket of water and Roxane nearly hysterical. Cathlina quickly unlocked the grate and issued her sister in, followed by several servants they happened to pick up in kitchen yard where they had gathered in an uncertain mass. Each of them had some kind of supply or possession with them, and the stable grooms were carrying more buckets of water.

When they had all entered the stairwell, Cathlina slammed the grate and locked it tightly again. Then, she followed the collection of people down into the vault and threw that gate as well, assisted by one of the grooms. Engaging the lock, she made her way back to her mother and sisters while the servants huddled over against the wall.

No one knew what to expect, or when to expect it. Buried deep in the ground as they were, they were insulated from the sights and sounds above. But if they had been able to see, they would have envisioned the Scots positioning three big ladders up against the gray stoned walls of Kirklinton in their attempt to breach the castle. Up above, the battle was in full swing.

The Kirklinton soldiers battled back, shoving the ladders away from the walls and sending dozens of zealous Scots crashing down with them. Those who weren't too badly wounded by the fall got back up again and up the ladders would go once more, only this time they were joined by two more ladders. And two more after that. Eventually, there were over a dozen ladders built from white oak or birch lined up against the walls and the Scots were making a strong push to mount Kirklinton's defenses.

This went on for the entire afternoon and into the night. Saer had positioned archers in the gatehouse and on the three turrets of Kirklinton's walls to shoot down the Scots. The longbows kept the Scots at bay for a while but there soon came a point that ammunition was running low. When that occurred, Saer called off most of the archers save a few who were more accurate with their arrows. As the sun set and the Scots showed no sign of relenting, Saer ordered the arrows lit and soon, flaming arrows were firing over the walls and striking the enemy below. But along with Saer's flame arrows, the Scots were firing fire arrows of their own. That was when things started to get critical.

The Scots were excellent marksmen and the stables and outbuildings were the first to catch fire. Saer ordered the horses and animals removed to the kitchen yards were they were corralled in with the chickens and goats. The stables, a long block of thatched roofs and piles of hay, went up in a ball of flame, burning hot and bright into the night sky. Embers carried over to the roof of the great hall, heavily thatched with sod as well as hay, and soon that began to smolder.

Saer had his men post ladders against the walls of the great hall in order to douse the smoldering spots but that soon became prohibitive because the Scots had made a major push and now several of them had managed to mount the wall. Dunstan, in charge of the north wall, was there with his men to fight off a horde of very angry Scots but after a lengthy and brutal battle, he fell victim to a big Scotsman with a bad attitude who grabbed him and threw him over the wall. Dunstan's life ended on the grass outside of the walls of Kirklinton when several Scots took their axes to him.

Meanwhile, Saer was trying desperately to keep the Scots from climbing off the walls and getting down into the bailey, but after a struggle that took almost until dawn, he was ultimately unable to achieve that goal. His legendary axe in hand, he had been swinging it steadily but there were simply too many Scots, a tide of tartan and flesh that overran Kirklinton in the end.

Saer and Beauson and the remaining Kirklinton soldiers retreated to the keep and bottled it up, hitting out at the Scots from the lancet windows as a group of men in tartans tried to break down the entry door. Unlike many keeps that had retractable stairs in case the castle was breached so the attackers could not get to the entry door of the keep, Kirklinton had a stone flight of stairs that led up to an iron and oak door that was as solid as stone itself. Still, the Scots were intent to break it down. They were also intent to destroy everything at Kirklinton, including the great hall.

The Scots plowed through the great hall, stealing anything of value and destroying anything they couldn't carry, including the feasting table. They ripped down tapestries and stole pewter plate. When they came to the servant's alcove, they drank whatever wine was there and smashed the pitchers. Then, the iron grate of the vault drew their attention and when the rattled it and realized they couldn't get in, they began savaging it with a vengeance.

Down inside the vault, Cathlina, her mother, her sisters, and the servants could hear the Scots at the upper door, howling and cursing. Abechail began to cry as Rosalund hastened to quiet her, but in truth, they were all terrified. Roxane clutched Cathlina, burying her face in her sister's shoulder as the Scots screamed their threats at the top of the stairs.

Because of the angle of the room, the Scots couldn't see if there was anyone in the room below but they suspected that whatever was locked up must be extremely valuable. Therefore, they set about trying to break down the iron grate any way they could manage. They even tried to unhinge it but the hinges were fused and well-placed, and they could not get to them.

Infuriated, they ran back into the great hall and grabbed pieces of the destroyed feasting table, propping it up against the iron grate and lighting it on fire. If they couldn't destroy or unhinge the gate, then perhaps they could build a hot enough fire to soften it to the point where they could bend it and get through. It was worth a try. Soon, there was a raging fire burning up against the iron grate at the top of the stairs, sending great billows of smoke and embers into the air.

The Scots thought they had been quite smart to try to soften the great iron gate with a white-hot fire, but soon enough the fire got out of control. The heat and embers ignited the great wooden roof support beams overhead and shortly thereafter, ignited the roof. Soon enough, half of the hall was going up in flames and the heat and smoke forced the Scots outside. After that, they could do nothing but stand there and watch the great hall of Kirklinton belch great smoke and fire into the night sky. The fire could be seen for miles, like a raging beacon in the night. At that point, there was nothing more to do but wait for the hall to collapse and see what they could scavenge. Those who raided the hall now turned their attention back to the keep, which was so far holding fast.

They went after it with a vengeance.

***

Down in the vault beneath the great hall, Cathlina and the others smelled the smoke from the fire. It was a strong smell but hardly unbearable. Cathlina, still huddled with Roxane, disengaged her clinging sister to go and take a look. Her mother stopped her.

"Nay, Cathlina," she hissed. "Sit down. Stay away from the door."

Cathlina gently pulled her hand from her mother's grasp. "I must see what they have done," she whispered. "Do you not smell the smoke? They have done something terrible and I must see what it is."

Before Rosalund could stop her, Cathlina crept away and stayed flush against the wall that contained the second gate at the bottom of the steps. One of the stable grooms, and older man who had been at Kirklinton for many years, joined her and together they carefully made their way to the iron grate so they could peer up the stairwell to see what was happening. Cathlina was very cautious, falling to her knees so she could peer from the bottom of the grate and hopefully be less noticeable if anyone was looking down. But the moment she looked up the stairwell, all she could see was a wall of flame at the top of it.

Shocked, she looked at the old groom, who had seen the white hot flames for himself. They looked at each other as if unsure what to say or do. The old man spoke first.

"We will be safe," he whispered. "Smoke and heat and flame travel upwards. It will not come down the stairwell. Aye, we will be quite safe down here."

Cathlina was truly and deeply terrified. "Won't the flame weaken the iron grate?"

The old man shrugged. "It would have to be very, very hot," he said. "Even if it is that hot, the Scots cannot get near it, so we are still safe. The best thing they could have done was set the hall afire. They will not be able to get near it now because it is so hot."

"And we will not be able to get out."

"The iron will eventually cool. We are still safe, my lady."

Cathlina wasn't so sure about the situation but his words brought her some comfort. He was older and wiser, after all. She glanced around the room of family and servants. "Be careful what you tell everyone, then," she said softly. "I do not want anyone to panic."

The old man nodded firmly and moved away. Cathlina scurried back to her mother and sisters.

"It seems the Scots are burning the hall down over our heads," she said quietly. "We are very safe because they cannot enter a flaming building to get at us, and the smoke and heat will rise. It will not come down the stairwell."

Rosalund was surprisingly calm knowing that a building was burning over her head. "I see," she said pensively. "I do not suppose there is anything we can do about it anyway. Come and sit, Cathlina. Mayhap... mayhap it is time to sleep a little while we can. You say the Scots cannot get at us now?"

"Not while there is a fire in the hall."

Rosalund seemed satisfied, although she was still visibly tense. "Then come and lay down," she said. "Sleep with Abbie."

Obediently, Cathlina crawled over to her little sister, who was quite weak and limp. Her breathing was slow and labored, but Cathlina didn't mention it to her mother. She suspected the woman already knew. Tears anew filled her eyes as she lay next to her sister and wrapped her arms around her, holding her tightly. Abechail hardly stirred and Cathlina thought she was somewhat comatose because when she whispered her name, she received no response.

Feeling great sorrow, and great fear, Cathlina began to whisper in Abechail's ear, telling her of the son she would bear in the spring and how she intended to name the child Magnus after Abechail's family of hawks. She told Abechail of the boy she intended to have and how he would be bold and cunning, and how much he would enjoy playing with his Aunt Abechail. But that was as far as she got before tears overcame her and she simply held her baby sister tightly, kissing the girl's cheek. Eventually, she faded off to sleep.

Rosalund remained awake, watching her daughters as they slept soundly. She knew that Abechail's condition had taken a turn for the worse; she had seen her deteriorate badly just within the past several hours and sleeping in a damp, dank and now smoky vault wasn't helping. Still, there was nothing she could do about it. She didn't pray because she and God had not been on speaking terms for quite some time, at least since the time Abechail had been diagnosed by the physics and Rosalund had prayed for a miracle. But no miracle had occurred and Rosalund had stopped praying. God ignored her, just as he was ignoring her now as her castle was under siege and the zealous Scots were burning the great hall over her head. Rosalund knew it was only a matter of time before the Scots broke through and were able to capture them, but she was determined not to allow that to happen. She would not see her daughters fall victim to the clans.

In her heavy robes she hid a bejeweled dirk, a wicked and sharp thing that she was prepared to use on her children if the situation looked hopeless. She would rather see her daughters suffer a few moments of pain rather than hours or even days of torture before they were killed. No, she wouldn't let that happen at all. As she had brought them into the world, she was prepared to remove them from it, too. Even the daughter that was pregnant with her only grandchild. She would be doing them both a favor rather than let them fall to the Scots.

As Rosalund sat against the cold wall of the vault that was both her prison and her fortress, she began to notice a haze in the chamber. Looking around, she realized that it was smoke, and she looked to the vault entry to see a significant stream of smoke billowing into the chamber. Her heart sank; somehow, someway, the smoke was flowing down the stairwell and into the vault. If the fire was bad enough, and burned long enough, the smoke would fill up the entire chamber and suck the air from it, suffocating them all. It was a horrible ending, choking to death.

Fingering the dirk, she knew what she had to do should it come down to it. If she thought praying to God for strength would help her do as she must, then she might have uttered a prayer. As it was, she couldn't bring herself to do it.

He wouldn't listen to her, anyway.

CHAPTER TWENTY FIVE

Kirklinton was in flames and the gates were wide open. Men in tartans were moving about freely. As Mathias and his army crested the road leading to Kirklinton from the north, he ordered shields slung for the knights and weapons in-hand. Nearly his entire force was mounted but he did have about seventy or eighty foot soldiers. He wasn't even going to be strategic about his method of attack; he was going to charge right into the sea of tartans and begin the killing trend. There was no time to waste.

With a battle cry, he urged his men forward and the charge was on. The Scots, hearing the cry, began to scramble as a hundreds of English soldiers descended upon them. Mathias headed right for the open gates and ended up lopping off the head of some idiot Scotsman who tried to challenge him. His big silver charger, so contributory in his wars with Mortimer, was again an instrument of death as the horse anticipated nearly every move of his master. Mathias was very thankful for the vicious, intelligent beast.

Once he entered the gates of Kirklinton, he could see the situation for what it was; the entire place was burning with the exception of the keep, which seemed to have held out. Off to his right, he could hear his brother's battle howl as the man plowed through several Scots with the relish of a man devouring a fine meal. There was a strange glee to Sebastian's manner and Mathias glance over at his brother as the man chopped and thrust at the enemy around him. Most of the Scots seemed to be on foot but there were a few mounted knights; it was those men that Mathias went after.

One of the knights was in fine mail and armor, astride an equally fine charger. He was near the keep, giving orders to the men trying to batter down the entry door, but he stopped when he saw Mathias charging at him. Startled to see English reinforcements, he met Mathias with equal strength as the two of them came together near the keep in a mighty clash.

Sparks flew into the early morning air as Mathias battled the Scots knight on horseback. He was as merciless as he was skilled, going after the man's limbs rather than his torso or his head. His strategy was simple; a disabled man was much easier to dispatch. The Scots knight, however, was quite talented and managed to stay away from Mathias' deadly broadsword for quite some time until Mathias managed to nick the charger, which nearly unseated the knight when it bolted off.

Mathias spurred his charger after the pair, catching up to them and using a massively heavy thrust to amputate the knight's left hand. When the knight howled and folded, Mathis speared the man right in the side, straight through the mail. His broadsword went in one side and out the other, and when he withdrew it, the knight fell to the ground, dead. Mathias didn't hang around to view his handiwork; he had more men to kill.

Thundering off into the heat of battle near the keep, he ended up helping Sebastian fend off a number of foot soldiers who were trying to pull Sebastian off his charger. The redheaded knight was furious with their attempts and men with hacked arms and heads fell back, victims of Sebastian's mighty sword.

Once his brother was safe from being unseated, Mathis ordered his men to secure the keep. An onslaught of English soldiers rushed the keep and the men trying to ram down the entry door found themselves overwhelmed. Soon, the vicious fight for the keep was in full swing and it was nasty hand to hand combat to chase the Scots away. It took a great deal of time and it wasn't simple in the least, but eventually, Mathias and Sebastian and a host of English knights were able to move the fighting away from the keep.

Meanwhile, a major portion of Mathias' army had swept through the stable yards and kitchen yard, engaging in heavy combat while trying to chase the Scots from Kirklinton's enclosure. Mathias sent some of his archers up to the gatehouse, protected by English soldiers, and the archers were cool and clean with their accuracy as they struck down Scot after Scot.

As the morning deepened and the sun rose, the remaining Scots realized that they were losing a great many men to the English archers in the gatehouse so they finally called a retreat. Mathias and Sebastian, along with several hundred English foot soldiers, chased the last of the Scots from Kirklinton's keep and scattered them to the countryside. Mathias ordered about a hundred mounted men to follow them to ensure that they did not turn for Carlisle while he and several soldiers attempted to gain entrance to Kirklinton's keep.

Mathias dismounted his charger at the base of the steps to the keep, taking the stairs two at a time until he reached the door. The old iron and oak panel had held admirable and he pounded on it, shouting up to the open lancet windows on the floors above.

"In the name of the King, you will open this door," he bellowed. "The enemy has fled and your walls are secured. Open the door in the name of Edward, I say!"

There was no response for several long moments. He pounded again, and yelled again, until he finally heard a voice overhead emitting from one of the long lancet windows. It was too narrow for a man to stick his head out of so he could see for himself that the English were at his door, so the person could only stand next to the window and yell.

"You will tell me your name!" the man inside shouted.

Mathias didn't hesitate. "Mathias de Reyne," he called back. "I have been sent by the Earl of Carlisle."

More silence. Mathias was growing just the least bit impatient; did these fools not realize that he was here to save them? He pounded on the door again, and shouted again, when he began to hear the bolt move on the other side. The door was fairly heavily damaged so it took those on both sides of the panel to actually open it. When it was open wide enough for a man to slip through, Saer appeared from the interior of the keep. His blood-shot eyes were wide on Mathias.

"*You!*" he said. It sounded something between an accusation and a sigh of relief. "You have come. I was told you were in Scotland."

Mathias stepped back so the man could emerge. "I was," he said. "But we have been following the Scots south because we knew they were intending revenge on Carlisle by attacking his properties. I am sorry we could not be here sooner."

Saer was exhausted, relieved. It began to occur to him that the siege was truly over and he slumped back against the keep, wiping the sweat from his brow.

"You came when you could and for that, I am grateful," he said. Then he took another step out onto the landing and caught sight of the flames and smoke billowing into the air as the great hall burned. His face went positively ashen. "Dear God; *no!*"

Terror filled every inch of his manner; he began to run down the stone steps leading to the bailey, hurling his armored body across the death and destruction of the bailey as fast as legs would allow. Mathias, caught up in the man's panic, was right behind him.

"What is wrong?" Mathias demanded. "Where are you going?"

Saer could barely speak; he gestured wildly to the hall. "They are in there!"

Mathias grabbed the man; he seemed nearly crazed with horror. "*Who* is in there?"

Saer was crazed; he was nearly incoherent. "My family," he gasped. "My… my wife. My girls. They are all in there!"

Mathias looked at the great hall, a great charred wreckage that was still smoldering and flaming. "Your… your wife?" he repeated, sickened as he looked at the structure. "My lord, if they are in there, they…."

"Cathlina is in there, you fool!" he screamed. "Your wife is in there, too!"

Mathias nearly fell over from the shock and grief of the harshly slung words; he stared at the hall, hardly able to comprehend what he was being told. His exhausted mind was wracked with disbelief and horror.

"Cathlina?" he repeated, hearing her name spoken in his shaken voice. His knees threatened to buckle but he fought it. "*My* Cathlina?"

"Aye!"

"But… but she was at Carlisle!"

"She came to Kirklinton a few weeks ago. We have no time to waste if we are to save them!"

That was all Mathias needed to hear. His training kicked in, his innate ability to deal calmly with any given situation. Panic would not do Cathlina any good; only calm heads would be able to save her if, indeed, she was salvageable. Brutally, he grabbed Saer by the arm and began yanking him towards the building.

"Where, for God's sake?" he demanded. "Where are they?"

Saer began to run, trying to enter the building at the main door but being sent back because of the heat and smoke.

"They are in the storage vault, down below the hall," Saer said, running to the west side of the structure with Mathias on his heels. "We must get them out!"

Mathias bellowed to the nearest soldiers, who came on the run. They all rounded the corner to the west side of the structure, which wasn't nearly as destroyed as the main entry. They raced inside the smoky servant's entrance to see that the roof had collapsed on the very doorway they needed to get to. Saer pointed at it furiously.

"There!" he screamed. "That is the door to the vaults! They are down there!"

Mathias rushed forward, shoving aside heavy beams and pieces of roof that were still smoldering. His soldiers followed him and quickly, they began to tear away at the debris that had fallen down against the old iron grate. In fact, the grate itself was twisted and soft from the extreme heat that had been burned against it. As a smithy, Mathias knew the heat factor well. It must have been intense. He struggled and coughed as he fought to clear the debris field near the vault entry.

"Cathlina!" Saer screamed as dozens of Englishmen tried to remove the carnage. "Cathlina, can you hear me? The key, daughter; we need the *key*!"

Mathias, fighting through a piece of roof that was still burning, looked at him curiously. "What key?" he asked, coughing as smoke billowed up in his face.

Saer pointed to the giant lock on the iron grate. "We need the key," he repeated breathlessly. "I gave it to Cathlina."

Mathias could see what he was referring to; the iron grate was heavy and old, and the key was needed for the massive lock. He gave a big shove to the burning debris so he could peer down the dark, steep stairwell into the vault. At the bottom, all he could see was more debris and darkness.

"Cathlina!" he roared.

There was no answer and his anxiety surged. Burning debris had toppled down the stairs through the iron grate and the steps were littered with it. Smoke was thick. In fact, it filled the stairwell and the blackness at the bottom. He turned to Saer.

"We must get in there now," he said, a panicked edge to his voice. "Do you have any smithy tools?"

Saer's mind was nearly gone, overwhelmed with what had happened to his castle and to his family, but he managed to nod to Mathias' question.

"We did," he said, lifting his shoulders helplessly. "I do not know what has become of it in the battle. It could be lost."

"Show me where it was. Mayhap there is something left I can use."

As the soldiers continued to frantically remove the debris, Saer and Mathias raced out to the bailey to what was left of the trade shacks near the stables. They had all been burned; the place where the smithy and the tanner's sheds once stood was now a heap of rubble. Saer began plowing through it.

"In here, somewhere," he said as he threw aside charred wreckage. "This is where the smithy and the tanner were. Any tools will be under this mess."

Mathias just kept digging through it, tossing wreckage aside as he tried very hard not to think of Cathlina. To do so would threaten his control and he needed that very badly if he had any chance of getting in to the vault. As he dug through the burnt timber and thatch, he saw Sebastian approach, covered with gore. The man was looking at him very curiously. Mathias waved him over.

"Cathlina is here," he told his brother, sounding edgy and winded. "She is in the vault but we cannot get to her."

Sebastian could see that his brother, his cool and collected brother, was verging on panic. "What are you doing?" he asked.

Mathias returned his attention to the ruins of the smithy shacks. "If I can find pliers and a measure of wire, I may be able to turn the tumblers on the old lock."

Sebastian was confused. "What lock?"

"The lock to the vault."

"But where is the key?"

Mathias looked up at him and Sebastian swore he saw tears in the man's eyes. "She has it," he muttered. "Her father gave her the key and told her to lock the family into the vault, the safest place during a siege. Now the vault is filled with smoke and we cannot rouse her. I must get to her, do you hear? *I must.*"

Sebastian began throwing aside burnt wood in an attempt to get to the bottom of the pile. He didn't even ask what Cathlina was doing at Kirklinton when she was supposed to be at Carlisle; he didn't ask any more questions because he was certain that Mathias would not take any delay, no matter how small, well. He'd never seen such terror in Mathias' eyes and it deeply concerned him. Therefore, he helped them clear out the debris.

Mathias located a long, slender pair of pliers that were red-hot. He nearly burned himself on them but tossed them aside. Saer was still digging through the debris and Sebastian was kicking aside charred wood and other remains. Finally, Mathias came up with two long, slender rods of iron usually used when repairing iron tools. With the pliers in one hand and the iron rods in the other, he bolted for the great hall. Saer and Sebastian followed.

The soldiers had managed to clear away a good deal of the debris by the time they returned. The arched entry to the vault was completely exposed and the old iron grate was torqued and hot from the fire. Mathias dropped to his knees in front of the old iron grate, his focus on the big iron lock in front of him.

"Can't we unhinge it?" Sebastian asked as he tried to gain a better look at the hinges.

Mathias shook his head. "It is impossible," he said. "Take a look for yourself; they are very nearly melted to the frame. Whoever built this built it to withstand a great deal. Nay, little brother, we cannot unhinge it. I must see if I can open this lock without a key."

Sebastian stood next to his brother as the man took the two slender iron rods and poked them inside the old lock, trying to move the mechanism inside. Saer stood at the grate, watching in fear and anticipation as Mathias attempted to unlock the grate. He kept turning his attention to the stairwell and the smoky darkness below. He'd never felt such anguish.

"Cathlina?" he called again. "Rosalund? Can anyone hear me? Roxane?"

It was pathetic, really. The poor man was trying to rouse his family when they more than likely would not be roused. He kept calling to them and the more he called, the more the silence was truly painful. Mathias could feel it even though he was struggling with all of his might to ignore it. If he succumbed to the bone-numbing grief that the silence provoked, then all would be lost. And he could not, would not, give up. Not when Cathlina's life hung in the balance. He would never, ever give up.

Please God, he silently prayed. *Please do not let anything happen to her. You have ignored me a great deal over the past two years but I beg that you not ignore me now. Give me the skill and strength to save the one person in my life who has given me joy and love above all else. Do not give her to me only to cruelly take her away.*

Tears filled his eyes as he prayed, clouding his vision as he struggled to manipulate the old tumblers. He tried blinking them away but they just kept coming. Soon, they were spilling from his eyes and he paused to angrily wipe them away. He didn't have time for tears. Cathlina was waiting for him.

But it was an agonizing wait. The minutes ticked by and he continued to twist the rods in an attempt to roll the tumblers. The roof overhead was still burning and twice, big hunks of debris had fallen dangerously close to him. Sebastian was watching him over his shoulder and a dozen English soldiers were standing around, watching and waiting while their commander tried to pick a lock. Saer could hardly take the strain and had taken to pacing in a circle, his head in his hands. Just as the stress grew too great to bear, the old tumblers finally gave way and the lock sprung.

Sebastian heard the click and saw the bolt lift. He reached out and yanked on the hot iron, pulling it back and nearly mowing his brother down in the process. But Mathias was quick on his feet, diving down the dark and cluttered stairwell, avoiding the debris as best he could with an army of men following him. When he came to the second grate at the bottom, he pushed his face against the slats to try and gain a better look at the room beyond.

"Cathlina!" he roared.

His voice echoed off the walls and he heard coughing. It was thick with smoke and bad air, and several pieces of burning debris had managed to fall in between the iron bars, now burning on the dirt floor of the vault. Mathias called her name twice more before a man suddenly appeared on his knees. Mathias, Saer, and Sebastian dropped to their knees also, moving to speak to the man but Saer reached out and grabbed him by the neck.

"My family!" he cried. "What has happened to them?"

Before the man could answer, Mathias snatched the man's arm. "The Lady Cathlina," he said calmly although his voice was shaking. "Do you know who she is?"

The man coughed and gasped. "Aye, my lord."

"She has a key!" Saer was frantic. "Get the key!"

The man nodded, hacking and gasping as he crawled back into the smoky darkness. They could hear him over at the far end of the vault, an area they could not see from their angle, and they heard a woman's voice lifted in fear.

"Nay!" the woman yelled, her voice guttural and hoarse. "You will not let them in! They mean to kill us!"

"Nay, my lady," the servant was saying. "It is your husband. He has come to rescue us."

The woman was evidently still reluctant. "It is a trick," she snarled. "It is a trap. They mean to kill us all! I will not let them have us, do you hear? They will not take us alive!"

Mathias and Saer looked at each other with great apprehension. Saer threw himself against the bars and called out.

"Rosalund?" he cried. "It is me! Cathlina has the key! Open the door!"

The woman didn't answer but they could hear her grumbling. Then the sounds of a struggle ensued and the manservant cried out.

"Nay, my lady!" he said. "They have come to rescue us! The knife… put it away, I say! Put it away!"

"Rosalund!" Saer cried again. "Get the key! Let us in!"

A woman's scream pierced the smoky haze. There were sounds of a struggle. They could hear grunting and thumping, as if people were fighting for their lives. Sounds of weeping filled the air and Saer went mad, yanking at the iron grate and screaming his wife's name. Meanwhile, Mathias had taken his two iron rods and was attempting to pick the lock with shaking hands when the man servant suddenly appeared again. A key was thrust into Mathias' face.

"Here," he rasped.

Mathias snatched the key and threw the lock, noticing that the servant was covered in blood. Heart in his throat, he had to crawl into the vault on his hands and knees because the smoke became very thick from the waist level on up. He could hear Sebastian and Saer behind him, all of them crawling towards the end of the room where a jumble of people seemed strewn about the ground. Mathias caught sight of his wife's hair before he ever saw her face, and that was his guide, like a beacon. He closed in on her in a flash.

Cathlina was pale and unconscious. Mathias grabbed her and, still on his hands and knees, somehow managed to drag her out of the vault. By the time he hit the stairwell, he was able to stand in the thinning smoke and he carried her out of the darkness and into the light above. All the while, he could hear panicked little gasps, unaware that they were his until he entered the destroyed hall above. Then, he realized he had been in an utter panic mode. Taking a look at his wife's unconscious face, he burst into tears of pure anguish.

Weeping, he carried his wife outside into the fresh air. Once he was free of the hall, he collapsed onto his knees and held Cathlina against him, so tightly that he was nearly squeezing her to death. All the while, he wept deeply, his face buried in her neck. There was no other way he could possibly react, finding his wife in a vault full of smoke and blood. He didn't even know if she was dead or alive, so he loosened his grip and lay her down on the soft earth of Kirklinton's bailey.

"Cathlina?" he sobbed, patting her cheeks to see if she would react. "Open your eyes, love; 'tis me. Open your eyes and look at me."

She lay as still as death. Mathias put his ear against her chest and he could hear a faint heartbeat. It was rapid and weak. He rubbed at her chest, trying to stimulate her into taking a deep breath, but she remained limp. Finally, he slapped her lightly on the cheek.

"Cathlina?" he said, gaining control over his tears. "Cathlina, open your eyes and look at me. All is well, I swear it. Open your eyes now."

As he continued to alternately pat and rub her cheeks, Sebastian came up beside him bearing another limp body. Mathias caught sight of Roxane as Sebastian laid her carefully on the ground.

"How is Cathlina?" Sebastian said, breathless with exertion.

Mathias shook his head. "She does not wake but she is breathing," he said, his voice trembling. "Is the sister dead?"

Sebastian looked at pale, unconscious Roxane. "This one is not," he said, "but it looks as if the mother went mad. The servants said that she thought the Scots were overtaking them so she stabbed herself before anyone could stop her. The servants prevented her from doing any damage to the daughters."

Mathias lifted his head, looking at his brother with his red-rimmed eyes. "Where is the father?"

"In the vault. He is trying to keep the mother from bleeding to death. Cathlina and her sisters are fortunate to have survived."

"Where is the little one?"

"Still down there."

"You had better bring her up into the clean air."

Sebastian stood up. "I will get her."

Mathias watched his brother walk away before closing his eyes for a moment, tightly, and muttering a prayer of thanks for God's infinite mercy. But he was jolted from his prayers when Cathlina began to cough violently. Startled, he sat her upright in an attempt to help her clear her lungs.

"There, now," he said, gently rubbing her back. "You are safe. Breathe easy, love. Take a few deep breaths and breathe easy."

Dazed and feeling ill, Cathlina continued to cough and hack, struggling for every breath. Eventually, she calmed enough so that she was able to breathe more evenly. She clutched Mathias, the steadying force as her world rocked, opening her eyes to his anxious, handsome face.

"Mathias," she gasped. "You... you *came*."

She sounded lucid and it was enough to drive him to tears once again. "Aye," he said tightly. "I came. Everything will be well again, I swear it."

Cathlina was struggling to clear her lungs and her mind. The situation was still very disorienting as she looked around, trying to gain her bearings. But her focus fell on Mathias once again and she put her arms around his neck, holding him as tightly as she could manage for all of her weakness. She still continued to cough even as she spoke.

"The Scots came," she told him. "My father said the vault would be the safest place for us so he locked us in and gave me the key. How did I get out here?"

"I brought you out," he murmured, kissing her smoke-smelling hair with the greatest satisfaction. "How do you feel?"

Cathlina coughed, her head on his shoulder because she was truly too weak to do much more than simply lean on him. His warmth and strength against her felt wonderful.

"Not very well," she admitted. "It is hard to breathe. What happened?"

Mathias was calming now that she was in his arms and, seemingly, not seriously injured. It was all he could do not to weep with gratitude. In fact, given the state of the hall and the situation in general, he could hardly believe it.

"The Scots burned the great hall," he told her. "The smoke traveled to the vault. I think you must have breathed in a fair amount before we were able to get to you."

She lifted her head and looked at him. "How did you know to come?" she asked, incredulous. "How did you know I was in danger?"

Mathias gazed into her beautiful face, thinking a lot of different things at that moment. But he was mostly thinking that his wife was safe, and in his arms, and that was the only thing that mattered to him. *She* was the only thing that mattered to him.

"I will always be there to keep you from danger," he said softly, stroking a pale cheek. "The first time I met you, I saved you from danger. I will always be there, Cathlina, no matter where you are. Look over your shoulder and I shall be there; look into the sky and I will be gazing down upon you. Do you understand that you drew me out of despair and gave me a reason to live again? You redeemed me, my sweet Cathlina, and I will always be there for you, in this life or any other, to keep you safe and love you until the end of time. That is my destiny in life; you have given that to me, and I am grateful."

Cathlina smiled at him, touching his stubbled face, watching as he tenderly kissed her fingers. "All I did was love you," she whispered. "As a smithy or as a knight, all I did was love you. As for your destiny, I am glad we will live it together."

Mathias kissed her, tenderly, sampling every taste and texture she had to offer. It was overwhelmingly intoxicating, and his joy and relief knew no bounds. She was safe and she was whole, and they had a future to attend to. His life, his future, was far richer because of her.

From the scandal of Roger Mortimer to the victory on the fields of Dupplin Moor, Mathias had found himself once again. He was no longer the Fallen One but the Redeemed One because no matter what, the confidence and strength that Cathlina gave to him could never be taken away, not by kings or princes or entire armies. What she gave to him couldn't be erased. It was buried deep in the heart of a knight, never to be tarnished again.

Scooping his wife into his enormous arms, he carried her off into the setting sun.

EPILOGUE

May 1333
Carlisle Castle

Thankfully, he was sleeping.

He slept a good deal of the time but in moments when he was awake, little Magnus de Reyne had lungs like a trumpet, louder than any baby Mathias had ever heard. He hadn't been around a lot of babies, in fact, but he was convinced his six week old son had a louder voice than any child alive and he was very thankful that the child was currently sleeping peacefully in his mother's arms. A crying baby made the new father nervous.

They were all crowded into Carlisle's chapel for Magnus' baptism on this sunny day in May; Tate, Toby, Kenneth, Stephen, Roxane, Rosalund, Saer, Cathlina and Mathias. The only people missing were Sebastian because he had been sent on an errand, and Abechail because she had passed away the previous winter.

It had been a rather difficult few months since the youngest de Lara daughter's passing with the grief of a young life cut short, but Cathlina's pregnancy and the subsequent healthy birth of a rather large boy seemed to ease the ache of Abechail's loss. Even Rosalund, who was still mentally unbalanced since the attack on Kirklinton and the loss of her youngest child, had helped deliver Magnus and took great pride in her grandson. It had been a good distraction for her.

Even now, Rosalund hovered over Cathlina and the baby as if fearful they were going to disappear. Roxane simply rolled her eyes at all of the fuss and wondered aloud when Sebastian was going to return. The two of them had struck up a courtship of sorts, strange as it was. They were both fickle, selfish people, so it made the relationship tricky at times. Aye, things were returning to normal.

Tate, Kenneth, Stephen and Mathias were all dressed in their finest armor as the priest recited the blessing in Latin and performed the baptism with blessed oil. Magnus had three Godfathers – Tate, Kenneth, and Stephen- and one Godmother, Toby, who was expecting her sixth child and lovely with the rosy glow of pregnancy. She stood next to Cathlina as the priest prayed, wiping the oil off of little Magnus' skin when it dripped off his forehead.

Mathias also stood next to his wife, never more proud of anything in his life. He had a beautiful wife, and a healthy son, and he wanted for nothing. Life was good. He had spent the past year at Carlisle Castle serving Tate with the king's permission. Although he had none of his titles restored, he understood the process and why he had been stationed with Tate even after his exemplary performance at Dupplin Moor; essentially the king wanted to keep an eye on him and not heap too much upon him, too quickly. He was, after all, once the fallen. But he didn't really mind; he was very happy to serve with Tate in a military capacity.

He lost himself in thought as the priest finished with the prayers and asked everyone to kneel while he gave the blessing. He helped Cathlina to her knees as Tate went to help his pregnant wife and they all bowed their heads as the benediction was given and the priest flicked more holy water on them. Some of it hit Magnus and Mathias cringed, waiting for the baby to let loose with his awesome wail, but the baby remained peacefully sleeping. Mathias breathed a sigh of relief.

When the service was over, they group moved from the chapel to the great hall where Toby had arranged for a lovely feast. The hall was warm and fragrant as the servants began to bring forth bowls of mashed fruit, or boiled carrots with dill, and big platters of freshly baked bread. Cathlina cradled little Magnus against her as she carefully sat and allowed her husband to serve her. When an enormous platter with a suckling pig was produced, everyone sat down and helped themselves.

All except Tate; he had disappeared once they left the chapel and even now was absent as everyone enjoyed the food. Toby had the nurse bring her children down from their rooms and soon the hall was filled with the voices of children. When the younger ones began to scream because Stephen was teasing them, Mathias watched Magnus to see if the baby would awaken, but alas, he remained quiet and asleep. Satisfied, Mathias dug into his food.

As they were eating and talking, speaking on things both humorous and trivial, Tate entered the hall. Mathias glanced up from his pork, noticing that the man had a vellum in his hand. When Tate drew close, he motioned at the scroll in his grip.

"What do you have?" he asked.

Tate eyed him. "I have an announcement to make," he said. Then, he lifted his voice. "I have something very important to speak of. Stephen, stop tormenting my sons and listen to what I must tell you. You will want to hear this."

Everyone quieted and Stephen stopped harassing the de Lara twins. He shushed them and made them sit on the bench beside him. When everyone was settled, Tate lifted the vellum in his hand.

"Good lords and ladies, I have received a missive from the king," he said, scanning the writing on the vellum. "For exemplary service and brilliant conduct at the Battle of Dupplin Moor which resulted in a great victory, and for a long and distinguished military history, Edward has fully restored Mathias' status as a knight of the realm. Furthermore, he has bequeathed upon him the following titles: Earl of Bristol, Baron Westbury, and High Warden of the West. Along with these titles comes more lands and property than I have the time to list, but it is all here on this missive. Congratulations, Mat. You are once again among the ranks of the nobles in good standing."

Cheers went up all around as Mathias sat there, looking rather shocked by the whole thing. It wasn't until he looked at Cathlina, beaming at him, that he began to process what Tate had said. He stood up rather uncertainly and took the missive that Tate was extending at him.

"Earl?" he repeated.

"Of Bristol," Tate said with a grin. "Good God, man, you nearly have as many titles as I have. How does it feel?"

Mathias had to shake himself. "I am not entirely sure," he said. "I do not know what to say except… thank you. I am sure you had a hand in all of this."

Tate grinned and slapped him on the shoulder. "I simply told Edward the truth," he said. "That you are the kind of knight all men aspire to be but seldom are. Everything you have been granted is well deserved."

As the news began to sink deeper, Mathias loosened up. He smiled at Tate. "I can hardly believe it," he said. "Is there anything in the missive about Sebastian? Is he restored as well?"

Tate nodded. "Baron Beckington," he said. "His lands border yours."

Mathias' eyebrows lifted in surprise. "A baron?" he repeated. "God's Bones, I will never hear the end of how great he thinks he is. I sincerely wish my father was alive to see his sons restored to a greater glory."

Tate's humor faded somewhat and he again slapped him on the

shoulder. "He knows," he said quietly. "Wherever Justus is, he surely knows."

"I hope so."

Mathias sat back down next to Cathlina and laid the missive out on the table, reading over the details. Kenneth and Stephen joined him, both of them very happy for their friend. They spoke of their past, their present, and their plans for the future; it seemed that Kenneth was headed for the Welsh Marches and Stephen was headed back to Berwick to battle the Scots. Mathias knew that wherever they all went, or how long they were separated, it would never dampen or weaken the bonds of their friendship. Men who had stood behind him through his darkest hour and who were as close to him as brothers.

The group remained in the hall well into the evening hours, enjoying de Lara's fine wine and speaking of things both important and trivial. Eventually, Saer took Rosalund to bed, for she needed a great deal of rest these days, and Cathlina sat in a chair near the hearth and gently rocked her son, who had slept most of the afternoon away. Roxane sat with her. Toby took her brood up to bed and they could hear the twins screaming two floors above them.

As Mathias, Kenneth and Stephen sat around the end of the feasting table and relived old times, the entry door to the keep swung open. Cathlina had her back turned to the door and couldn't see who it was, but she didn't have to; Mathias let loose with one word.

"Sebastian!"

Sebastian the Red looked weary and dirty as he walked into the hall bearing an enormous box. He eyed his brother as he approached the feasting table and set the box upon it. Mathias looked at the box with great anticipation.

"Did you get it?" he demanded.

Sebastian was tired and irritated. "I did."

"Are you sure?"

"See for yourself," he said. "You know how much I hated that beast. He came right up to me and kissed me, so I knew it was him."

Mathias grinned as he collected the box and went over to his wife. Carefully, he set the box down at her feet. She looked at him curiously.

"What do you have?" she asked, glancing over her shoulder at Sebastian. "What did you bring, Sebastian?"

Mathias' smile broadened. "I made you a promise last year that I was unable to keep until now," he said. "With the battles, the rebuild of Kirklinton, and Magnus' birth, it completely slipped my mind.

Therefore, in honor of Magnus' baptism, as my gift to you, I sent Sebastian back to Scotland to fulfill my promise."

Cathlina genuinely had no idea what he was talking about. "What is it?"

Mathias pulled off the top of the wooden box and immediately, a dark furry head popped up. Beady brown eyes looked at Cathlina and, for a moment, she was speechless. But in the next instance, she was gasping with delight.

Midgy the otter gazed at his former mistress with as much happiness as an otter could muster. When Midgy slithered out of the box, he wasn't alone; three little baby Midgys slithered out after him. It would seem that Midgy had returned home to breed and now, in late spring, had three little ones in tow. Midgy, as it turned out, was a girl.

"Midgy!" Cathlina squealed.

Magnus awoke to his mother's happy voice, raising the roof of Carlisle's keep with his lusty and loud cry, and Mathias couldn't have been more thrilled… with all of it.

The Fallen One had had been reborn, richer than before.

ABOUT THE AUTHOR

Kathryn Le Veque is the author of 39 novels published on Amazon. Out of the 39, 31 of them are Medieval Romance.

Mathias' story was truly one of redemption for a man who had been stripped of everything. Even though he had been reduced to living as a peasant, he still retained that innate sense of the knighthood, of battle and passion, so even though he lost his titles, he never lost his sense of self. The Battle of Dupplin Moor really was a massive battle and the details contained within the novel are historically accurate. Want to read more? It's a very exciting bit of history – the best explanation is here:

http://skyelander.orgfree.com/dupplin.html

As for Cathlina, she was a sweet and level-headed girl most of the time, but she had tendency to let her imagination run wild. Still, she was a good match for Mathias because she believed in him. More than that, she loved him regardless of if he was a smithy or a knight. That's unconditional love. And in speaking of unconditional love… don't forget Midgy! Want to read a great story about an otter in Ireland, the inspiration for our Midgy? Read RING OF BRIGHT WATER by Gavin Maxwell.

Lastly, this novel is related to the DRAGONBLADE TRILOGY, although it is not 'officially' a part of it. Chronologically, it actually takes places between the novels DRAGONBLADE and ISLAND OF GLASS. This novel is pre-Aubrielle (Kenneth St. Hèver) and Joselyn (Stephen of Pembury). If you have not yet read that series, then it's a must-read. Will Sebastian and Roxane get their own story? Probably not. It would be a train-wreck; passionate, I am sure, but full of selfish and silly people.

Please visit Kathryn's website at www.kathrynleveque.com to subscribe to her blog and get the latest Le Veque information.

CPSIA information can be obtained at www.ICGtesting.com
Printed in the USA
BVOW04s1222241113

337188BV00013B/634/P

9 781492 982869